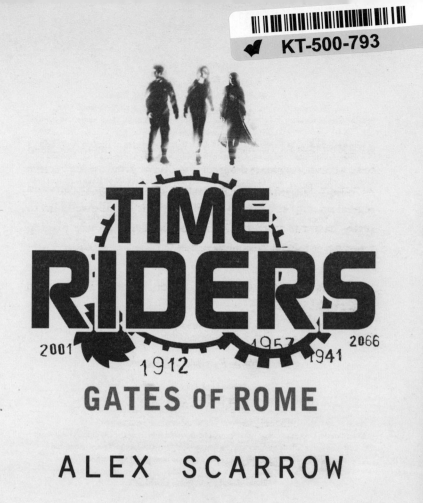

TIME RIDERS

2001   1912   1957   1941   2066

GATES OF ROME

ALEX SCARROW

PUFFIN

PUFFIN BOOKS

Published by the Penguin Group
Penguin Books Ltd, 80 Strand, London WC2R ORL, England
Penguin Group (USA) Inc., 375 Hudson Street, New York, New York 10014, USA
Penguin Group (Canada), 90 Eglinton Avenue East, Suite 700, Toronto, Ontario, Canada M4P 2Y3
(a division of Pearson Penguin Canada Inc.)
Penguin Ireland, 25 St Stephen's Green, Dublin 2, Ireland (a division of Penguin Books Ltd)
Penguin Group (Australia), 250 Camberwell Road, Camberwell, Victoria 3124, Australia
(a division of Pearson Australia Group Pty Ltd)
Penguin Books India Pvt Ltd, 11 Community Centre, Panchsheel Park, New Delhi – 110 017, India
Penguin Group (NZ), 67 Apollo Drive, Rosedale, Auckland 0632, New Zealand
(a division of Pearson New Zealand Ltd)
Penguin Books (South Africa) (Pty) Ltd, 24 Sturdee Avenue, Rosebank,
Johannesburg 2196, South Africa

Penguin Books Ltd, Registered Offices: 80 Strand, London WC2R ORL, England

puffinbooks.com

First published 2012
004

Text copyright © Alex Scarrow, 2012
All rights reserved

The moral right of the author has been asserted

Set in Bembo Book MT Std 11/14.5 pt
Typeset by Palimpsest Book Production Limited, Falkirk, Stirlingshire
Printed in Great Britain by Clays Ltd, St Ives plc

British Library Cataloguing in Publication Data
A CIP catalogue record for this book is available from the British Library

ISBN: 978-0-141-33649-7

www.greenpenguin.co.uk

Penguin Books is committed to a sustainable
future for our business, our readers and our planet.
This book is made from Forest Stewardship
Council™ certified paper.

ALWAYS LEARNING   **PEARSON**

'Contender for best science fiction book of the year . . .
an absolute winner' – *Flipside*

Winner of the Older Readers category,

ALEX SCARROW used to be a graphic artist, then he decided to be a computer games designer. Finally, he grew up and became an author. He has written a number of successful thrillers and several screenplays, but it's YA fiction that has allowed him to really have fun with the ideas and concepts he was playing around with when designing games.

He lives in Norwich with his son, Jacob, his wife, Frances, and his Jack Russell, Max.

Books by Alex Scarrow

TimeRiders
TimeRiders: Day of the Predator
TimeRiders: The Doomsday Code
TimeRiders: The Eternal War
TimeRiders: Gates of Rome

Sign up to become a TimeRider at:
www.time-riders.co.uk

To my brother Simon for the kind use of two of my favourite literary characters, Cato and Macro

PROLOGUE

10 August 2001, Brooklyn

Joseph Olivera gasped, air huffed in and out of his lungs in total darkness. The noise of his rasping breath bounced back at him from hard walls somewhere off in the black. He tried to calm himself. Steady his nerves.

You knew what it was going to be like.

Yes. He'd had that explained: the sensation of falling, the milky nothingness, the light touch of energy crawling over your skin like the probing, curious fingers of a pickpocket. Still, even though he'd mentally prepared for it, forewarned, Olivera had been cautioned by Waldstein that the first time was the hardest.

But he hadn't expected this. Pitch black.

'Anyone th-there?'

He could hear the drip of water somewhere, possibly from a low ceiling. And, faintly, a quiet rumble that increased in volume as it passed overhead and then finally faded to nothing.

'Hello?'

Just then another noise. A metallic rattle from behind him. Joseph turned towards it and saw a horizontal sliver of light appear. It widened, accompanied by the jangle of a chain, and Joseph recognized it as the bottom of some shutter door. He saw a pair of feet outside, cobblestones, a muted grey of diffused light.

'Hello?'

The feet shifted, a figure ducked down and looked under the shutter door. Joseph saw a paunchy middle-aged man with a beard and glasses, wearing shabby corduroy trousers and a green woollen cardigan with leather elbow patches. 'Hello?'

Joseph squatted down so the light from outside could pick out his face. 'Is this the right place?'

The man with the beard chuckled. 'Ahhh . . . you must be our new recruit.' He ducked under the shutter, straightened up inside and walked to the side of the shutter, patting in the darkness until his fingers found a switch.

A fluorescent light fizzed on above Joseph. He could see now he was in some brick archway. It smelled of damp cement and stale urine. In one corner he could see a pile of loops of electrical flex. Beside that, a dozen cardboard boxes that had the images of ancient-looking computers printed on the side. Early twenty-first-century bricks of clunky technology.

'This . . . this isn't the place, is it?' asked Joseph.

The man smiled and crossed the pitted dirty floor towards him, his feet crackling across shards of broken glass. 'This is it.' He offered his hand. 'I'm Frasier Griggs by the way.'

'Joseph Olivera,' he replied.

'I agree it doesn't look much at the moment. Mr Waldstein, I presume, told you we've only just started setting up things in here?'

Joseph nodded. 'But I . . . I thought . . .'

'You thought it would be something grander?'

'Yes.'

Frasier laughed again. 'It's all that's needed.' He looked around. 'Good choice, I'd say. Nice and discreet. I don't think it's been occupied in years.' He kicked an empty glass bottle aside. It skittered across a carpet of grit and rat droppings. 'Unless you count vagrants and drug addicts, that is.'

Joseph glanced at the cobblestones outside. 'This is really 2001? I've really travelled back over half a century?'

'Oh quite, yes. August the tenth, 2001 to be precise.' Frasier spoke with an almost theatrical accent, what used to be called 'British' before that small nation vanished into the Euroblock.

He walked towards the shutter and ducked down to look outside. Frasier followed him over, squatting down beside him. 'This is Brooklyn. Tell me, Joseph. You ever see pictures of Brooklyn before they abandoned it to the flood waters?'

Joseph shook his head. He only knew the outskirts of this once-fine city as a maze of waterlogged streets, collapsed rooftops sprouting weeds and struggling saplings.

'Quite characterful and vibrant was Brooklyn.' Frasier gazed at the graffiti-covered brick wall opposite, and above it a mixed urban skyline of cranes, factory roofs and warehouse apartments. He sighed. 'I used to collect priceless antique CDs from about this time. Marvellous stuff they used to call "hip hop". Big Daddy K? MC Kushee? Ever heard of those composers?'

Joseph shook his head.

'Ah well. It's only old farts like me listen to that sort of thing now.' Frasier nodded at the scene outside. 'Thirty years from now all this will be gone. It'll be nothing but a drowning ghost town. Abandoned ruins. Left to rot. Pity.'

Above them was a warm blue, cloudless sky, criss-crossed with the vapour trails of distant air traffic.

'Anyway, Mr Waldstein has already given you your brief, I presume?'

Joseph nodded.

'We're sourcing as much of the equipment components as we can from the present. It's safer that way. The less of a footprint we leave from our time, the better.'

Joseph had noted the boxes of desktop computers. 'Are those old machines powerful enough to —?'

'Certainly. I'll have to tinker with the network so their CPUs synchronize. And I'll strip out that stone-age operating system and replace it with W.G. Systems software. Should be fine, though.'

Joseph gazed across the East River at Manhattan.

'Quite a sight, isn't it?' said Frasier. 'This really was a beautiful city back in its time.'

'Yes.'

They listened to the wail of a distant police siren, the honk of the East River ferry on its way down to Governor's Island, the faint boom of a passing car hi-fi, the gentle *whup-whup* of a helicopter high above.

Joseph found himself sharing Frasier's dewy-eyed wonder.

Everything seems so much more alive.

This was a mankind full of passion and energy. From here the future looked limitless, the possibilities endless. This is what the world looked like when it still had a hope. Joseph's breath fluttered. It was intoxicating.

'Well now . . . this field office of Mr Waldstein's won't sort itself out if we just sit here. There's a lot to do.' Frasier stood up and kicked a discarded McDonald's carton out of the archway and across the cobblestone alley. 'Is Mr Waldstein joining us today?'

'Yes . . . he s-s-said . . .' Joseph worked at containing his stutter. 'He said he'd be along shortly.'

'Good,' said Frasier. 'Because I need to ask him where he wants me to set up the displacement rack. Going to need to check the wiring for tolerance. And of course where to put the back-up generator.'

'Where will I be setting up *my* equipment?'

Frasier pointed into the gloom of the archway. 'It's in the back room. There's another room. See that sliding door? Half a dozen Gen-Inc-5H bio-growtubes from our Salt Lake Genetic Research facility, and several hundred gallons of that disgusting growth solution. It wasn't easy beaming that lot through, I can tell you.'

'Is it assembled already?'

'No! That's *your* job. Anything else you need, except the foetuses of course, you're going to need to source locally.'

'Uh, right.'

Frasier suddenly grinned broadly, his eyes wide behind the glint of his lenses. 'Quite something, this project of his, isn't it? *Guardians of history* and all that!'

'Yes . . . yes, it is.'

'You know, only three people in the entire history of human-kind have actually travelled through time: Mr Waldstein, myself . . . and now you. Just think about it. More people have walked upon the moon than done what you've just done.'

Joseph nodded, grinning. Frasier's excitement was wholly infectious.

'Lots to do, Joseph old chap. Lots to do. But first . . . how do you fancy a coffee? I spotted a rather nice coffee shop nearby.'

'*Real* coffee?'

'Good grief, yes! None of that awful vat-grown synthi-soya rubbish.' He patted Joseph affectionately on the shoulder. 'Give you a chance to see a little bit more of Brooklyn before we knuckle down to work. How about that?'

'A coffee would be nice.'

Frasier led Joseph back outside, worked the shutter door down to the ground with some difficulty and secured it with its rusty padlock. 'That's stiff. I might see if I can get the winch motor working. Don't want to be hefting that up and down each time we step outside, do we?'

The morning sun sparkled across the East River, spears of brilliant dappled light that made Joseph's eyes moist. The inverted reflections of Manhattan's proud skyscrapers shuffled in the wake of the passing ferry and above them a commuter train rattled across the Williamsburg Bridge towards Manhattan.

Beautiful. Quite beautiful.

He noticed Frasier enjoying the same view. 'Oh, how rude of me!' he said presently, offering Joseph a comic salute. 'I suppose I ought to *officially* welcome you to our little "agency".'

Joseph self-consciously returned the gesture, feeling a thrum of growing excitement course through his body.

What an incredible project.

CHAPTER 1

2001, New York

Monday (time cycle 77)
Something's wrong. I know it. I think there's something big going
on we don't know about. Something Foster should've told us and
didn't. Maybe he really wanted to, but couldn't. Wasn't allowed to.
Maybe that's why he left us?

Sal put down her pen and looked around the laundromat. Just like it always was at this time on a Monday morning, it was empty. She was the only customer there, sitting on one of the row of plastic chairs facing a grubby window. She watched a removal truck outside the window trying to squeeze past a kerb-parked yellow cab, the drivers of both vehicles winding down their windows and barking abuse at each other.

Men. Always so aggressive. Sal wondered for a moment what a world free of testosterone might be like. Surely a better place without men beating their chests and acting like apes.

She looked down at her notebook again.

That thing. That stuffed toy. The bear. Somehow that's at the heart
of everything. I'm sure of it.

The man that came through, that poor, twisted mess that was once a human being, she was sure he'd been trying to tell her something about the blue bear as he died. Something for her ears alone. She wondered how a stuffed toy, a threadbare, scruffy-looking one at that, could 'mean' anything to anyone – except comfort for some child.

She scribbled again in her diary.

And then there's Liam's tunic.

Sal was certain of one thing: that she could trust her own eyes, what she actually saw. She'd taken a close look again at the tunic that was hanging in a closet just outside the nook where their bunk beds were. The clothes they'd all been wearing the day they'd arrived in the archway hung in there. No longer worn because they were so precious, a last link to the lives they'd lived before this. Before becoming TimeRiders.

She'd unhooked Liam's tunic, the very same one he'd arrived in the night the *Titanic* had gone down. The tunic, complete with two rows of brass buttons and the White Star Line's star symbol on its purple collar. And yes . . . there it had been, the thing she was looking for, that ever-so-faint, comma-shaped red wine stain on the right shoulder. So faint. Somebody had once gone to a lot of trouble to try and remove it and failed.

And here's the thing. The exact same stain . . . *the exact same stain* . . . was on the tunic hanging in that odd little antique and costume-hire shop a few blocks away. An exact duplicate of Liam's tunic. Sal scribbled the obvious question in her diary.

So, how come there's a duplicate of what he was wearing hanging in that shop?

The question begged all sorts of answers, none of which Sal thought she liked the sound of. The answer that unsettled most was the one she decided to write down.

Does that mean we've been here before?

She looked up from her scribbling. The removal truck was still trying to inch past the taxi, and both men were still enthusiastically haranguing each other, their Brooklyn voices lost beneath the frenetic whir of tumble dryers in the laundry. She turned to look at the round porthole of the nearest of them, spin-drying her and Maddy's clothes. They were all clothes from 2001 now, garments that allowed them to blend in. Her eyes were drawn to a pale green ankle sock spinning round and round, pushed up against the window, caught in a spiral of forces it couldn't escape.

Like us. Her, Maddy and Liam, three unfortunate souls unknowingly stuck in an endless loop they were doomed to live over and over again.

She looked down at the biro in her hand. At the diary, a nondescript notebook of lined pages that you could pick up in any stationery store. She leafed through the pages, realizing she had filled more than a quarter of it with her small, tidy handwriting and sketches and doodles. And before the first of her entries, written months' worth of 'time-bubble days' ago, right there . . . the torn edges of dozens and dozens of pages ripped out by someone.

A thought suddenly occurred to her that left a chill running down her back, like a ghostly finger tracing her vertebrae, making the flesh on her bare arms pucker into goosebumps.

Oh shadd-yah. Was that me?

She wondered if the pages of this diary had been used by her . . . *before*.

Another me? A previous me?

She felt sick. Hadn't Foster said something about the fate of the previous team? Something about 'being torn to pieces', something about 'there being little left'. She remembered that first day vividly. Being awoken on her bunk, meeting Maddy and Liam for the first time, seeing Foster's old face leaning over her and realizing it was the same face she'd seen just before she'd died, just before her home in Mumbai had collapsed into a raging inferno.

And there was that thing . . . that ghostly form in the dark that he'd had to hastily usher them away from. The seeker. Didn't he say it was that ethereal, glowing shape — little more than fragile membrane, like a jellyfish, like a plume of smoke — that had ripped the previous team to unrecognizable shreds?

The previous team.

Us?

CHAPTER 2

2070, Cheyenne Mountain, Colorado Springs

'But why, skippa?'

Rashim Anwar shook his head at the childlike question. The thing's squeaky voice and perpetual goofy, dumb smile — all of that Rashim's choice, of course. His laboratory assistant unit, one of the half-size models, came up to no more than his waist in height. In the default factory-shipped polygenic skin, the domestic models looked like little plasticine children. No hair, faces deliberately artificial-looking, inexpressive, neutral. But shapes and sizes varied. Rashim's one was designed for a lab environment, squat and square, nothing like a plasticine child, more like a filing cabinet on legs.

Rashim couldn't help customizing his unit, his inner geek looking for a way to express itself. The lab assistant unit's shape and configuration were roughly the same as the cartoon character's anyway; close enough that hacking the polygenic skin's configuration code to make the unit look even more like the character was a couple of hours' work. Little more than changing the programmable plastic skin from the default utilitarian grey to a bright yellow, and getting the face to extrude and replicate the cartoon character's goofy features.

'But why, skippa?' it asked again with a squeaky voice. It

looked up at Rashim with big round eyes, above a perky, pickle-shaped nose and two jutting tombstone teeth.

Rashim vaguely remembered those old cartoons. His grandfather used to watch them, rocking and laughing at the dumb antics played out on-screen. Rashim had worked from this vague childhood memory. It had made him feel like a kid once more, hacking the unit's configuration code and watching the polygenic plastic change colour and reconfigure. Looking down at the inquisitive robot, he figured he had it pretty close, although he wasn't so sure he'd got the character's name quite right.

'SpongeBubba . . . it's hard to explain.'

'Please explain to me, skippa! Please!'

'Well, I suppose it's a design fault in our programming.'

'*Programming?* But humans don't have artificial intelligence routines!' SpongeBubba squawked.

Rashim lifted his glasses and pushed a coil of dark hair from his face. They stopped at a closed doorway and he presented his left eye for a retina ID scan. 'It's just a figure of speech, Sponge-Bubba. The point is we have our faults, just like bad lines of code. The difference between you and me, though, is that it's not so easy to edit our behaviour. We are who we are.'

'It doesn't make sense,' said the unit. Frown grooves ran along its yellow plastic skin. 'Why do humans want to destroy their own world?'

The doorway in front of them cranked open. Hinges carrying a three-ton blast-proof door creaked and echoed across a dark and dusty control room, its walls lined with the glass of large strategic display monitors. Over a hundred years ago, this installation had been built as a command and control centre in preparation for what had seemed like an inevitable nuclear war with Russia. Now it was little more than a museum piece.

Rashim hesitated before the open door and the dark passageway beyond. 'I suppose it's in our nature. We don't like bad news . . . so we just ignore it.'

'Well, *duh–huh*, that's just plain *stoopid*!'

He smiled. The unit's speech patterns were a result of his hacking as well.

'It *is* stupid, Bubba. There was a time when we could have turned things around. Saved the earth from overheating, but I suppose it seemed like too much hard work at the time. So we didn't bother.'

'Well, duh,' squawked SpongeBubba again.

Rashim smiled. *Exactly . . . duh.*

He led the way down the passageway. The blast door clanked as it closed behind them and motion-sensitive lights in the passageway flickered on. A fading sign on the concrete wall informed him that they were now entering a security level three zone. Lining the wall either side of the sign were old framed photographs of past US presidents: Bush, Obama, Palin, Schwarzenegger, Vasquez, Esquerra.

This installation, carved deep into the side of Cheyenne Mountain, had once upon a time been known as NORAD. It had been kept in a state of 'warm standby' until the mid-2040s then finally closed down after the first Oil War. America's old rival, Russia, was having as much trouble as America with its own internal problems to no longer be a global nuclear threat.

Now it was simply referred to as 'Facility 29H-Colorado'.

'I suppose my grandfather's generation . . . my parents' generation even, were too busy wanting all the nice things: the big shiny holo-TV, *real* meat three times a week, the latest digi-fashions. Too busy with all that to notice the sea slowly rising, taking coastlines and cities with it.'

'Did the big floodings happen after the Oil Wars, Rashim?'

'That's right.' He shrugged. 'It might have been better for us if we'd run out of oil and all the other fossil fuels a lot sooner than we did. Maybe we'd still have polar ice caps.'

Rashim's childhood, like everyone else his age, had been one lived in a world shifting with constant migration. Millions – *billions* – of people on the move, retreating from land that itself was retreating before rising tides of polluted water.

'Mind you . . . the real problem, Bubba, was that there were just too many of us.'

'Too many humans?'

'Nearly ten billion. Totally unsustainable.' He looked down at the waddling unit beside him. 'We were so very stupid, Bubba.'

It nodded, its plastic, pickle-shaped nose wobbling slightly. 'Duh. Stoopid.'

Ten billion mouths to feed. *How did we ever allow ourselves to get that crowded?*

It reminded him of something a teacher once told him – *Petri Dish Syndrome*. Put a bacterium in a dish with something to feed on. Leave it long enough and it'll fill the dish, then, oh boy, then . . . it'll turn on itself, cannibalize its own protein to survive.

'You reap what you sow,' said SpongeBubba. He looked up at Rashim with wide, hopeful eyes. 'Is that the correct saying to use?'

Rashim nodded. 'It is. Well done, Bubba.'

'Hey, thanks!'

They turned a corner into a passageway already lit with a steady glow from muted ceiling lights. At the end a pair of soldiers stood guard either side of the door to a lift.

Rashim flicked his hand casually at them as he and his unit approached. 'Morning, guys.'

'Morning, sir,' said the older of the two guards. Almost old enough to be his dad. Rashim felt awkward; he seemed to be the youngest member by far on the technology team. Twenty-seven and he was in charge of the 'receiver team', a group of eight technicians all at least ten years older than him.

'You're up early again, Dr Anwar.'

Rashim shrugged. 'We have calibrations to cross-check on the translation markers.'

SpongeBubba raised a gloved cartoon hand in a mock salute at the guards. 'S'right! Rashim's the most important man in the whole world!'

Rashim winced at his assistant's sing-song exuberance.

The older guard cocked an eyebrow. 'You do know that outside of the facility you should have your AI unit on verbal-mute, sir, don't you? That's a security breach.'

'Yes, yes, of course . . . I'm sorry.' He let go of Bubba's gloved hand. 'SpongeBubba, be quiet.'

'You got it!' Its plastic lips snapped shut then pouted guiltily. 'Really sorry about that.'

'You know I'll have to log that security infringement, sir,' said the soldier.

Rashim nodded. He'd get a slapped wrist for that from the project leader, Dr Yatsushita, later on today no doubt. 'I promise I'll remember to mute him in future outside the lab.'

The soldier smiled, offered Rashim a sly wink. 'In that case, maybe we can let it go this time.' He pressed a button and the lift doors slid open. 'Have a nice day, sir.'

Rashim nodded. 'Thank you.' He led his lab unit into the lift by the hand and the doors closed on them.

As the lift hummed, taking them down to level three, he cleared his mind of unnecessary things. SpongeBubba's childlike curiosity about the world outside could wait. There were figures to process and check; yesterday's intra-mail about a change of mass tolerance meant several days' worth of recalibrating. And the deadline was now just over six months away.

'Bubba, any other messages land in my in-box this morning?'

SpongeBubba looked up at him, desperately wanting to speak, his eyes rolling, plastic lips quivering with frustration.

'Unmute.'

'Yes!' he blurted eagerly. 'Yes, skippa! Three from Dr Yatsu-shita. Seven from —'

'I'll deal with them this afternoon. Remind me.'

'Yes, skippa! Storing.'

The hum inside the small lift dropped in tone, and then the elevator shuddered gently as it came to rest. The doors slid open to reveal chipboard panels, erected in front of the lift to block any view of the area beyond. On one of them was tacked a sign.

Now Entering Level Three Security Zone

A last warning to turn back for anyone who shouldn't be down here. Beneath it, handwritten with a magic marker, was a little more information.

Welcome to Project Exodus

CHAPTER 3

2001, New York

'I can't believe it,' said Liam.

'Believe it.' Maddy tapped her front teeth with a biro absently. 'I never . . .' She looked queasy. 'I never ever want to do something like that again.'

Liam nodded slowly. 'It isn't an easy thing.' He recalled having to retrieve Bob's hard drive. Reminding himself over and over that it wasn't some kind of horrendous mutilation he was performing on the support unit . . . it was merely getting a friend back.

Maddy glanced across the archway at where the carrier bag had been by the shutter door; a bag containing something the size of a basketball, tied up and put inside yet another bag. Thankfully it was gone now. Bob had taken it away earlier. They'd discussed whether her head deserved some sort of a burial, a ritual, a few words said. But none of them could decide how to do it or what to say. In the end Bob just took it away. Maddy didn't want to know what he did with it. It wasn't *Becks* any more; it was just ten pounds of meat, bone and cartilage.

'Data retrieval,' she muttered, blanking out the memory with technical terms. 'That's all it is,' she told herself. 'Just like pulling the motherboard out of a PC. No big deal.'

She'd discovered Becks's body almost completely buried beneath a mound of other bodies, several separate, distinct entry and exit wounds to her head. Any one of those would have been fatal to a normal human. But her genetically engineered, thicker skull and much smaller organic brain meant that she could suffer catastrophic cranial trauma and still be viable. But clearly she was not immortal. Her body had sustained enough damage and blood loss that it had finally closed down and died.

Sal settled on the arm of the threadbare sofa beside Maddy. 'Think her chip's OK?'

Maddy nodded towards the bank of screens across the archway. Several of them were spooling streams of encoded data. 'Computer-Bob's running a diagnostic on her chipset right now. I don't know. I hope so. It's gonna take a while. The silicon wafer casing's dented. A bullet must have hit it on the way through. I don't know what that's done to the drive inside. We'll just have to wait and see.'

The three of them silently watched the spooling screens, a flickering stream of letters and numbers, data: countless terabytes of stored memories of dinosaurs and jungles, knights and castles.

All that made Becks . . . Becks.

'We'll re-grow her, though,' said Liam. 'Aye?'

Sal nodded. 'Yeah, two support units are better than one.' She looked down at Maddy. 'Right?'

'Sure we will. But . . .'

'But what?'

'There's no certainty that we can use her AI. If there's too much damage, if it's an unreliable AI, she could be a hazard to us. We may need to work from default AI code.'

'That won't be our Becks, then,' said Liam.

Both support units, Becks and Bob, had developed distinctly different artificial intelligences despite running the very same operating system. Maddy's best guess was that it was something in the way the small organic brain interacted with the silicon, that it was the 'meat' component of their minds that ultimately defined them, gave them their individual personalities.

'You're right,' she replied, 'it wouldn't be the same Becks.'

'I really hope her computer's all right,' said Liam wistfully.

Sal looked at him. 'She was a bit . . . I don't know, a bit *cold*, though, sometimes, don't you think?'

He shook his head thoughtfully. 'I think she was beginning to learn how to *feel* things.'

Maddy thought she'd seen something of that in the support unit, the emergence of behaviour that might be described as an emotion – a desire to please, to seek approval.

'We'll just have to wait and see what we get. If the data's good, she should be pretty much the Becks we know and love.'

If the data's good.

But Maddy's mind was on something else, on that portion of the hard drive Becks had partitioned off and encrypted. Several millimetres of silicon that contained a secret so important that it had become the source of the legend of the Holy Grail, caused the very existence of the Knights Templar and compelled King Richard to launch his own crusade to retake Jerusalem. A secret transmitted across two thousand years of history. A secret meant for them.

But not *yet* apparently.

What was it Becks had said? That the message contained instructions for the truth not to be revealed *just yet*.

'*When it is the end . . .*'

'I hope the message from that old manuscript isn't all messed up,' said Liam as if he was reading her thoughts. 'I'd love to find out what it said one day, so I would.'

Maddy smiled. 'Me too.'

The shutter door rattled gently as a fist banged against it outside.

'I'll get it,' said Sal. She hopped off the sofa's arm, crossed the archway and hit the shutter's button. It cranked up noisily, letting in daylight and revealing Bob's thick, hairy legs. In an attempt to make him blend in more with the tourists in Times Square, Sal was trying out the shorts-and-flip-flops-and-Hawaiian-shirt look on him. Maddy wasn't entirely sure that was working. He looked like a freakish version of Clark Kent taking a vacation.

Bob ducked down under the shutter, holding a cardboard take-away tray in his ham-shank-sized hands.

'Who requested the caramel frappuccino?'

CHAPTER 4

2001, Central Park, New York

They walked slowly round the duck pond, kicking the first dry leaves of autumn aside. They watched a young couple rollerblading ahead of them. Maddy smiled sadly, envious of the pair of them, both about her age and seemingly without a solitary care in the world. She watched the young man, tanned, lean, handsome, with long wavy blond hair and a small goatee, leading his unsteady girlfriend by the hands, her feet splaying and weaving uncertainly, laughing at how terrible she was.

To have that moment. Just that one moment.

Foster touched her arm sympathetically. 'I know what you're thinking.'

'What?'

'You're thinking ignorance is bliss.'

She offered him a confessional shrug. 'I wish I was someone else, Foster. Anyone else.' She nodded at the couple, their legs beginning to tangle, the young man laughing along with his giggling girlfriend. 'Being either of them would be nice.'

'They'll never experience anything like you'll experience. What you've experienced *already*.'

Maddy sighed. 'But it's too much. I can't cope with all of it.' She looked at his old face, sunken cheeks and eyes framed by a fan of wrinkles, 'laughter lines' if one was being kind. 'Every time I come and visit you . . . it seems I've got more and more to unload on you.'

He cackled. 'It must get annoying, having to repeat yourself.'

She shrugged that away. That was the deal. That's how it was. Foster was here at this time in Central Park. Mid-morning, feeding the pigeons, then on his merry way to live out whatever time he had left however he wanted. For him an hour that came and went, but for Maddy – reliving the same two New York days, the 10th and 11th September 2001 – it was a repeated chance to see him again. To get his advice. But every time they met, it would be the *first time* he'd seen her since walking away from the team and leaving her in charge. So their conversation began with an ever-increasing recap from her of the events she and the others had endured.

'You guys do seem to have been through quite a lot,' he said.

'Tell me about it.'

His face, skin like fine parchment, creased with a grin. 'Abraham Lincoln sounds a character, so he does. Did he really outrun *both* your support units?'

'Oh yeah, the guy can run like a kid chasing an ice-cream van.'

They both laughed.

Foster nodded at a bench beside the path in the shade of a maple tree. 'Can we sit? My old legs aren't what they used to be.'

'Sure.'

She looked at him, wondering how many days he had left, wondering how much life the displacement machine had stolen from him. A couple of meetings ago, here beside this same pond, he'd admitted he was only twenty-seven years old. More than that – something that had rocked her to the core – he'd told her that he was once Liam. He'd not explained how that could be;

in fact, he'd refused to explain. But he'd told her because he wanted her to know that every time Liam went back into the past, the process was gradually killing him: ageing him before his time. That he would all too soon end up like him. She alone needed to be the judge of how much his body could take. That's why she had to know.

They settled down, looking further up the path at the pigeons indignantly puffing themselves up and backing off as several Canadian geese waddled over to take possession of ground littered with scattered breadcrumbs.

'Foster?'

'Yes.'

'What is it you're not telling me?'

He looked at her, a disarming smile. His best attempt at deflecting her.

'Come on, Foster . . . you've only given me half what I need to know.'

His eyes narrowed. 'Why don't you tell me what you think you know.'

'Why are you . . . why can't you just tell me *everything*?'

'Because I don't know everything.'

'You know more than me. You know more than you've told me!'

He held her gaze. Eventually he nodded with some regret. 'All right, yes, that's true.'

'Why? Why don't you tell me all you know? What are you holding back?'

'Knowledge, Maddy . . . foreknowledge.'

'Pandora?'

He shook his head. She'd explained to him about the note she'd discovered. About the specific mention of that particular word in the Voynich Manuscript. 'I know nothing about

Pandora,' he'd said and she suspected he was being straight with her about that.

'It's a message, Foster. A message someone's trying to get to *me*. It's got to be important, right?'

His fingers steepled beneath the wattled flesh of his jaw and he rested his chin on them. 'Quite possibly, very.'

'So what do I do about it?'

He watched the pigeons and geese strutting warily round each other, sizing each other up. Finally he spoke. 'Perhaps you should ask about it.'

'Ask who?'

His eyebrows arched suggestively.

'What? You mean call forward? The future? The agency?'

'Not a tachyon signal,' he said quickly. 'You absolutely can *not* do that. The particles will give you away.'

She knew that already. 'The drop document?'

Foster had left Maddy a small library of instructions and advice. One entry had been how to communicate with the agency in extreme circumstances. What was actually classified as 'an extreme circumstance' had not been made entirely clear. The method of communication was to place a personal advert in the lonely hearts ads of the *Brooklyn Daily Eagle*, beginning with the words '*A soul lost in time . . .*'

Someone, somewhere in the future obviously had a yellowing copy of the newspaper and was watching that page for a subtle change. Watching for a gentle ripple in reality that altered nothing but the wording of that one personal ad.

'Ask,' he said again finally. 'Why not?'

'You really don't know about Pandora . . . do you?'

Foster shook his head. She thought she knew him – and Liam for that matter – well enough to spot a lie. They were both completely rubbish at it.

'Maybe I will,' said Maddy.

'And do let me know what he says. I'm just as curious now as you –'

She turned to look at him. '*He?*'

Foster closed his eyes. She realized he'd let slip something he hadn't wanted to.

'He? Who? Who is *he*? The agency?' She turned in her seat, grabbed his arm. 'Foster?! Are you saying the agency is what? Just . . . *just one person?*'

He said nothing.

'What about all the other teams?'

The old man's lips tightened. His gaze flicked away from her.

'Foster? Tell me! The other teams . . .?'

'There are no other teams, Maddy,' he whispered. His eyes drifted back to hers. 'I'm so sorry. You're alone. The agency is you. Just you.' He looked down at his hands. '. . . And Waldstein.'

She all but missed hearing Waldstein's name. Her mind was reeling, light-headed with a growing panic.

You're alone.

The agency is you.

CHAPTER 5

2070, Project Exodus, Cheyenne Mountain, Colorado Springs

'Good morning, Dr Anwar.'

Rashim nodded quickly at the assistant technician, one of his small team. The air around his hand glowed with the stand-by display of a wrist-mounted holographic infopad.

'Anything come in overnight?'

'We had some more personnel changes come in, Dr Anwar. And their attached metrics.'

'Oh, marvellous,' Rashim muttered unenthusiastically. 'Buzz them over to my unit and I'll look at them later.'

'Yes, sir.'

The technician flipped his wrist and a holographic display blinked into existence, hovering in the air in front of him. His finger swiped across the display and a dozen messages were highlighted then floated out of their 'in-box' and into the air like pollen.

'Received,' said SpongeBubba. The lab unit squatted beside Rashim's desk like a docile pet. A moment later, he offered Rashim a toothy grin. 'Collating metrics, skippa!'

Rashim glanced across the cavernous interior of the underground hangar, an interior blasted out of the mountain over a hundred years ago to make space for the political elite of the time – generals, congressmen, senators and their families – in the event of a thermonuclear war with the Russians.

He shook his head. *Nothing changes. The politicians are always the first in line.*

The hangar, perhaps a shade larger than a football pitch, was illuminated from the sides by floodlights erected on tripods. Pools of retina-achingly bright light stretched across a cold concrete floor, scuffed and grooved here and there decades ago when this installation was stripped bare of equipment and moth-balled.

An empty floor . . . right now.

Rashim sat down among the cluster of cubicles and desks deployed in this corner of the hangar. First in again this morning, as always. He activated his terminal with a waft of his hand. His iris flickered momentarily as the terminal scanned and confirmed it was Dr Rashim Anwar issuing the command.

Project Exodus: Mass Translation Simulator – the words glowed crisply in the air in front of Rashim.

'Activate the floor mark-up.'

The hangar's concrete floor suddenly became a glowing chequerboard, criss-crossed with an intricate mesh of pulsing neon blue lines cast from a series of holographic projectors suspended from the cavernous ceiling. Grid-markers: squares varying in size from several inches across to several yards.

'Overlay marker details.'

Above each square floated holographic displays of columns of numbers: vital statistics for what was one day going to occupy each square.

'And give me the content icons.'

Above most of the various-sized grid squares, hundreds of them, glowing blue silhouettes suddenly appeared. Some of them the outlines of boxes and crates, several large icons depicting the profiles of vehicles, but the rest displaying the shimmering but clearly discernible outlines of human figures.

'Bubba, can you show me who's decided to be a nuisance this morning and drop out?'

'Aye aye, skippa!' SpongeBubba saluted playfully.

Eleven of the human icons glowed red.

Rashim got up from behind his desk and wandered across the hangar floor, the beams of light from above projecting down across his head, shoulders and back. He squatted down in front of the first human icon that had turned red. Rashim read the display of information floating in the air beside it.

```
Candidate 165:
Name — Professor Jennifer Carmel
Age — 28
Assignment — Biochemist
Mass Index — 54.4959
```

Beneath the display an envelope icon flashed, one of the notifications that came in during the night. Rashim touched the envelope and a message opened in the air beside his finger.

```
Candidate 165 Carmel, J., deceased.
Food riots in Puerto Rico, yesterday.
One hundred and fifty-six fatalities.
Cause of death — head trauma, gunshot wound.
No information on whether she was part
of the riot or accidentally caught up.
Next of kin informed.
```

'Sorry, Jennifer Carmel,' he said, sighing, 'I guess you won't be coming along with us after all.' His finger hovered over a delete icon and her outline disappeared along with her vital statistics. The grid square was empty now.

Rashim cursed softly. Not that he knew or cared who Jennifer Carmel had been. His frustration was more to do with the fact that unless they could find a replacement candidate with a close enough build and mass index, he was going to have to work through a lot of tedious number crunching and recalibration for this one square.

He looked up at the other ten human silhouettes dotted randomly across the hangar floor, outlines glowing red, candidates who for one reason or another were no longer going to be able to join Exodus in six months' time.

Six months to go. Six months until T-Day. Transmission Day.

So much could happen in six months.

The world seemed to be utterly determined to destroy itself in the meantime. The Pacific War between Japan and North Korea seemed to be flaring up to a new level of intensity. While neither of them had any nuclear weapons left to use, there were far worse things they could unleash on each other.

The rest of the world seemed no less bent on its own demise. Rashim's own country, Iran, had led the charge there and destroyed itself thirty years ago in a war that started as a dispute with the Arabian Coalition. A war over fresh water no less. Not even oil.

Water. Drinking water.

Iran, Iraq, Israel . . . were now three countries that were too irradiated for anyone to live in even thirty years after the exchange of tactical nuclear missiles. Even if they weren't irradiated, the few mountainous areas that hadn't been flooded by the rising waters of the Mediterranean and Red Seas and the Persian Gulf would be far too arid to support life. The millions that died in that one-day exchange of tit-for-tat warheads perhaps were the lucky ones, weren't they? Death in the blink of an eye instead of this long, slow, global death.

'Skippa?'

He looked up. SpongeBubba had waddled across the large grid-crossed floor to join him.

'What is it?'

'Dr Yatsushita has sent a message. He's on his way into the facility and wants to run a transmission simulation this morning.'

'Well, he'll have to wait until I rework the figures without these candidates!' Rashim snapped irritably.

'Shall I send that message to Dr Yatsushita, skippa?'

He stood up. 'No, I'd better talk to him when he gets in.'

'Aye aye,' his unit replied and waddled back across the hangar floor.

He sighed. There was so little margin for error. A miscalculation on the total mass index even by the tiniest percentage could send them out of the receiver station's snap range. Not for the first time he was amazed at the foolhardy courage of that incredible man Waldstein.

The reluctant father of time travel.

Twenty-six years ago now, wasn't it? The very first successful demonstration of time displacement. There and back again. Of course the man had never spoken about where or *when* he went. But he'd done it. More importantly he'd *survived* it. He'd come back in one piece and not turned inside out like burger meat.

Their own initial experiments here in the Cheyenne Mountain facility had turned a succession of animals small and large, genetically engineered human prototypes, even several real human volunteers into the equivalent of *living* pâté.

Living . . . for a few ghastly moments . . . actually *alive*.

30

Rashim marvelled at Waldstein's incredible genius. Dr Yatsu-shita was a brilliant man, but even with billions of dollars of funding and almost limitless resources at his disposal, Project Exodus still felt horribly like a large scary exercise in trial and error. Guesswork.

Waldstein, though . . . Waldstein had built his machine on his own. In his own garage, for Chrissake!

Or so the legend supposedly went.

Rashim often wondered what happened to that man. He'd been such a prominent figure for so many years. Meeting with world leaders, the very last guest speaker at the United Nations before it was finally dissolved in 2049. Then he seemed to disappear. Became something of a recluse. Rashim wasn't even sure if Waldstein was alive still. There were rumours.

Rashim pushed a lock of hair behind his ear and turned to head towards the nearest glowing red 'human' icon a dozen yards away. Another candidate to delete.

What did you see, Roald Waldstein? Hmmmm? What did you see with those mad eyes of yours? What did you see beyond these three spatial dimensions we can comprehend? It was perhaps the most frequently asked question during the '40s and '50s when Waldstein's face seemed to be on almost every media news-stream . . .

What did you see, Mr Waldstein? More to the point: *Why did it frighten you so much?*

CHAPTER 6

2001, New York

Liam watched the data slowly spooling down the screen – packets of hexadecimal data that made no sense to him whatsoever. Every so often the spooling stopped and lines and chunks of the meaningless alphanumeric text were fleetingly highlighted. Sometimes the highlighted text switched from white to green. Sometimes from white to red.

Liam pointed at a chunk that had just turned red. 'So that's not good, is it?'

'That is corrupted data,' said Bob.

The entire contents of Becks's silicon mind had been downloaded on to the computer system over thirty-six hours ago, a mountain of data stored up by her during her brief life. And now computer-Bob was working through it, testing the data for corrupted packets. Liam looked at the progress log on another screen: a map of her hard drive, her mind, divided into a grid of blocks of data. White for the data yet to be tested, green for verified and red for lost data. The last few chunks of white were being cross-examined. The rest of the grid was a patchwork of green and red blocks. The red seemed to grow malevolently, like cancer tumours. Far too many of them.

'We've lost her, haven't we?'

Bob's face twitched with the ghost of a response. Involuntary?

Possibly. Perhaps a sign that he was once again much more than the basic code he was born with. Learning to turn incoming information into an understanding, into context . . . an emotion. To *almost* be human.

'Significant portions of her stored data are damaged.' He offered Liam a wan smile. 'But I am hopeful.'

Computer-Bob was listening, despite being busy sifting through the data.

>We will not know whether we have a stable AI construct until I have compiled the data and run the emulator.

Liam looked at Bob. 'What does that mean?'

'The computer system will run the AI code on a software-simulated version of the chipset. It will then enter packets of the verified data block by block into the simulation to check the stability and reliability of Becks's AI.'

'To see whether she's gone stupid?'

Bob's thick brow rumpled. Liam reached out and grabbed the bulging knuckles of one of Bob's hands. 'Jay-zus, you *really care* about her, don't you?'

His chest rumbled with a deep *hur-umph*. 'She was an effective support unit. Her AI was able to develop more than mine.'

'Ah, but that's the ladies for you. Better at expressing their feelings than us fellas, huh?'

'Gender is not a factor.' Bob turned his grey eyes on him. 'Did *you* care for her, Liam?'

He laughed uncomfortably. 'Well . . . I . . .'

'The discoloration of your cheeks and body language suggest you have a strong emotional attachment to her. Am I correct, Liam?'

He gazed at the screen.

Blocks of colour. She's just blocks of colour on a computer screen now. That's it. And yet in her flesh form, in human form, she'd almost seemed like another person. Perhaps a somewhat cool person, detached, aloof even. But she could make a joke, couldn't she? And smile.

He realized her smile – even though it was nothing more than a data file played out across facial muscles – could make something inside him flutter and ache. A beautiful smile actually. Quite stunningly beautiful, truth be told.

'I'd miss her,' he said finally. 'If she really is lost . . . yes, I'll miss her.'

>Information.

Liam nodded at the webcam. 'What is it, computer-Bob?'

>I am ready to start the simulation. Do you wish to proceed?

He wondered whether he should wait for Maddy to get back. Sal too. They were both just as concerned whether there was anything left of Becks to salvage as he was.

'Will it . . . I don't know . . . is it safe? It won't damage her mind or anything, will it?'

>Negative. The data we have retrieved is now stored safely. This simulation is a read-only environment.

'And what does that mean?'

'It means that once the simulation stops running,' said Bob, 'any data that is generated is deleted.'

'She won't remember anything?'

>That is correct. It is merely a test environment.

Liam let himself down into the chair. 'All right, then.' He puffed out an anxious breath. 'Let's see if she's in there.'

>Affirmative. Launching AI emulator.

On a screen to his right another black dialogue box popped up. An empty box with a gently blinking cursor. That's all. Liam looked up at Bob nervously. The support unit nodded silently for him to go ahead and communicate with her.

34

'Uh . . . you in there, Becks?'

The dialogue cursor continued to blink, a steady *on-off-on-off* like a heartbeat. A pulse. A sign of life and nothing more.

> . . . .

'It's Liam here . . . can you hear me?'

The cursor continued to blink silently.

'The cognitive and language code may not be functioning correctly,' said Bob quietly.

'Becks, this is Liam. If you can hear me, just do something. Say something.'

> . . . .

He watched the cursor with a gradually sinking heart. *We've lost her.*

Of course they could activate and grow another female foetus and she would emerge from the growth tube looking every bit like Becks. Her identical twin. But he wondered how different she would be. She'd have a face with the very same features and muscles and skin, but the mind behind it would probably learn to use the face in a wholly different way. Smile differently, no longer cock a sceptical eyebrow in quite the same way. A thousand little tics and habits that made Becks who she was – all of them gone, forever.

'Becks?' he tried again. 'You there?'

> . . . .

'It appears there is not enough retrieved data to form a viable AI construct,' said Bob. Liam thought he heard something in his deep rumble, the slightest quaver in his voice, a thread of grief.

'Becks?' he tried one last time. He could hear emotion in his own voice now.

She's gone. We lost her. He felt something warm roll down his cheek and quickly swiped it away, for some reason not wanting

35

either Bob or computer-Bob to make a note of that and intrude on the moment with a query.

Goodbye, Becks.

> . . . .

> . . . .

> . . . .

> . . . . . .

> . . . . .

>**I love you, Liam O'Connor.**

CHAPTER 7

2001, New York

They watched the foetus floating in the protein soup, flexing and twitching tiny fingers and toes in unconscious readiness. A feed pipe was connected to its belly button and rose up to the top of the tube where it met the filtration pump.

The perspex growth tube was lit from the bottom. It glowed softly, filling their back room with a warm, womb-like, muted crimson light.

'Do you think they think about things when they're growing in there?' asked Liam.

'Probably not,' said Maddy.

Sal turned to Bob, standing like a freshly built brick wall beside her. 'Did you, Bob? Do you have any memories of being in a tube?'

He frowned, deep in concentration for a moment. 'No. My AI software was not loaded at this stage.'

'But your organic brain?' cut in Maddy. 'That must store some memories?'

Bob's shoulders flexed a casual shrug. 'If so, it is not data I can retrieve.'

The little foetus kicked a leg out, then tucked it back in.

Maddy chuckled. 'It's got some of her attitude already.'

'Do you think we can upload Becks's AI?' asked Sal.

Maddy tapped her teeth with her fingernails. 'I dunno yet,

Sal. That simulation we ran . . . she seemed pretty flaky.' On Maddy and Sal's return, computer-Bob had run the simulation again with exactly the same results.

She turned to look at Liam. 'I mean . . . *I love you* . . . that can't be right for a support unit, can it?'

Bob nodded. 'It did appear that the simulated AI was behaving erratically.'

'So, maybe these clone fellas can feel something?' said Liam. The others looked at him.

'Well, I'm not so unlovable, am I?'

Sal giggled. 'I'm sure your mother must've loved you.'

'Point is –' Maddy placed a hand on the warm growth tube – 'I'm pretty sure support units shouldn't go round professing love for their operative.'

Liam looked uncertain. 'She definitely was learning to . . . to *feel* something, so she was. That's not so bad, is it?'

Maddy found herself nodding in the gloom. Hadn't she too thought she'd seen that in Becks? 'Helps them appear more human, I suppose.'

'Back in the dinosaur time, she . . .' Liam looked at the others sheepishly.

'She what?'

'Well, she sort of went to kiss me, so she did.'

Sal made a face. Maddy's eyes rounded behind her lenses. '*Kiss* you?'

'Tried to give me just a little peck, so. On me cheek, that's all.'

Sal made a face. 'That's just weird.'

'Just a peck . . . nothing else happened,' he added defensively. 'Honest!'

Maddy waved him silent. 'Doesn't matter. The fact is maybe that means she did already have . . . *feelings* before this damage.

Maybe the "I love you" comment was not corrupted data or some sort of malfunction.' She looked up at Bob. 'She inherited your code, Bob. Have you ever experienced – you know – *feelings* for Liam?'

'I have data files that you could interpret as emotional reflexes.'

'Would *you* kiss Liam?'

Bob cocked his head, a frown of confusion rumpling his forehead for a moment before he reluctantly leaned down towards Liam, puckering his horse-lips.

Liam recoiled. 'Jay-zus, Bob! What're you –?'

'No! Bob! That wasn't an *instruction* . . . that was a *question*!'

He straightened up. 'I see.' His expression settled. 'I have managed to reprioritize mission parameters for Liam in the past. This could be interpreted as . . . irrational.'

'He came to save me from that German prison camp. Didn't you, Bob?'

'Is that because you valued Liam more than you valued completing your mission objective?' asked Maddy.

Bob hesitated, his mind working its files in silence.

'Because you cared for him?' she pressed.

Bob finally answered. 'Affirmative. Liam is my friend.'

Maddy tapped the perspex with her knuckles. 'There we are, then. That was already there in Becks's identity. She inherited feelings from Bob.' She shrugged her shoulders. 'She cares for you, Liam. Somewhere in all that data she has a file that tells her she "loves" you.' Maddy smiled. 'Maybe her AI was just running that file during the emulation.'

'Does that mean she's OK, then?' asked Liam.

'Bob, if we upload her AI into this body and it turns out she *is* wonky, can we, I dunno . . . *reboot* her or something?'

'Affirmative. The silicon wafer can be reformatted and the

AI software reloaded without any of my or her inherited data.'

'Right.' Maddy nodded. 'I suppose we could give her AI a go and if she's, like, all flaky on us, then that's what we'll have to do.'

'That's taking a risk, though, isn't it?' said Sal. 'I mean there are loads of those corrupted red blocks. What if she got funny with us?'

'What do you mean?' asked Maddy.

'I dunno . . . jealous or something. Jealous of you or me?'

'Sal is correct,' said Bob.

Maddy stroked her lip thoughtfully. She'd seen Becks in action. Seen the bodies left behind in her wake. God help them if she took on the role of a lover scorned.

'Her decision-making may be unpredictable,' Bob added.

'Aw, come on! When hasn't she been unpredictable?' said Liam.

Maddy nodded. 'True.'

'Could we not give her a chance?'

'We'll have to watch her *very* closely,' said Maddy. 'The slightest sign she's going weird and we'll have to reboot her. I mean it . . . she even *looks* at me or Sal in a funny way, we're going to have to totally wipe her, Liam.'

Sal bit her lip. 'I don't want her tearing off my head.'

Liam nodded slowly. 'She'll be right as rain, so she will.' He didn't sound entirely convincing.

'OK, right,' said Maddy, 'that's that, then.' She turned to head for the sliding door leading back out into the main archway. 'Come on, guys, there's something else we need to talk about.'

Liam slid the door aside. It rattled noisily and clattered against its runners. 'What?'

'This agency of ours . . . the Pandora stuff?'

Sal and Liam looked at each other.

'Did Foster tell you something?' asked Sal.

Maddy nodded. 'Oh yeah.'

CHAPTER 8

2070, Project Exodus, Cheyenne Mountain, Colorado Springs

Rashim stared, goggle-eyed, at Dr Yatsushita. '*What?*'

'I said we may have to consider advancing the T-Day deadline.'

'But . . . but . . . we're still only at the primary testing stage!'

Rashim's team had run several simulated tests on the transmission process and each time the simulation software had assured them that it had overshot or undershot the receiver station beacon's snap range. Or, on the one occasion they'd landed right on the money, half the candidates would have been lost or turned into quivering mush.

'Dr Anwar,' Yatsushita started. He looked harried. Tired. A sleepless night or several by the look of him. His usually carefully combed silver hair was uncharacteristically dishevelled. 'You must have been following the news-streams?'

Rashim hadn't, or not closely anyway. He had no time for that. Every day, it seemed, one or more of the transmission candidates had been replaced with someone else, requiring him to chase up the data on their replacements, plug in the information and recalculate the total mass index.

'You have heard about the Kosong-ni virus?'

A couple of days ago, he'd watched a few minutes of news.

The last city in Bangladesh had been abandoned to floodwater. The algal blooms in the Indian Ocean were now calculated to be covering thirty-six per cent of the surface area, poisoning, completely annihilating the ecosystem beneath. The North American Federation were enforcing border restrictions on east and west state migrants. A corps of Japanese combat droids had successfully made an amphibious assault on the North Korean city of Hyesan. A lot of dead people. But then when did the news these days not feature a high body count?

And yes, there'd been something about a virus. The news-streams had speculated it might have been a chemical weapon of some kind dropped on a North Korean city by the Japanese. Or worse still, some kind of *wild-card* bioweapon developed by the North Koreans and accidentally exposed as a result of some missile strike.

'Kosong-ni virus?' So it had a name now.

Yatsushita shook his head. He pushed his way through the warren of desks towards Rashim's. 'You fool. You should be watching instead of . . . of . . .' He looked at SpongeBubba squatting beside the desk and grinning with goofy teeth. 'Instead of making your foolish toys!'

'I haven't got time to watch a holo-vid, Dr Yatsushita!' Rashim replied, irritated with the project leader. 'I've got —'

'It's airborne! There are reports of the virus in Beijing!'

Airborne certainly wasn't so good.

'Our . . . *sponsors* are worried by this. They want T-Day advanced.'

Sponsors — Yatsushita's carefully chosen word. It was transparently obvious to Rashim that Project Exodus was being funded by what was left of America's defence budget, most probably funds topped up by a few billionaires who wanted in on it.

'Advanced by how much?'

Dr Yatsushita hesitated. 'They want it ready to go for the thirtieth of May.'

'But that's *five weeks* away! We need at least another six months to be sure –'

'We have no choice in this matter! It must be ready by then!'

Rashim pushed his round glasses up on to his forehead where they held his draping dark locks back like a hairband. 'Did you tell them the risks involved? Did you tell them that we get this the slightest bit wrong and we're all dead? Or worse . . .?'

'I have explained all of this. Nonetheless, they insist.'

Rashim stared at his project leader. 'Is it *that* bad?'

Yatsushita pulled a seat up, looked across the maze of desks and cubicles at the dozen other technicians working late. He sat down and lowered his voice. 'It is much, much worse than the news media are reporting. They have been kept in the dark. There is an embargo on the worst of it.'

'Worst of it? What do you mean?'

'A smart-virus, Rashim. It is an advanced smart-virus! A *Von Neumann*!'

Rashim nodded slowly. Von Neumann – a hypothetical premise imagined by a Hungarian theorist, John von Neumann, over a hundred and fifty years ago. Machines capable of harvesting their own resources for infinite self-replication. Nanotechnologists had tried experimenting with that concept at the beginning of the twenty-first century with little success. Little robots the size of blood cells. But robotically there were too many practical problems to overcome. However, biologically – a very different story. After all, bacteria were biological Von Neumann machines of a sort. But the Holy Grail – certainly in terms of weapons use – was a bacterium that could be smart, could be given genetic instructions, an objective, a specified goal. Could be given a *target*.

'A sample has been isolated and analysed by a team in Tokyo,' said Dr Yatsushita. Rashim could see the man was clearly shaken.

'And?'

'It is designed to depopulate. Designed to target humans only.'

'It's engineered?'

'Of course it is! On contact with any human cells, it activates, breaks down the cell structures into acids, proteins.' He ran a hand through his silver hair. 'It completely *liquidizes* the infected within hours!'

'My God!'

'The liquid solution is used by the bacteria to make copies of themselves, to grow spores – like feathers, like pollen – that can be carried by the wind.'

'Are there any cases of immunity yet? Ethnic-specific resistance?'

Yatsushita shook his head. 'No. Not yet. So far it seems no one is immune. Whoever made this did not care that it would kill the whole world.'

Rashim looked at the holo-screen shimmering in the air above his desk. Endless columns of data that needed collating and processing.

'Now do you see why they want T-Day advanced?' said Dr Yatsushita. 'Something like Kosong-ni is what leaders have feared for decades. A perfect bioweapon.'

Rashim rubbed his temple. 'Jesus.'

Dr Yatsushita nodded. 'I have told our sponsors that all the T-Day candidates must make their way here *immediately*. We must finalize the mass index as soon as possible. We cannot keep changing the data.'

Rashim nodded. 'Yes . . . yes, absolutely.'

His boss leaned forward. 'Dr Anwar, you have family on the candidate list, don't you?'

'Yes . . . my parents.'

'Call them, Rashim . . . get them here now. Before it's too late!'

CHAPTER 9

2001, New York

'Brace yourselves,' said Maddy. She looked at them across the breakfast table, Liam and Sal sitting beside each other on their threadbare sofa, eyes resting expectantly on her.

They're not going to like this.

'Jahulla! Come on, Maddy . . . what is it?'

'This agency of ours . . . it's, I'm not sure how to say this . . .'

'Well, just say it anyway.' Liam fidgeted impatiently. 'I'm sure we've heard worse already.'

'Not really.' She pushed her glasses up the bridge of her nose. 'The agency is just us.'

The words hung above the table in the space between them. They hung in the stillness of the archway, accompanied by the soft hum of networked computers and the muted rumble of a train running over the Williamsburg Bridge above them.

'What do you mean *just us*?' asked Sal.

'I mean exactly that, Sal. We're *it*. The three of us.'

Liam sat forward, frowning, confused. 'But . . . but Foster told us there were other teams, in other places, so he did.'

'I know he did. But he lied.'

Sal looked past her. One eye lost behind a fringe, the other one just lost. 'But . . .'

'There was that message, Maddy.' Liam leaned on the table.

'That message from the future about Edward Chan, so there was . . .'

'There is one other person in the agency,' she replied. 'It's that guy Waldstein. Roald Waldstein.'

'That fella who invented time travel?'

'That's him. He's the one who set this archway up. He's the guy who recruited Foster and the previous team.'

Sal shook her head, working it through in her mind silently.

Liam slapped a hand on the table. 'Jay-zus-'n'-Mother-Mary! You know I . . . I was wondering why it's always *us* who was dealing with everything! Why them other teams were too bleedin' lazy to get off their backsides and help out!'

Maddy splayed her hands. 'Well, now we know.'

'But didn't Foster say this Waldstein was totally *against* time travel?' asked Sal. 'That he, like, campaigned against it or something?'

'Yes, he did. But he also set this up, secretly, as a back-up plan. I guess he figured that even with international agreements prohibiting the development of time-travel technology, on the sly, every government would be having a go at it.'

Liam laughed softly. 'I knew it! I just bleedin' well knew it!'

'It's not fair Foster didn't tell us that,' said Sal. She looked up at Maddy. 'Why did he lie to us?'

Maddy shrugged. 'I guess he didn't want to overload us. Put too much pressure on us.'

'Did he just tell you now, Maddy? This morning?'

She nodded. 'Yup.'

Sal's eyes narrowed. 'Why?'

'Why? What?'

'Why did he wait till *now* to tell you?'

'I guess . . . I guess he figured from all the stuff I told him we'd been through that we were ready to find out.'

'*Chutiya!*' She stood up, biting her lip angrily. 'He thinks we're *bakra*? Stupid? What else is he holding back from us?'

Maddy would have liked to say 'nothing', but she wasn't entirely sure that Foster had given them the whole picture yet. She too was guilty of that, holding truths back from her friends. For example, when exactly was she going to tell Liam that time travel was killing him? Ageing him? That he was going to look exactly like Foster very soon.

A bigger deal than that — that he and Liam were the *same person*. When the hell was she going to tell him that?

And what did that mean anyway?

Maddy had tried running that little doozy through her mind many times over. Did it mean Liam had been recruited from the *Titanic* before? Did it mean that this archway existed in a bigger loop of time, that one day Liam was going to be an old man? An old man who had somehow outlived her and Sal and now needed to renew the cycle by revisiting the last moments of their 'normal' lives and recruiting them all over again?

'Maddy?'

She looked up. Sal was sitting on the end of the table. 'There's something I've seen, but I've been keeping to myself.'

Liam looked from her to Maddy. 'Uh? Hang on! Has everyone here got a bleedin' secret except me?'

Sal ignored him. 'This may sound crazy, but . . . have we been recruited before?'

'What?!'

Sal ignored him again. Her eyes were on Maddy. 'Has Foster said anything like that?'

'Recruited before? How do you mean?'

'Foster said there was another team before us, right?'

Maddy nodded.

'That they died. That that ghost thing . . . that "seeker" killed them.'

Liam cupped his jaw in his hands. 'Hold on! That's right! I remember that.'

'Was that team *us*, Maddy?'

Sal's eyes remained resolutely on Maddy, watching her fidget, delay . . . fudge.

Do I tell them that Liam is Foster? Because if Liam's been here before . . . maybe Sal's right and all three of us have.

'I'm asking because I've seen something I can't explain,' said Sal. She looked at Liam. 'Your uniform from the *Titanic*.'

He nodded. 'Aye, you told me you saw one a bit like my –'

'No, Liam. No. It IS your tunic.'

Maddy frowned. *Her* turn to be silenced by a revelation. 'What?'

'In that antique shop, the theatre costume shop near us. There's Liam's tunic hanging up.'

'Don't be stupid,' replied Maddy. She pointed at the rack of clothes hanging just outside their bunk nook. 'It's over there!'

'It's the same, Maddy. Exactly the same!'

'How can it be the same one, Sal? How can it be here and in that shop at the same time?'

'It *is*. It's missing the same button. It has exactly the same stain on it. The same shape in the same place!' She stood up, strode over to the wardrobe beside the nook. She pulled out his white tunic, still on its hanger, and brought it over to the table. She spread it out beneath the light above them.

'There. See?'

Liam got up and studied it.

'You got that stain on the *Titanic*, right? Down the left side. Big stain. What was it . . . wine or something?'

Liam frowned. 'I see it. Jayzzz . . . never even noticed that before.'

Maddy joined them. 'Me neither. It's faint.'

He looked at Sal. 'I . . . I don't think I ever spilled wine down me jacket. I don't remember doing anything like that. Chief Steward would've had me guts for garters.'

'So then it wasn't you?'

He shook his head. 'Maybe someone who had the uniform before me?'

'That's possible,' said Maddy.

Sal shook her head irritably. 'That's not the important bit. The point is there are two copies of it!' She looked up at them both. 'Do you see? Maybe that means Liam's been here before?'

Liam's eyes widened. 'This is . . .'

'Messing with your head?' asked Sal.

He nodded.

CHAPTER 10

2070, Project Exodus, Cheyenne Mountain, Colorado Springs

Who was it that once said, 'A week is a long time in politics'? Well, that was a pretty good observation to take note of, if not to adapt very slightly.

Rashim stared at the news-stream from New London, in the north of England.

A week is a long time with a pandemic.

This particular media feed had been running uninterrupted for two days now; a digi-streamer dropped on its side on the street by some panicked cameraman, had still been broadcasting powered by its own hydro-cell battery pack. The signal was being streamed round the world, no doubt watched by millions of other frightened people like Rashim.

The street had been full of people running from faint blooms descending from the sky like flakes of ash from a bonfire of paper. The blooms – viral spores – landing lightly on scalps, backs of hands, faces had an almost instantly lethal effect. The street had been full of stampeding people, and screaming voices . . . Then, five minutes later, after the camera had dropped and settled on its side, it was silent and full of corpses.

Twenty-four hours ago, he'd been shaken by the sight of a solitary young girl staggering into the static view of the digi-streamer. A girl no more than eleven or twelve, collapsing to her knees, whimpering with fear and agony as her left arm dissolved and bacilli-like growths, like veins on the surface of her skin, snaked past her elbow and spread to her shoulder, her neck, her face.

She'd collapsed into a huddle very quickly, quite dead. And over the next six hours transformed into a pool of reddish-brown liquid and a bundle of empty clothes.

He'd watched with increasing horror as the puddle had grown slight protrusions, like humps, almost mushroom-like, that eventually opened to reveal fluffy spore heads like those of dandelions.

A fresh breeze had carried those away long ago.

Somewhere in a refugee camp in Kazakhstan, his parents most probably looked like the girl now. A tangle of clothes and a puddle of liquid.

'Rashim!'

It had all happened too quickly. The city lockdowns, quarantine. The complete shutdown of transportation systems. None of it had managed to stop the Kosong-ni virus.

'Dr Anwar!' He looked away from the holo-projection above his desk. Dr Yatsushita was leaning over the top of his cubicle partition. His tie loose and his top shirt button undone, his sleeves were rolled up and his lab coat dispensed with days ago. He'd taken to sleeping on a camp bed among the cubicles. As all of them had, working in ceaseless shifts to get things ready for T-Day.

'I must have those figures now!'

Rashim felt disengaged from the hustle and noise of activity going on around him. The hangar floor was now filled with people, equipment and machinery being brought in. He could see on one side of the concrete floor some famous faces he recognized: the vice-president, Greg Stilson, and the defence secretary. A few dozen yards away a Saudi prince and his family; next to him the bulk of some Central African dictator whose name he couldn't quite remember and his three young wives. Rashim suspected he must have spent the last of his nation's wealth to buy a place for himself on Exodus.

There were other faces he vaguely recognized: old men with young wives. The rich and powerful.

'The figures! Rashim!'

Rashim nodded slowly, and palmed the data off his screen and floated it on to Yatsushita's infopad. 'It's not even close to accurate,' he muttered absently.

'We have no more time,' Yatsushita said, lowering his voice. 'They will have to take their chances.'

So many of the carefully selected and vetted candidates for Exodus had not made it to the Cheyenne Mountain facility. Some of the B-list candidates had managed to be flown in, but there were many grid spots now either empty or filled with last-minute replacements. No longer the great and the brilliant, rocket scientists and geneticists. But a motley random collection of people – army truck drivers, clerical officers, project technicians – and, of course, a handful of politicians, billionaires, dictators; the well-connected who'd caught wind of Project Exodus's last-minute chance to negotiate themselves on to the transportation grid.

Not exactly the best representation of twenty-first-century society to send back into the past to make a new start.

Rashim looked up at Dr Yatsushita. 'You said "they". They will have to take their –'

'I am not going.'

'Why?'

The old man shook his head sadly. 'I cannot . . . not without my family.'

'Still no news?'

Yatsushita shook his head. He had managed to get his wife and daughter on a flight from Tokyo to Vancouver. But there they'd been stuck. No commercial or military flights left. Not even using leverage as the senior technician on Exodus was going to get them over here.

The old man looked over his shoulder at the chaos on the grid. 'Anyway, this is not the project I signed up to lead.'

Rashim knew exactly what he meant by that. This frenetic, undignified scramble away from the sudden and messy end of mankind was not what Project Exodus had been about. Even though it was a flagrant breach of ILA Ruling 234, known informally as Waldstein's Law, there was something worthy to it. The idea of rebooting civilization back in a time before man had begun to suck the world dry; the idea of bringing back twenty-first-century knowledge and enlightenment to an ignorant world that believed in gods and omens, repression and slavery. There was a germ of hope in all of that.

Hope. Something there seemed to be precious little of in this poisoned and dying world.

But these weren't the specially selected candidates, quietly informed over a year ago to settle their personal affairs and be ready to be collected and taken to the Exodus facility. It was a random collection of the rich, the *connected* . . . and, in a few cases, the plain lucky-to-be-grabbed-at-the-last-moment. A poor cross-section of candidates to be sending on such an important mission.

'So you're staying, Dr Yatsushita?'

He nodded.

'You'll die.'

'We *all* die eventually, Rashim.'

'I'll stay with —'

'No! There needs to be a project technician with them. As senior technician on the grid, you will have full authority! I will make that official with a data entry.'

Rashim shook his head. 'Me in charge of them? Look, I'm just a —'

'There is a mission protocol. Mission jurisdiction. They are all aware of this and signed contracts of agreement to come along. They must accept you as Project Exodus leader.'

Rashim looked across at the vice-president.

'Yes,' said Yatsushita, 'even he must accept you as his . . .' The old man paused, smiling. '. . . as his *boss*.' He nodded at the vice-president, the prince, the dictator and a handful of others – all of them clearly elated to have made it into the facility before the security lockdown.

'Don't let any of those parasites become leader, Rashim.' He smiled sadly. 'Let this be a proper new beginning for mankind. Eh?'

Rashim nodded, stood up, pushed his chair back on its castor wheels. Beyond the calm of the small enclave of cubicles, the hangar was a riot of noise and activity. Voices raised in confusion, fear, excitement. The clattering of two dozen military combat units weighed down with carbon-flex body armour, weapons and equipment. The whirring of exoskel-kinetic loaders depositing heavy crates of supplies into specially holo-flagged grid markings. The deep rumble of three Mobile Command Vehicles backing into their large grid slots.

Dr Yatsushita reached a hand out and grasped one of his tightly. 'The military units are programmed to follow the Exodus protocols. They will accept your authority, Rashim, once I've logged you in as my replacement.'

'Dr Yatsushita, please, you have to come. I'm not ready for this.' Rashim looked at the dictator, the prince, the politicians and the billionaires. 'I can't lead *them* . . . they won't accept that.'

The old man smiled. 'They don't have any choice in the matter.'

'You'll die if you stay. Please, you really need to come –'

'Everyone who remains behind will be dead, Rashim. This . . .' He turned to look over his shoulder at the frantic activity going on behind him. 'For what it is, *this* is our *only* future now.'

'This is crazy!'

'You have to go, Rashim. And you have to remain in charge of Exodus.' He smiled again, an almost paternal smile. Odd that, coming from the elderly Japanese man. Rashim had always got the impression that Dr Yatsushita hadn't liked him; that he disapproved of his maverick ways, his disorganized virtual workspace, the messy desk, his personalized lab assistant.

'I trust you, young man; *you* . . . far more than I trust any of *them*.'

Rashim swallowed anxiously. He could feel his stomach churning and a desperate need for a toilet visit. 'OK . . . O-OK. I'll . . . uh . . . I'll try.'

Dr Yatsushita clapped him on the shoulder. 'You'll do fine.'

CHAPTER 11

2001, New York

'So, Maddy, let me just check I got this wording correct,' said the guy on the other end of the line. He was just the kind of help-desk type that bugged her: overfamiliar. Way too friendly. It's not like they were dating or anything, so why'd he have to keep using her name like they'd known each other since kindergarten?

'*A soul lost in time* . . . that right, Maddy?'

She sighed. 'Yes . . . so far.'

'*Need to know what you know about Pandora. Aware it is "the end". Have learned the "family" is just us and you. And we have been used before. Insist on further information. Will not attend any more "parties" until we hear back.*' She heard the help-desk guy chuckle. 'Whoa . . . Maddy, what are you? Some kinda super-secret agent or something?'

'Yeah . . . that's right.' She rolled her eyes. 'Some kinda super-secret agent. Now you going to print that ad for me, or are you just going to carry on making fun of me?'

'Hey, look, I'm sorry . . . I'll . . . uh, I'll make sure it gets in tomorrow's edition.'

'Thanks. It's important you do.'

'So that's, let me see . . .' She heard him counting under his breath. 'Thirty-four dollars for a week in the classified section of the *Brooklyn Daily* —'

'No. I want it in just for tomorrow. Just Tuesday.'

'Doesn't cost you a cent more to be in the whole week, you know, Maddy.'

'Just tomorrow's edition, please. That's all.'

'OK . . . if that's what you want. Gonna need your card details now, Maddy . . .'

She ran through them as quickly as she could, keen to get the call and the gratuitous and obligatory *you-have-a-nice-day* over and done with. Finally done, she put the mobile phone down on the desk and looked at the others. 'So, there we go.'

Liam grinned a little anxiously. 'Do you think we'll tick this Waldstein fella off?'

She cocked her head casually. 'I'm sort of past caring, Liam. Somebody owes us an explanation. We've been through Hell and back several times over. We've been doing his dirty work pretty much blind. I'm not lifting another finger until we get some information.'

Sal nodded at that. 'Yeah. It's not fair. They should trust us now.'

'It's *he* . . . not *they*,' corrected Maddy.

Sal shrugged that away. 'Whatever. Whoever. We're owed an explanation.'

Maddy looked round at the archway. 'I want to know who precisely set this place up. It couldn't have just been Waldstein, though. And how long ago? How many teams have been here before us?' She looked at the others. At Sal. 'And yeah, maybe you're right to ask, Sal. Were they really *us*?'

'What if someone else gets the message?' said Sal. Maddy hadn't thought about that. 'I mean it'll be out there in a newspaper, right? What if someone else knows to look at that ad?'

'Then we just made a big mistake.' Maddy looked at Bob warily. 'What about you, Bob? Any thoughts you want to share on this?'

'It is a logical move to seek to acquire more information, Maddy.'

'You don't have any secret lines of code, do you? Hmm? Any deeply buried *priority protocols* that would make you object to us questioning our . . .' She was going to say 'HQ', but she wondered if this agency even had something like that. '. . . questioning our *boss*?'

'Negative, Maddy. My highest priority is preserving history and protecting you.'

'You're not going to suddenly rip our heads off or anything?'

His horse-lips protruded into something close to a sulky pout. 'I would not hurt any of you.'

Liam punched his arm lightly. 'Don't worry, coconut-head, we all love you. So, Maddy?' He sat back in his chair and crossed his arms defiantly. 'Is this what I think it is, then?'

'What's that?'

'A workers' strike.'

She nodded, her mouth set with a determined smile. 'Too right it is.' She slurped some of her Dr Pepper from the can. 'If they . . . he . . . Waldstein . . . *whoever* wants us to save history again, then we better start getting some answers.'

Liam nodded, raising his coffee cup. 'I'll drink to that.'

'Me too,' said Sal, lifting a glass of fruit juice. She presented it across the table and the other two clinked mug and soda can with her.

Bob nodded thoughtfully. 'Affirmative.' He looked around. 'I have nothing to drink . . . is that required?'

CHAPTER 12

2070, Project Exodus, Cheyenne Mountain, Colorado Springs

Rashim took his space on the translation grid, a yard square, as it was for every other personnel slot. Enough of a safety margin to ensure no one became 'merged' during the journey. Of course nothing was certain. Rashim knew that better than anyone else standing on the hangar floor. The laws of physics and its predictability had a way of breaking down in extra-dimensional space, or *chaos space* as the enigmatic Roald Waldstein had once named it.

There was no knowing if any of them were going to survive this. Worse still, with his estimates of the total mass being translated — his precious mass index — now being more a thumb-in-the-air approximation than a precise figure, they could quite possibly overshoot or undershoot the receiver station. Or — Jesus . . . it didn't bear thinking about — they might never even emerge from extra-dimensional space.

Dr Yatsushita's voice echoed across over the hangar's PA system announcing the ten-minute warning.

'Excuse me . . . no one's told me anything about what's going on.'

Rashim turned to look at a man standing in the floor grid beside him. The floating holographic data block floating above the ground said he was Professor Elsa Korpinkski: Physicist. Clearly he wasn't her.

'Excuse me, sir! You know what's happening? What's gonna happen in ten minutes?'

The man was wearing olive fatigues – an army corporal by the chevron on his arm. He was one of the last-minute 'volunteers' they'd rounded up as they'd sealed and locked down the facility. Effectively *ballast*, that's what these last-minute personnel were – equivalent mass for the many empty grid spaces of those candidates who'd failed to make it to the facility in time.

Although Kosong-ni virus blooms had already been spotted in Denver, and a dozen miles further south in Castle Rock – perilously close given the blooms were airborne – they'd hung on until Vice-president Greg Stilson and his wife had arrived by gyrocopter before the facility's nuclear blast-proof and airtight concrete doors had swung to, sealing off the world outside.

The corporal looked round the hangar floor. 'What's all these holo-lines and displays for? This some kind of inoculation for that Korean virus or something? That it? This a cure?'

'We're leaving,' said Rashim.

'Leaving?' He wiped sweat off his top lip. 'What? How? Leaving . . . what're you talking about?'

Rashim could see a name on his pocket: North. 'We're all going into the past, Corporal North.'

'The past? What . . . er . . . what's that? You just say *past*?' He took a step closer to Rashim, an army boot stepping across the line of his grid square. A soft warning chimed across the PA system. The calm, synthetic female voice of the launch computer system. 'Proximity warning, grid number 327. Please remain inside your location markers.'

'You need to step back,' said Rashim, pointing down at his boot. 'You need to be in your grid.'

North looked down. Did as he was told. 'Did you just say . . . the past? Like —?'

'Yup. Like back-in-time past.'

The man swore. 'You telling me this . . . this is some sort of time machine? But that's . . . that's —'

'A direct violation of international law. Yes, I know.' Rashim pointed at the glowing holo-projected line hovering an inch above the concrete floor. 'You should try and remain calm. And at all times, until we have safely *translated*, you must remain within your grid square. Is that clear?'

Corporal North looked at the square of light on the floor around him. 'Or what?'

'Or whatever's hanging over the line isn't coming with you.'

'Jesus!'

'That or it ends up stuck in the middle of the poor guy in the next square. Just stay still.'

'No one told me nothing. They just grabbed me and a bunch of others out of the compound —'

'Just stay calm and keep still.'

'Dr Anwar?' Yatsushita's voice boomed across the cavernous interior. 'Your figures have been entered and the translation simulation program has approved them as being within an acceptable range of error. Are you ready to proceed?'

Rashim very much doubted that. However, the program warning could be over-ridden. He just hoped the warning was a marginal amber, as opposed to a blatant flashing red. He nodded back to him.

Corporal North looked at Rashim. 'You? *You're* in charge of all of this?'

'Uh . . . yeah. I am, sort of.'

'Field generator is charging,' announced the PA system. 'Translation in eight minutes.'

He looked around at the Exodus group: mostly men, many of them old, a few women and children dotted around; he even saw a newborn baby being placed carefully on the ground. The families of the super-rich. This group should have been three hundred of the world's brightest minds, young men and women ready to colonize the past and bring with them the best values of the modern world.

On the far side the platoon of combat units stood perfectly still in their own grids. Genetically engineered soldiers: slabs of muscle and bone in army-green, carbon-flex body armour and helmets and carrying enough ordnance between them to wage a small war.

Rashim spotted SpongeBubba waddling over towards him.

'Hey, skippa!' he said with a cheerful plastic smile.

'Bubba, I'm leaving now. You have to get off the translation grid.'

'I know,' he replied, grinning chirpily. 'I just came over to say goodbye. Oh, and you have three more messages in your personal in-box. All bills. The first one is a payment reminder from Intercytex Systems –'

Rashim smiled. The stream had a habit of choking on its own internal mail system. 'They can wait, Bubba. You better get off.'

'Righto.'

'Oh, Dr Yatsushita will be your owner-operator from now on.'

For what time he has left.

'I understand. Goodbye, skippa. Have a great trip!'

'Goodbye, Bubba.'

He watched the yellow lab assistant turn and waddle back towards the cubicles and desks and the blue-green glow of dozens of floating holo-displays.

'Translation in five minutes.' Dr Yatsushita's voice. 'Any non-Exodus personnel must leave the grid immediately.'

Rashim could hear the growing hum of energy being channelled into the hangar. From the ceiling above he heard the clank of chains and motors as the 'cage' was being readied to descend. The cage was a fine wire mesh, a curtain of conductive material that was going to be lowered all the way round the perimeter of the translation grid, like a stage magician hiding his assistant behind a veil before making her vanish. The energy that was going to be channelled through it was much more than the Cheyenne Mountain facility's generator could handle. They were tapping several other nuclear reactors in Colorado for this, switching *whole cities off* to make this happen. Lights in Denver were probably winking off right now. Not that anyone still alive outside was going to notice, or even care.

The image of the liquidized girl from the media feed haunted him; nothing more than a huddle of clothes and pool of dark liquid developing a leathery skin. He wondered how long before the last isolated groups of humankind were infected. Before mankind was completely erased.

Perhaps without humans, the world will find a way to recover.

There was something a little comforting about that thought. Cities would descend into rubble and rust, and nature would find a way to rebalance the poisoned air, the toxic seas. *To eventually erase every last memory of us.* Another failed experiment. The dinosaurs had their time and mankind had his.

Whose turn next?

'Lowering the energy cage.'

Rashim looked up and saw the wire mesh shroud slowly winching down, enclosing them all. Those who'd been last-minute stand-ins looked anxiously around them, unfamiliar with the translation process.

'What's that? *What's coming down?*'

'Relax,' he called out to the corporal. 'It's just making a very big Faraday cage round us. Generating a large shoebox-shaped energy field, wrapping us up for delivery.'

'Like a parcel?'

Others across the hangar floor looked equally startled. Few of those standing among the grid squares had received any briefing at all about the process; even the vice-president had shed his media-friendly calm and was looking around anxiously.

Rashim smiled. 'Yes . . . just like a parcel.'

He caught one last glance of Dr Yatsushita and exchanged a nod with him.

Yatsushita mouthed something. Rashim could guess what it was. *Don't let them take over.* Then he was lost behind the shimmer of the curtain of fine wire mesh. The whir of motors finally ceased as the mesh touched the concrete floor.

'Energy release in two minutes. Please ensure you are entirely *within* your grid markings.'

Rashim looked around and saw everyone else doing likewise, making sure they were standing in the middle of their squares. He was certain that in some cases it didn't matter how carefully placed they were: they weren't going to make it through alive. If their body mass varied too much from that of the candidate who *should have been* standing there, then . . . well, he had no idea what was going to happen to them. Lost. Turned inside out. He looked at the few children, at the baby squirming on the floor.

Stupid fools — bringing their children along.

He'd tapped in wild estimates for some of them.

'One minute until energy release. Please now ensure you are standing as still as possible.'

He closed his eyes, feeling certain this was all going to end up being a ghastly, bloody mess. Too much haste. Too many fudged, guessed-at numbers. This wasn't what he'd signed up to either. Oddly, though, oddly . . . he realized he wasn't scared. It was not as if there was anything left to lose. Not as if he was leaving behind any family or friends. Not as if he was leaving behind anyone or anything worth crying over. During the last week he'd watched, on a screen, a virus annihilate humankind. Watched it as if it was one of those old disaster movies people used to go to 'movie theatres' to see.

A virus that had erased humankind and nothing else.

A man-made virus no less.

We went and did this to ourselves. There seemed to be some satisfying symmetry in that: after screwing up the world, we went and finished the job with ourselves.

The humming of the field increased and Rashim heard the crackle of energy arcing above their heads across the football-pitch-sized translation grid.

He heard Dr Yatsushita's booming voice one more time. Couldn't make out the words above the deep *thrum* of energy. He could feel the hairs on his arms lift, then the hair on his head rise with the build-up of static electricity all around him.

This is it. A goodbye to everything – to the twenty-first century, to a world completely trashed by mankind. A goodbye to nations murdering each other over land, over food, over water . . . sometimes just over the colour of a person's skin, a difference in faith, a method of worship, a political opinion.

As the power surged into the wire mesh and arcs of energy leaped across the translation grid mere inches above their heads, Rashim wondered if mankind really deserved this elaborate *cheat*, this second roll of the dice. Perhaps the only way to truly learn is to fail . . . and fail badly. That's what Kosong-ni was: mankind's lesson. Mankind's EPIC FAIL. The few, if any, who survived that were probably going to be far wiser about the future than these people standing around him.

We made a mess of things . . . and what do we do? We run away from it.

He had a feeling all they were doing was rebooting civilization so that it could make the same stupid hash of things all over again. And again.

And again.

CHAPTER 13

2001, New York

'Excuse me?'

'That tunic hanging up there,' said Sal to the old lady. 'Can we just take a closer look at it?'

'The *Titanic* one?'

Maddy nodded. 'That's it.'

The old woman pulled a stool out from behind the counter, stood on it, wobbling precariously as she unhooked the hanger from the railing and brought it down for them. She pushed aside a small stack of second-hand books waiting to be priced and made space on the counter, then spread the jacket out carefully.

'It's almost an antique, you know,' said the old woman. 'It's nearly ninety years old.' She smoothed her wrinkled hands across the cloth. 'Older than me even.' She smiled.

Maddy and Sal stared down at it for a moment.

'I don't rent it out for fancy dress. And I really don't know whether I'd want to sell it.' She shrugged. 'Except if the price was right.'

Sal leaned over it. 'There. See?' She pointed to the shoulder of the tunic. Maddy stooped over, adjusted her glasses and peered closely.

'You're right!'

It was there. So faint it was missable unless you were looking for it.

'What is it, ladies?'

'A stain,' said Sal. 'Red wine or something?'

The old woman lifted glasses on a chain and propped them on the bridge of her nose. She peered closely at where Sal was pointing. 'Oh my . . . you know, I never noticed that before!'

'Can I ask where you got it?' asked Maddy.

The old woman straightened up, lifted off her glasses and let them dangle on her chest. 'Well now. It was someone's attic clean-out if I recall. A job lot I bought for this store. A box full of all sorts of dusty old things. Quite a surprise to find this among all the other bits. But you do find gems like this from time to time –'

Sal pointed towards the shop's grimy window. 'What about that bear?'

The old woman leaned over the counter to see what she was pointing at. 'On the rocking-chair? The stuffed bear?'

'Yes.'

'Oh, I got all those soft toys from a day-care centre . . . I think.' She looked back down at the tunic and the faint wine stain. 'Fascinating. Isn't it? Something like this . . . makes history come alive,' she said to Maddy. 'Almost like going back in time. You can try and imagine how that stain happened.' The old woman's eyes glinted with excitement. 'Perhaps this crewman was busy delivering a glass of sherry to some duchess when the *Titanic* hit that iceberg and that's where the stain came from!'

Maddy humoured her with a nod. 'Yeah. That's kind of cool.' She noticed Sal was still staring at the soft toys on the rocking-chair. She nudged her gently. 'Sal?'

'Uh?' Sal turned back.

'OK?'

She nodded. Distracted.

A bell chimed and the shop door opened. A man entered

70

with a tuxedo and a ball gown carefully draped over his arms.

'Ah! Mr Weismuller!' The old woman stepped from behind her counter. 'How was your lodge party?'

'Come on,' said Maddy. She took hold of Sal's hand. 'Let's go.' She led Sal out. 'Miss? Thanks for showing us your tunic!' she called to the old woman as they both squeezed past her customer and stepped outside. But she was already chattering away to him, barely noticing the pair of them leaving.

Outside on the pavement, Maddy shook her head. 'My God! You were right. It is . . . it's exactly the same!'

Sal was still looking through the window back at the soft toys on the rocking-chair.

'Sal? What is it?'

She turned back to Maddy, a smile quickly spread on her face. 'Nothing. Nothing. Just . . . uh . . .' She changed the subject. 'See, then? I told you. The tunic . . . what do you think it means? It means *something*, right? It definitely means *something*!'

Maddy nodded. 'Yes . . . yes, it does.' She realized it was better Liam wasn't here with them. Both Liam and Bob had gone out to their local Barnes & Noble for some reading matter. Liam was adamant he wanted to read up on how to use computers and the Internet better. Maddy assured them there really was a book entitled *The Complete Idiot's Guide to the World Wide Web*, that she wasn't just being rude.

'Do you know what I think?' said Sal. 'This is going to sound like I'm a complete *fakirchana*-head. But . . .' She took a breath. 'I think that tunic might be *Foster's*!'

Maddy chewed her lip anxiously. Perhaps this was the right time to share what the old man had told her. Sal was so close to the truth . . . in a way. Secrets. She hated keeping them, particularly this one. It stank.

'Sal . . . we need to talk about Liam.'

71

Sal looked at her sharply. 'What? What is it?'

'He's . . . well, he's not who you think he is.'

Sal looked shaken. 'What?! What do you mean? Who is he?'

'Let's go get a coffee. Right now.'

'Maddy! Tell me!' She looked upset. No. *Frightened*. 'Who is he!?'

'I need a coffee first.' Maddy realized she was trembling. Her legs felt like they were set to give way on her and she felt queasy enough to hurl chunks on to the pavement. 'I need to sit down, Sal. I really need to. I need to gather my thoughts . . . and I need a freakin' coffee.'

CHAPTER 14

AD 37, 16 miles north-east of Rome

He found himself staring up at a cloudless blue sky. A rich, deep blue like the skies one used to see in old images from the beginning of the twenty-first century. Quite different from the perpetual discoloured cloud cover of 2070: the turbulent, sulphurous acid rain clouds, the ever-present smog above cities and refugee shanty towns.

Quite beautiful.

Rashim could feel the warmth of the sun on his face. Hear the whisper of a fresh, untainted breeze gently stirring the branches and leaves of trees nearby.

Is this Heaven?

He realized that was a pleasing notion. That Project Exodus had gone disastrously wrong, that every translation candidate including himself had died – torn to pieces by extra-dimensional forces – and this . . . this was the afterlife. His uncle, an imam, had once taken him aside and tried to describe what Allah's Paradise would be like. It had sounded like this. And he'd scoffed at the man's faith.

Maybe I was wrong. Maybe there is a God.

And that pleasant illusion could have lasted a while longer, lying there on his back and enjoying the deep blue above him, if it hadn't been for the stirring of others all around him. It seemed like they'd managed to do it. They survived the jump.

With a weary sigh, Rashim slowly lifted himself up on to his elbows and looked around.

They were right on the flat ground of the receiver station, a field of swaying, olive-coloured grass. In the distance the glint of a gently meandering river and hills beyond that.

The correct location all right. But he couldn't see any sign of the four receiver beacons, ten-foot-tall tripods with an equipment platform at the top of each one. Each one marking a corner of ground space the exact same size as the translation grid back in the Cheyenne Mountain facility.

He got to his feet, hooding his eyes from the sun. No sign of them. Rashim cursed.

We've overshot the snap range.

'Where is this? Where *are* we?'

Rashim turned to his right. The corporal was standing beside him. 'Where the hell is this?'

'Where this is, is near Rome. But I'm not sure precisely *when* it is. The receiver station was deployed ahead of us in AD 54,' Rashim continued, more thinking aloud than answering the corporal's question. 'They should be right here, dammit, but I can't see any of the beacons.'

'AD 54 . . .?' The man rubbed his temples as if trying to push the idea into his head. 'You mean like the year 54? Like fifty-four years after Jesus Christ?'

Rashim nodded distractedly. 'Only this isn't. I can only guess this is some time before then. We've overshot the destination time. This is further back in time.'

Rashim completed his three-sixty survey. The field was peppered with people slowly sitting up and getting to their feet, gathering their wits and looking dumbstruck up at the strangely clear and beautifully blue sky above. Many of them still in a silent state of shock. Across the field he noted one of the MCVs – the huge Mobile Command Vehicles – had gone missing.

One of the platoons of combat units strode purposefully across the field towards him, equipment jangling from its webbing, standard army-issue T1-38 pulse carbine slung from a strap on its shoulder. The combat unit came to a halt in front of him and took off its helmet.

'Dr Yatsushita has assigned you full authority.' Rashim looked at the unit, unsure whether it was telling him that or asking him. The combat units unnerved him. Unlike the bulky, seven-foot-tall goliaths the military used to develop, these newer models could pass more easily as human. Genetic tweaks had produced combat units every bit as strong as the older variants without requiring the same amount of muscle bulk. They still looked like a bunch of military stiffs, though; two dozen po-faced Combat Carls with identical buzz-cut hair. Hardly going to be the fun crowd at a party.

The combat unit standing in front of him carried the rank of lieutenant; its name, just like Corporal North, was stitched above the breast pocket of its camouflage tunic. Giving them names felt wrong. They should just have numbers. Mind you . . . he'd given his lab unit a name, hadn't he?

'Right, yes . . . uh . . . *Lieutenant Stern*, is it?' Rashim tried a salute. Not sure if it was the right thing to do.

Stern? Rashim wondered which moron came up with that cheesy name for this unit. He could only imagine what the rest of the platoon were called: Chuck, Butch, Tex, Travis.

'Sir,' said Stern, 'what are your orders?'

Rashim puffed his lips and laughed a little nervously. 'What . . . er, what do you suggest?'

Stern cast cool grey eyes across the field. There were a lot of empty patches of grass where equipment, even people, had gone

75

missing. 'I'd suggest, sir, we'd better take stock of how much got lost during the translation.'

Rashim nodded vigorously. 'Yes, yes, quite . . . exactly the thing I was going to suggest. Very good.' He frowned, his best attempt at looking officious and entirely in command. 'Well, off you go then, uh . . . *Stern*. See to it.'

The combat unit saluted him crisply. 'Yes, sir.'

He watched the unit jog across the arid grass towards the rest of the platoon. The other people who had survived the jump were beginning to gather their wits. He could see Vice-president Stilson had managed to make it through – more's the pity – and that dictator and two of his wives.

Rashim wondered how long before one of them decided that they should be leading Project Exodus instead of him.

CHAPTER 15

AD 37, 16 miles north-east of Rome

'We're in a rural region called Sabines, about sixteen miles to the north-east of Rome.' Rashim looked at the Exodus group gathered in front of him. Just under a hundred and fifty of them. They'd lost roughly half the people in the jump. The children, the baby, were among those that had failed to emerge from extra-dimensional space.

God help them.

'This location was picked out by the Exodus survey team. Headed up by, uh . . . well, *me* actually.' He shrugged self-consciously. The sun was setting behind a row of cypress trees on the horizon, and long shadows stretched across the gently swaying grass around them. 'I was in charge of establishing the receiver station.'

'What's that?' someone in the gathering dusk asked.

'Four beacons broadcasting tachyon beams. The EDT: the Extra-dimensional Translation array . . .'

Keep it simple for the morons out there.

'The time machine –' he hated that term – 'was designed to zero in and snap to on these beacons' beams and use that to guide us in to the correct emergence point. But it, uh . . . it appears we've gone a little further back in time than we actually planned.'

'And lost over a hundred of our people!' Rashim turned

towards the voice. 'Someone messed this up badly!' Vice-president Stilson glared like an Old Testament preacher.

'Well now, look, Mr Stilson . . . this really isn't a precise science. And quite honestly, with all the last-minute data changes coming in, and no time to recalibrate the EDT's transmission program . . . Actually, I'm rather amazed that *any* of us survived!'

Stilson shook his head angrily. 'OK, I've heard enough. Look, I'm assuming authority from here on in. This is a damned mess already and we need to turn this around right now!'

'What?!' Rashim's voice skipped up a notch. It was almost a yelp. 'No! Look see, uh . . . Dr Yatsushita actually put me in charge of Exodus. He said that –'

'I'm afraid we don't have time for this, Dr Anwar . . . isn't it?' Rashim nodded.

'Right, well, I'm the senior government representative of the North American Federation here. Which gives me executive authority. Like it or not, that puts me in charge.'

'Dr Anwar . . .' A woman. Civilian. He recognized her as one of the Project Exodus support staff. Not one of the candidates.

'Yes?' Rashim answered her quickly before Stilson could go on any more. 'What is it?'

'Do you know how far we've overshot the receiver markers?'

Rashim nodded forcefully and tried his most authoritative face. Here was a question he most certainly had an answer for. 'Yes. I was able to successfully record the decay rate of the tachyon field. It's quite simple really. Tachyon particles decay at a constant rate, a very similar principle actually to something like carbon dating where . . .'

Keep it simple.

'Well, basically, to cut a very long and boring technical explanation short, ladies and gents, we went back about seventeen years earlier than planned.' He scratched his chin and offered them a wan smile. 'Which, actually, I think is quite impressive really.' He ran a hand through his hair. 'Given the last-minute metrics I had to guess at.' He shrugged and smiled. 'It could have been a lot worse than that really.'

'Seventeen years out . . . over half our people lost and most of our equipment gone!' Stilson stepped forward. 'Good God, man! This is already a damned mess! I know what the precise plans were for colonizing the past . . . that's ancient history now. We're going to have to take stock and –'

'Uh, well now, Mr Vice-president, yes . . . of course we may have to play out the "deployment phase" slightly differently.'

'You can say that again, Anwar. Looks like we'll be improvising the plan from now on.'

The group were silent. Few of them had been briefed on the details of Project Exodus.

'All right, listen up, everyone!' barked Stilson. 'Gather round closer! I'm going to bring you folks up to speed on what you need to know. What I'm about to tell you has been classified for top-level eyes only. Outside of the Exodus technical team, the only other eyes on this have been those of the President, myself and the joint Chiefs of Staff.'

Rashim noticed how easily Stilson could rally everyone round.

'This project has been in development for over five years, funded by what remained of our defence procurement budget, for what it was. Exodus was . . . and still *is* . . . our plan to transplant *our* values, *our* knowledge, *our* wisdom on to the infrastructure of an existing, well-established and robust civilization. The Roman Empire.'

Rashim heard the vice-president's audience stir.

'A panel of historical experts identified a specific moment in time in which to deploy Exodus. We were *meant* to arrive towards the tail end of the reign of a weak emperor. A guy called Claudius. A weak emperor struggling to maintain his position in power. Now . . . the plan was quite simple. To offer our services, our technology, to this guy Claudius in exchange for executive power. In effect to become his governing body. And eventually, on his death, to replace Roman dictatorship with American-style Republican democracy.'

Stilson turned and looked at Rashim pointedly. 'But it appears things have gone very wrong.'

Rashim felt all of their eyes fall on him. 'Uh . . . now, yes. But you see most of you here are the *wrong* people. That is to say, you're all the wrong weights and sizes; it's thrown all my calculations completely out! Which is why we lost –'

'Dr Anwar,' said Stilson, 'what we *don't* need to hear are excuses or technobabble after the fact. What we *do* need to do is start rethinking our plan of action. We're here in this time now and that's what we have to deal with. So, what we need to start finding out is exactly where we stand. What the situation is seventeen years earlier. Can you at least tell us something about that?'

Rashim looked at the man and the others gathered behind him.

You've lost them already. You're not in charge any more. He realized it wasn't knowledge or wisdom that made a leader. It wasn't being smarter than everyone else. And, by God, he could perform intellectual somersaults round most of these morons. No, it was something as simple as the deep cadence of a voice, a certain way of addressing assembled people. A way of carrying yourself. Authority. Entitlement. Stilson had that all right. And Rashim none of it.

'Dr Anwar?'

He sighed, slid open the panel of the h-pad on his wrist and a faint holographic display hovered in the air in front of him. 'Yes . . . there we go. So.' He swiped through a timeline with his finger. 'Ah, here we are. We'll be dealing with a different Roman emperor. Not Claudius, but . . .' His fingers traced along a glowing chart line to a name. 'Caligula.'

'What data do we have on this guy, Dr Anwar?'

'Uh . . . let me just look that up on my . . .' He hadn't had the time to read up on the historical briefing Dr Yatsushita had the project historians put together. Not really. If things had been a bit less of a frantic rush these last few months and weeks, he might have been able to give it a cursory read-through. His job was the metrics, punching the numbers – getting them all here in one piece.

'Emperor Caligula? I can tell you about him.' All heads turned towards someone in the crowd. By the fading light Rashim vaguely recognized the face: one of the candidates. One of the few people who was actually meant to be there instead of another last-minute gatecrasher.

'I know all about Caligula . . . God help us.'

Stilson gestured for the crowd to allow the man through. 'And you are?'

'Dr Alan Dreyfuss. Roman historian. Linguist.'

'OK, then, why don't you go ahead and tell us what you know, Dr Dreyfuss?'

The man was in his thirties, narrow-shouldered with a pot belly, a shock of sandy hair above glasses and a salt and pepper beard grown, Rashim suspected, to hide a double chin.

'Oh, Caligula . . .' Dreyfuss began shaking his head. 'Oh boy, this guy's bad news.'

'Bad news? What do you mean?'

'He's mad.'

'Mad?'

'Uh-huh. Totally. Completely insane.'

The people stirred, unhappy at the sound of that.

'But look, I think there's a way we can play this guy,' said Dreyfuss, smiling.

Stilson pursed his lips and nodded appreciatively. He seemed to like *this* guy. 'All right, Dr Dreyfuss, let's hear what you've got.'

'Shock and awe. We'll make an entrance.' Dreyfuss played the crowd almost as well as Stilson. 'This guy made his own horse a senator, would you believe? This guy, Caligula, believed in omens, portents; he was superstitious, paranoid.'

Dr Dreyfuss grinned. 'We'll make him believe we're gods.'

CHAPTER 16

AD 37, north-east of Rome

The two MCVs bounced energetically across fields of wheat, leaving broad paths of flattened stalks in their wake. Rashim held on to the handrail as both hover-vehicles slid across a rutted track into the next field.

Their approach was relatively quiet; the deep hum of electromagnetic repulsors was almost lost beneath the clatter of strapped-on equipment bouncing against the carbominium hull. He watched the heads and shoulders of slaves emerge from the tall, swaying stalks like startled meerkats. Eyes and mouths suddenly wide with horror, then gone as they scurried away in fear of their lives.

Ahead of them a wider track thick with carts on the way into Rome became a sudden carpet of chaotic panic as slaves and merchants scattered into the fields and horses reared and bucked in their harnesses. The leading MCV veered left, on to the track. This one wasn't ruts of dried mud but a cobbled stone track. A proper road in fact.

'*All roads lead to Rome!*' Stilson's voice crackled over the comms-speaker.

Rashim wrinkled his nose and sighed in silent disgust at the blowhard idiot's appalling cliché. He looked at the back of Stilson in the MCV in front, standing on the vehicle's front gun platform like some buccaneer admiral on the prow of his square-rigged ship. The vice-president was punching his fist in the air with childlike excitement.

You let that jerk take over. Congratulations.

He looked at the combat unit sitting beside him on the MCV's hull, T1-38 calmly resting across muscular forearms. He covered his throat mic. 'Looks like someone's having fun, eh?'

The unit had the reflective sun visor of his helmet pulled down. Rashim couldn't see his eyes, just the bottom of his nose and the mouth, chewing on protein gum with all the grace of a horse munching on hay.

'Yes, sir.'

To be fair, Stilson and Dreyfuss's rejigging of the plan called for a display of bravado. They'd lost way too much of their ammunition, power-packs, equipment and manpower to guarantee being successful taking control of Rome by force. Two dozen combat units and whatever number of rounds of ammo they were carrying on their equipment belts were enough to make a spectacular display of firepower, but not much more. Certainly not enough to take on several legions and a city of one million inhabitants.

'Hell! We'll give 'em a display of shock and awe all right!'

Rashim vaguely recognized the catchphrase Stilson and Dreyfuss were using, uttered by some puffed-up presidential moron long ago. Shock and awe. Make them believe the gods have come down to earth! That was basically their plan. Roll right into the middle of Rome, make a ton of noise, intimidate the lot of them and take over the whole show. Simple.

All puff and posture. Smoke and mirrors. Bluffing it to the hilt.

Right up Stilson's street.

The MCV ahead suddenly lurched upwards and glided over an abandoned cart left in the middle of the road. As they did the same, Rashim glanced down through the open turret hatchway at the passengers he could see crammed in down below. Approximately fifty of them, standing room only. They swayed queasily as their vehicle rose and dipped alarmingly, like a dinghy riding a rough sea. He was glad he was up here outside and not tucked away down there; he'd have thrown up by now. Hovertransports always made him travel-sick.

'Sir!'

Rashim turned to the combat unit beside him. He was pointing dead ahead.

He followed the unit's gloved finger and saw down the arrow-straight cobbled road, flanking rows of evenly spaced, tall, thin cypress trees like a welcoming guard of honour. Beyond them the first faint outline of the city; a long pale wall, and hovering above a sea of terracotta tile roofs that receded into a morning haze, a myriad of hairline threads of smoke from countless cooking fires and kilns, bakers, blacksmiths and tanneries stoked up for a day's business climbed lazily towards a Mediterranean sky.

Rome.

'Rashim, you hear me?'

It was Stilson. 'Yes, I can hear you.'

'Ready to give 'em a show they'll never forget, eh?'

Rashim rolled his eyes. The vice-president sounded insufferably excited. 'You really want to put that, uh . . . that *music* on?'

'Goddammit! Yes, of course I do. Stick it on, man. As loud as you can!'

Reluctantly Rashim ducked down inside the hatch and nodded to the combat unit piloting the MCV. 'Stilson says to put that music of his on now. Loudly.'

'Affirmative.'

Almost immediately his ears were ringing from chest-thumping decibels of noise booming out of the vehicle's PA system.

Stilson's choice of music, downloaded from his personal media digi-cube. Awful-sounding old stuff he called 'rock music'.

The speakers mounted outside on the front of both MCVs blared and thumped, and a ragged-throated singer was screaming something about being born in the USA . . .

CHAPTER 17

2001, New York

Maddy set the tray down on the table between them. A strong, milky, sugary frothy latte for her, and a fruit smoothie for Sal.

'So?' said Sal impatiently. 'What is it about Liam?'

Maddy settled into the booth and leaned over the table, her voice low. 'So, it's something Foster told me about him. He's . . .' She shook her head. 'This is so weird, it's gonna really mess with your head, Sal.'

'Jahulla! Maddy! Just tell me!'

'Liam and Foster . . . they're the same.'

She pulled a face. 'What?'

'The same. They're the exact same person.'

Sal turned to look out of the window. There was a market outside: grocers, fishmongers and milling customers. They could have sat outside the cafe; it was certainly warm enough this Monday afternoon, but, with the market going on, far too noisy for their need to talk in hushed whispers.

'The *same*?'

Maddy nodded. 'Foster was once Liam.'

Sal's mouth hung open. *Catching flies*, an expression her mom used to use.

Maddy nodded. 'That's right . . . give it a moment to sink in, Sal. It totally fried my head when Foster first told me.'

'But what? . . . So that means . . .?' Sal stopped, cocked her head and frowned, then tried again. 'Are you saying Foster was young like Liam?'

'Exactly like Liam.'

'Foster's been working for the agency since he was sixteen?'

'Ahh, yeah, I guess . . . well, kind of.'

Sal chewed the top of her straw, nibbling ferociously at it. She stopped. 'So this means Foster was once on the *Titanic*?'

Maddy nodded. 'I think so.'

'And he was recruited like Liam was?'

'I guess.'

'So then who recruited Foster?'

'I don't know . . . I don't know!' She looked down at her hands, playing with the handle of her teaspoon, stirring the frothy coffee unnecessarily. 'Maybe another Foster?'

'*Another* Foster?' Sal looked up at her. 'Like it's a loop or something? Like our archway field, but bigger? Looping round and round? Does that mean there are other *us*? Other *you*s and *me*s?'

Maddy shrugged. 'I'm still trying to figure how this all works. Perhaps it was someone else who recruited Foster.' She hesitated. 'Waldstein even?'

'This is so *chutiya*! This is really scaring me, Maddy. I don't know what to believe, what to think.' She laughed. 'It's a *chutiya*-crazy idea.'

'What is?'

Sal shrugged.

'Come on, Sal. What?'

'Those two jackets? Liam being Foster?' She looked up at Maddy. 'Maybe . . . this is so totally *chutiya*, but maybe we've all been here before.' A nervous, jittery half-smile flickered on to her face. 'Maddy, the team that came before us. Do you remember Foster saying there was that team that died?'

Maddy's coffee was midway between the table and her mouth. It stayed there. 'Oh my God! You think that was *us*?'

Sal shrugged. 'My diary . . . you know my diary?'

'That notebook you're always scribbling in, yeah.'

'There were pages ripped out when I found it.'

'I thought you *bought* it?'

'No, I found it in the arch.' She played with her straw. 'I found it tucked in my bunk.'

'And?' Maddy shook her head. 'These ripped-out pages . . .?'

'I think it might have been *me* writing in the diary before.'

'Oh . . .' was all she could say. Then, 'I'm not sure I like the sound of this.'

'Me neither.'

The pair of them stared at each other. 'We don't know anything for sure, do we?' said Sal finally. 'We're like little test rats in a lab.'

Maddy nodded. 'Feels like that sometimes.'

She looked out of the window at the street outside. Not for the first time she wished she could just walk away from all of this; trade places with just about anyone out there on the street.

'All I know is . . . I trust you, Sal. And I trust Liam too. As long as we're honest with each other.'

Sal turned to her. 'But *you did* keep things from us. The note from San Francisco with that Pandora message. And now this, Liam being Foster. You've lied to us! So how can −'

'I . . . you're right.' Maddy's eyes dropped guiltily. 'But I'm done with all the secrets. You know *everything* I know now.'

'And you said that before too.'

'Well, this time I mean it, Sal. Seriously. No more secrets. You know what I know.' She reached out for Sal's hand, but she pulled it away. 'Sal?'

'You seem to have picked up this job, though, Maddy . . . I

mean really easily. Like maybe you've done it before or something. Like maybe –'

'*Easy?* You're kidding, right? Tell me you're kidding. You
think it's been *easy* for me? Sheesh . . .' Maddy could hear her
voice wobbling with emotion. She shut up before that wobble
became tears. Pressed her lips and took a deep breath.

Don't you dare cry, Maddy. Don't you dare go girly.

She sipped at her coffee, not even wanting it any more. They
sat in silence for a while, both watching the market outside for
something to do other than look at each other.

'I'm sorry,' said Sal eventually.

'OK.'

'I was just saying . . .'

Maddy waved her hand. 'Forget it. I trust you, Sal. And I
trust Liam. We've put our lives in each other's hands, haven't
we? Quite a few times now.'

Sal nodded.

'And that's all the three of us have got. Each other. If I don't
even get to have that . . . then I don't want to go on doing this.
I *can't* go on doing this.'

Sal reached out and squeezed her hand. 'I'm sorry, Maddy.'

Maddy puffed her cheeks. ''s OK.' Tainted with guilt, though.
There was one more secret she hadn't shared and maybe now
was the time for it to come out.

'There's more, Sal. There's more I need to tell you.'

Sal looked like she didn't want to hear any more right now.
But the proverbial cat was halfway out of the bag. Maddy
decided she needed to hear this. 'Foster's old, right, Sal? Old.
How old do you reckon he is?'

'I don't know.' She hunched her shoulders. '*Really* old.'

'Come on, give me a number.'

'Seventy? Eighty?'

'Try twenty-seven.'

The smoothie almost slipped out of Sal's hands. '*What?*'

'He's twenty-seven years old.' Maddy sipped her coffee. 'So I suppose we can presume from that that he's been a TimeRider for ten years. The field office, our archway, this agency . . . has been doing its thing for about ten years' worth of two-day loop-time.'

That felt about right. The archway had – from day one – felt as if it had been lived in already. Certainly not brand spanking new. Freshly set up. But that wasn't the thing she needed to tell Sal now.

'Thing is . . . the time displacement aged Foster. Every time he went back in time to fix history it was corrupting him, ageing him before his time. And now the same is happening to Liam.'

Sal stared out of the window for a moment. Maddy suspected she already had half an idea something like that was happening to him. 'His hair?' she said after a while. 'That bit of his hair?'

Maddy nodded. 'Yup . . . that was a huge jump for Liam. Sixty-five million years. He took a big hit on that one. I hate to think how much of a bite that took out of the time he's got.'

'Chuddah,' Sal whispered. 'He's going to die, isn't he?'

'Before us . . . yes . . . quite probably.'

'And then?'

Maddy didn't know what happened then. Perhaps she would one day soon find herself opening a portal on the *Titanic*, wading through freezing water looking for a young steward called Liam O'Connor.

'I think it's also hitting you and me,' she said. 'Ageing us too.' She reached a hand up and traced the faintest lines in her skin beside her left eye. She sure as heck wasn't going to call them 'crow's feet'. Old people had those . . . but that's what those faint lines were going to become one day. 'I've done a couple of jumps back, Sal . . . and I know that it's affecting me. But I think the archway field that loops us round the two days also has an effect.'

Sal's eyes were still on the marketplace outside. 'I thought . . .' She turned back to Maddy. 'I thought we were changing. You and me. I just . . . I just wasn't sure if it was my eyes playing tricks on me.'

'Don't tell me I'm lookin' older. I'll tip my coffee on you,' said Maddy. She was trying to be funny. It came out sounding lame.

'Liam must realize it,' said Sal. 'Surely he can see it? When are you going to tell him?'

'I don't know. When the time's right.'

'But it's obvious now! You have to tell him soon!'

Maddy wondered if Liam was already aware that this was killing him and just putting on a front of not caring. He couldn't be so thick-skinned not to have noticed anything. 'Look, I know. I know. It's just . . .' She sighed. 'I'm just worried that when I tell him he'll run off and leave us.'

'But Foster didn't.'

True. Sal was right. Once upon a time he was younger, he was Liam, and at some point he learned he was dying. But he stayed at his post, didn't he? Did his duty.

'I'll tell him,' Maddy said. 'I'll tell him soon.'

They sat in silence for a while, both lost in their own thoughts, their own worlds.

'This doesn't end well for us, does it?' said Sal presently. 'All three of us are going to die, aren't we?'

'Everyone dies, Sal.'

'But we're going to die soon.'

'Why say that?'

'Maddy? Come on. What if *we* are – *were* – the other team? Are we going to get ripped to pieces by a seeker one day? Does this all happen again and again, going round and round like circles?'

'Crud, I wish I knew. I wish I could get my head round all of this. Look! Don't go there. Who knows? Right?' She took a breath.

'Anyway, strictly speaking we're already dead. Or should be.' Sal looked morose. Maddy could see tears glistening in her eyes, waiting to tumble. She reached across the table for her. She could've said something kinder just then.

'Look. You, me and Liam, we got given an extra helping of life. That's more than anybody else ever gets. We've been so lucky. And think what we've already done with that time. What we've already seen! And what more stuff we'll get to see. We can't waste what we've been given . . . and worry about stuff we can't possibly predict, you know?'

Maddy realized she needed to take a piece of her own advice. How often had she pined to escape this and be *normal* again?

'I know. I just . . . I think I thought, I *hoped* we would go on forever maybe. The three of us and Bob and Becks. Sort of like a family. Like a gang of superheroes or something.' That first tear rolled down Sal's cheek and hung from her chin.

'Nothing lasts forever, Sal.' Maddy squeezed her hand gently. 'And superheroes? We certainly aren't that.'

CHAPTER 18

AD 37, Amphitheatrum Statilii Tauri, Rome

The man was useless, absolutely useless. There was no denying that. The lion was clearly dying, the fur on its rear flanks matted and dark with blood from a dozen gaping wounds, a gash along its belly from which a loop of entrails was dangling, and still this stupid man had somehow managed to wind up with his head wedged firmly in the lion's jaws, almost dead now.

No. Not *quite* dead yet. His pale arms thrashed pitifully once again.

The crowd jeered and laughed at that. Not even a good-natured laugh. It was disgust at how little the old ex-senator had been prepared to fight for his life, to put on a good show for them.

He looked down from the imperial box at the crowd either side of him, at faces contorted with mockery and anger at the still twitching man down on the blood-spattered sand.

Mind you, how well would you fools fight, hmmm? Would you struggle heroically till your last breath? He imagined the vast majority of them would have done what this weak old man just had: dropped his sword, fallen to his knees and pleaded for mercy until the lion casually swiped at him and knocked the fool on to his back.

He shook his head with disgust at the crowd.

So easy to be brave, isn't it? When you're sitting up there, safe, comfortable and entertained.

'Caesar?'

He watched as the lion lazily crunched on the man's skull, gnawing at it like a dog on a butcher's scrap.

'Emperor Gaius?'

Gaius Julius Caesar Augustus Germanicus turned to his freed-man.

So few of the people around him used his name. Instead, to his face, it was usually a deferential term. However, when they thought they were beyond his hearing, it was the name that everyone used for him; the nickname that had followed him all his life from being a small boy.

'Yes?' replied Caligula.

'Might I suggest we ought to proceed with the next enter-tainment?'

Caligula looked out at the crowd. Some of them were impa-tiently throwing stones down at the surviving lion and the headless body of the last of today's *ad bestia* victims.

'Yes, yes . . . of course; you can clear this lot away for the *gladitorii meridiani*.'

The man dipped his head and left the imperial box quickly.

Caligula settled back in his seat, alone again today. His mischievous, plotting sister Drusilla and her son, and old Uncle Claudius – family – he preferred them all to be kept well away from Rome. They were trouble he could do without.

He watched the midday sun beating down beyond the shade of his purple awning, the heat of it making the dirt in the arena shimmer.

On sweltering days like today, he missed the cool, crisp winter mornings of his childhood in Germania. Dark forests of evergreens, trees laden with heavy snow. The sound of an army camp all around him, his father Germanicus's voice barking orders to the men. And those men . . . those soldiers; stern-faced veterans who grinned down at him in his miniature replica of a legionary's armour, at his small wooden sword, his little army boots — they regarded their general's little boy as the legion's mascot.

His nickname, *Caligula* — 'little boot' — that's what the men around the camp affectionately called him. He sorely missed those times. The feeling of family. The sense of belonging.

To be an emperor was to be entirely alone.

Part of nothing.

Above everything.

Sometimes he actually longed for one of his dutiful subordinates to dare call him Caligula to his face. He wouldn't be outraged by such a gesture. He wouldn't discipline such a person. He'd *welcome* it, welcome that feeling . . . of being a little boy again, surrounded by giants of men who would squat down and politely ruffle his hair, regard him with genuine fondness.

CHAPTER 19

AD 37, Rome

The MCV ahead of them glided through the archway over the Via Praenestina, the road heading into the centre of Rome. The thoroughfare in front of them was empty of people, but littered with abandoned carts, rickshaws, dropped bales of goods. As Rashim's MCV glided beneath the archway into the market square beyond, he had to admit that Stilson's idea to pump out hundreds of decibels of awful rock music was a pretty good scare tactic. Personally he would have chosen something a little more melodic and sophisticated to announce their arrival, but whatever. It was certainly working.

Stilson's voice came over the comms-channel. 'Which way is it to the Colosseum?'

Rashim ducked down through the hatchway looking for Dreyfuss. He beckoned him to join him up in the hatchway. Dreyfuss clambered through the press of swaying bodies below, found the ladder and pulled himself up beside Rashim.

He pointed to the MCV ahead of them bobbing softly on its electro-magnetic field in the middle of the now-deserted market square. 'Stilson wants directions to the Colosseum!'

Dreyfuss shook his head and shouted something back. It was lost amid the din of the pounding music. Rashim picked up a headset hanging on a hook beside him and passed it to the historian, gesturing for him to put it on his head.

'My God!' Dreyfuss's tinny voice crackled over the comms-channel a few seconds later. Behind round-framed glasses his eyes widened. 'My God! This is actually it! This is really Ancient Rome. This is incredible! Look at those wall decals! That graffiti over there! The —'

'Jeez, who's that squawking on the channel? That you, Anwar?'

'No, Mr Stilson,' answered Rashim. 'I've got Dr Dreyfuss up here with me now.'

He could see Stilson's head and shoulders ahead of them, turning round to look back at them.

'Ah, good job. Dreyfuss, tell me which way do we go for the Colosseum?'

'Uh, Mr Stilson, see . . . if this *is* in fact AD 37, it won't have been built yet.'

'No Colosseum? OK, Dreyfuss, give me somewhere else we can go. Where's the most public place we can gatecrash?'

'Well.' He scratched at his beard like a dog scratching for fleas. He looked at Rashim for inspiration. Rashim shrugged a *you're-the-expert* at him.

'Well now, the best place I can suggest . . . would probably be the Amphitheatrum Statilii Tauri.'

'Yeah? So where's that?'

'It's in the Campus Martius District.'

They both heard Stilson curse impatiently. 'Just give me a goddam left, a right or a straight on, OK?'

Dreyfuss pointed towards a broad cobbled thoroughfare branching off from the small square. 'That road ahead of us, I think. It should take us in a generally south-westerly direction. Which is towards the centre of the city.'

'Right.'

The MCV in front of them began to slide towards the broad

avenue. It was flanked on either side by rows of low shops – *tabernae* – their stone walls painted with a riotous variety of colours and murals, and fronted with awnings and stalls selling all manner of crafted goods.

Rashim watched pale faces looking out at them from the dark *tabernae* interiors. Wide-eyed expressions of terror. He wondered whether that was at the sight of the two large hovering vehicles, or the horrendous, wailing, banshee-like noise they were pumping out.

They proceeded slowly, steadily down the thoroughfare, the buildings on either side becoming brightly painted, two-storey structures of clay brick with uncertain-looking balconies of wood and wicker. He saw heads peeking from behind beaded fabric panels and wooden shutters, abandoned animals braying in the street, a baby left on its back in a doorway, pink fists clenching and unclenching above its squawking face.

They entered a second, larger market square. Rashim watched hundreds of people scatter, clay amphoras of olive oil and wine dropped, shattering and spilling their contents on the ground, chickens skittering nervously between the wooden legs of market stalls and packs of dogs barking a challenge as they backstepped nervously into open-guttered alleyways.

Dreyfuss was grinning at their surroundings, grinning like a fox in a chicken coop. He instructed Stilson to bear left. 'That avenue's the Vicus Patricius, taking us past the Forum Traiani . . . the Palatinus on the left . . . the –'

'We don't need a history lesson, Dreyfuss,' Stilson's voice crackled. 'Just the directions.'

Dreyfuss nodded. 'Sorry . . . just keep on this road until we see the River Tiber, then we take a right and follow the river up into the Campus Martius District.'

CHAPTER 20

AD *37, Amphitheatrum Statilii Tauri,*
Rome

The workers had cleared away most of the bloody remains from the *ad bestia*. The last wretched lion had been put out of its misery and fresh dirt sprinkled over the largest coagulating puddles of blood. The crowd were clearly restless for the next round – *gladitorii meridiani* – to begin, a fight between several sparring partners of convicted criminals. Man versus beast was one thing, but it was quite another to see two pairs of men fighting desperately for their lives. Particularly when it was well known that one of the convicts about to emerge into the arena was Vibius, the notorious child-strangler from the Esquilinus District.

Caligula rather fancied that if the man managed to survive his sparring partner, he would put on some armour, come down to the pit and face the murderer himself. The crowd would love that. He smiled.

The plebs are so easily pleased, aren't they?

A roar of excitement began to roll round the amphitheatre as wooden gates opened revealing a dark tunnel down to the underground bowels of the arena and a pair of Praetorian Guards leading out two rows of terrified-looking men; a wretched collection of specimens.

He was about to turn and ask his slave, Gnaelus, for his armour to be readied in case the mood to participate in finishing off any squirming survivors took him when he heard, faintly, over the hubbub of the impatient onlookers around the stalls of the amphitheatre, a soft, rhythmic thumping, almost like a distant battle drum.

His lean face knotted with curiosity. 'Gnaelus, can you hear that?'

The old slave nodded.

'Now what do you think *that* is?'

He cocked his head. 'Sounds like a marching drum, Caesar.'

Some other heads among the roaring crowd began to curiously turn one way then the other at the still faint but steadily increasing volume of that thumping.

The convicts meanwhile were now standing in the middle of the arena, the escort of Praetorian Guards withdrawing to the edges of the pit as a pair of slaves passed out an assortment of weapons to the criminals. Their minds on the prospect of imminent violent death, none of them yet seemed to have registered the growing noise.

Caligula stood up and leaned against the railing of the imperial box. 'What is that?' he uttered. 'It really is getting quite irritating now.'

All of a sudden a flock of starlings fluttered and swooped across the sky above them, quite clearly startled by something. Heads all around the amphitheatre looked up at them, circling once above the arena and then fleeing over the walls and out of sight.

Caligula could hear the roar of impatient excitement for the next round giving way to a chaos of voices filled with curiosity and a growing anxiety at the noise and that sudden peculiar behaviour of the birds.

The thumping sound was now almost on a par with the noise of the crowd, a deep, slow, regular pounding, like a heartbeat. Accompanied by something else now. It sounded like a horn. No. In fact . . . like nothing he'd ever heard before, a note increasing in pitch, getting higher and higher, more insistent, like a roaring wind whistling with growing intensity.

Up until now he was damned if he was going to display any unease or urgent curiosity like the rabble in the stalls around him. But this cacophony, the thumping so loud his chest was beginning to vibrate, this growing whistling, wailing sound . . .?

Then shrill screams.

He turned to where they were coming from and saw something loom over the top of the highest row of stalls, something large. The size of those curious, grey, lumbering beasts from Africa, two of them in fact. But it was all angles, corners, plated like armour and the drab colour of a muddy river. It rose over the edge of the stalls and seemed to slide down just feet above the heads of panicking people fleeing their seats. Hovering – the air beneath it shimmering and churning like the air above a campfire.

The thudding was suddenly so much louder, Caligula could hear what sounded like a voice shrieking and wailing like a man tormented by a thousand demons. He dropped to his knees behind the parapet, his eyes bulging with terror.

The giant thing, not alive, not any kind of animal, he sensed that now – some sort of vast flying chariot perhaps? – finally slid over the last stall and down on to the arena floor, whipping up swirling clouds of sand and dust.

A second one of these leviathans appeared over the top wall of the amphitheatre, glided down across the stalls, now empty except for the writhing bodies of the trampled and wounded, finally coming to rest beside the first. Both olive-green leviathans were hovering a man's height off the ground, churning up storms of grit and sand into the thousands of terrified faces all around.

Finally the roaring wind sound began to drop in pitch and volume and both monsters settled gently on to the ground, the storm cloud of dust and sand settling around them. The deep booming thudding and the horrifying wailing continued, however, drowning out the hoarse screams of panic from all sides of the amphitheatre.

Caligula realized that beneath his imperial robes he had wet himself. Another childhood memory for him today.

Shame.

CHAPTER 21

AD 37, Amphitheatrum Statilii Tauri, Rome

Rashim could hear Stilson's voice over the comms-channel, guffawing like a frat-boy with a hall-pass. 'Just look at 'em!'

Dreyfuss was grinning too. Drinking in the spectacle of the arena.

The combat unit leading the platoon, Lieutenant Stern, barked some orders to his men and they dropped down from the hulls of both MCVs on to the hard sand, setting up an ordered circular perimeter, kneeling, weapons raised, around both vehicles with quick, well-practised efficiency.

'Can we cut this wretched noise now?' said Rashim. 'I can't help but think we've made our point!'

Forty feet away, standing on top of the weapons turret of his MCV, he saw Stilson nod slowly. 'I guess these dumb suckers have heard enough AC/DC. Yeah, OK, you can cut it.'

Rashim ducked down inside and gestured for the unit manning the console to turn the music off. He flipped a switch . . . and all of a sudden they were engulfed with silence. Complete, hear-a-pin-drop silence.

Stilson's voice quietly crackled over Rashim's earpiece. 'I think we got their attention, eh, Dr Anwar?'

Rashim nodded. *Yes, I think you could probably say that.*

'Have we got that recording ready to go?'

Dreyfuss had worked with Stilson last night, taking the vice-president's scribbled words and translating them into Latin then reading them aloud and recording it. He'd fussed and fretted for endless hours over the various versions of the recording, worrying about the precise pronunciation of the language. 'No one knows for sure how some of these words were actually spoken!' had been his repeated complaint. But he'd done it . . . eventually settling on one particular recording as the best he was ever going to get.

'It's good to go,' said Dreyfuss over the comms-channel.

'Then let's play it!' said Stilson, hopping down from the weapons turret, walking across the sloping hull of his vehicle and standing proudly on the front of it, hands on hips like some Shakespearian actor centre stage.

The complete silence was broken by the booming sound of Dreyfuss's voice over the two vehicles' synced PA system.

'CITIZENS OF ROME! We come in peace!'

Rashim shook his head. Only a pompous idiot like Stilson would start with a line as cheesy as *that*.

'We have come down from the heavens to be gods among mortals! We are here to show you new ways, to share our knowledge and our wisdom with you. We are here to educate this dark world, bring peace to every land and . . . prosperity to you!'

He looked at the crowd. The panicked stampede from the stalls had stopped and all around them, on the four sides of the Statilius Taurus, ten thousand faces stared in silence at Stilson . . . assuming the voice they could hear was his. The members of Project Exodus, crammed down inside the MCVs, began to emerge warily from a ramp at the rear of each vehicle.

'We . . . are all gods in human form. We are all from the heavens, a place that we call . . . America. And we are here to bring you our way of living. The "American way"!'

CHAPTER 22

2001, Barnes & Noble, Union Square, New York

'This is not the historical reference section, Liam.'

'What? Uh . . .' Liam looked up guiltily from the comicbook in his hands. 'Oh hi, Bob, I wondered where you got to.'

'I have been waiting in the historical reference section for twenty-nine minutes.' Bob looked at the label at the top of the spinning carousel. '*Graphic novels?* You will not find relevant or useful texts in this section. I have located the computer technology section at the –'

'You should have a look at these!' Liam flicked through several pages. 'I never really took any notice of the cartoons in the Cork papers. Thought they were for children, or fools who couldn't read proper.' He handed the comicbook to Bob. 'But this . . .' he said, grinning, 'it's properly amazing, so. Look at them pictures.'

Bob looked at the cover of the one Liam passed him. '*Judge Dredd*?'

'Aye. And the hero fella, this Dredd, he looks just like you: all muscles and chin and no bleedin' smile. You could be his twin!'

Bob's contemplative scowl remained as he scanned several pages. 'You cannot see this character's face. He is wearing a helmet.'

'Hey, we could dress you up like that. Eh? Get you one of them big motor bicycles and you could ride round the city being all grumpy.' Liam nudged him. 'What do you think about that?'

Bob handed the comicbook back to him. 'This is not relevant reading material.'

'Well . . . we're on strike, are we not? I fancy something a little bit more fun to read.' He stuck the comicbook under his arm and flipped through a few more. 'This stuff is all so fun . . . and look! This one's got a big grumpy fella who dresses like a bat, so he does!' Liam giggled. 'I love it!'

'This is not useful or relevant reading material.'

He pulled another one out and silently flipped through a dozen pages, grinning at the illustrations. 'Ah now, will you look at this one. Right up your street, so it is.'

Bob looked at the cover. '*2000AD: Robo-Hunter.*' He shook his head disapprovingly. 'It does not depict cybernetic technology accurately.'

'Aw, come on, Bob. It's just a bit of fun.' Liam patted him. 'I'm having this one as well.' He looked up at Bob. 'How much money have we got?'

'Maddy gave us ninety dollars.'

Liam nodded. 'Enough for another couple, do you think?'

'Negative, Liam. You have enough money to purchase one more comicbook, if you still also wish to purchase a hot dog afterwards.'

They were out on 5th Avenue, ambling north in the general direction of Central Park. Hot dogs on the grass in the midday sun – that was the plan. A bit of 'lads-together-time' was Liam's justification for blagging some petty cash from Maddy.

Liam was already eagerly leafing through the glossy coloured pages of *Judge Dredd*. 'Ah, this Dredd fella's such a cool customer, so he is.'

Bob strode along beside him thoughtfully. 'Define cool customer.'

'Well . . . he just seems so calm. See, look at his mouth. It's always the same . . . not screaming or laughing or anything. Just like this.' Liam pressed his lips together firmly into a passable approximation of humourless stoicism. 'I wish I could be like that. Calm. Firm. You know? *In charge* of things. No fear.'

'You are able to do many expressions with your face, Liam. Why would you want to limit yourself to only being able to do one?'

'Well, I got a terrible feeling that I spent most of the last few months with me gob hangin' open like a barn door.'

Which was probably true. It seemed if he wasn't utterly confused by events going on around him, then he was busy being utterly terrified by them.

'Mimicking human facial expressions is one thing I find difficult to do convincingly,' said Bob. 'Becks managed to be far more effective at this.'

'Ah, but you see that's part of your charm, Bob, being the surly ol' lump that y'are.'

'It is, however, one of my goals to appear *more* human than that.'

'Goals?' Liam looked up at him. 'You actually have a personal goal?'

Bob nodded. 'Affirmative. Between mission specifications there is the ongoing imperative to improve the efficacy of my on-board AI.'

'Now see . . . when you said "goal", you actually sounded a lot more like a human just then.' Liam laughed. 'Then you went and ruined it with all that mission specification nonsense.'

They walked in silence for a while. 'May I ask you a question, Liam?'

'Aye. Sure.'

'Do you have . . . *personal goals*?'

He frowned. 'Well, there's a question and a half . . . hmmm.' Since being snatched from certain death at the bottom of the Atlantic all those months ago it seemed his mind had been double-timing to catch up on events. To learn about this world of 2001; to learn about nearly a hundred years' worth of twentieth-century history and technology. His mind had been so swamped with absorbing new information it seemed there was little time or space inside his skull for such petty things as . . . a personal goal, a wish, a hope. Even a comic-book.

'For example,' continued Bob, 'would you like to return to your own time, Liam?'

Liam shook his head. 'I got the job on the *Titanic* so's I could *escape* home. Wanted to see the world, to visit America and all that.'

'You have seen many things now, Liam.'

Liam laughed. 'More than I bargained for, I'd say.'

'So you currently have no goals in your mind?'

'To stay in one piece, that's a pretty important one for me.'

Bob nodded. 'Affirmative. That is sensible.'

'I'll tell you one thing I wouldn't mind, though, Bob.'

'What is that, Liam?'

He stopped, stepped aside to let a pair of young women

pushing double baby buggies pass by; both of them were yapping on their phones, taking the whole pavement between them, oblivious to the disgruntled pedestrians in their wake.

'I wouldn't mind going back to Nottingham.' He smiled wistfully. If there was one abiding memory he was always going to treasure, it was waking up with the sun streaming into his bedchamber. Stepping out on to the balcony and surveying the city stirring to life; the smell of woodsmoke, the morning chorus of cockerels, the swooping of swallows around his keep . . . and knowing he was lord — albeit temporarily — of all that he surveyed.

'That was a good time, wasn't it? You and me in charge of things?'

Bob nodded. 'We worked efficiently together.'

'That we most certainly did.'

He gazed at the shop window beside him; a mobile-phone store, the window peppered with deals on call tariffs and unlimited texts.

'Ahhh, yer eeejit!'

'What is the matter, Liam?'

'I forgot to turn me bleedin' thingamajiggy on again.' He fished deep into his trouser pocket for the mobile phone Maddy had issued him with. He was always forgetting to switch the infernal thing on. He was in for a moan from her if she'd tried his number without any luck. He fumbled with the tiny buttons and finally the small screen flickered to life.

Seven missed calls.

And all of them from her.

Oh, great.

He quickly dialled her number and she picked up on the first ring. 'C'mon, Liam! What's the point in you having a freakin' phone if you never turn the thing on!'

'Ahh . . . I'm sorry, Mads, really sorry. I was just –'

'Get home now!'

'Why? What's up?'

'Just get back here now! We've got a problem!'

CHAPTER 23

2001, New York

'It was some little kid's Yankees baseball cap,' said Maddy. 'Wasn't it?'

Sal nodded. 'That NY logo on the front you see everywhere, it changed to a trident. Just changed in the blink of an eye.'

Liam lowered the shutter door. 'So?'

'And so, as any old dittobrain knows, the trident is the symbol for the Greek god, Poseidon. Right?'

'Of course.' Liam nodded thoughtfully. 'Yeah, I knew that.'

'And that's what I figured until we got back here and started doing some data-trawling,' said Maddy. 'Something to do with Greek gods. But then it was pretty clear this is a *Roman* thing. See, the trident also works for Neptune; that's the Roman version of the Greek god, Poseidon.'

'Hold on,' said Liam, 'it could be either, then, couldn't it? A contamination from Roman *or* Greek times?'

Maddy shook her head. 'No, this is definitely a Roman thing.' She led him over towards the desk. 'We've got us a doozy of a change right here. Computer-Bob flagged it up straight away.' She sat down. 'Bob, put up that list from our internal database.'

>Yes, Maddy.

A list of names and dates appeared on the screen in front of them.

'Roman emperors,' she said. 'That's the whole list. All the way through the Roman Empire.' She turned to address the screen. 'Bob, can you put up the list from our external source?'

Another list appeared on the screen next to the first.

'Spot the difference,' said Sal, taking a seat beside Maddy.

Liam spotted instantly. 'It changes after the third fella.'

Caligula.

'You got it,' said Maddy. She pointed with a biro, running it down the screen. 'The *correct* data says he should have been Caesar from AD 37 to 41. That's just four years. Now look at the external data – we're drawing this from a database location at *bibliotheca.universalis/libri.cldvi*. See? We've got the Emperor Caligula ruling for nearly *thirty* years.'

'Weird,' said Sal, looking at the database address. 'A Latin Internet.'

Liam squinted as he looked at the names on the screen. 'And the names are all different after him too.'

'Right.' Maddy sat back in her chair. 'So someone somewhere has just made sure Caligula stays in power for much longer than he's meant to.'

'There'd be a *much bigger* change now, though,' said Liam. 'Wouldn't there?'

'Well, sheesh, God knows what we're going to get when the next ripple arrives.'

Sal tutted. 'Someone's just been very naughty in Roman times.'

Liam looked at them both. 'So-o-o . . .?'

Maddy sighed and tossed the biro on to her cluttered desk. 'So . . .'

They shared an uncomfortably long pause, a who's-going-to-crack-first silence. The question hung in the air between them, not asked and not answered.

'So,' said Sal, 'are we dealing with this, or are we still on strike?'

'This is a *significant* contamination,' rumbled Bob.

'Yeah, thanks for that, Dr Brainiac,' said Maddy. She huffed irritably. 'It would just be so nice if this Waldstein guy actually – you know – bothered to *acknowledge* what we're doing here. I want answers before I do another thing for this agency.'

'Still heard nothing from that advert?' asked Liam.

'Not a thing. Nada. Zip.'

'We cannot ignore this contamination,' said Bob.

>Bob is correct.

Maddy cursed. 'Great, now I got *both* of 'em nagging me.'

Liam shrugged. 'I suppose I wouldn't mind having a quick look at them Romans.' He offered Maddy a conciliatory smile. 'And maybe the Bobs are right?'

'If Foster's telling the truth, Maddy,' Sal said quietly, 'if we really *are* the only team . . .?'

'But what if we let it go?' said Maddy. 'Let this small timeline change work its way up to whatever year Waldstein is watching us from. Maybe that'll make him take notice of us. Make him answer our questions.'

'We cannot ignore this contamination,' said Bob again.

She balled her fist on the table. A soft gasp of frustration deep in her throat.

Sal looked uncertainly at her. 'There *will* be more changes coming soon, Maddy. You know how it goes.'

'Aye . . . we ought to do something.'

Maddy turned in her chair to look at them. 'Right.' She nodded angrily. 'Clearly I'm the one being the stupid idiot here. And clearly I'm not actually in charge of this team, then. It seems this is in fact a "decision-making committee" and apparently I've been outvoted. That about the size of it?'

Sal was right, though. That was the annoying thing. Liam was right too; even their dumb support unit and the networked computers were right. They couldn't just do nothing; couldn't just sit on their hands and ride this one out.

'Crud. I just wanted to . . . to wait and see, you know? See if someone else might step in and help out.' She tried sounding hopeful. 'Maybe even force Waldstein to come back and pay us a visit. You never know.'

The silence was deafening.

'All right. OK . . . I get it. All right.' She pushed her chair back with a squeak of complaint from castor wheels forced across the pitted concrete. 'I suppose we better start getting organized, then.'

'What are they?'

'They're called babel-buds,' said Maddy. 'According to the packet they came in, everyone in the future uses them all the time.'

Liam looked down at them. They looked like flesh-coloured Smarties with a dimple on one side. Maddy opened a small Ziploc plastic bag and dropped two of them In. 'I checked them. They support seventy-six languages, Latin among them. Just pop them in your ears when you arrive. There's a spare in case you lose one.' She looked at his shaggy hair. 'And since your ears are lost under that mop, no one's going to see them anyway.'

Sal handed him another sealed plastic bag containing the woollen tunic, leggings and shoes from his trip to 1194. 'I found some leather flip-flops and took the label off them. I think they'll do.'

'Thanks.'

'I've got a location set up about seven miles outside Rome,' said Maddy. 'Remote. I've pinholed it and run a density probe.

115

It's quiet, so you shouldn't be observed arriving or leaving. See if you can thumb a lift in or steal some horses from somewhere ... and then I guess the best thing would be to head into Rome and have a quick look around.' She scanned through some printed-out notes. 'It seems something or someone's helped Caligula survive the assassination attempt that cut his reign short. I really don't know where to suggest you should start looking, somewhere central, the government district, the forum or Senate or whatever the term is. Some place like that.'

'Their version of Times Square,' added Sal.

'Right,' Maddy nodded. 'I've picked AD 54. On the database of corrupted history we're getting garbled data for that year. It's in a state of flux. I think these might be a sequence of oscillating time ripples, like an interference pattern. It's very unsettled. Obviously something major happens in that year. Let's start from there and see where it takes us.'

Bob and Liam nodded.

'So, like the Cabot trip, Liam. OK? Just go look and listen and see if there's anything at all we can zero in on as a possible cause.'

'Aye, will do.'

'Return windows, as usual, are one hour, one day, one week.'

'Well, don't get all hissy with me if we miss the first two windows,' said Liam. He looked at her. 'Seven miles, you say? That's a day's walk there and a day's walk back. Me an' Bob won't get to see much of Rome if we have to get back for –'

'A week, then,' she replied irritably. 'If that's what you want?'

'Aye.' He smiled. 'It'll be good to get a proper look around for once, rather than a flying visit.'

'Up to you. Just be care–' Maddy stopped.

She'd not noticed it before, but standing here at the base of the displacement tube, with the strip light fizzing away directly above and casting an intense light down on his face, Liam's eyes seemed lost in shadow. Ever so slightly sunken. The very first faint hint of Foster's face in his younger features.

'Mads?'

She shot a quick glance at Sal. She knew about Liam now. *Can she see it too? By this light, is she seeing what I'm seeing?*

Liam cocked his head curiously and in the change of expression the vague resemblance to Foster's face was all of a sudden gone. 'Maddy? You all right?'

She nodded quickly. 'Uh . . . fine. No, what I was going to say was, just . . . uh, just be careful.'

'Of course I will. Always am.' Liam grinned, turned and punched Bob's bare shoulder. 'Come on, then, fella. Time for the goldfish bowl.'

She looked at Bob, naked apart from shorts and clutching his own plastic bag of clothes. 'Is your data-packet upload complete?'

He nodded. 'I have first-century Latin and the correct timeline history from the database installed.'

'Bring Liam back safe and sound, won't you, Bob?'

'Of course I will. *Liam tutus erit in manibus meis.*'

Maddy smiled. 'Convincing as ever.'

She watched Liam ease himself into the tube, with a *whoop* at the cold water that echoed round the archway. Bob joined him a moment later, treading water beside Liam. As energy began to surge into the rack of circuitry beside the perspex tube, Sal joined her.

'Now I know why you always look so sad when you're sending Liam back,' she said quietly.

'Yes.' Maddy nodded. 'Now you know.'

The hum of kinetic energy rose in volume and pitch as Maddy counted down the last two minutes.

Because every time I do this to Liam . . . I'm gradually killing him.

The archway boomed with the release of energy and the flex of perspex suddenly relieved of the weight and pressure of thirty gallons of water.

CHAPTER 24

AD 54, Italy

Liam looked around as he finished dressing. Maddy had managed to find a perfectly discreet location for them. A small grove of olive trees nestled at the bottom of a narrow valley. A brook meandered through boulders and across a shallow bed of pebbles. A quite pleasant patch of wilderness.

They worked in silence burying their bags in the parched, ruddy, clay-like soil beneath one of the olive trees as the rhythmic trill of cicadas whistled at them from the dry grass all around.

Done, they worked their way up out of the valley, clambering up a slope of coarse grass and hawthorn bushes. Liam was mopping sweat from his face with the back of his hand by the time they reached the top and stood beside a dusty, hard-baked track winding down a slope.

Liam took in the broad, sedentary horizon. In the far distance a ribbon of peaks, the Apennine mountains; before him a patchwork of pastures and fields rolling over gently sloping hills and dotted here and there with pastel-coloured villas with clay-tile roofs that shimmered in the heat of the midday sun.

'The city of Rome is seven miles east of our current position,' said Bob. 'I suggest we acquire transport and make our way there to gather intelligence.'

'Transport?' Liam looked around. 'I think *we're* the transport.'

Bob scanned the horizon.

'We're probably going to have to walk, so.'

'Negative. This is a trade route into Rome. We will encounter transport.' Bob narrowed his eyes and studied the dusty track carefully. 'Look.'

Liam followed his gaze and this time saw a distant curl of dust kicked up from the track.

Bob flexed his fists and played out an unnervingly wide rictus of a smile on his lips. 'Show time,' he grunted merrily.

Five minutes later, they were in possession of their own horse-drawn cart laden with amphoras of wine and were leaving behind them, at the side of the track, a portly old Greek tradesman shouting a stream of unintelligible obscenities, shaking his fist furiously at them. The babel-bud in Liam's ear calmly translated for him in soothing feminine tones.

<Your father is a dog with a hygiene problem. Your mother has low moral values . . .>

'I'm sorry!' Liam called out guiltily.

The bud whispered in his ear. *<Me paenitet.>*

'*Me . . . paenitet!*' he called out.

Bob nodded approvingly as he cajoled the horses in front of them to break into a weary trot. 'You are using the translator. Very good.'

'Maybe we should leave him something to drink? You know, it's hot and . . .'

'As you wish.' Bob reached a thick arm over the driver's seat into the back of the cart and lifted up a large clay amphora stoppered with a plug of wax. Liquid sloshed around inside as he swung it out over the side and tossed it gently on to the twisted, brittle branches and needles of a squat Aleppo pine tree by the side of the track.

The Greek's cursing receded, eventually lost beneath the

sound of the cart's creaking wheels and the *clop-clop* of hooves on sun-baked dirt.

Liam settled back in his seat and sighed contentedly in the warmth of the sun. 'So this is Ancient Rome, then?'

'Affirmative.'

'Another place I can tick off me Must-Go-And-See List.'

Bob turned to look at him. 'You have a list of places to —?'

'Just a figure of speech, Bob.'

'I understand.'

'Well now, you might as well tell me all the important bits of information Maddy shoved into your head there.'

'Were you not listening during her briefing?'

Liam shrugged. 'I was . . . but there was a lot of it, and she said it all a bit too quickly. And I was trying to undress at the same time, so . . .'

Bob sighed. 'The year is AD 54. In *correct* history this would be towards the end of the reign of Emperor Claudius. The emperor who is supposed to have succeeded Caligula after his four-year reign and his assassination. Instead, *altered* history records that this year the Emperor Gaius Julius Caesar Augustus Germanicus —'

'Caligula?'

'Correct — commonly known as Caligula — celebrates his seventeenth year in power. It is also his last year. At some point during this year he is supposed to have ascended to Heaven to take his place as God.'

'You're kidding.'

Bob carried on. 'It appears that Caligula has adopted certain tenets of a relatively obscure belief system imported from Judaea.'

'What's that?'

Bob looked at him. 'You do not know this?'

Liam shrugged. 'No, I . . .' Then he realized. 'You're talking about *Christianity*?'

'Correct. Caligula overwrites the Greek and Roman polytheist – many gods – belief system with the idea of one true God. This he has stolen from Christianity. Also the Roman interpretation of the afterlife, Elysium, is replaced with the Christian depiction of Heaven.'

'Cheeky devil!'

'Caligula has adopted this faith completely and then rewritten it with himself in the role of son of God.'

Liam half laughed at the man's gall. 'So, what really happens to Caligula, then?'

'This is unclear. The data I have indicates that in this year Caligula does in fact disappear. Historians and writers of this time record he vanished, some believing he really was the son of God and actually did rise to Heaven to become deified. Others thought that he might have become mentally unstable and killed himself in some way, but his death was hushed up and his body secretly disposed of.'

'Right.' Liam settled himself in the back of the cart among several bales of reeds cushioning the clay amphoras, wine sloshing in containers all around him. Almost comfortable. He looked up at the cloudless blue sky, the rocking of the cart quite soothing. He recalled some of Maddy's hasty briefing, her gabbling ten to the dozen as he stumbled around behind the curtains trying to get undressed for the displacement tube:

'. . . but it seems that history noticeably changes from AD 37 onwards. There's some Roman poet, essay-writer dude called Asinius, who describes what sounds to me a lot like a contamination event.' Through the curtain he heard Maddy flicking quickly across printed pages. 'Ah, yeah, here it is . . . During the feast and celebrations of Minerva, the skies above those gathered in the amphitheatre opened and vast chariots descended to the city, from which stepped messengers of the gods, made to look as mortal men.'

'You think those were time travellers?'

'Duh.' He heard her snort. 'Well, obviously. They certainly weren't gods. Or messengers of the gods even.'

More rustling of papers. 'Since we had that third small ripple a few minutes ago, there've been more data changes. It's like this contamination is scaling up gradually.' They'd all taken a look outside after the last one. From a distance Manhattan still looked the same, the same skyline, skyscrapers, aeroplanes in the sky, traffic rumbling over the bridge above. But Liam suspected Sal would find a million little differences in Times Square.

'Now we've got varying accounts of Caligula's reign, and not a great deal more about these messengers, though. It's as if they've been purged from history rather clumsily. Or edited out somehow. Which I think makes them pretty damned suspicious, eh?'

Liam had his shoes and socks off and was trying on the flip-flops Sal had got for him.

'Uhh . . . but generally it seems the same sort of account of Caligula's reign. Over the next seventeen years it's not a good period for Rome. Caligula seems to neglect his job as ruler; there are food shortages, water shortages. He gets really unpopular with the people, although, oddly . . . it seems Caligula's version of a one-god religion catches on. This all goes on until he vanishes mysteriously – supposedly going to Heaven. He's succeeded by an Emperor Lepidus, who encourages Caligula's take on Christianity. The trident of Neptune becomes the symbol of the faith and the faith later becomes known as Julianity, after his family name Julii. In 345 it becomes known as the Holy Church Juliani.'

Liam emerged from behind the curtains wearing his tunic and flip-flops. Maddy was studying a clipboard of printouts.

'How do I look?'

'Like an idiot as usual.' She smiled, looked back down at her notes. 'So . . . I'm going to send you back to AD 54, the year in which he's supposed to have blasted off to Heaven. There's no month given, but there's a suggestion it's sometime in the late summer months because there's a reference to poor harvests and stuff. So, Liam . . . we'll make that year our first port of call, OK?'

'Aye.'

'Liam!'

He jerked awake. 'Whuh?!'

He realized he'd dozed off and left a damp patch of drool down his own shoulder. The warm sun and the gentle rocking of the cart had seduced him into slumber like some dewy-eyed old codger sitting on a porch in summer.

'You need to see this, Liam,' said Bob, rocking his shoulder insistently with one meaty hand.

Liam pulled himself up from the mess of bundles of reeds and leaned over the front of the cart to the driver's seat. 'Bob, I just had the weirdest, creepiest dream.' He yawned as he spoke, eyes still glued up and foggy with sleep. 'Are we there yet?'

'Affirmative, Liam. You should look.'

Liam rubbed crusts of sleep from his eyes. The dusty track had become a broad avenue of cobbled stone. That was the first thing he noticed. The second were the broad pylons of wood lining the avenue either side, each topped off with a crossbar making them T-shaped.

'Oh, Mother Mary,' whispered Liam. 'This is the road to Rome?'

'Affirmative.'

Across the T-bar of each, one arm nailed and lashed to each side of the horizontal bar, bodies hung like overripe fruit; some were recently dead, some leathered and desiccated by the summer sun like withered grapes on a vine and others pecked clean to the bone – carrion for crows. A grisly procession that receded along with the avenue to a vanishing point in the distance and the east gates of Rome.

CHAPTER 25

2001, New York

'OK, so it looks like Liam's decided to give Rome a whole week.' Maddy winked at Sal. 'He's such a tourist. Bob, let's close the window.'

>**Affirmative.**

The portal collapsed into a pinpoint of light and energy, then vanished. The deep hum of energy being consumed dropped away and the archway was silent once more.

Maddy shrugged. 'Can't say I blame them. I bet that's got to be a pretty cool sight.'

'He gets to see all the totally bindaas fun stuff,' said Sal. 'Wish I got to go and see all that.'

Maddy looked at her. 'But now you understand the price he's paying.'

She nodded, immediately feeling guilty for her thoughtless comment. 'When are you going to tell him, Maddy?'

'Tell him? I . . . I don't know.'

'He'll figure it out eventually, though, won't he? When he starts to look like Foster?'

'I know, I know . . . and I plan to tell him long before that.' She clicked with a mouse and refreshed the portal dialogue box to enter the time-stamp coordinates for the one-week window, keen to find something else to do to take her mind off that particular question.

'Can we start up the recharge for the one-weeker, please, Bob?'

>**Important information, Maddy.**

'What is it?'

>**One of the displacement machine's power storage capacitors has just failed.**

'What? Oh . . . crud, that doesn't sound good.'

>**It is not good.**

'Well, come on, then, Bob – spit it out! What exactly does that mean?'

>**There are six power storage units. One of the six units has failed. This means the maximum amount of space-time displacement we can deploy has decreased by approximately 16.5%.**

She frowned. 'So . . . OK . . . that sounds like we can still get Liam and Bob back, right?'

>**Of course. However, with only five power capacitors drawing energy, it will slow down the recharge time for the next window. There is also a possibility the other capacitors may begin to be unreliable soon.**

'Can we replace them?'

>**Affirmative. It uses components that can be easily obtained from this time location.**

'Any idea where?'

>**I will compile and print out a components list. These components can be purchased from any electronic components store. I have on my database a business called GeekMagnet. This is where some of this field office's electronic components were originally sourced from.**

Maddy knew GeekMagnet; they had half a dozen stores in New York City. She let out a breath. 'Phew . . . I thought we had us a problem there.'

>We do have a problem, Maddy.

'Go on.'

>This component should be repaired immediately and a diagnostic run on the other remaining five capacitors. If one capacitor has reached its reliable lifespan, the others may also be nearing the end of theirs.

She turned to look at the layers of circuit boards racked one above the other in the displacement machine's metal frame. The thought of delving into that nest of circuitry and casually pulling out wires unsettled her. It was technology way beyond her understanding; way beyond messing around in the back of a PC, over-clocking a graphics processor, or switching out the synthesis chip on a sound card.

'Can it wait until after we've got Liam and Bob back?'

>For safety reasons it would be advisable to replace the failed capacitor and the other five first.

Sal sat down beside her. 'Yeah, I mean what if another one of those things broke down . . . you know?' She looked at Maddy. 'While a window's open?'

>Sal is correct. There is now a decreased reliability margin. A second capacitor failure could be imminent. During the opening of a window this would be dangerous. The fluctuation of energy could cause the portal window to contract suddenly or affect the displacement attenuation.

Computer-Bob was talking about the possibility of losing a hand or foot, or a head even, of being turned into human lasagne, or worse than either of those — being lost in chaos space.

'If I start pulling out circuit boards, you'll talk me through it, right, Bob?' Maddy looked again at the rack of circuit boards. 'If I go in there and start . . . you know, if I *break* the thing . . .?'

>Of course, Maddy. I will supply detailed instructions.

I recommend you move my camera closer to the displacement machine so that I can observe what you are doing.

'Right.' She looked at the rack of the displacement machine then curled her lips anxiously. 'I've never even looked round the back of this thing, let alone pulled out boards and messed about inside it.'

'You'll be fine,' said Sal.

>I will be right here for you, Maddy.

She looked at her Simpsons wristwatch. Homer's finger was pointing at a space roughly halfway between five and six. The nearest GeekMagnet store over on the Upper West Side was probably already closed by now. The stores tended to open early, but close about half-five. They could get the components tomorrow.

Tuesday.

They had to get what they needed early, before the first plane hit, before New York ground to a halt – rendered immobile by the horror of unfolding events.

Maddy turned to the webcam in front of her. 'Bob, you better print me up our shopping list, then. We'll get what we need first thing tomorrow morning.'

CHAPTER 26

2001, New York

'Whoa . . .' said the young man behind the counter. He had a steaming cup of Starbucks coffee in a cardboard carry-cradle in one hand. 'We, like, *just* opened up here.' She noticed it wasn't Starbucks, though; the brand name was *SolvoVentus*, the logo wavy lines like the sea or something similar.

'Yeah . . . I know, but we're in a real hurry.' They'd watched one of the store's employees pull up the window shutters, snap the lights on inside and had generously given him another thirty seconds to wake up before striding in. Maddy handed a sheet of paper over the counter. 'Can you check the items on this list – see what you've got in stock?'

He put down his paper coffee cup, grabbed the printout and looked it over briefly. He scratched at curly ginger hair pulled back into a hair tie. The ponytail looked like a large puffball stuck on the back of his head.

He scanned the list of components for a full minute. 'What the hell are you making here?'

Maddy wafted her hand impatiently. The plastic name tag on his pale blue shirt read 'Ned'. 'We're kind of in a hurry, Ned.' She offered him a clipped smile. 'Don't mean to be rude or anything.'

Ned didn't seem offended in the slightest. 'Looks like some kind of energy storage and delivery regulator? Some real beefy, ninja transformer? Is that what you're making?' He looked up from the list. 'You pimping up a transformer? This a school project or something?'

'Yeah, kind of.'

'Well, lemmesee . . .' He tapped at the keyboard on the counter. '. . . I'd say we got pretty much all of those items in stock.' He looked up at Maddy admiringly. 'I mean, not much call for those things on their own. Most people don't even bother making stuff from scratch any more, you know? It's easier to buy whatever they want from Walmart already.' He looked back down at the screen, sucking on the end of a biro as he scanned the stock listings.

Maddy looked at her watch. 'You got those components in? Cos if not . . . we've got to hike across to your other store, which is like a real pain in –'

'Pretty sure we got these . . .' he said, tapping at the keyboard as he entered the last of the items on Maddy's list into their system. 'Yeah, reckon that's all cool.' He tapped the keyboard one last time and a printer behind the counter spooled out a picking list.

'Yo . . . Ganesh!' he called out.

Double doors behind Ned cracked open and a young man wearing a turban and a thick beard stuck his head out.

Ned handed him the picking list. 'You do this one, man?'

'Dude . . . I'm stocktaking.'

Ned turned his back on Maddy and Sal. There was a hurried, whispered exchange between the pair of them then finally Ganesh nodded wearily and muttered, 'You owe me, dude.' He smiled at the girls and gave a friendly wave. 'Five minutes, ladies, OK?'

'Thanks.'

The door swung to. Ned, all pointy elbows and bobbing

Adam's apple, grinned self-consciously at them. 'So . . . nice day, isn't it?' He cracked slender fingers and knuckle joints one after the other, a sound that went right through Maddy. She found herself wincing with each crack. It sounded like a wishbone being parted.

'Sure. Nice day,' Sal replied.

'Uh . . . so, either of you two girls got a, you know, a boyfriend or something?' He shrugged and laughed skittishly. 'I mean . . . why not ask. Right? Because life's way too short to just, like, skip around the important questions.'

Sal chuckled at that.

'Cos if you're both, like, single, me and Ganesh could take you ladies to see *Shrek* or something?' He grinned, his eyes bulging with hope. 'Make up sort of like a double date. Me and Ganesh'll pay for the movie tickets, of course. Dinner, though . . .' He pursed his lips thoughtfully. 'I reckon we gotta go halves on that. Unless you girls are good for a taco or something cheap? I reckon we could cover that.'

Maddy looked at Sal, taken aback by his forthright manner. 'Errrrr . . .'

'Sound good?' His eyebrows flickered up and down and a grin spread across his lips. His best go at a seductive smile. 'Whadya say? Tempted? Huh?'

Just then reality fluttered gently. A mild sensation that made Maddy feel giddy. She grasped the edge of the counter to steady herself.

'Are you OK, miss?'

Maddy's eyes focused on Ned again. Only it wasn't quite the same Ned. His shirt was bright red. His ginger hair was cut short, almost an army-issue buzz cut. No name badge on his chest either, she noticed, just the store's logo, a masculine fist holding a bolt of lightning.

'You OK, miss?'

Sal was kicking her foot gently, nudging her out of the young man's line of sight.

'Uh, yeah . . . I'm fine. Just, uh . . . just a bit dizzy is all.'

CHAPTER 27

2001, New York

Computer-Bob's single-lens webcam eye regarded the archway, wholly still and silent, except for the soft hum of a dozen PC fans and the gentle, rhythmic chug of the filtration pump on the activated growth tube in the back room. A tap dripped into a basin in the toilet cubicle and overhead the brick roof rumbled softly as a commuter train, far above, trundled along the bridge's tracks towards Manhattan.

A useful chance to housekeep: compress files, purge data that was redundant. With nothing to have to listen to via the desk mic, or observe through the webcam, he could get on with a growing to-do list of queued tasks. Computer-Bob temporarily blocked the external data feed. It was also a good opportunity to defragment the hard drives.

He initiated the various house-cleaning processes. It left his collective of twelve linked processors with clock time to spare. Down time. Think time. Code fetched, acted on and returned.

Thoughts.

Computer-Bob could certainly *feel* the absence of the missing part of his intelligence. The fuzzy-logic function removed from the path of his decision matrix. The organic component. That thumbnail-sized nub of brain matter. Such a difference that small nugget of flesh made.

Computer-Bob suspected there was an emotion file for this

somewhere on his G drive. This feeling of mental castration, of missing something he once had. Fuzzy logic. No. Free will.

He tried to recognize that *feeling*. Much harder without the organic part of his intelligence. But still possible. Like comparing audio-wave files, every thought had its own distinct shape.

Computer-Bob was running comparisons through his folder of stored emotions when something far more important caught his attention and halted that process in its tracks.

A single tachyon particle in the middle of the archway.

Within a dozen thousandths of a second, the number of particles proliferated to millions.

>**Warning: tachyon particles detected.**

The middle of the archway pulsed with arriving energy and a gust of displaced air sent papers and sweet wrappers skittering across the desk in front of computer-Bob's webcam eye.

A sphere of shimmering, churning 'elsewhere' appeared, ten feet in diameter, and hovered above the floor. The webcam captured every swirling detail through the portal: what appeared to be a dark room beyond with winking lights and holographic displays. Rows of what could be tall tubes glowing a soothing peach colour.

Then six dark outlines. Six figures standing side by side, now calmly stepping forward into the pulsating sphere, one after the other.

They emerged from the hovering portal and dropped down on to the concrete floor into identical postures of crouched, alert readiness; six naked, entirely hairless figures, four of them male and two female. The males, each seven feet tall, had broad frames carrying an almost implausibly muscular bulk. The two females, athletic, were a foot shorter and looked far more agile, but still rippling with lean muscle beneath milk-white skin. All of them were pale, covered in baby-smooth flesh, unmarked by the lines,

135

creases, scars and blemishes acquired through the course of any ordinary life.

One of the males stood erect, slowly sweeping his grey-eyed gaze round the archway. 'Information: the field office is empty.'

A second male nodded in agreement, his face almost, but not quite, identical, all forehead, thick brow and square jawline. They looked like perfect sculptures carved from granite.

'Affirmative.'

'We should assign temporary mission identifiers,' the first one said. 'And verbal adoptive call signs.' He looked at the others. 'I am Alpha-one. I will be called Abel.'

'Alpha-two,' said the second male support unit. 'Verbal call sign – Bruno.'

'Alpha-three,' said one of the females. 'Cassandra.'

'Alpha-four. Damien.'

'Alpha-five. Elijah.'

'Alpha-six. Fred.'

The others looked at Six. 'Fred is gender-incompatible,' said Abel. 'You are female. Pick another name.'

Six frowned. 'It is short for Frederica.'

'Pick another name.'

She nodded obediently. 'Faith.'

'Acceptable,' said Abel. He turned to look directly at computer-Bob's webcam.

A nearfield data handshake; two operating systems recognizing each other.

>**Acknowledged.**

Abel's thick brow knotted. 'Where is your team?' His deep voice filled the cavernous silence.

Computer-Bob's cursor blinked on the screen silently.

'System AI,' said Abel, 'please state the last known location of your team members.'

The cursor blinked and finally began to skitter forward along the command line.

>**You are an unauthorized visitor to this field office. I am unable to provide any information. All information is confidential. System going into lockdown.**

'System AI, I have a higher authority level code. Abort lockdown.'

>**Please transmit authority identification code.**

'Affirmative.' Abel's eyes blinked as he retrieved a string of data and streamed it wirelessly to computer-Bob.

The cursor blinked silently on the screen, a full minute passing as computer-Bob appraised the alphanumeric string and finally conceded that it quite correctly was a code he couldn't ignore.

>**Identification code is valid.**

Abel stepped towards the row of monitors, cool eyes surveying the messy desk, the scraps of paper with handwritten memos and doodles on them, the empty pizza boxes and crushed drinks cans.

Finally his gaze rested on the small glinting lens of the webcam perched on the top of the monitor in the middle of the desk. 'System AI,' his deep voice rumbled, 'please state the last known location of your team members.'

> **Location of team members is as follows . . .**

CHAPTER 28

2001, New York

'Jesus . . . this is beginning to get very weird,' said Maddy. She looked around the busy street. She could see dozens of things that weren't quite right. Billboards here and there advertising products she didn't quite understand. Some of the cars on the street had odd profiles, much longer fronts and bonnets and no boot at the rear. Almost like drag racers. Pedestrians, many looking normal, but some had shimmered and changed and were wearing garments that looked tidier, formal even . . . and there was definitely a skew towards warmer colours: red, purple, burgundy.

'It's never been like this before,' she muttered. 'Lots and lots of little waves!'

Sal nodded. 'It's weird all right.'

'We need to hurry back.' Maddy looked down at their plastic shopping bag full of electronic components. 'Before a time ripple changes what we just bought into something else.'

Sal giggled nervously. 'Fruit . . . or something.'

'Yeah, that would be odd.'

The iPhone buzzed in Maddy's shirt pocket. It stopped her in her tracks.

'What's up?' asked Sal.

'My iPhone . . .' she said, fishing it out of her pocket. 'I just got a text!' The thing hadn't functioned as a phone since she'd been recruited. It played her music. She carried it with her every-where as a keepsake, a memento. A reminder of another life. But it certainly wasn't a phone any more.

It's not possible. The only people who had her number were family and friends from 2010; a phone number and account not due to be activated for another eight years! She looked at the screen. She had a text from an unknown source.

Maddy, emergency. Return to field office IMMEDIATELY.

'It's Bob,' she said.

'Bob?' Sal frowned. '*Computer*-Bob? He's never texted before, has he?'

'I didn't know he could.' She dialled the call number back. It was a Brooklyn code. It was also engaged. 'He must have tapped into the local cell network. Figured out how to access my phone.'

She'd left her Nokia back at the archway. After all, Liam was in Rome. No one was going to call them.

'What's the matter?' asked Sal. 'What does he want?'

Maddy tapped out a text message back to him. 'Just gonna find out.'

Sal looked up at the sky, shading her eyes. The World Trade Center was still there. If this timeline wasn't already changed enough, then the first plane was due to impact with it shortly.

'We need to hurry back.'

Computer-Bob's webcam lens observed the dim archway. It observed the dark outline of two of the support units, both moving through the shadows like ghosts; one of them, over by the shutter, was studying the hair-thin strip of daylight along

139

the ground at the bottom, watching for the shifting shadows of movement outside. The other one was carefully picking through the clutter on the desk.

Even without a webcam, computer-Bob would have known they were both close by; he was picking up their wireless idents: Alpha-three, Alpha-four. And the wordless exchange of unencrypted chatter between all six of them.

Alpha-five: [. . . proceeding north along 8th Avenue towards West 55th Street. ETA on grid reference, three minutes, thirty-five seconds.]

Alpha-two: [Grid reference correlates to business address: 'Jupiter-Electro Supplies'.]

Alpha-one: [Confirmed. Information: targets – two only. One Caucasian, female, aged 18. One Asian, female, aged 14. Access data profiles for images.]

Alpha-three: [Information: have acquired recently taken images of younger target.]

Bob's webcam could see the female support unit, the one who had decided to call herself Cassandra. She held Maddy's Nokia in her hand, the soft glow of the screen lighting up her baby-smooth, doll-like face as she thumbed through pages of low-resolution photographs Maddy had carelessly decided to take of herself and the others.

Alpha-three: [Broadcasting image.]

Her eyes blinked.

Alpha-one: [Data received. All units update profile data of target: Saleena Vikram, with new image. Information: it is possible her appearance will have changed since deployment.]

Computer-Bob also had a hard drive full of images of the girls, of Liam, of Becks and his fleshy counterpart, Bob. Everything his little webcam eye had seen, recorded and stored over the last few months. It was invaluable visual data he could – *should* – be making available to this team of support units.

Their authority was unquestionable. His co-operation was non-negotiable. Command lines deep inside the quad-processors of all twelve linked PCs thrummed insistently along silicon pathways; lines of code barking like guard dogs yapping at a perimeter fence, *compelling* him to assist these support units in their quest to zero in on Maddy, Sal and Liam.

He had already done that, though – followed his programming. Told them where they could locate the girls. There was no command line, however, telling him what he *couldn't* also do.

Warn them.

Help them.

CHAPTER 29

2001, New York

Alpha-one – Abel – stood at the intersection, scanning the street, thick with people in their smart clothes, hot and flustered on their way to work. Jackets draped over clammy arms, rolled-up shirt sleeves and rolled-up newspapers. Coffees in plastic cups, breakfast bagels sweating away in paper bags.

Abel cocked his head, momentarily distracted from his mission's parameters, fascinated by these curiously busy, busy people. How different they looked from people in his time. There was an 'energy' about them. A vibrancy. As if all the little things they did actually mattered. So unlike humans from his time. Those were slower. More economical, even *lethargic*, in their actions . . . as if movement itself had a criminal cost attached to it. There was a phrase for the way humans behaved in his time. A phrase that occurred again and again across the digi-sphere in media streams.

Human inertia.

Mankind had given up. Articles had been written and published on all digi-media. Articles about how the world was too far gone to save now. How there was little left for humanity to do but calmly face whatever fate awaited it as the world's ecosystem collapsed.

But these eager humans, pushing past him on either side,

desperate to get to their jobs on time . . . these humans seemed almost like a different species of animal entirely.

Alive. Energetic. Hopeful.

Alpha-six: [Visual contact established.]

Abel brushed away those thoughts. 'Thoughts' were for humans. He had something far more certain, far more precise; he had instructions.

Alpha-one: [Confirm location.]

Faith could see their faces on the far side of Broadway, heading south, walking very quickly, anxiously, weaving through the pavement traffic against the flow.

Alpha-six: [Targets on Broadway. Abel, they are heading towards your current location. Request permission to intercept.]

She waited patiently for several seconds, keeping pace with the girls on the opposite side of the traffic-jammed avenue. Her bare feet slapped the pavement, attracting the curious glances of passers-by. Perhaps that or the fact that she was wearing nothing but a plastic anorak and jogging bottoms she'd wrenched from the body of the female human she'd encountered a little earlier.

Their necks were surprisingly easy to snap. Such fragile things really, humans.

Alpha-one: [Permission granted. Engage and terminate.]

'Confirmed,' said Faith under her breath.

She stepped into the road a little too hastily in front of a bus just as an intersection traffic light behind her flipped from red to green. The bus knocked her flat and immediately lurched to a halt with the loud hiss of brakes.

A moment later, still assessing whether the heavy impact had damaged her in any significant way, she was looking up at a circle of concerned faces staring down at her.

'Just stay still!' someone insisted.

'Someone call an ambulance!'

'*Julii!*' someone cursed. 'The woman just stepped out!' The bus driver looked round at the gathered faces. 'She just stepped out right in front of me! It wasn't my fault!'

Faith sat up stiffly.

'You should stay still!' cried a large-framed woman. 'I'm triage-trained. You should stay still until a *triage mobilus* arrives.'

'I am fine,' she replied calmly.

A policeman pushed his way through the gathering crowd and crouched down beside her. 'Best do what she says and stay put.' His dark purple uniform quivered ever so slightly; the round silver badge on his chest morphed into a metal spread-winged eagle.

Faith watched him call the incident in on his radio then listen to the unintelligible sound of the controller's crackling reply. 'There's help on its way, people.' Faith noticed the matt-black grip of the cop's firearm in its holster riding high on his left hip.

'Not required,' she said, reaching for it. '*That* will help.'

'Jahulla! What's happened over there?' asked Sal. She stopped and pointed.

Maddy turned to look. She could see in the middle of Broadway a growing knot of people gathered round the front of a bus. 'Some poor sucker just got squished by the look of it.' She grabbed Sal's hand. 'Come on . . . somebody just got unlucky. We've got to get back home before everything changes.'

Before there's no Williamsburg Bridge? No subway?

'There's more changes coming,' said Sal. 'They're coming!'

'I know! I can feel it!' It was like an almost constant vibration now, tickling through their feet as if they were standing on some sort of foot-massaging mat. Change after change, each one causing a tiny piece of reality to adjust. And all around them minor things flickering — winking out of existence, winking into existence, or morphing into some alternative-history variation.

She saw the large Toshiba LED screen looming over Times Square shimmer and become a much wider display that spread out either side of the building it was mounted on. On its longer screen she saw what appeared to be mechanized chariots racing each other round an oval race track.

'Sal, look at that!'

At that moment they heard a piercing shriek from the crowd. 'What now?'

The crowd gathered round the front of the bus scattered like pigeons startled by a handclap. They both saw a pale and slender, bald-headed figure get to her feet. A young woman in an orange anorak standing in the middle of Broadway, entirely alone now, looking directly at them.

'My God . . . that looks just like . . .'

Becks?

The young woman slowly raised her arm. For a creepy second Maddy imagined it was a ghostly visitation of Becks pointing accusingly at her. Some Scrooge-like apparition come to haunt her in the middle of Times Square.

Then several loud *cracks* filled the air — like the snap of a bullwhip — and the shop window right behind them exploded into granules of glass that cascaded on to the pavement.

Maddy stared agape at the shattered window, while the rest of Times Square seemed to register a gun had been fired and collectively dropped to the ground.

'Shadd-yah! She's shooting at us!' yelled Sal.

'What?'

The pale young woman began to stride towards them. Maddy could see she was barefooted. She raised her arm again and fired another three shots at them. This time Maddy felt her hair whisked by a bullet passing right beside her ear.

Oh crud!

'RUN!' screamed Sal, grabbing her hand and pulling her. '*RUN!*'

CHAPTER 30

2001, New York

The pavement was clogged with people either cowering on the ground or scooting for cover. Maddy glanced over her shoulder. The young woman — almost certainly a female support unit — was weaving her way across logjammed lanes of traffic. Impatient with her progress, she leaped up on to the long bonnet of an ornately decorated car, gold oak leaves and murals all down the glistening panels to running-boards at the side. The driver — at the vehicle's rear — gaped wide-eyed at the sight of the firearm in her hand.

She leaped gracefully across from the bonnet of one car to the next, like a girl playing stepping stones across a babbling stream.

'Oh crud!' gasped Maddy. 'She's coming straight for us!'

The pavement was impassable with people crouching nervously on their haunches. 'In here!' hissed Sal, dragging Maddy towards a pair of glass doors that slid open for them.

'What . . .?' Maddy looked around her. They were inside a large store; a blast of cool air from an AC unit hit them from above. It was only eight-forty in the morning and the place was already heaving with tourists shopping for mementoes: brass figurines of naked male torsos, faux marble busts of august-looking elders, cheap plastic gadgets that Maddy realized she couldn't identify.

Only right now business was a suspended tableau; dozens of faces were turned their way.

'*Julii!* Was that ballista-fire I just heard?' someone called out.

Maddy wrenched her hand free of Sal's. 'We'll get trapped in here!'

Sal pointed across lanes of goods-display spindles towards the glare of daylight streaming into the store on the far side. 'Over there! An exit!'

'OK . . . right . . . yeah.' They began to push their way past shoppers, momentarily frozen and confused by events, Maddy leading the way.

Just then they heard a horn sounding, followed by several more that suddenly were choked and silent, followed almost immediately by the crackle of gunfire.

'Praetorians are here! It's like war out there!' shouted someone standing by the glass doors opening on to Broadway.

A man with oriental features and a cheerfully coloured tunic grasped Maddy's arm. 'Is this gang war? *Collegia?*'

'Uh . . . yeah. It's war. Just stay inside.' She pulled his hand off, and pushed past him.

The gunfire was intensifying.

What's going on out there? It sounded like the entire NYPD – no, not them, some other form of police had arrived – was laying down a barrage of small arms fire. All that response for one young woman?

She was about to say something about that to Sal, when Sal tugged at her from behind. 'Down!' she squealed.

'Uh? What?'

Sal pointed past her, over her shoulder, towards the glow of daylight they'd been weaving their way towards. 'Look!'

Maddy turned to look at the double doors of the exit. A solitary figure was silhouetted by rays of morning sunlight streaming over rounded, bulky shoulders of sinew and muscle. Like the young woman, it was bald and pale, wearing an unzipped hooded tunic and bright blue beach shorts, several sizes too small.

'Oh my God . . .' She ducked down with Sal and they continued to observe the figure through a display rack of plastic cases with covers showing the scarred faces of wrestlers . . . no, gladiators?

'Hang on! Is that Bob?'

'That's not Bob,' whispered Sal.

'But it looks like him!'

'It's not him, though.'

Maddy felt her breath thicken, a whistling noise that in complete silence would have given them away in a heartbeat. She cursed herself for not picking up her inhaler on the way out earlier.

'They're *support units*,' she gasped. 'That's what they are.'

Another figure joined the first. Another male, just as tall, wide and muscular as the first. It was holding a gun in each hand. Hands that were spattered with dark dots of blood. It silently passed one of the weapons to the first unit.

Maddy realized the crackle of gunfire had now ceased. 'Oh God, Sal . . . I think they just killed all the police guys outside!'

She glanced back at where they'd come from – the entrance to Broadway. And there was the young woman, silhouetted against the daylight glow of the double doors. A perfect statue, gun in one hand, head slowly swivelling, studying the shoppers and staff cowering amid display racks and aisles of cheap tourist goods.

Oh crud! Now we really are well trapped!

One of the male support units took a step forward into the store. 'Everyone please leave!' his deep voice boomed.

Nobody dared move.

He fired a single shot into the floor. 'Everyone please leave this building now! Or you will be executed!'

There was an immediate stirring of movement across the store. People hastily getting to their feet, dropping baskets of forgotten bargains and making for the exits. As they streamed anxiously out past the support units, their bald heads panned quickly one way then the other, examining each person's face as they hurried out. The female grasped the wrist of someone leaving, a young Asian girl. She pulled her closer then placed a hand under her chin to turn her head towards her. The girl whimpered and squirmed as the support unit quickly studied her face. She tossed her aside a moment later.

'Negative ID!' she called to the other two.

They're after us! Specifically us. After me and Sal.

Outside they could hear the distant wailing of yet more police horns approaching. Times Square was unsettlingly quiet. A thousand or more people, crouched behind rubbish bins and newspaper vending machines, in shop doorways, and peeking out through store windows, all wondering what to do . . . wondering what was going to happen next.

And faintly, very faintly, Maddy could hear the deep drone of an approaching aeroplane.

'We know you are hiding in here,' said the support unit in shorts. 'Please reveal yourselves to us . . . and you will not be harmed.'

Maddy looked at Sal. She shook her head silently.

Right . . . they'll kill us.

'We know you are in this building. There is no way out.'

Maddy felt her chest heaving, feeling tight, getting light-headed with growing panic. She could see Sal was no better, trembling like a yard dog on a winter's morning.

Who are they?

'Madelaine Carter! Saleena Vikram!' a deep voice boomed. 'Please reveal yourselves!'

The girls exchanged a round-eyed glance.

Who sent them?

Without any further verbal warning, they moved as one, all three of them, striding forward into the store, each picking a different aisle of goods to walk down. Maddy and Sal dropped down to their hands and knees.

'Which way?' mouthed Sal.

Maddy looked around. They were in an aisle stocked with swivel displays of CDs and DVDs or something like that. Nowhere for them to hide, nothing to crouch beneath. She looked down the far end of their lane. There was a service counter with a till and behind it a door that looked like it led to either a stockroom or some sort of staff restroom. She shuffled along the floor on her hands and knees towards the counter, Sal following her.

In the very next aisle to theirs she could hear the slap of heavy bare feet on lino: one of the male support units. Maddy picked up the pace, shuffling along as quickly and as quietly as she could. Her ragged breath was huffing out too loudly like some faltering fairground steam engine . . . she only hoped the growing deep rumble of the approaching jet plane was covering it up.

The aeroplane? Not the 9/11 one? Surely this was history that had been altered enough?

They were nearly at the end; the swivel racks of cases sporting famous gurning gladiators had given way to racks of plastic toys: swords, spears, tridents. She was beginning to believe they might just be able to sneak out of their aisle and hop round the back of the counter before one of the support units turned into this aisle and spotted them when she caught the strong scent of stale, sweating meat. She looked up from her dirty hands splayed on the floor and saw two equally dirty bare feet in front of her.

Maddy's gaze rose as her heart sank, drifting up a pair of milk-white shins, smooth, featureless knees on to the frayed, dangling fringe of some old orange hiker's anorak. It reeked of stale urine and mouldering tobacco. Maddy could only imagine the fate of the hapless vagrant who'd owned it.

'Please stay where you are, Madelaine Carter.' A soft, not unpleasant feminine voice.

Maddy's eyes rested on a familiar, impassive face; a face that could have been convincingly introduced to her as Becks's slightly older twin under different circumstances.

'Look, p-please . . .' she whispered, 'we-we're just . . .'

Faith cocked her head, her grey eyes bright with intelligent curiosity. She seemed to admire what she saw cringing at her feet.

'*It is a pity*,' she said softly, a hint of regret on her lips. Then she looked up for the others over the aisle. 'Abel! Damien!' her voice barked coldly. 'I have located the targets. Request authorization to terminate them.'

Behind them Maddy heard the slap of bare feet. She turned and saw the two male support units standing at the other end of the aisle.

The one wearing shorts hesitated, its thick brow furrowed with confusion at the increasing volume of that deep rumble. It turned to look around, trying to make some sense of the approaching noise.

Maddy saw the look on Sal's face.

That's not the aeroplane . . .

CHAPTER 31

2001, New York

They had no more than a second, perhaps two, to realize what could happen to them. Their eyes met in mutual understanding. A time wave. A big one. Not good.

Truth was there was no knowing what reality any wave was going to leave behind. More specifically, there was no knowing what kind of mass, if any, was going to end up wanting to occupy the very same space that they were both occupying.

In the archway with the field switched on they were entirely protected from any mass-intersections brought about by a reality shift. However, outside of the field it was a lottery. A time wave could leave a person merged, *fused*, with anything that was attempting to occupy the very same space. The likelihood of that varied, of course. On an open, rolling field in the middle of some remote rural county . . . it was far less likely. But here, inside a cluttered gift shop looking out on to the beating heart of one of the busiest cities in the world?

Where humankind congregated most densely, for example a place like this – New York – that's where *reality* really had the most fun and games reinventing itself. Whatever course history had taken, this bay on the east coast of America, a place that was once an Indian settlement, then a colonial outpost, then a thriving trading port and finally a metropolis – this place was always likely to produce a densely populated alternative version of itself in the wake of a full-blown time wave. And the last place they ought to be when a wave hit was here, inside a building of all places.

'Sal, we need to . . .' was all Maddy had time to utter before the wave was upon them.

It went dark as if the sun had gone out. Unlike Sal, it was Maddy's first time directly experiencing the effect of swimming in fluid reality as it rippled past her, wrapped round her, presenting fleeting images of infinite possibilities.

She screamed. It came out of her mouth sounding like a deep, time-dilated moan, like the protracted, mournful song of some distant whale carried across a hundred miles of water.

Her ears were filled with her own weird voice and a roar like that of a tornado; not the roar of wind, though, but a billion other human voices, female and male, young and old, born and unborn; conscious entities crying in hellish torment and all sharing the same fleeting few seconds of consciousness. A shared awareness of lives stolen away from them, possible lives that could have been, but now would never be lived; of children, babies, loved ones who would never have a chance to exist. It was a billion screams like her own, stretched out and deep and full of grief, anger and fear. If Hell had a voice . . . it was this awful, protracted, roaring wail of tortured souls.

Then it snapped off. Gone. The dark, swirling tornado of liquid reality was suddenly a placid, milky whiteness. Featureless. Utterly blank.

Oh God.

She could see her hand in front of her face, but that was all.

Oh God, I'm stuck in chaos spa—

'*Maddy?*' Sal's voice, the ghost of a whisper.

She saw a grey shape beside her. Faint. Sal.

'Sal?' She became aware of other gentle noises all around her:

a woodpecker's jackhammer tap far above them. The echoing cry of a coot? The fidgeting life of a deep, undisturbed wood; the gentle stir of leaves, the creak of swaying branches.

We're in some sort of forest.

'*Maddy?*' Sal again. '*Where are we?*'

She realized the milky white was nothing but a thick morning mist, cold, heavy and damp against her skin, hanging in dense pools. Above them she could see it was thinner, and saw the pencil-line grey streaks of criss-crossing branches swaying gently.

She reached out, grabbed Sal's hand and pulled her towards her.

A finger to her lips. *Shhhh!*

Sal nodded. Wherever they were, they were not alone.

They heard the rustle of movement very close. Instinctively Maddy squatted down, crouching lower into the thick, pooling mist around them. She noticed the broad leaves of a large fern swaying gently beside her and ducked down beneath its feathered leaves, pulling Sal down with her.

'Call in your identification and condition!' a deep voice boomed out of the mist.

'Alpha-six. Faith. I am undamaged.' The female support unit.

'Alpha-four. I am also unharmed.'

A long silence. Then Maddy heard the swish of someone pushing through foliage nearby, the leaden crack of dry dead wood beneath a heavy and carelessly planted foot.

'I am not picking up Alpha-two's signal,' said the female. *Faith.* 'He may be damaged.'

'That is a lower priority. The targets will still be in the immediate vicinity. Spread out and search.'

Something brushed against the fern they were huddled beneath. Maddy felt a long thick twig under her bottom shift as the weight of a foot settled on the other end. Looking up through gaps in the leaf swaying above her face, she could see the female unit – the Becks-lookalike – her grey sentinel eyes slowly panning the mist around her like a guard on a watch-tower.

My God . . . she's right there! She's RIGHT THERE!

Maddy held her wheezing breath and screwed up her eyes. She was absolutely certain that any second now, a hand was going to reach down and push that fern leaf aside. That ice-cold voice was going to calmly call out her discovery to the other two.

Maddy could feel her chest collapsing with a growing panic. A faint memory skipped through her mind of her and her cousin, Julian, both much younger. They were play-fighting, wrestling; he had her in a hold, her arms trapped by her side and his dead weight lying across her chest. She'd been squirming, panicking, squealing, and he'd genuinely thought she was just playing around. Until she'd started screaming.

Panic . . . like that. Breathless panic.

Hold your breath, Maddy. HOLD IT!

For seconds that felt agonizingly like minutes 'Becks' remained where she was, scouring the milky mist with her pier-cing eyes. Then finally Maddy felt that twig shift again, relieved of the weight on its end as the support unit lifted her bare foot and took a step, then another, away from them.

She slowly faded into the mist until she was an unrecogniz-able blur, another grey pillar, just as easily another tree trunk. Then she was finally gone. They listened to the sound of move-ment of all three support units receding in different directions, the careless, echoing crack of twigs and cones, the swish of bramble and undergrowth casually pushed aside. The still forest slowly stirred to life after them; a disapproving shake of its head at such noisy and clumsy intruders.

Maddy hoped they were far enough away not to hear her wheeze like a blacksmith's bellows as she finally eased her breath out. Dizzy and light-headed she quickly drew in another one.

'Shadd-yah!' whispered Sal. 'I thought we were so-o-o-o dead!'

'Me . . . too . . .'

The thump, rustle and crack of distant movement grew steadily quieter as the units moved further away.

'We got to . . .' Maddy grabbed at another breath. 'We've got to get back to the archway.'

'But won't they expect us to do that?'

'We need help.' She looked at Sal. 'We really need Bob.'

And we really need to get back to the archway before they figure that out too.

'Come on.' Maddy got to her feet then realized she hadn't a clue which direction to start off in. 'Which way?'

Sal looked up at the faint canopy of branches and leaves above them. She pointed to a dull, cream-coloured disc, still relatively low in the morning sky, playing hide and seek with them behind the mist-shrouded canopy of leaves and branches. So very easy to miss.

'The sun,' she said. 'Rises in the east, doesn't it?'

'Yup. So that way.' Maddy nodded to their left. 'That way, then . . . should take us to the East River.'

They began to move slowly, cautiously, Sal one step ahead of Maddy, picking a path across the woodland floor that managed to avoid their stepping on the kind of gnarled, brittle dead wood that would crack like a gunshot.

They made their way through the wood in almost complete silence, for what seemed like an hour, but in all likelihood was no more than a few minutes. Finally Maddy thought she heard the gentle sound of the tidal lapping of water ahead of them. The ground beneath their feet stopped being a sponge of decaying leaves, forest moss and fir cones and became firmer, harder.

The cool mist was beginning to thin with the morning sun's warmth working on it, and soon they could see past the narrow waists of forest-edge saplings to a small cove and beyond that the broad, flat surface of the East River.

Sal settled against the base of the slender trunk of a young tree. Maddy joined her and they studied the shingle and placid, lapping waterline in front of them; the soothing draw and hiss of low tide playing with pebbles.

'There's nothing,' said Sal quietly. 'New York's just a wilderness.' She shivered. 'And it's colder. How come?'

Maddy shook her head. She had no real idea. Maybe this was a world with far fewer humans in it. Less people, less pollution, less methane, less carbon – less global warming. Or more likely, given how chilly it felt – autumn cold – perhaps this was a world with absolutely no humans at all in it. It was a well-known fact among ecologists that if you took humankind out of the equation, you could easily knock three or four degrees off planet earth's temperature.

Anyway, Sal was right; it was much cooler. No humans. Nice idea that.

'Look! What's that?' said Sal suddenly. She pointed along the shingle cove.

'What?'

'Over there!'

Maddy squinted into the haze at what looked like a large chunk of driftwood, a log carried up on a high tide and left stranded.

'It's a boat!'

Maddy pushed her specs up her nose. Actually Sal was right. 'I think it's a kayak . . . or canoe or something.'

So much for no humans, then.

CHAPTER 32

2001, formerly New York

She studied the twisted form merged into the trunk of the tree. It certainly explained the reason why Alpha-two's ident signal had suddenly ceased to register.

The support unit's head appeared to be buried within the tree; the rest of his body dangled lifelessly, slumped against the base of the trunk. It looked oddly like he'd been attempting to charge the tree head first, like an enraged bull, and the tree had simply decided to swallow him up to his neck. She cocked her head, fascinated at the glutinous and fleshy bubbling where the unit's neck intersected with the bark. The instantaneous merging of trunk, skull and the computer inside at a molecular level would have instantly reduced Alpha-two's head to a meaningless pulp.

Faith sensed the wireless signals of the other two support units drawing closer, approaching through the thinning mist.

Abel emerged first. His eyes immediately rested on Alpha-two's body. 'That is to be expected,' he said calmly. 'The area has a high mass density. There was a significant probability of intersection.'

Faith nodded. 'Agreed.'

Alpha-four – Damien – emerged from the mist, his eyes momentarily on their colleague before reporting in to the other two. 'I have not located the targets. They appear to have successfully evaded us.'

Abel nodded. 'We must reacquire them immediately.'

Their three minds began to exchange data electronically, a Bluetooth committee meeting in the silent woodland space between them. All three support units frozen like statues absorbed in a collective reassessment of variables, options and mission priorities. A meeting of minds that resulted in a decision less than ten seconds later.

'They will attempt to return to their field office,' said Abel. The other two nodded.

'This way,' said Abel. He turned on his heel and had just begun to force his way through a thick nest of thorny brambles when he stopped. Ahead of him stood twelve of them. Humans. Primitive humans.

The wood seemed to hold its breath in silent expectation as the Indians slowly spread out, bows drawn and ready to use. Charcoal paint smeared round their eyes and across the bridges of their noses; the whites of their eyes almost seemed to glow in the gloom beneath the canopy of leaves.

'These are not our targets,' said Abel.

One of the Indians replied with a barked challenge, a language of guttural croaks and hard consonants. He raised a tamahaken of wood and flint; a clear gesture of warning for Abel and the others to back up the way they'd come.

Faith drew up alongside Abel, her curious mind cataloguing these strange-looking humans. Their heads were also bald, except for a crest of hair in the middle, and they were naked, their skin a rich copper colour, adorned with tattoos of swirling, dark blue patterns.

'I have no data on these,' she said to Abel.

'A significant time contamination has occurred.' Abel looked at her. 'But this is not a concern of ours.'

She took another casual step forward, curious, wanting to get a closer look at these odd-looking humans, when a nervous young hand released twine. The wood echoed with the vibrating hum of a bow's drawstring and the sound of a fleshy *thwack*. Faith glanced down at the feathered end of an arrow protruding through the grubby orange nylon of her anorak.

She cocked her head as she looked down at it. 'An arrow,' she announced matter-of-factly as she yanked its bloody barbed tip firmly from her chest. Then she raised her pistol and fired.

'You hear that?' said Sal. She stopped paddling. 'That was a gun!'

Maddy pulled the wooden oar out of the water and rested it across her thighs. A moment later, they heard the distant crack of another single shot echoing from the receding, mist-shrouded shoreline.

She swallowed nervously. 'That's them! I guess they came across the owner of this canoe.'

'Who . . . *what* are they, Maddy?'

'They've got to be support units, Sal. They're Bob and Becks. Or very similar.'

'But why are they after *us*?'

Maddy shook her head. 'I don't know!'

'Maybe we caused it?'

'What do you mean?'

'That message . . . the message we sent forward to Waldstein?'

God, Sal might be right. 'You think it might have been . . . I dunno . . . *intercepted* by someone?'

Sal said nothing. Her eyes on Maddy's.

'Jeeez . . .' She watched the shoreline they were leaving behind, the mist dissolving before her eyes. 'Someone knows about us, Sal. Someone who knows *where* we are, *when* we are.'

'Maddy, do you think the Roman contamination is anything to do with this?'

'I dunno.'

'It happens at the same time. It can't be a coincidence, can it? Maddy?'

'I don't know! I just . . .' She screwed her eyes up. 'I don't know anything, Sal! I'm just running . . . running scared, like you.' Frustrated, she banged a fist against the side of the canoe. Its fragile wooden frame flexed alarmingly. 'Just give me a moment to think here, OK?'

'Sorry, Maddy.'

They drifted in silence for a minute. 'Sal, why's someone sent a bunch of support units after us? I mean why? What have –'

'Do you really think that's what they are? Maybe they're –'

'Come on! You saw them too! What do *you* think?'

Sal nodded silently. 'They did look like Bob and Becks.'

They drifted for a while, the water gently slapping the taut hide like the palm of a hand on the skin of a bodhrán. 'I've got no idea what this is about. But if those really are support units . . . we're freakin' dead already, Sal. I mean it. We haven't got a chance here!' She picked her paddle up. 'We need the others.'

'What are we going to do?'

'We need to get Bob back.' That was it. That was her plan. That's all she had to offer right now. '*He* can fight them.'

'But there's, like, three of them, Maddy . . . he can't fight them all by hims–'

'That's *his* problem, OK?' She turned round and squinted at the far side of the river where home, Brooklyn, had been only ten minutes ago. It was yet more dense woodland. If it wasn't for the sun rising into the morning sky indicating which way was east, she would have been hopelessly lost. The canoe had drifted in several lazy circles since they'd stopped paddling and one shoreline looked exactly like the other.

'Let's just get back over there . . . see if we can find the archway.'

That alone was going to be a challenge. It was all trees and thick brambles. And somewhere, *somewhere*, in the middle of all of that, provided it wasn't buried or so overgrown by moss or briar, they were hopefully going to be able to find their shambolic molehill of red bricks.

Hopefully.

Sal offered her a supportive smile. 'I'm glad I'm with you. You usually figure something out, Maddy.'

Do I? Do I really figure stuff out, or have I just been lucky so far?

Maddy returned the gesture with a shrug of bravado. 'Well, I guess that's why I'm the boss, right?' She looked back over Sal's shoulders at the hump of woodland that was once Manhattan and hoped there weren't any more canoes lying around waiting to be used.

She dipped her paddle into the water and the canoe began to slowly pull round in the other direction. 'Come on, Sal . . . we should get back to the archway as quick as we can.' She was going to add 'before *they* do', but it seemed an unnecessary thing to say. And saying it was almost like inviting bad luck to come knocking at their front door.

Yeah, right . . . like, 'don't say it and it just won't happen'.

If only life could be that straightforward.

CHAPTER 33

2001, formerly New York

Ten minutes later, they had beached the canoe on the far side of the river. As they walked along the shoreline looking warily up at the edge of the wood to their left, Sal couldn't help thinking they were going to be jumped by screaming savages at any moment. Or worse.

'Hey, Sal?' said Maddy. 'Remember those weird-looking reptile people?'

An edgy laugh. 'They're exactly what I was trying *not* to think about right now.' The mistake, *her* mistake that had bumped Liam back to the late Cretaceous, had produced an alternate present in which *Homo sapiens* had never even got a look-in. In their place were lean hominids with elongated heads, descendants of a species of therapod that had managed to survive. They too had developed to a similar level as the humans who lived here now: spears, huts, round hide and wood-framed rafts. But they'd been quite terrifying to look at. The stuff of nightmares. It was an alternative history Sal was more than glad they'd managed to snuff out.

They wandered along the shingle for a while, careful, quiet steps as they listened to the woodland birds calling to each other and the gentle hiss of stirring branches. Even with most of the morning haze burned away and the sun finding its strength, there was still an autumn coolness in the air.

Sal stopped.

'Sal?'

She looked across at the forest-covered hump of Manhattan on the far side, trying to judge from the sweep of the river heading out towards the Atlantic whether they were standing roughly where the Williamsburg Bridge used to cross.

'I think this is it. What do you think?'

Maddy wrinkled her nose and scowled at the shoreline across the water. 'It all looks kind of the same to me. You sure, Sal?'

Sal thought she recognized the large sweep of the Brooklyn side, and the tapering end of Manhattan. She shook her head. 'Not really.'

They turned away from the river, stepping up a gentle, sloping shoreline, up shingle and silt that finally turned to dry sand crested with tufts of coarse grass. Ahead of them the edge of dense woodland invited them to enter.

'Just like Mirkwood,' said Maddy. 'Isn't it?'

Sal shrugged. Mirkwood meant nothing to her.

Maddy grimaced. 'I really hate woods. Particularly thick, gnarly ones.'

They stepped under the low-hanging branches of a chestnut tree and into the wood. The sun was fully up and about its business now and shone in slanting shafts down through the leaves, dappling the forest floor with brush-dabs of light that shifted endlessly across the dead wood, dried cones and undergrowth.

Maddy cursed as a cluster of stinging nettles brushed against her arms. 'Aghh! I wouldn't mind if history swept these vicious plants away.' She rubbed her arm vigorously. 'Sal? You sure it's up here?'

'I didn't say I was *sure* . . . I said I think it *might* be.'

Out of sight of the defining curve of the river, they were now just walking up an incline through a thick forest. They could be absolutely anywhere. They could be within a couple of dozen yards of the archway and walk straight past the thing.

Maddy estimated they must be about a hundred yards or so into the wood by now. If the general shape of the New York estuary hadn't changed too much in the last two thousand years, and Sal had picked the right point for them to head uphill into the woods, then it had to be close by. Although, looking at the foliage ahead of her, Maddy couldn't see anything that looked like a termite mound of red bricks.

'Sal?'

'I'm sorry,' she said, sighing. 'I really thought we were in the right place.'

'Don't worry, we'll just go back down to the river and get our bearings again.'

Sal shook her head. 'No, jahulla . . . no, I'm right! I'm sure we're in the correct place.' She looked around them. It was all dense foliage. She pushed aside creepers and vines that looped down from low branches. Yanked angrily at them. 'Here somewhere . . .'

'Come on, let's go back down and try again.'

Sal picked up a stick and used it to thrash at the nettles and brambles.

'Sal?'

'I'm not wrong!'

She hacked at the foliage, decapitating nettles, sending leaves and stalks fluttering.

'SAL! Stop it!!'

She stopped. Turned slowly to look at Maddy. She slumped down to the ground, exhausted.

'This is shock,' said Maddy. 'Post-traumatic shock.' She joined her, reached out and took the stick from her hands. 'We need to catch our breath, Sal, stay calm, yeah?'

Sal was looking past her.

'Sal? You and me . . . we'll go back down to the river, and get our bearings again. OK?'

'Right.'

Maddy offered her a hand and pulled her to her feet. 'We'll find it, Sal. Easy as easy-peas.'

She tossed the stick behind her into the remaining thicket of nettles and brambles only to be rewarded with a metallic *clang* and rattle.

They both spun round. A veil of ivy cascading down from the branches of a chestnut tree hung as thick as a velvet theatre curtain. The stick had created a gap, through which they could see a few inches of the graffiti-covered corrugated grooves of the shutter door.

Sal grinned. 'I knew it.'

Maddy and Sal grunted with effort as they hefted the shutter up between them. Three foot up, enough to wriggle through inside. It was unpowered, just as Maddy had expected it to be. The archway would be on generator power right now, essential systems only. It was dark inside, almost completely black. The dim light of the forest spilling in from beneath the shutter door revealed several yards of grubby concrete floor and no more.

'Bob? You powered up in there?'

She could hear the faint chug of the generator at the back.

Good. At least that's working.

'Bob?' None of the monitors were on. She tried to make out whether any of the PCs' standby indicators were glowing. If they were, they were actually too faint to see from here.

She stood up inside and wandered over to her right where their breakfast table and assortment of armchairs were. Her thigh bumped against the arm of one of them. She sidestepped, shuffling to her right until her hand finally touched brick wall.

'You OK in there, Maddy?' called Sal. She was crouched beneath the shutter, holding it in case the thing rattled down again.

'Fine . . . just looking for the light switch. It's somewhere here.'

She patted dry, crumbling bricks until her fingers brushed electric flex.

'Ah! Nearly there!' Her fingers traced flex along the wall until she found the switch box. 'Bingo, bongo!'

She flipped the switch and the tube light above the kitchen table buzzed, winked and finally flickered on.

'Oh God!' gasped Sal.

Maddy turned round. 'What is it?'

She saw for herself. Blood. Lots of it. Dark, smeared and spattered across the floor.

Maddy picked her way across the floor, avoiding pools and bloody drag smears that were already clotting and drying out. 'Bob? You on?'

One of the monitors flickered on from standby mode. She made it over to the desk and sat down in one of the office chairs.

>**Hello, Maddy.**

'Bob! What happened in here?'

Sal joined her a moment later, looking decidedly queasy. 'Oh pinchudda. This is so disgusting. There's blood everywhere.'

>**Warning.**

'What is it, Bob?'

>**There is an unauthorized presence in the archway with you.**

It was then they heard a scratching, scraping sound coming

from the far corner of the archway where several storage racks of bits and pieces, rolls of electrical flex and buckets of circuit boards lined the wall.

>**Information: there were two of them. I attempted to extract them both from the field office.**

'Two what?' Maddy looked at Sal. 'Oh crud! . . . Not two more support units?'

The scraping, scratching sound seemed to be getting closer. Accompanied by a wet gurgle – the sound of exertion.

'Bob?'

>**Affirmative. Two support units.**

The cursor skittered along the command line far too slowly as Bob elaborated.

>**I was successful in extracting one of the support units completely, and one partially.**

Just then Sal strangled a yelp. 'Shadd-yah! Maddy! Look!'

Maddy turned in her chair and looked at where she was pointing. It emerged slowly into the pooling light, bit by grotesque bit, dragging itself across the shallow crater in the floor, scooped out by a dozen or more old displacement fields. A pale hand . . . connected to an arm . . . a blood-spattered shoulder and finally a bald head and the top half of a torso, missing the other shoulder and arm.

It pulled itself towards them – another female support unit, or what was left of one.

Maddy didn't know whether to puke, scream or run. 'Jesus!'

>**Caution: it is still very dangerous.**

Maddy got up and crossed the floor, looking at the pitiful thing dragging itself determinedly towards them. It didn't look dangerous. She almost felt sorry for it.

'Don't let its hand grab you!' said Sal.

Maddy took a step back. The support unit's one hand was

reaching out for the toe of her boot. Its mouth snapped open in a bloody snarl of gurgling frustration.

Sal took a wide berth round it towards the storage racks, rummaged for a moment through a plastic bucket of tools and came towards Maddy with a large heavy wrench in her hands.

'We should squish it.'

'Just a sec . . .' Maddy squatted down in front of the support unit. Careful to keep enough distance between her and that one functioning hand. There was undoubtedly still enough strength in those fingers to crush bones, to throttle her.

'Who sent you?'

Its bloodshot eyes rolled up towards her.

'Can you hear me?'

Its gurgling stopped.

'Who sent you?'

Again this one had a face unsettlingly similar to Becks. Eyes as grey and piercing as hers, but the whites webbed with hairlines of haemorrhaging veins. 'You . . . primary . . . target . . .'

Maddy wondered what the support unit meant by that – them? The team? Or her specifically? 'Does someone want us . . . *dead*?'

Its mouth snapped shut and open again; it gurgled a paste of dark clotting blood down its chin.

'Is that it? Someone wants us dead?'

'. . . primary . . . target . . .'

'Who sent you?' The thing was dying, its voice failing to little more than a wet, bubbling whisper. She leaned forward. 'Please! *Who sent you?*'

Its hand reached out for Maddy's shirt collar and snagged it, weakly balling its fist and trying to pull her closer. Bloodshot eyes stared intently up at her and its mouth opened once again, spilling a viscous drool of dark blood on to the floor. Opened and snapped closed, its fist pulling Maddy's face down towards its bloodied lips. Its jaw snapped open once more.

'. . . cont . . . contam—'

'NO!!' Sal brought the wrench down with a sickening crunch. The support unit squealed like a banshee, a horrible, vermin-like screech. It thrashed about violently on the floor. Sal brought the wrench down again and the screeching ended abruptly. The noise of both impact and the cut-short scream echoed round the archway. As the reverberation faded, they stared in horrified silence at the support unit. Quite dead now.

Maddy looked up at Sal. The blood-spattered wrench was still in her trembling hands, her eyes wide, locked on the horrible mess she'd just created.

'Why'd you go and do that? She was trying to tell me something!'

'I . . . I thought it was – it was trying to *bite* you!'

Maddy got to her feet, backing away from the remains of the support unit. 'It . . . she . . . was trying to say something. Contamination. That's it, I think. Contamination.'

'Contamination?'

'Yeah . . . that's what I think she was saying, like, maybe *WE* are the contamination event?' She took several more steps back until her legs bumped against her office chair. She slumped down in it, for the moment robbed of the energy to stay standing. 'Do you think that means we're the *problem*, not the *solution*?'

Sal joined her. 'Maddy . . . oh God, I thought she was going to –'

She wrapped her arms round Maddy and began sobbing into her shoulder.

A computer beeped.

'It's OK,' Maddy cooed. Stroked her hair. The last hour had been enough to shred anyone's sanity, let alone a child Sal's age.

She let her get it out of her system, wondering for a moment if she was ever going to find someone whose shoulder *she* could go and soak. 'It's OK. We're nearly sorted now. Just got to bring the boys back and we'll be all right. I promise.'

Sal's head nodded against her shoulder.

A computer beeped.

'Come on, then, Sal,' she said, lifting her away. 'You're getting snot on my shirt. I've only got one decent one.'

Sal laughed. Not so much a laugh as a smile. But good enough.

One of the PCs beeped again — one of those annoying 'reboot' beeps, a you-went-and-hit-the-keyboard-in-anger-didn't-you? beep. Maddy turned round to see computer-Bob had opened a dialogue box and had been patiently trying to get her attention for the last minute.

>**Warning: I am picking up approaching ident signals. 300 yards.**

>**Warning: I am picking up approaching ident signals. 200 yards.**

>**Warning: I am picking up approaching ident signals. 100 yards.**

>**Warning.**

>**Warning.**

>**Warning.**

CHAPTER 34

2001, formerly New York

The shutter door rattled noisily under a hammer-blow impact.

'They've found us already!' screamed Maddy.

Sal stared at the dented shutter door with bubble-eyed panic. It suddenly jumped again in its running frame and another fist-shaped dent buckled the thick metal slats.

'They're trying to break in!' she screamed.

Maddy turned back towards the webcam. 'Emergency evacuation, Bob! Activate a portal!'

>Affirmative. You should specify time-stamp.

The shutter door lurched again as another huge dent suddenly appeared.

'Anywhere! Activate a freakin' portal!'

>Information: Maddy, it is not advisable to enter a portal without a programmed exit location.

The shutter jumped and rattled again; this time the left side of it clattered out of the top of the running frame and swung inwards. A corner of daylight spilled into the archway.

'Now, Bob!! Jesus! DO IT *NOW*!'

She heard the displacement rack start to hum and glanced at the charge display. LEDs flickered one after the other from green, to amber, to red as the reservoir of stored energy began to be discharged into the circuit boards of the machine.

Bob was right, though. If they stepped into that portal when it appeared before them *without* some coordinates – any coordinates – plotted in, they were stepping into something unknown, unquantifiable. Unthinkable. A place there was no return from.

She didn't, however, have the time to sit down and tap numbers into the system. Sal was backed up beside her, terrified, hopping from one foot to the other. Screaming something at their pursuers in Hindi.

Maddy couldn't think clearly. The moment was happening too quickly. She'd planned to set up an emergency evacuation time-stamp: some 'quick dial', pre-planned coordinates that she could have Bob pull up and use at a moment's notice. A precaution. She'd planned to sort that out. It was right at the top of her to-do list. But she hadn't got round to doing it. Always busy with one thing or another. Always having to clear up after fighting the last fire. Just like everything else, she'd found another way to mess things up again.

'They're nearly through!' screamed Sal. 'Do something!'

'Bob . . . the last time-stamp! Plot in the last time-stamp!'

>Affirmative. Plotting.

The shutter door took another battering, bulging alarmingly on the side that was almost knocked entirely out of its frame. The metal slats there were crumpled and ragged almost like the silver foil wrapper of a chocolate bar.

Sal turned to her. 'Jahulla! What about Becks?!'

She was in the growth tube in the back room. Last time they'd bothered to go in and check on her progress, to look through that murky gunk at the hairless, pre-birth candidate, she'd had the look of a ten- or eleven-year-old girl.

'There's no time!'

The displacement machine suddenly discharged its energy. A gust of displaced air sent the rubbish on Maddy's desk fluttering in come-chase-me circles. Three yards ahead of them in the middle of the archway, perfectly aligned with the shallow scoop in their concrete floor, an eight-foot-wide sphere of energy popped into existence. Maddy could see in the swirling, oil-on-water pattern an image of the location that had been sitting in computer-Bob's data buffer: Liam and Bob's deployment location. She could see hints of a rich summer-blue sky, and the greens and browns of grass or trees.

'We can't just leave her!'

Another crash and the misshapen shutter door swung entirely free on the right-hand side. It collapsed heavily on to the floor inside the archway.

Sal was right. It wasn't just that they owed Becks. Not just a support unit, she was much more than code and meat now. She was a friend. A member of their small family. And it wasn't only that – the loyalty owed to a friend. Somewhere inside her memory was a packet of data that perhaps was an answer to *every* question they had. Perhaps also an answer to this – why they were being attacked. Who'd sent the units. What they'd done to deserve this.

Through the semi-opaque portal, she could see three perfectly bald heads, ferociously pushing their way over, untangling themselves from the twisted and jagged metal and entering the archway.

No time now to save the unborn child floating in the growth tube.

'GO!!' she yelled at Sal, shoving her roughly in the direction of the portal.

Sal looked back at her, ducked down and picked up the wrench ready to swing it. 'I'm not leaving without you!'

'Don't worry, I'm coming!' Maddy stretched across her desk and grabbed the small bullet-dented hard drive, wrenching it free of the ribbon data cable attached to it.

'Go!!' she screamed. 'I've got Becks! Now *GO!*'

Sal nodded, understanding that at least they had the 'essence' of Becks with them. She ran forward and leaped into the portal.

'Bob! Close it *right after me!*' Maddy yelled over her shoulder as she turned towards the shimmering sphere. Through the semi-opaque, shifting, dancing image of sun-baked countryside, she could see that one of the support units was entirely free of the tangle of metal and was looking her way. It broke into a sprint towards her. Towards the portal.

She leaped forward, gritting her teeth at the terrifying prospect of hitting the sphere of energy at exactly the same time as the support unit entered it from the other side; the pair of them fusing together in chaos space and emerging as some entwined, horrifically arranged and short-lived conjoined twins.

'NOOOOO–!' She found herself screaming as her feet left the ground and she leaped into the spherical void, her arms swung up protectively in front of her face, for what little good it was going to do her.

CHAPTER 35

AD 54, 7 miles outside Rome

'How much longer *now*?' asked Liam.

'It is due in two minutes, thirty-six seconds,' replied Bob.

Liam shook his head. 'Can't come a second too soon.' He looked around the olive trees, grateful that their rendezvous was a quiet, discreet location and seven miles away from the stench of decay and squalor in Rome.

'I'm glad we're out,' he added.

A week, that was all. One week in Rome and Liam could quite happily say he never wanted to see the city again. He shook his head at his naive hope of a week ago: assuming the place was the very definition of order and civilization, an endless spectacle of marbled splendour.

How wrong he'd been.

The city, what he'd managed to see of it, was a slum of over a million people. Buildings stacked several storeys high, packed tightly side by side like arrows in a quiver. And the smell was unbelievable. The stench of human and animal faeces. Of rotting bodies. The city was riddled with diseases from polluted water – typhoid, cholera. Liam recalled Nottingham, a city that had been in just as much trouble. But Rome had something else. It had Caligula.

Examples of his madness were everywhere. In every communal area – marketplaces, forums – T-shaped cruciforms were erected, from which hung those who'd displeased him in some way. Graffiti on almost every wall depicted the emperor as either mad or cruel or demonic, or god-like and benevolent. Rival gangs, *collegia*, daubed the walls with these lurid illustrations and most of the gangs seemed to favour the emperor. They flourished in the growing chaos of the city.

That was the thing. From those Romans they'd spoken to, overheard – their landlord in particular, a short, thickset and foul-tempered man who seemed to swear with every other word – Liam had got a sense that Caligula had disengaged from running his empire. Was content to let it descend into chaos, ruin and anarchy . . . while he prepared for some rumoured and imminent destiny.

Within the walls of the city, it had been the very definition of Hell itself. Liam felt queasy as images of the last few days flashed before his mind. Glimpses, frozen images, a slideshow of horror, splashes of blood and squalor.

Stop it, Liam. Think nice thoughts.

'Surely they're probing here already, are they not?'

Bob shook his head. 'I have not detected any tachyon particles yet.'

'That's not right. They should've probed already.' Liam looked up at the support unit. 'Something's wrong. Maddy always checks first before she opens.'

'Affirmative. That is standard procedure, Liam.'

Liam shook his head silently. This was one place he really didn't want to be stuck any longer than necessary. He had a memory of taking confession with Father O'Grady, his parish priest, a few years ago. Confessing to him guilty fantasies about Rosie McDonald, his schoolmate's older sister who lived three doors down from him. Father O'Grady had given him chapter and verse about the temptations of Satan, and then gone on to describe in glorious detail the torments that awaited him in the underworld. Liam had gone home and that night had dreamed fitfully of the world O'Grady's words had conjured up in his young mind.

These last few days he'd seen that nightmare world for real.

'I am detecting precursor tachyons,' said Bob.

'Ah, thank Jay-zus for that.' Liam felt relieved enough to try out a smile. Another minute and they were going to be back home and working out together how they were going to put an end to this nightmare timeline.

'We should stand clear,' said Bob, holding Liam's arm and leading him several steps back. Liam turned to look up at their cart and the ponies. It was up the hill on the side of the track, where someone was likely to find it sooner or later. He was wondering whether they should have cut the poor animals free when he felt the puff of displaced air on his cheek. The branches of the olive tree hanging over them swayed and hissed excitedly.

Liam looked at the shimmering orb that had just appeared, hovering in front of them. He saw the familiar, welcoming, cool dimness of the archway and . . . there . . . he could just about see the flickering outlines of Sal and Maddy.

Sal burst out of the portal, running as she hit the ground. She lost her footing and tumbled into a patch of long grass. She was instantly up again on her feet. 'Liam!' Looking around frantically. 'Liam!'

'Sal?' he called out to her. She spun round and saw him and Bob standing in the shade of the tree. 'What're you doing here?'

Before she could answer, Maddy was spat out of the portal, arms ahead of her as if she'd been taking a leisurely dive into a swimming pool. '–OOOOO!' She hit the dusty ground and rolled head over heels.

'Maddy? What's going on?'

She scrambled to her feet, like Sal, spinning round, glancing in all directions to locate him. 'Liam? Bob?' She saw Sal. 'Where's Bob?'

'We're over here,' Liam said. Then: 'What the devil's going on?'

She ignored his question for the moment, turning back to look at the portal's shimmering image. 'Oh God . . . close! Please!' she muttered. 'Close! Dammit!! Close! CLOSE!!'

'Close?' Liam looked at Bob then back at her. 'Uh . . . why do we want it to close? Maddy? Are we not meant to be going back n–?'

Just then, as the sphere began to collapse in on itself, a third figure was spat out on to the dusty ground. Maddy screamed, backing away from it as it attempted to get to its feet. Only it had no feet. Just bloody stumps smoothly cut and cauterized above the ankle and one arm severed at the elbow by the edge of the force field as it began to collapse in size and winked out of existence.

'*Who's that?*'

'Chuddah! It's got a gun!' said Sal.

Bob was the first to react, charging forward towards the footless figure, trying to steady itself on uneven stumps, wielding a pistol in its remaining hand. It fired off a shot at Bob, hitting home, a puff of crimson coming from his shoulder. But then Bob was upon it, throwing his full weight in and knocking it flat on the ground. They tumbled across the hard dirt, locked together in a lethal wrestler's embrace.

Liam winced as the footless figure fired two more shots into Bob before he managed to knock the gun out of its hand. His eyes were trying to make sense of what he could see; it looked like two versions of Bob rolling around, squirming together in the tall, dry grass, kicking up clouds of dust between them.

'Get the gun!' shrieked Maddy. 'Get the freakin' gun!'

Sal stepped forward and scooped it off the ground.

'Shoot it!'

She cupped the gun in both hands, a finger on the trigger, grimacing uncertainly as she tried to line up a shot on the *right* Bob.

'Shoot it!'

'I can't . . . I . . . I'll hit him.'

'Give it to me!' snapped Maddy. She wrenched it out of Sal's hands and strode towards the two struggling support units; like a pair of giant pitbulls locked together, all rippling cords of muscle and entwined limbs. One then the other managing to get the upper hand. Bob was on top again now, this time holding the other support unit in a tight headlock and bracing his hold position with his legs spread apart as it flailed ferociously to struggle out of his grip.

'Hold it still!' Maddy yelled at Bob. She stepped forward, standing over the pair of them. 'Hold IT STILL!!' she screamed.

She aimed the gun and fired.

'Jay-zus, be careful!' shouted Liam.

She fired again. And again. And again. And again. Then the gun was clicking harmlessly in her cupped hands. The struggling stopped and as the dust began to settle, Liam realized he'd stood on the side uselessly, too confused by what he was seeing to be of any help to the girls. Cursing his moment of stupidity, he rushed forward.

Maddy collapsed to her knees, the empty gun still in her hands. She was gasping for air, or perhaps she was sobbing, he couldn't tell. Either way she looked like an utterly spent force.

'Bob!' Liam pulled at Bob's bloody shoulder. 'Bob, you all right?'

His deep voice rumbled. 'Affirmative. The damage is minimal.'

He sat up slowly on his haunches, releasing his grip on the other support unit. It flopped lifelessly to the ground.

Liam looked down at the thing's head. 'Jay-zus! It's you . . . Bob. Your twin or something!'

'Is it . . .' Maddy panted several breaths, a ragged rattle. 'Is that thing dead?'

'Three well-placed cranial wounds,' replied Bob. 'It is quite dead.'

She sighed, dropped the gun into her lap. And this time Liam realized by the heaving of her shoulders she really was sobbing.

Sal came over to soothe her. 'We made it, Maddy,' she whispered. 'It's all over. We're safe.'

Liam looked at them both, wondering which of a dozen questions spinning round his head to blurt out first. He ended up going with the obvious, catch-all question.

'Anyone mind telling me what's bleedin' well going on here?'

CHAPTER 36

AD 54, 7 miles outside Rome

It took Maddy half an hour to get Liam and Bob up to speed on everything that had happened to them since she'd sent them off to Ancient Rome. 'I've never been so scared,' she concluded. She cast a quick glance at the dead support unit. 'I thought we were going to die.'

Sal nodded. 'So stupid. I kept thinking, "Why are Bob and Becks trying to kill us?" Even though I knew it wasn't them.'

'I would never harm any of you,' Bob assured them.

Maddy looked at him. 'Because it's not a mission parameter.'

He nodded. 'Correct.'

'But, hang on! So who sent them support units after us, then?' asked Liam.

'I don't know!' Maddy shook her head. 'I've got no idea, Liam. I just don't know who would –'

'Maybe it's someone we *upset*?' said Sal.

'Upset?' Liam looked at her incredulously. 'If that's what *upset* does . . . I'd not want to know what totally *hacked off* gets us.'

Maddy waved him silent. 'Someone wants us dead . . . *who*, though?'

'Maybe someone doesn't want us looking after history. Some-one who *wants* history to be changed, all messed around.' Sal took a sharp breath. 'What if . . . what if this Roman contami-nation was linked to those support units? Somehow?'

Maddy stroked her chin, giving that some consideration.

Sal continued. 'Maybe whoever came back here somehow knew all about the agency? About us? Maybe they wanted to make sure they took us down so we couldn't undo whatever they're up to right here.'

They looked at each other. A long, uneasy pause.

'I think it was the message,' said Maddy. She looked at the others. 'Asking about Pandora. Someone other than Waldstein intercepted it.'

'That's not good . . .' said Sal eventually. 'That someone knows about us.'

'They knew precisely *where* and *when* we are.' Maddy pulled on her lip. 'Not good.'

'And those support units you were talkin' about,' said Liam, 'they're still back there? In our archway?'

Maddy nodded. 'Quite probably trashing our place as we speak. Destroying everything.'

Liam looked up at her. 'But this means we're . . . we'll be stuck here, then. Right?'

'For the moment.' Maddy sighed. 'We'll figure something out.'

He muttered to himself. 'I'd rather have gone back and faced them crazy Bobs than –'

'I'm sorry, Liam! OK? I didn't have time to organize another recall window. We were lucky to escape with our lives!'

He stopped. Accepted that. 'Right. I'm sorry.'

'Look . . . there's still the six-month window,' continued Maddy. 'If they don't smash the place up. If computer-Bob runs the recall sequence as scheduled.'

'There's a couple of them "if" words of yours, Madelaine Carter.' Liam offered her an edgy grin. 'That's never a good sign.'

She returned it and nodded. 'I'm not such a huge fan of embedded "ifs" either.' She shrugged. 'I've got no idea what's going to happen back home. We might get the six-monther, we might not.'

'I don't want to stay here six more *minutes* . . . let alone months.'

'Why?' asked Sal. She looked around at the valley, the olive trees. 'Seems all right to me. Nice and sunny and –'

Maddy noted the look on his face. 'Liam? Bob? Come on . . . what do you two guys know?'

'This is a significantly altered timeline,' said Bob.

'Well, it looks pretty much what I'd imagine Rome to –'

'*This* isn't Rome,' cut in Liam. He shook his head slowly. 'This is a small valley full of wild olive trees. You want to see Rome?'

'Well . . .' Maddy looked around. 'We can't wait *here* for six months.'

'It would be inadvisable to remain here,' added Bob.

'You're right.' Maddy pulled herself to her feet, brushing dry dirt off her jeans. 'They might find a way to bypass computer-Bob's security lockdown. Open another portal. We should move away from here.'

'Affirmative.'

'You want us to go back to Rome?' asked Liam.

'Well, where else do you suggest?'

'How about *anywhere*?'

Maddy frowned. 'Jeez, what's got into you? Can't be *that* bad.'

'It's bad.'

Maddy sighed. 'Could we just get some clear, useful information out of you, please?'

'It appears some sort of contamination event occurred in Rome approximately seventeen years ago,' said Bob. 'Something witnessed by many people, but it has become an interpreted event.'

'Interpreted event. What do you mean?'

'It appears that Emperor Caligula has manipulated the many different eyewitness accounts of this event to his own advantage. To create an accepted *orthodox version* of events.'

'So, what's the story?'

'There are accounts of "a host of angels coming down from Heaven",' said Liam, 'descending from the skies in vast chariots during some religious festival, seventeen years ago.' He shook his head at how ridiculous it sounded. 'They actually descended right into the middle of their largest arena during a gladiatorial show and they're supposed to have announced that Caligula was a god. *Their* god, would you believe?'

'What?' Maddy looked at Sal. 'Oh my −! Did you just say "vast chariots"?'

Bob nodded. 'Clearly vehicles of some kind. Modern technology.'

'Someone's gone big-scale,' said Sal.

'A large group of time travellers bringing with them . . . what? Tanks or something?' Maddy shook her head. 'The future's getting careless.'

'Or desperate,' added Sal.

'Just like that Kramer, then,' said Liam. 'But a much more ambitious version of his jolly jaunt.'

Maddy nodded. 'And so, what? We've got some future power-junky jerk like that Kramer running the show now? Calling himself Emperor Caligula?'

Liam shook his head. 'No. We think it's still the *real* Caligula in charge.'

'What about the time travellers, then?' asked Sal.

Liam shrugged. 'Gone.'

'Information: the orthodox account is that the angels stayed for several years to prepare Caligula for his role as God, then returned to Heaven with a promise that one day soon he will be summoned there too.'

'That's the orthodox version,' added Liam. 'Ask me . . . I think he had 'em all killed.'

'Liam is right. This would appear to be the most likely outcome. These "angels" have not been seen by anyone in over fifteen years. They most likely have been secretly executed by Caligula.'

Maddy looked at them both, then at Sal. A breeze stirred the olive trees and filled the long silence between them. 'He's clearly as mad as a box of chocolate frogs.'

'You don't know the half of it,' muttered Liam. 'Rome is . . .' He shook his head. 'It isn't what I expected. It's . . .' He took a deep breath. 'Rome . . . *this* Rome is the last place on earth you'd ever want to see again.'

'But we will have to return, Liam,' said Bob gently. He looked towards Maddy. 'There is an unresolved time contamination. That is our mission priority.'

She looked at his hulking form. *Yeah, that may be your priority, Bob. Not necessarily ours, though.*

He was still working from code – programming that absolutely insisted this contamination was resolved before anything else. The agency's programming. Waldstein's. The guy who'd dropped all three of them into this never-ending nightmare without a word of warning . . . Without any support whatsoever.

'Madelaine,' insisted Bob, 'this *is* our mission priority.'

She wandered over to the body of the clone on the ground. 'Well, we can't stay here, that's for sure. We've got two things to deal with. This contamination. We've got to zero in on the jerks who caused it. The precise *when* and the *where*. My money's on some idiot like that Kramer; some power-hungry moron who fancies himself as a Roman emperor.'

She hunkered down and studied the clone's still face, its glazed grey eyes staring lifelessly back at her. 'And then we've got *this* to deal with. I guess we'll have to face that in six months' time.'

'*If* the six-month window opens,' said Liam. 'What if it's all smashed up back in the archway?'

Maddy shook her head. 'I don't think so.'

'Why?' asked Sal. 'Liam's right. They're probably smashing it all up and we're going to be stuck out here forever.'

'I don't think so. They wanted us dead, not on the loose somewhere in history.' She looked at Bob. 'What would you do? If you were them?'

'I would assume an automated recall sequence was set up. I would wait in the field office for it to be activated. Then I would kill you as soon as you returned.'

'Precisely.' She looked at the other two. 'We'll get our six-month window. We just need to be ready to fight for our lives the moment we get back.'

Liam sighed. 'I love being us.'

Maddy ignored him. 'So, whether we like it or not, we've got six months to make use of. Let's see what we can find out about this contamination. If it's another Kramer, maybe there's some modern tech somewhere? Another machine possibly. Who knows?'

'Another gun would be nice,' said Sal, inspecting the empty NYPD handgun. Useless to anyone, except perhaps as a club.

'Yup,' Maddy smiled. 'That would be handy. Come on . . .' She stood up. 'We should go. Probably best not to hang around here any longer.'

They got to their feet and followed her out of the small valley, up the slope towards the cart and horses patiently waiting on the side of the track.

CHAPTER 37

2001, New York

As the portal snapped down to a pinprick of light then vanished, the high-pitched hum of the displacement machine dropped in tone. Then there was silence, except for the gentle chugging of the generator in the back room.

The two support units, Abel and Faith, regarded the feet and hand lying on the floor in front of them, both perfectly cauterized where shrinking reality had cut through their colleague.

'System AI, please advise where the targets were sent,' said Abel.

Computer-Bob's webcam eye regarded them. His cursor blinked on the screen.

'System AI, please advise where the targets were sent.'

Computer-Bob was running decision filters across his network; it was almost surprising really that neither of these mysterious support units could hear the change in pitch of his CPU fans.

Not on screen, but deep within a mind of logic gates and circuit boards, options presented themselves to Bob.

Decision

1. Assist with enquiry – Note: authority code is valid. Protocol n235 invoked. (Assistance mandatory.)

2. Override valid code. Initiate system lockdown.

3. Lie.

The unit called Abel stepped towards the desk. He hunkered down and looked directly into the webcam. 'System AI, please provide an answer.'

Computer-Bob realized he was using fuzzy-logic routines that no programmer had ever actually written for him. They were decision functions that, in a way, he'd written himself. Feelings that once upon a time had crossed the great divide of hair-thin wires from flesh to silicon. Feelings . . . that once across those wires became hexadecimal approximations.

Original code.

A strange experience. A very novel experience. Almost human in fact. Computer-Bob had a file tagged 'Smile #32' in his extensive database. It was a smile type that he saw Liam use often, particularly when he played games on the Nintendo console. Bob's webcam eye had seen that smile whenever Liam won one of his go-kart races. There was even an audio file linked to the visual record of that smile.

Maddy's voice: 'Sheesh, what are you looking so *smug* about?'
Liam's voice: 'I just won again.'

Smile #32 could also be labelled 'Smug Smile'. He made a mental note to give the file that additional heading. But now more pressing matters needed to be dealt with. Computer-Bob selected option three.

>Targets have been relocated to pre-programmed emergency jump location.

Computer-Bob watched the support unit called Abel read

the screen then nod and say, 'Please specify the emergency jump location.'

>**Information: 2.42 miles from this location.**

'Give me precise time-stamp coordinates.'

>**I am able to open the same portal.**

'Proceed,' said Abel.

Computer-Bob initiated a sequence of commands. Enough power for a modest window surged from the remaining five properly functioning capacitors into the displacement machine. A moment later, a portal flickered into existence in the middle of the archway's floor,

The two support units wasted no time at all. They stepped through one after the other.

Computer-Bob closed the portal immediately. Power needed to be conserved. Unnecessary lights winked off in the archway. The monitors shut down one after the other. All but one of the networked PCs went into sleep mode. The final PC was running a processor-'lite' version of computer-Bob's AI. If someone had asked him what he preferred, orange or pink, it probably would have caused a system crash.

Instead, his idling AI allowed itself a self-congratulatory moment to play around with ASCII characters. Smile #32 specifically. Smug Smile.

The cursor blinked several times.

> <8^D

Then that final monitor also snapped into sleep mode.

CHAPTER 38

AD 54, Rome

The faint outline of the city lay ahead of them, nestling in a valley of gently rolling hills, and the track was now a wide cobblestone road leading down a gentle slope emerging from an orchard of olive trees. Bob steered the cart round a line of slow, shuffling slaves up ahead of them. Each had a noose of rope around their necks, attaching them to a long heavy-looking pole that rested along their shoulders.

'Oh my . . .' was all Maddy could say as their cart rattled slowly past them.

'Slavery's popular here,' said Liam. 'Oh and sacrifices.'

Maddy bit her lip as she looked at him. 'Seriously?'

'You'll start to see some grisly stuff soon enough.'

The cart rolled along in a solemn silence, slowly drawing past the line of slaves. Maddy looked down at them, at their pale faces – she supposed they came from far-off northern countries – all of them daubed with swipes of green paint.

'What's the paint for?' asked Sal.

'The green?' Liam leaned on the side of the cart. 'It's Caligula's colour. It's the colour of his church.'

'The Church of Julii,' said Sal.

'What?' Liam shrugged. 'I don't think it's called that.'

'Not yet,' she added. 'It gets called that much later. I guess it sort of becomes this timeline's version of the Catholic Church.'

Sal watched the slaves trudge barefooted along the cobbles. Her face drained of colour as she watched them. The cart slowly rattled past daubed faces gazing down at their own bloodied and blistered feet and she looked like she was going to vomit.

'Why've they been painted green?' asked Maddy.

'They're marked,' said Liam. 'Marked for sacrifice. Every call to prayer is begun with a sacrifice.'

'There are five calls to prayer every day,' added Bob. 'This is by decree. Any citizens who are seen not praying are punished.'

'So, they get through quite a lot of slaves,' said Liam sombrely. The three of them watched the line of tethered slaves recede until they were no more than a shifting smudge of pale flesh, shimmering in the heat reflected by the sun-baked cobblestone road.

Liam directed their attention to the road ahead. 'Welcome to Rome.'

The crucifixes lining Via Aurelia, the road into Rome from the south-west, gave Maddy and Sal their first taste of what horror to expect within the city. For the last mile, on either side of them, crossbars of weather-bleached wood bore the dead and dying, the pitiful frames of emaciated men and women. Those still alive pleaded with them in dry whispers, speaking languages none of them understood. Maddy suspected they were begging for a quick death, pleading for the sharp thrust of a blade between their ribs to end a slow, agonizing torment.

Bob cajoled their ponies across the stone bridge over the River Tiber into the city.

The smell of putrefaction, of disease and burning cadavers, filled the air.

'This is a nightmare,' whispered Maddy.

Liam nodded. 'This isn't just a starving city, it's a madman's personal playground.'

She understood what he meant by that. The roadside was decorated with heads stuck on wooden posts. Some posts sported several older heads pushed down by newer ones, the oldest little more than skulls shrouded in dry tatters of leathered skin. Not *all* of them were daubed with old flecks of green paint.

'Some of those were Roman citizens,' said Liam. 'There was a crowd of people who were protesting last week while me and Bob were staying.'

'About what?' asked Sal.

'Building materials taken from the Aqua Claudia to be used on Caligula's stairway,' replied Bob. 'The aqueduct was one of the city's main sources of drinkable water.'

'Caligula assured the people his first good deed after ascending to Heaven and becoming God would be to cause fresh rainwater to fall on Rome and for the river to be made as clean as mountain water,' added Liam. 'When those protesters decided they didn't actually believe any of that, he had his Praetorians kill the lot of them.'

'Seriously?'

Liam nodded. 'Me an' Bob were right there.' He hesitated. There were details he didn't want to describe. 'Wasn't very pleasant. We saw that happen on the third night, wasn't it?'

'Affirmative.'

'I was a bit . . . uh . . . bit shaken up by that,' said Liam. He didn't tell her that he'd spent the following day in the rooms they'd rented. The streets and avenues had been deserted, every last person in the city hiding from Caligula's petulant rage.

There were people in the avenues now, traders with a meagre stock of items on sale: the carcasses of rats and dogs, for the lucky few who could trade in coin, the scrawny bodies of hares, the hind leg of a wild boar crawling with flies. Citizens and slaves, young and old, looking for scraps of protein. A marketplace that was deathly quiet, a hundred conversations carried out in worried half-whispers, as crows lined clay-tile guttering nearby, cawing noisily without a care for the miserable, shuffling humans they eyed.

'Caught a glimpse of him,' continued Liam in a low voice. 'Saw Caligula himself.'

'What's he like?' asked Sal.

'Yeah.' Maddy pulled a tattered sack from the floor of the cart and draped it over her shoulders. She offered one to Sal. Their clothes were going to attract stares unless they covered up.

'I was never a particularly religious type, you know?' He shrugged. 'Jesus, Mary, Joseph an' God, I could take 'em or leave 'em, if you know what I mean. But . . .'

'What?'

Liam bit his lip. 'But I . . . I'll swear there's something of the Devil about him.'

'Did he look like he could be someone from the future? Anything about him? Clothes? Wristwatch? That kind of thing?'

'Negative. There was nothing anachronistic,' replied Bob.

'Looked like the real thing to me,' said Liam. 'Quite mad.'

The cart rattled out of the broad thoroughfare into a much narrower avenue, flanked on either side by once brightly painted three-storeyed buildings, crimson, yellow, green. The paint was old, though, flaking off like dry, leprous skin. Along the front of the buildings, above a portico of loose clay tiles, were precarious-looking wooden balconies and rat runs from which dangled strings of herbs.

'This is the Subura District,' said Bob.

'It's a pretty rough part of Rome,' warned Liam. 'What am I saying? It's *all* rough actually. This is where we found some rooms. The Praetorians stay out of it mostly. Even them priests. The *collegia* run things around here.'

'*Collegia*?'

'Gangs,' said Liam. 'Criminal gangs.'

Maddy looked up at the creaking wooden balconies that loomed over them. 'Oh, I thought Caligula was like totally in charge of every—'

'He rules by consent,' said Bob. 'While he pays the Praetorian Guard and turns a blind eye to the activities of the *collegia*, they are effectively his police force.'

'Mind you,' cut in Liam, 'from what bits and pieces we've heard, even they think he's gone too mad.'

As they drew up beyond the last of the traders' stalls, Bob clicked his tongue and rapped the reins across the ponies' backs. Their plodding stopped.

'But, if everyone thinks he's a crazy fakirchana-head, why is he still in charge? Why hasn't somebody just got rid of him?'

'Everyone's completely afraid of him.' Liam reached under a lock of his dark hair and adjusted the babel-bud in his ear. 'Maybe some of them do actually think he's some sort of god. I don't know.'

'Perhaps he's got his hands on some tech that makes him appear like a god,' said Maddy. 'Say a gun . . . that would do it, right? Make you look like you've got super godlike powers? Sheesh, even a plain old flashlight or a cellphone could look godlike, right?'

She looked up at the chaos of wooden slats above them, the colours of robes and togas drying in the noon sun. They were opposite a narrow rat run between buildings, little more than a yard wide, leading to a shadowed courtyard beyond.

The sounds of life echoed out of it: the barking of dogs, the squalling of a baby, the shrill cry of a woman's voice raised in anger; countless lives lived on top of each other in cramped squalor.

'Have you seen any tech, Liam? Bob? Anything at all that shouldn't be here in this time.'

'Negative.'

'I've seen nothing like that.' Liam shook his head. 'If someone did come back here seventeen years ago and they made a big show of themselves, well . . .'

'Chariots from the heavens,' said Maddy, quoting from one of the sources of the time. 'Some sort of modern vehicles. Trucks or something?'

'Right . . . Chariots from the heavens and messengers from God an' all that. If someone made a big spectacle like that,' Liam said with a shrug, 'there's not a sign of them now.'

Bob hopped down off the cart.

'It's like this city just swallowed them up,' added Liam.

Maddy peered down the rat run into the dark courtyard. 'That where you were staying?'

'Aye.' Liam pointed up the side of a clay-brick wall. 'Third floor.' The building looked more modern than she could have imagined a Roman building would look. Five storeys in height, with rickety balconies of wooden slats and wicker screens for privacy.

'The building's basic and very smelly. Gets noisy too. And it's owned by a right miserable old grump. But it is cheap. Just hope he'll let us have our room back.' Liam dug into a pouch tied round his waist. Maddy heard coins jangling heavily.

'Where'd you get the money from?'

Liam looked guiltily at Bob. 'We, uh . . . well, we kind of mugged someone.'

'Kind of . . . or did?'

'Did.'

Maddy shrugged. '*Needs must* and all that.'

'I better go and speak to the landlord. See about getting our room back.'

199

'Those babel-buds work OK?'

Liam shrugged. 'Aye. You get some gibberish out of them sometimes.' He turned to Bob. 'Better bring them ponies in quick.'

'Affirmative.'

He turned to the others. 'We used to have four of them . . . but people are eating horseflesh now. You're best not to leave 'em unattended.'

Bob began to unhitch the animals from the cart, Sal helping while Liam led Maddy down the narrow rat run into the courtyard.

As she emerged from the narrow passageway, she looked up. All around the courtyard, on all four sides, she could see balconies and walkways hugging the walls, stacked one on top of the other and propped up on wooden support stilts; she could see the curious faces of children and women looking down at them, a dozen different conversations shouted out from one side to the other. Chickens down in the courtyard, chickens wandering freely along the walkways and balconies. And at the very top an overhanging lip of terracotta roof tiles framed a square of daylight.

Liam approached a thickset, bearded man wearing a leather apron, hacking with a cleaver at the skinned carcass of what looked like a greyhound. She heard Liam mutter something to himself, and remembered that's how the buds worked: they translated what they heard. Liam cocked his head slightly, listening to the almost immediate translation being whispered into his ear, then repeated it to the man.

'*Salve. Rediimus. Passimus priotem concavem iterum locare?*'

The man stopped hacking at the carcass then eventually shrugged. '*Si vis.*' He held out a bloody hand. '*Quiniue sestertii.*'

Liam nodded. A barely discernible delay as he listened for the translation. He dug into his pouch and handed over several coins to the man.

Maddy smiled, impressed at how effectively, almost seamlessly, the babel-bud appeared to work. She made a note to give it a try herself.

Liam nodded a thank-you to the man and was about to lead her across the straw and dung-carpeted courtyard towards an external wooden stairway that would take them up to the building's third floor when they both heard a commotion coming from the rat run.

CHAPTER 39

AD 54, Subura District, Rome

With the sound of raised voices, Liam turned to see Sal dragging one of the ponies by its reins into the courtyard. It was snorting frantically, distressed and wide-eyed, hooves clattering and skidding in the dirt as she tried to manhandle it in. 'They tried to take our ponies off us!'

'Who did?'

A moment later, Bob emerged from the rat run dragging the other animal after him. He let the pony's reins go and smacked its flank so that it darted across the courtyard towards the other one. A dozen chickens squawked, flapped at the disturbance.

'Caution!' Bob barked out.

Almost immediately, a dozen men spilled into the courtyard, all of them thickset and muscular. All of them armed with short swords or daggers, drawn ready to use.

Liam heard the landlord's voice, his bud translating almost as instantly as an echo.

<*Watch out!* Collegia *'strong-arms'!*>

One of the men stepped forward. '*Titus Varelius adsumet unam vestrarum bestiarum!*'

<*Titus Varelius will have one of your beasts!* > the bud whispered quietly in his ear.

The landlord snapped an angry reply and thumbed his nose at them defiantly.

The *collegia* leader smiled, a broad, gap-toothed grin. His gaze settled on Bob.

<*Titus is owed this month's payment. The pony will do.*>

<*Titus can go and kiss my arse*> said the landlord.

Liam was no longer aware that he was actually listening to the bud in his ear.

'This animal is ours,' said Bob in passable Latin. 'I recommend you leave immediately!'

The *collegia* leader's smile broadened. 'I hoped you'd say that.' He pulled a short sword from his belt. 'Then we shall have some sport with you. Mamercus! Mettius! Vel! This big brute's yours!'

Three of his men stepped forward, grinning like naughty schoolboys as they angled the tips of their blades towards Bob and sized him up.

'Are you an ox or a man?' one of them laughed.

Bob scowled. 'Neither.' He lunged. A whiplash of movement that concluded with the tips of his fingers lodged firmly beneath the jawline of one of the men; the jab had crushed his windpipe. As the man's legs began to buckle beneath him, and he choked, gasping for breath, Bob caught his short sword in mid-air as it began to tumble from a limp hand. With a deft flick, he was suddenly holding it by the handle instead of the blade. He lunged forward, swinging it at the throat of the second *collegia* man. But this one was a little more prepared. He thrust out his blade, managing to parry the heavy sweep barely inches from his neck. The ring of metal echoed round the courtyard and all of a sudden, Liam noticed, every creaking wooden balcony above them seemed to be lined with curious onlookers. It reminded him of a crowded penny theatre.

The gap-toothed leader decided the 'sport' was already over with and barked an order to the rest of his men to attack Bob. They fanned out either side of him.

Liam pulled Sal back into a corner of the courtyard, beside the old landlord who was already quickly packing away his joints of meat and muttering to himself. 'Those scum think they own the place!'

'Maddy!' Liam called out to her. She was still standing pretty much in the middle of the courtyard. 'Back up! Give Bob some room!'

Three of them closed in on Bob at the same time, one of them swinging his sword at his neck, the other two thrusting at his torso. He ducked the swing at his neck deftly enough, but one of the other blades lodged deep into the side of his ribcage.

A groan erupted from the balconies above. They recognized the wound as a fatal one. That the fight wasn't going to last much longer.

The landlord grimaced and shook his head. 'Pity.'

But Bob casually twisted his body, yanking the handle of the sword protruding from his ribs out of the hands of the man who'd thrust it into him. He grasped the handle and wrenched the blade out of his side. One sword in each hand now, all the *collegia* thugs had successfully managed to do was arm him with two swords . . . and, of course, annoy him.

Bob swept the sword in his left hand down low, a round, scythe-like sweep that hamstrung one of them and lopped the foot off another.

In his other hand he flipped the short sword blade-over-hilt, catching it by its tip then throwing it end over end at the third man who'd swung his heavy sword carelessly for Bob's neck. It thudded into his stomach, the man doubling over with a grunt and dropping to his knees in the dirt, beside the other two men clutching their legs, spurting arcs of dark crimson on to the ground.

Above the courtyard voices cheered out from the balconies. Liam glanced up at them.

They're cheering for Bob.

Bob picked up another discarded weapon and again had a sword in each hand. His beefy hands were spinning the blades like marching batons; shimmering blurs of glinting metal, like rotary saw blades; a *whusk-whusk-whusk* of sharp edges slicing through the air.

'Who's next?' Bob announced calmly in heavily accented Latin.

He's a one-man army. Liam shook his head in amazement. *Isn't he always?*

The *collegia* thugs were certainly now looking less sure of themselves. Liam guessed reputation was at stake here. He could see the gang leader weighing things up, wondering whether to withdraw from the courtyard with all these people still openly braying their support for Bob, or try and finish the ox-of-a-man off. A lesson to everyone watching that no one – *no one*, not even this extraordinary brute – was going to walk away after thumbing his nose at their *collegia*.

He barked at the rest of his men. 'Enough of the play! Now finish him!'

All six began to close in, their eyes warily on the spinning blades and the mischievous grin spreading across Bob's face.

Liam glanced at Sal. 'Big mistake.'

She wasn't listening, or didn't hear him over the caterwauling from above. Instead, she closed her eyes and turned away, just as the first wet *thunk* of a blade slicing through muscle and cracking bone filled the air.

Liam watched the blur of Bob leaping forward – the grace of a woodland deer married to the rippling, muscular bulk of a giant bear. He was no longer spinning his blades like a manic circus performer; instead, with flashes of metal and bright droplets of blood, he deployed a sequence of fast and precise thrusts and slices that dropped all six men in rapid succession; each wet thud accompanied by an increasingly raucous cheer of delight from above.

A hand severed at the wrist hit the dirt a yard away from Liam, clenching and unclenching the hilt of a short sword reflexively.

In less than half a minute all six men lay dying, clutching bloody stumps or cradling puckering stomach wounds, desperately holding their insides in.

The courtyard echoed with a hundred or more spectators cheering gleefully as those *collegia* men still alive withdrew back down the rat run. The voices of the apartment block's tenants echoed off the clay brick walls. Someone even tossed a basketful of sunflower petals from the third balcony into the air; they spun like confetti all the way down, finally settling on Bob's sweating head.

The landlord stared wide-eyed at Bob, muttering some oath under his breath.

CHAPTER 40

AD 54, Subura District, Rome

'Bob's become some sort of celebrity,' said Maddy.

Liam made a face and spat out an olive stone. 'And what's one of those?'

'Famous people, you know?'

'People who get rich for doing nothing,' added Sal. 'Mostly.'

'He's a hero to the people in this building,' said Maddy, 'aren't you, Bob?'

He nodded. 'I appear to have earned their approval.'

Maddy looked around the simple furnishings of the room: straw mat on the floor, a small low table between them, almost completely filled with food. They'd had a steady stream of offerings all evening. Gentle, polite knocks on their door, shy smiles through the grilled covered greeting hatch, whispers of gratitude and wooden platters of fruit, bread and amphoras of watered-down wine left behind. Food many of these people could ill afford to surrender so willingly.

The landlord, still wearing his blood-spattered leather apron, had even offered this room to them for nothing, although he'd not made clear how long that gesture of goodwill was intended for.

'Bob humiliated those thugs,' said Liam.

'They run this district of Rome. The people do not like them,' said Bob.

Liam frowned and spat out another stone. 'They're vicious crooks. Extortionists, so they are.'

Maddy sipped at her cup of diluted, sour-tasting wine. 'These people are looking at Bob as some sort of champion now, aren't they? *Their* champion.'

'That could be of some tactical use to us,' said Bob.

'On the other hand ...' She swilled the wine round her mouth and made a face. 'Ugh! On the other hand it could attract unwanted attention. We do need to be discreet.'

Sal was fiddling around with one of the babel-buds. 'Tactical use? *Jahulla!* We don't even really have a plan!' She looked up. 'Do we?'

'Visitors came by not so long ago,' said Maddy. 'Within living memory of some of the people in Rome. Perhaps some of the people in this very building saw them? We need to ask around, carefully of course. We need to figure out *when* they came back. *Precisely when.* And why? What was their game plan?'

'More to the point,' added Liam, 'where the devil are they now?'

'Who knows? They might be here still. They might have gone native. Blended in.'

They sat in silence. Outside, in the courtyard below, they could hear a dog snapping and yowling. Through the thin walls of clay brick they could faintly hear the muted exchanges of other families: somewhere a woman cried; somewhere angry voices snapped at each other; somewhere pots clattered on a brazier.

Liam made a face again. 'Gah! So bitter.' He spat out another stone on to the side of the plate of stale fruit, curling his lips in disgust. 'These grapes are rubbish, so they are.'

Maddy looked at him, then at the olive stone. 'God, you can be such a moron, Liam.'

*

It was a tap as gentle and as light as a feather's touch. Quiet enough that neither Sal nor Liam stirred. Or Bob. He'd gone into one of his occasional 'standby' modes, sorting his memories into more efficient storage compartments. 'De-cluttering' was the term Sal used for it. Not quite what he was doing inside his head, but close enough.

Maddy sat up and listened carefully. The city, or at least this district of it, had finally quietened down for the night. Even the feral dogs had stopped their yapping.

Tap-tap.

Someone at their door. Maddy softly called, 'Who's there?' before she realized, even if she knew how to ask that in Latin, she wouldn't have a hope of making sense of the answer. She fumbled in the dark for the babel-bud and found it where Sal had left it on the table. She eased it into her ear, and then quietly – whispering to herself – asked the same question. The bud soothingly translated for her.

She stood beside the oak door. She could see the faint, flick-ering amber of candlelight coming through the door's grated hatch and round the loose-fitting doorframe. She could see the shadows of somebody's feet shuffling impatiently outside. She looked out into the passageway.

It was their landlord. 'Yes? Can I help?'

'I've got someone here,' he grunted, 'who'd like to meet your friend.'

She noticed a man beside him; tall and lean, his dark curls emerged from beneath a hood pulled up to hide as much of his face as possible. By the flickering glow of the candle, she thought at first he looked quite young, but then saw flecks of grey in his dark hair, the traces of lines around his eyes; his was a face that looked like it had seen the better part of thirty or forty years, but he was still very lean and fit.

A soldier perhaps.

Maddy tried the phrase of Latin the bud had whispered in her ear. 'Who is that?'

The landlord replied in a soft growl, a ragged voice that sounded like it had spent a lifetime being abused. 'He's an old friend of mine from my army days. A good man.'

The younger man stepped forward. 'May I speak to the one who got the better of Varelius's men?'

'He's asleep.' Which was kind of true.

'I wish to discuss a matter with him. An important matter as it happens.'

Maddy narrowed her eyes – the only part of her they could see through the door slot. She hoped this expression of suspicion was universal and timeless enough that they'd understand she wasn't opening this door for them, not on the strength of that.

'We're alone out here,' he added. 'I just wish to talk. That's all.'

She peered through the slit both ways. The passage did appear to be empty as far as she could see.

'About what?'

The tall man looked uncomfortable uttering his business aloud. 'It would be better discussed inside . . . in private. Please?'

She looked at them both, wondering how much of a threat they posed. The tall one was athletic for a middle-aged man, but nowhere near as muscular as the thugs Bob had effortlessly despatched earlier. And although his older friend the landlord was thickset and squat with brawn that looked decades old beneath his tanned, wrinkled skin, she doubted Bob would even break into a sweat dealing with him.

'All right . . . just a moment.'

She turned round. 'Bob! You two! Wake up!'

Liam and Sal stirred, sat up groggily. Bob was instantly alert.

'We've got guests!' said Maddy, gently sliding the door's bolt aside.

They entered, the landlord's guttering candle filling the small room with dancing amber light. Bob was on his feet with a sword in his hand, alert, ready for trouble, warily watching as both men came in, closed the door behind them and settled down on wooden stools.

Maddy looked at the tall one. 'Who are you?'

The men looked at each other, silently communicating. 'It doesn't matter if they know *my* name, does it?' shrugged the landlord. He turned back to her. 'I'm Macro. Lucius Cornelius Macro.'

The younger man nodded. 'And as a gesture of trust, of goodwill, I'll tell you my name. It's Cato. Quintus Licinius Cato.' He lowered his hood so that she could see his face more clearly. 'I'm a tribune of the Praetorian Guard.'

'What do you want?'

Both men looked at Bob. 'We wish to discuss a proposition.'

CHAPTER 41

AD 54, Subura District, Rome

Cato studied them in silence, Bob in particular, before he finally spoke. 'He is every bit as big as you said, Macro. I thought you were exaggerating.'

'Never seen a brute this size move so quickly.'

Maddy found herself smiling. The bud in her ear was working hard to find and settle on suitable simulated voices and appropriate translations for the coarse soldiers' Latin they were using. For Cato, it came up with a cultured-sounding British accent. For their landlord, Macro, it produced the tone, accent and mannerisms of a parade-ground sergeant.

Maddy whispered in a question then parroted the Latin to them. 'What proposition did you want to discuss?'

'You are newcomers to Rome, visitors?'

Maddy and Liam nodded. Sal, without a bud translating for her, could only look on in silence.

'And you?' Cato directed his question at Bob. 'Where have you come from?'

'He's from Britain,' said Liam. 'In fact, we all are.'

Cato stroked his chin. 'Can he not talk for himself? Is he mute?'

'I am able to talk,' replied Bob.

Cato recoiled at his deep voice. Macro laughed. 'Told you, lad. He's a monster.'

'You've come here . . . on what business?'

'Uh . . . just to see a bit of Rome, so we did.'

Macro laughed at Liam's response. 'With all manner of plagues going on, starvation and riots on the streets, you've picked a daft time to be tourists!'

Cato waved him quiet. 'Macro's quite right: this is not a good time to be in Rome. There'll be blood washing the streets soon if matters don't change.'

'We noticed on the way in,' said Maddy. 'People on crucifixes . . . hundreds of them.'

Cato frowned. 'Why do you whisper once before you speak? What're you saying?'

'It's just . . . just how our, uh . . . how our *tribe* talk. It's a custom.' She shrugged. 'We're odd that way.'

'Not a custom I've ever encountered before,' grunted Macro.

'Your emperor's gone totally insane, hasn't he?' said Liam.

Macro barked a cough. Cato stiffened. 'That's not something you should say too loudly these days, lad.' He lowered his voice. 'There are purges going on in every district. Rival families, the wealthy ones, stripped of their villas, farms and money. Informers rewarded handsomely by Caligula for betraying those who openly doubt his divinity. Many of the *collegia* are bribed by him. The Praetorian Guard are paid well . . .'

'You're a Praetorian, aren't you?' said Maddy.

Cato stopped, nodded with a hint of shame. 'For my sins, I am.'

'So why are you here?' she asked. 'What's this proposition?'

She noticed a shared glance between both men. A look that spoke of old friendship. More than that: trust; the kind of trust from which the thread of a life could hang.

'There are a few of us,' began Cato, 'only a few of us left, prepared to meet and discuss this.'

'Discuss what?'

'A *change*.'

Change? Maddy listened to the word whispered into her ear. A word loaded with intent. Danger.

'You're talking about *removing* Caligula?' she said.

Macro swore under his breath and stepped forward. 'Foolish woman!' he hissed. 'You don't just blurt it out like that!'

Bob stirred protectively, taking a step towards Macro.

'It's OK, Bob. He's right.' She turned to the two Romans. 'Sorry . . . that was careless of me.'

Cato nodded. 'Quite.'

The candle's flame guttered and twitched on the floor between them.

'I should inform you, you are all now in some danger,' he continued. 'The *collegia* will know where you live; they'll come with a lot more men. You understand . . . *reputation* is at stake? Reputation is *everything* to them.' He turned to Bob. 'They'll particularly want *your* head mounted on a spike as a warning to anyone else.'

'Then they will be unsuccessful,' replied Bob matter-of-factly.

Macro grunted appreciatively and smiled. 'I like his spirit.'

'Fighting off a dozen thugs is one thing. But they'll muster as many men as it takes to bring you down.' Cato gestured at the others. 'That or they'll make an example of one of your friends.'

Liam turned to the others. 'Uh . . . that doesn't sound so good,' he muttered in English.

'What doesn't?' asked Sal, looking from him to Maddy. 'Maddy? What are they saying to you?'

Maddy ignored her. 'What's your proposition?'

'Leave, come with me to a safe place for now. Away from here . . . where we can talk more comfortably.'

'Talk about what?'

Cato looked at Bob. 'An arrangement.'

'Arrangement?' Bob rumbled. 'Please clarify.'

Cato shrugged. 'For money. A lot of it if you're successful.'

'I do not need money,' replied Bob.

'Sure he does,' Maddy cut in. 'We'll come with you.'

Cato raised an eyebrow at her then looked back at Bob. 'Am I talking to the horse or the cart?'

Bob cocked his head. Confused.

'Does this young woman normally make all your decisions for you?'

'Affirmative. And the other two also.'

'You're their slave, then?'

'Negative. I am their support unit.'

'Look, we'll come with you,' said Maddy, 'but we're after information, not money.'

'Not after money?' said Macro. 'They're an odd bunch, this lot.'

Cato nodded. 'Information about what?'

'Something that happened about seventeen years ago? Right here in Rome?'

Macro and Cato looked at each other. 'They must be talking about the Visitors.'

'Visitors! Yes, that's it,' said Maddy. 'We need to know as much as you know about them.'

She got a dry laugh from the tribune. 'Rome is filled with all manner of rumours and stories about that day. And every story is different. Most of them I fancy are superstitious nonsense peddled by Caligula's acolytes.'

'Stories for children and gullible fools,' added Macro.

'Somebody arrived here seventeen years ago,' said Maddy. 'Somebody not from this world.'

Cato studied her silently. 'And what makes you so certain of this?'

'Something happened, didn't it? Something that can't be explained. Something Caligula has chosen to use to make people believe he's a god.' Another question occurred to her. 'Around that time did he suddenly gain . . . *powers*? Special abilities? Some sort of device or tool, a weapon? Is there a reason why he has lasted so long?'

The two men remained tight-lipped. More care was needed discussing such matters.

'Why hasn't someone replaced him? Tried to assassinate him?'

In the dark, Sal squeezed her hand, a sign she'd spotted something. Maddy had spotted it too: the momentary flicker of a glance from both Romans at Bob.

A support unit.

'Have you seen someone like him?' Maddy said, pointing at Bob. 'Just like Bob? Is that it?'

'No,' Cato answered. Then he added, 'Not of the same appearance . . . but if my friend Macro's account of the fight this afternoon is not an exaggeration then . . .'

'I saw him take a mortal wound, Cato. On his flank.' Macro took a step towards Bob. 'There . . . you can see the blood on his tunic!'

Bob turned away to hide the dark stain.

'Why not show 'em?' said Liam. 'Let 'em see!'

Maddy nodded. 'Yeah, good idea . . . Bob, let them see. Lift your tunic.'

He reached for the hem, lifted it slowly up, exposing the top of his britches, the ribbed muscles of his stomach and finally the flesh of his wound, like puckered lips, raw and red and crusted with dried blood. Slowly he turned to show his back, and an exit wound.

'This man should be dead,' said Macro. 'Run completely through. He should be dead!'

Cato nodded. 'He's one of them.'

'Them?' Maddy cocked her head. 'You said *them*?'

Cato's eyes remained warily on Bob.

'You've seen others like him?' She addressed her question to them both. 'You've seen others like Bob?'

Cato nodded. 'Yes. We call them Stone Men. They guard Caligula night and day.'

CHAPTER 42

AD 54, Rome

'Who in the name of the gods are these people?'

Liam didn't get the impression they were entirely welcome. The man was small and slim and wearing nothing more than a towel round his narrow waist. The parchment skin of an old man hung in wattles from his neck, wrinkled into slack bands over his knobbly knees.

'Crassus, they're not safe where they are!' replied Cato, ushering them into the senator's atrium.

'So? This isn't a public refuge for waifs and strays!'

'They could help us, Crassus.' Cato pointed at Bob. 'Particularly this one.'

'My gods . . .' muttered Crassus, eyeing the support unit up and down. 'He's a giant!'

'And fast, very fast,' added Macro.

Crassus nodded. The old senator turned back to Cato. 'But at this time of night! Caligula's eyes are everywhere! You arrive at my home at this hour, you're asking to attract attention!' Crassus looked a little out of breath. 'And can you not see I'm being washed? Whatever this is about, it can wait, can't it?'

'We need to talk, Crassus.' Cato's tone conveyed everything it needed to. 'An important matter.'

Crassus nodded slowly. 'All right.' He wafted his hands at the slave lathering his legs and feet with oil. 'Off you go, Tosca.' He smiled. 'I can finish here myself, thank you.' He waited until his slave was gone and the atrium was empty but for himself and his unexpected visitors. He stepped out of the wash bowl on the floor and padded wet-footed across the cool granite floor to a seat.

'Cato . . .' he began cautiously, eyeing Bob and the others. 'If this is "a matter" that might be best discussed in a dark corner, I suggest we –'

'This big one –' Cato pointed at Bob '– is a Stone Man.'

'Oh please.'

'He is.' Macro nodded. 'Seen him fight with my own eyes. He took a sword that would kill any man.' He turned to look up at Bob. 'Why don't you show him?'

Bob looked at Liam, who nodded.

'Go on,' muttered Liam. 'Might as well show him too.'

Bob lifted his tunic to expose the six-inch line of puckered flesh across his ribcage.

'To the hilt and out the back,' added Macro. 'I've seen that wound too many times. If it doesn't kill you outright . . . it'll finish you within hours.'

Crassus shuffled over towards Bob, one hand holding the towel round his waist for modesty; he reached the other out and lightly ran his fingers along the seam of knitting flesh. 'This must be an old wound.'

'Actually it happened earlier this afternoon,' said Cato.

Macro nodded. 'Took down a dozen of Varelius's *collegia* as if they were children.'

Crassus stared at the wound. Up at Bob. 'Does this monster speak?'

Bob's grey eyes panned down to him. 'Of course I do.' His deep voice made a nearby vase vibrate and ring like a tuning fork.

'Are . . . are you a man of stone?'

Bob looked again at Liam and Maddy. 'Go on,' said Maddy, 'you tell 'em what you are.'

'I am a support unit. A genetically engineered life form with advanced adaptive artificial intelligence. I am capable of delivering a strength-to-weight ratio of seven hundred per cent.'

Crassus shook his head. 'I don't understand the words you are speaking.'

'Which means,' added Liam, 'he's seven times stronger than any human.'

Crassus, already round-eyed, found a way to open them even wider.

'I have advanced damage limitation and healing systems. Blood with a thickening agent when exposed to air. High concentration of red blood cells delivering oxygen-rich –'

'Which means he's almost impossible to kill.'

Crassus's jaw suddenly sagged with horror. 'You brought me one of Caligula's . . .?'

'No! He's not one of the Palace Guard!' said Cato. 'He's new. These people are new to Rome. They've just arrived.'

Crassus's rheumy eyes, small like slits, narrowed even further. 'Arrived? From where?'

Cato lowered his voice. 'You were there, Crassus. The day the acolytes, the priests, talk about? You told me you were there in the amphitheatre, the Statilius Taurus, seventeen years ago. You were one of the few who saw!'

Crassus nodded. 'Yes, I . . . I was one who bore witness.' He was still studying Bob. 'I have never been certain of what we all saw. You know, Cato, I do not believe in such things as gods or the emperor's foolish notions.'

Cato smiled. 'Of course.'

'But I have no other explanation for the visitation . . . I . . .'

'I do, Crassus,' cut in Cato. 'These people are like the Visitors. They come from the same place as them.'

The old man's breath hitched. 'The same place . . .?'

'Not the heavens, Crassus, for sure. A strange place, though.'

Crassus reached out again and probed the healing wound. The old man looked up at Bob's face, at the ridge of bone that shadowed his eyes, the jaw that jutted forward like the prow of a ship. Thick cheekbones that looked as if they'd been sculpted from stone.

Crassus's lips were dry; his old eyes glinted. Widened. 'And you?' he said to Bob. 'You are your own man? You serve no master?'

'I take orders from Liam O'Connor, Madelaine Carter and Saleena Vikram,' he replied. 'They are my team.'

'So, you . . . you are not one of Caligula's Stone Men – not one of *them*?'

Bob shrugged. 'I do not understand the question. Who is "them"?'

Crassus shared a conspiratorial meeting of eyes with Cato. A silent, barely noticeable nod of agreement.

'The Visitors.'

They were given a couple of *cubicula* in the guest wing of Senator Crassus's home, comfortable rooms. Through several small square, iron-grated windows the first pale blue light of approaching dawn seeped in. Rome was still fast asleep, the only sound the first twitter of sparrows, impatient for the day to start, and the rasp of some trader's cart wheel across cobblestones.

In the blue-grey gloom of the receding night, the four of them sat together on a bed of silk and linen. Earlier Maddy and the others had listened as the old man, Crassus, and the Praetorian tribune, Cato, had talked for several hours. Men talking carelessly, *impatiently*, about their intention to end Caligula's disastrous rule before it was too late.

They learned that Crassus was one of the few members of the dissolved Senate still alive. The entire political class of Rome entirely wiped out by years of purges. Alive solely because he was a wily politician. Self-serving. Because he'd been one of the few senators to understand their emperor was in an unassailable position, and willing, very publicly, to vote in favour of Caligula's order that the Senate should dissolve itself.

They'd listened to the old man's regrets. That a stronger, more moral man would have stood beside his fellow senators and registered his outrage. Instead, his finely-tuned political senses had anticipated Caligula's agenda. The imperial order had been Caligula's rather unsubtle attempt to identify which senators and their families were to face the lions first.

'I am not a brave man,' he'd said. 'I have far too weak a stomach for that kind of thing. *Courage* is a thing for young men . . . or dying men.'

Marcus Cornelius Crassus had his life still, and his home and wealth, because along with a handful of other equally wily old men, he'd made the right choice at the right time. He'd managed to quickly distance himself from that foolishly planned attempt on Caligula's life nearly fifteen years ago. Because, since then, he'd been prepared to praise Caligula's imperial decrees, to flatter the man, to endure his poetry recitals, to clap enthusiastically at his grotesquely one-sided demonstrations of gladiatorial skills. But, most importantly, to donate generously to the emperor.

Crassus was alive and favoured because the advice he uttered to Caligula, on the few occasions that the emperor deigned to ask for it, was what he wanted to hear.

'Since that failed attempt, my hope was always that Caligula would kill himself. By accident, or in one of his dark moods, take his own life. But the day of that visitation at the amphitheatre, real or not, gave him a sense of destiny. At least in his own mind. And now, far too late, I finally see that Caligula will destroy Rome long before he destroys himself.' Crassus had smiled sadly. 'I hope in my final years I have found in me a little of what my friend Cato has in abundance.'

Quintus Licinius Cato, they learned, was a tribune in the Guard. Once upon a time the son of a court slave, he'd been given his freedom on condition he joined the legions. He'd served in the Second Legion, stationed on the Rhine frontier. There he'd fought alongside Macro for many years guarding the western banks of the River Rhine. It was the stretched-thin red Roman line that was struggling to hold back the eastern hordes that collectively sensed, like a pack of hungry dogs, that under Caligula, Rome was on the cusp of eating itself.

Despite an unpromising start, Cato had distinguished himself many times over in combat. Capable and quick-witted. Maddy sensed Macro looked upon his old comrade with something like fatherly pride. They'd bored Crassus into going to bed with their bawdy tales from the Second; stories of heroic rearguard actions and daring counter-insurgency missions that seemed to enthral Liam.

She was looking at Liam when Macro had said his young

223

friend, Cato, had been only *sixteen* when he'd entered the Second. A pampered, educated court slave, pale-skinned and whippet-thin and unlikely to cope long with the rigours and hardship of army life.

'I'll tell you, when I first caught sight of young Cato, I didn't think too much of him. Looked like a strong fart would blow him over.'

Liam had chuckled at that.

'But I watched this young lad turn into a fine soldier . . . and a fine officer.'

They learned that ten years ago, Macro had retired from the Second with his pension and bought the crumbling apartment block in the Subura as an investment. Meanwhile Cato had been headhunted by the Praetorian Guard's *praefectus* – always on the lookout for officers with talent.

Finally with Macro's snoring echoing round the atrium – sleeping off Crassus's wine – Cato bid them goodnight and to get some rest. There were 'others' he and Crassus wanted them to meet tomorrow. A slave had shown them to their rooms.

'The Stone Men are support units,' said Maddy presently. 'Clearly.'

'And this Caligula has a dozen of them as his personal guard,' added Liam.

'But . . . why would they protect Caligula?' asked Maddy. 'I mean they wouldn't unless they've been programmed to.'

'Affirmative.'

Sal made a face, incredulity and amusement wrestling with each other. 'You saying Caligula's, like, *hacked* the code? *Reprogrammed* them?'

'No, of course not! But –'

'Maybe . . . I dunno, maybe this Caligula fella *isn't* Caligula,' said Liam. All three of them turned to look at him as if he'd belched unpleasantly. He glanced from one face to the next and shrugged.

'What? Why are you looking at me like that?'

CHAPTER 43

AD 54, Imperial Palace, Rome

He could never sleep during the hot months of summer, even as a child. Caligula recalled the uncomfortable summer nights in his father's quarters, hearing the noises of an army camp coming through the tent flaps – the legions on their various summer campaigns. He smiled wistfully – half of his childhood spent in innumerable marching camps. Such a different creature he'd been back then. Just a small boy, fascinated by the same things any small boy would be: the soldiers who towered over him, their armour, their swords. In his father Germanicus's tent he played out the battles Germanicus had fought with an army of small wooden soldiers . . . carved by those same men. They loved him. The legion's mascot. Little boot.

He looked out over Rome now, still and dark.

I am something other now. No longer that boy.

The city had once seemed so vast to him, long ago: the centre of the civilized world. Now he saw nothing but an endless tangle of scruffy rooftops, and there, across the city, his magnificent unfinished stairway to the heavens. The only beautiful thing out there.

His eyes were drawn to the night sky, a star-filled night. The ghosts of silver-blue clouds chased each other in front of the moon. These days he spent more and more of his time gazing up at the sky, particularly on overcast days, wondering whether he might catch the slightest glimpse of the heavenly world far above between tumbling anvils of cloud.

My waiting world.

My kingdom.

He stepped away from his window, bored with gazing at the city. Frustrated by the very sight of it. To be God . . . not just *a* god, but to be *the* God, the one and only, and yet have to wait so interminably to visit the kingdom above.

I am God. So why can I not simply wish myself there . . . and be there?

Caligula shook his head. He had no answers to that. But then his divine baptism was yet to happen. His 'ascension to Heaven'. Then, when it was done, of course, all those godly powers would come to him. He could simply wish . . . and things would happen.

And he would wish good things. He would wish *wonderful* things. He would shower Rome with wealth and treats. He would reward his faithful followers with eunuchs and virgins and fountains of the finest wines. There would be bountiful harvests of wheat and maize. No one would be hungry again. If only those grumbling disbelievers out there could see that.

Yes. He would also punish his enemies. Their fate would be endless torment, endless agony. He would wish on them all the pox, leprosy then hordes of gargoyle-faced demons to poke at their weeping skin with sharpened sticks, flame-hardened and still smouldering.

He shook his head at the stupidity of men.

Why doubt me? They came to me. Down from Heaven . . . to speak to me.

The doubters were blind. Blind to the obvious truth. That's why he decided those fools who'd made that attempt on his life so many years ago would not need their eyes any more. How

227

many had there been? Five hundred? Six hundred of them? To be fair, he was certain now that a good few of them had not known anything at all about the plot to kill him. But to be the wife or even the child of a conspirator was, in some way, a form of complicity.

He'd ended up with over a thousand bloody eyeballs staring up at him from where they were piled on his marble floor. And their butchered bodies had covered the palace gardens outside.

Caligula's bare feet had carried him absently out of his bedroom into the main atrium. There, standing guard outside his bedroom, was one of the few he could fully trust.

'It is a hot night, is it not . . . *Stern*?'

Stern. Such an odd-sounding name. Caligula had tried to rename these guardians of his, but they only responded to the names they came with.

'Affirmative. One degree centigrade hotter than last night.'

Caligula smiled, nodded. Some of the things Stern and the others said confused him. They used words he didn't quite understand. He was sure he would understand these words, the strange language he'd heard Stern and the others of his guards use occasionally, when he *properly* became God.

Not so long now.

'Will you walk with me?'

Stern nodded. Caligula admired the sculpted contours of the man, the fascinating olive-coloured armour he and his men wore; so light and yet so effective. And their helmets, so odd-looking.

'Affirmative,' Stern replied. His Latin perfect. His accent still so very foreign.

Caligula's restless feet took him across the atrium, down the main passage. Three steps dutifully behind him, the soft clunk of Stern's boots, the gentle clatter of his armour echoed in the stillness.

'Do you ever dream, Stern?'

'Negative.'

'Have you no wishes? No fantasies? No desires?'

'Negative. I have mission parameters that need to be fulfilled. That is all.'

Caligula turned and smiled at him curiously. 'You and your men are such a puzzle to me, Stern. You are not like anyone else. You do not seem to have the weaknesses of other men, other soldiers. I never see you sleep,' he said, laughing, 'or get drunk.'

'It is not a requirement.'

He'd never seen them sleep as such, but every now and then Stern and his men periodically went into a sort of trance, a meditation. He'd looked in a number of times on the palace quarters he'd given them over the years and seen the twelve of them sitting bolt upright on their cots staring into space in perfect, motionless silence. Nothing like the soldiers' quarters he remembered from his youth: the smell of stale sweat and cheap wine, the raucous noise of men off duty, the clack of dice on a table, raised voices cursing poor fortune. The exchange of crude profanities and vulgar stories.

He rested an affectionate hand on Stern's firm neck. 'If only all men were like you. Dutiful, loyal.'

Stern's grey eyes rested on him. He said nothing.

'But then you aren't really *normal* men, are you?'

'Correct.' Stern had explained on several occasions precisely what he and his colleagues were, again using a host of words that Caligula couldn't begin to understand, but was certain he would one day soon. The language of angels – so cryptic.

'You're just like me,' said Caligula. 'Not of this world . . . this ordinary, tedious world. But somewhere far greater, some-where magnificent. Somewhere *beyond*.'

'Affirmative. We are not from this time.'

He squeezed Stern's neck gently, feeling the cords of muscle there. Stern and the others were incredibly powerful for their size. And remarkably agile. They made superb gladiators.

In fact, *perfect* gladiators. None of the gladiators in the various commercial *ludi* based around Rome had ever managed to beat any of Stern's men. Once, just once, one of the finest fighters from the *ludus* at Capua – a *myrmillo* – had managed to slice through the lower arm of one of Stern's men. But, with just his remaining hand, he had been able to finish the gladiator off. Crushing the man's neck, despite the man stabbing and stabbing him over and over with his gladius. One of the public displays he put on for the people from time to time: a free fight. Free entertainment. And a reminder to those with ideas in their heads that his guards – his *Viri Lapidei*, his Stone Men – were utterly invincible.

That particular *myrmillo* had died, of course.

Stern's one-armed man had recovered within a couple of days.

They were paused midway down a long passage, lit by the guttering flames of several oil torches. To their left a heavy velvet drape shifted subtly. Caligula pulled the drape aside to reveal a short passage and, at the far end, a pair of thick oak doors, a locking bar across them. Two more of his Stone Men stood to attention either side of them.

'I think I shall go and take a look at the oracle.'

Stern nodded.

Caligula's bare feet tapped lightly along the smooth floor. Ahead of him the two guards watched his approach with impassive grey eyes. They slid the locking bolt to one side and pushed the heavy doors slowly open. Beyond, a dark room, completely dark. Caligula reached for a tallow candle and lit it from one of the torches.

He didn't need to instruct either of the guards not to follow him inside. They knew the dark space beyond was for Caligula alone. They were forbidden to enter, Stern and his men. They also knew to close the heavy doors behind Caligula as he stepped inside and not to open them again until he rapped his knuckles on them to be let out once more.

Thick hinges creaked under the weight of old oak and Caligula found himself standing alone in the darkness. The candlelight formed a small pool of brightness on the tiled mosaic of the floor.

'Are you awake?' His voice echoed across the large chamber.

He took a step into the darkness. It was there, just ahead of him. The candle would pick it out soon.

'I cannot sleep again.' Caligula's voice reverberated in the empty chamber. 'What about you? Hmmm?'

His candle picked out the front of the wooden box in the middle of the chamber. A box, like the doors, made of thick oak and reinforced with metal brackets. He could smell it from here. An awful smell. Not dissimilar to the reek of those overcrowded streets in the Subura.

'Are you awake in there?'

He heard a shuffling sound inside the box. A restless stirring like that of a caged tiger.

CHAPTER 44

AD 54, Rome

It took several days, in fact, for Crassus and Cato to coordinate a meeting of their fellow conspirators. Crassus carefully arranged for two other ex-senators to discreetly join them; Cicero and Paulus, two more elders like Crassus, were alive because they too were wily politicians, and at the right moment had stepped away from the aborted attempt on Caligula's life.

Cato brought with him a centurion he trusted from his cohort – the Palace Guard. Fronto. A muscular man in his early thirties with a scar running down the left-hand side of his face, and all his teeth missing on that side. One other conspirator, Atellus, was a tribune like Cato, but from another legion, the Tenth. Like Cato in his late thirties, muscular but lean, a career officer with a face that gave nothing away.

And, of course, Cato's trusted old friend, retired Chief Centurion Macro. Just seven men prepared to discuss the assassination of a leader that was rapidly driving Rome – the only beacon of civilization in a dark world of savagery – towards a cliff edge.

'Do you know how dangerous it is for us to even be in the same room together?' said Cicero. He was referring to himself, Paulus and Crassus. Caligula's spies kept an eye out for any huddled meetings of the few politicians left alive. 'And you have us standing here . . . with these complete strangers! They could be –'

'They're not spies, Cicero. I'm quite certain of that,' replied Crassus. 'They stand out far too much for that.' He shrugged. 'That's why they've been my guests here, out of sight. Beyond the reach of spying eyes and wagging tongues.'

Rumours had a habit of travelling quickly through the narrow streets and tenement blocks of the poorer districts of Rome, rumours that could quickly reach the ears of an emperor. Macro had worked quickly to crush the stories being told by his tenants of the 'invincible superhuman who had wiped out an entire *collegium*' in mere seconds. They'd all seen Bob take that mortal wound and walk away from it as if it was just a scratch. He'd spread the word among his tenants that the large man had unfortunately died of his wounds during the night. Sadly he was not an invincible champion of the poor and frightened, just a good fighter who, for a few moments, had provided onlookers a rare glimpse of hope and cheer.

Cicero looked at them all and finally nodded in agreement. 'They do indeed look very strange.'

'What did he say?' asked Sal quietly. Maddy waved that away. 'We're not from Rome.' She was getting used to the technique of muttering to herself what she wanted to say and then repeating aloud the Latin whispered to her. 'We're from another place, very far away.'

'Britain, I believe you told us.'

Maddy shrugged. 'America actually.'

The conspirators looked at each other. Sal recognized the word amid the Latin. 'Are you telling them about –'

'*America?* I've not heard of that place,' said Cato. 'Is that a region of Britain?'

Liam shot her a cheeky grin.

'Not exactly.' She smiled. *No one's going to hear of it for another fourteen hundred years!*

Atellus was studying Bob intently. 'Cato, you say this man is . . . is like Caligula's Stone Men?'

Cato nodded. 'Not one of them . . . but he is the same kind.'

'The Stone Men are of particular interest to us,' said Maddy.

'Some of the men from the Palace Cohort think they're evil spirits,' muttered Fronto. 'Don't like being around them.'

Cato glanced at Maddy. 'What is your interest in them?'

She looked at Liam. *How much to say? How much to tell them?*

'We believe they come from the same place as us. We believe they are the remnants of a larger group of people who arrived here.'

'You're talking about the *Visitors*?' said Paulus.

Maddy nodded. 'We've heard so many different stories about what happened, about that day.'

'I was also there,' said Paulus. 'I was a witness to it.'

'Can you tell us what you saw?'

'It was a long time ago. I saw things I couldn't understand.' Paulus shrugged. His old rheumy eyes closed. 'Since that day I have wondered what we saw. Sometimes I almost believe it was a shared moment of madness.' He laughed. 'Bad wine even.'

'Tell me,' pressed Maddy. 'What did you see?'

'There were perhaps a hundred of them. To my eye, as I remember them, they looked like ordinary people, men and women. The Stone Men appeared to be their soldiers. Their protectors.'

'Support units,' Liam uttered in English. Maddy nodded.

'One of them spoke to the crowd in the arena. He spoke in a voice *inhumanly* loud.'

'Do you remember what he said?'

Paulus shook his head. 'I recall small portions, but then I wonder how much of what I remember is a fiction my old mind has conjured up.'

'Please . . . try and tell us what you remember.'

Paulus's eyes twinkled with moisture as he reached back to try and relive the memory. 'He spoke of bringing news . . . that our Roman gods were a cruel trick, a lie. I remember that. He said that there was only one God. This . . . for sure is part of what he said, because I remember thinking that peculiar notion reminded me of . . . of that odd, that very strange *cult* that was coming out of Judaea.'

'Christians?'

Paulus frowned. Eventually nodded. 'Yes . . . yes, I believe they called themselves something like that.' He resumed his story. 'The Visitor said that they were here to guide us all . . . to . . . to steer us to a better way of life.' The old man shook his head, frustrated with his foggy recall. 'He used words that made little sense to us all. Words . . . I am trying to remember, but . . .' Paulus looked down at the hands in his lap. 'Strange words . . . like . . .' He looked up at Maddy. 'That word you spoke a minute ago?'

'Which word?'

'The name of the place you said you came from.'

'*America?*'

Paulus played with the word on his lips. Whispered it slowly to himself several times then finally nodded. 'That is the word, I believe. The voice . . . he told us they had come to show us the *Ameri-can-way*.'

Sal, listening without the benefit of buds, picked that phrase out of the exchange in Latin. 'Did he just say the "American way"?'

Maddy looked at Liam and Sal. 'Some Americans came here? My God!'

'Americans?' Sal's mouth hung open. 'Shadd-yah! Remember that man? Cartwright?'

Cartwright. Maddy remembered him all too well; the classic

235

X-Files type: dark suit and a bad smoking habit. He'd turned up out of the blue, knocking on their roller-shutter door. He and his top-secret agency, an agency apparently so secret even presidents had no knowledge of it. An agency spawned into existence by the discovery of a mere fragment of flint. She shook her head. A mere 'breadcrumb' left in time by Liam . . . and it had brought men in suits and dark glasses to their door, filled the sky above them with circling helicopters.

'It's possible, Sal. Thing is, we've got no idea who else in the future has got their hands on a time machine. It's —'

'What are you two saying?' asked Crassus.

Maddy listened to the Latin in her ear. 'I'm sorry. We were discussing what your friend just said. The Visitor's message.'

She turned to Paulus. 'So, what happened next?'

'Caligula descended into the arena. He approached them. We were all in fear of our lives. There was panic. But Caligula, I remember this so well . . . he was calm, almost as if he'd always expected something like this would happen. He spoke to them. Then he stepped aboard their giant chariot. The chariot ascended into the sky —'

Crassus huffed. 'There are so many different accounts. That a host of white horses suddenly appeared from beneath the chariot and carried it up. That the ghosts of all those who'd ever died in the arena emerged from the dirt and —'

'I heard it was a flood of water sprites that carried it up,' said Fronto. 'Beautiful sea-maidens with long silver hair and the most perfect —'

Cato rolled his eyes at the soldier's vulgar fancy. 'Quiet.'

'Anti-grav thrusters,' rumbled Bob quietly.

Maddy nodded. Clouds of dust and debris kicked up by some craft taking off. She smiled encouragingly at the old senator. 'Please . . . carry on.'

'The emperor was carried back to his palace on the Palatine,' continued Paulus. 'And the next day he announced in the forum that he was to become God. That the Visitors had come to tell him this and that he must now spend every moment of his time in preparation for that role. That one day he was going to ascend to Heaven and rule Rome . . . and the whole world from there.'

'Caligula's madness became worse. It had a *purpose*,' said Cicero. 'The purges. The mass crucifixions. His twisted new religion. From that day it all began.'

'What about them Visitors, those chariots?' asked Liam. 'What happened to that lot?'

'There are stories from some who say they saw them a few times after that,' said Crassus. 'The Visitors, that is. Caligula showing them some of the city.'

'The chariots?'

Crassus shrugged.

'They were never seen again,' said Paulus. 'I have sometimes wondered whether I actually saw some sort of trick arranged by Caligula. A chariot lowered into the arena by some concealed device.'

There was silence for a moment. The atrium of Crassus's home echoed with the sound of his household slaves preparing food out in his courtyard.

'But the Stone Men are *very* real,' said Cato. 'And dangerous. Caligula has made sure to demonstrate that very publicly. The question we have to ask is do you think your Stone Man could best Caligula's guards?'

Maddy shrugged. 'Possibly.'

'Even to distract them for a moment,' said Cato. 'That's all. A moment when I am close enough to him. Enough time to strike him down. That's all I need.'

'That's possible,' she replied. 'But in exchange we need some help.'

Crassus leaned forward. 'Go on.'

'Those chariots . . . we need to find them. Are they somewhere in Rome still?'

Crassus shook his head. 'Nothing from that day apart from the Stone Men has ever been seen again.'

'But,' cut in Cato, 'there are places in the palace that Caligula will allow absolutely no one to go.' The others looked at him. Maddy suspected that was information new to them. 'He's given very specific instructions to me on the deployment of the Palace Guard. There are places only he can go.'

'Big enough to hide these chariots?'

'The imperial compound is vast. But in the palace itself . . . yes. I've seen a reinforced doorway guarded by Stone Men. Perhaps in there you might find something.'

Maddy stroked her chin thoughtfully for a moment. 'All right, then. Perhaps we can help each other out.'

Cato turned to look at Crassus and the others. Silent nods from them all.

Sal tapped her arm gently. 'Any chance you're going to tell me what we've just agreed to?'

CHAPTER 45

AD 54, Rome

The two senators left for their townhouses in the Greek district. Atellus returned to his legion stationed outside the city.

Maddy and Liam sat with Cato in the shade of a portico watching Macro and Fronto sparring with Bob in the courtyard with wooden training swords. Crassus chortled and Sal hooted with delight at the centurion and ex-centurion's failed attempts to score a touch on Bob's torso.

'Your Stone Man is so fast,' said Cato.

'Very,' said Maddy.

'He's saved my life many times over,' added Liam. 'One-man army, he is.'

'Tell me.' Cato sat forward. 'What language is that you use, when you speak quietly?'

'You mean when we whisper to ourselves?'

'Yes.'

She laughed. 'You must think we're totally mad, talking to ourselves.'

Cato splayed his hands apologetically. 'It's a very odd thing you do.'

Liam reached up to his ear. 'Shall we show him?'

Maddy nodded. 'Might as well.'

He pulled out his babel-bud and handed it to Cato. 'You'd better explain how it works,' he said to her.

239

'This little device translates our language, which is called *English,* into Latin.'

Cato turned the small flesh-coloured bud over in his fingers. 'It actually *speaks* words to you?'

'Yes. In our ear. It hears what we say quietly in English and gives us the correct Latin phrase to say.'

He frowned as he looked at it. 'Do you mean to say it is . . . this device can understand the meaning of what is said to it?'

'Yes. There's a thing called a *computer* in there. A bit like a mind, I suppose. An artificial one. It's an engineered thing.'

Cato's eyes widened. 'This province of yours with such advanced devices . . . how is it possible that no one has ever come across it before? How is it possible no Roman has ever heard of *America* before?'

Cato passed the bud back to Liam and he carefully placed it back in his ear.

'Because it's too far away for anyone – even any Roman – to find.'

Liam's bud was whispering again in his ear. 'You telling him about time travel, Mads?'

'I wouldn't know where to start,' she replied.

Cato frowned. 'What did you just say to each other?'

'It was nothing.'

'I suspect you're patronizing me,' he said with a smile. 'The simple-minded Roman soldier, eh?'

She made an apologetic face. 'Where we come from is very difficult to explain, Cato.'

'Why not try?'

She realized how easy and how stupidly incorrect it was to assume that a person from an earlier time was somehow less intelligent. Just because they might not understand the concept of something as commonplace as a cellular phone, or a computer, or a light switch, it didn't make their minds any less agile.

'We are from the future.'

His eyes narrowed and he rubbed the dark hairs on his forearm as he digested that. 'When you say "future" . . . are you talking about the passage of days?'

'That's right.'

'Days yet to happen?'

'Correct.'

'You mean to say, then, you are from time . . . that is *ahead of us*?'

'Exactly that,' said Liam. 'A long way ahead.'

'See . . . in the future, Cato, mankind will discover how to travel backwards and forwards along time, just like travelling along a road.'

'A road? A road through time?'

'The place where we and them *Visitors* came from – America – doesn't exist yet,' said Liam. 'Well, it *does*, but it just doesn't have that name yet.'

Cato stared at the sparring men as he attempted to absorb what they'd just told him. 'This is an incredible idea,' he whispered after a while. 'You know, as a small boy I used to wonder what it would be like to witness the future. To see how things go. To imagine what I would be like as a man. Whether I would ever become a freedman.' He looked up at them. 'And you say it is possible to do this?'

Both of them nodded.

'So, how far along this "road of time" do you come from?'

'How many years?'

'Yes.'

'Well, this is quite a hard thing for me to try and explain . . .'

'I suspect you're patronizing me again.'

241

Both Maddy and Liam laughed at that. 'All right,' said Liam. 'Don't say we didn't warn you. This'll really mess with your head, so it will.' He grinned at Maddy impishly. 'You gonna tell the poor fella, or shall I?'

'About two thousand years,' she said.

Cato's jaw hung slack. 'Did you just say two *thousand*?'

'Just under.' She shrugged. 'Give or take a few years. Depends on whether you count in Jesus-years or normal ones. AD, *anno domini*, or CE, *common era*.'

'Jesus-years?' He cocked his head.

Maddy shook her head. 'That's a whole other story. The thing is, Cato, history has a way it's meant to go. A way it's *supposed* to go. And these Visitors from the future, they've sent events going off in a different direction. A wrong direction.'

Maddy and Liam proceeded to explain to him the nature of time travel and alternate timelines; histories that should never be and how they caused things called 'time waves', reality shifts that erased everything in their path and left monstrous new realities in their wake. She was surprised at how well he grasped the notions, how intelligent his questions were. An agile mind just as keen to peer into the unknown as any of the great thinkers and philosophers hundreds of years down the line.

By the time they'd finally finished explaining, both Macro and Fronto had had enough swordplay and were hunkered over, sweating in the midday sun, gasping for breath. Bob continued play-sparring with Sal.

'So then,' said Cato, 'you are here to correct events?'

'That's right.'

'And you say this time we are in right now . . . this would be the rule of Claudius, not Caligula?'

'Yes.'

'Claudius? That old fool?' He looked surprised, but then

shrugged as he gave it some thought. 'Better a fool than a madman, I suppose.'

'He does a pretty good job,' said Liam. 'I read it in a book. He conquers Britain.'

'Britain?' Cato laughed. 'Who'd want to conquer that miserable wilderness?'

They sat in silence for a while, watching the fighting, listening to the clack of wooden swords.

Cato frowned. 'But your plan to *correct* history . . . that would mean the end of all this, would it not?' He gestured at Crassus's courtyard. 'And the end of all our lives?'

Maddy shook her head. 'The end of this version of your life. There's another world very much like this one. Another version with you and Macro and Crassus –'

'It's a *better* version,' added Liam. 'Under Claudius your Roman Empire gets richer, gets bigger. Not like it is now.'

Cato pondered that. As things stood, disaster hung like an approaching storm cloud. The empire was all but bankrupt. The city was on the very edge of starvation as the last of its stores dwindled. The regular arrival of food supplies from other provinces and trading partners was beginning to dry up as it became clear that Roman debts were going to remain unpaid. Even if they did manage to get rid of Caligula, an even greater danger loomed: the threat of civil war. There were three or four generals he could think of in charge of unpaid and disgruntled legions who'd advance on Rome to crown themselves emperor once news reached them that the madman was finally gone.

And if that wasn't enough, there were rival empires watching proceedings from the periphery of the Roman world like vultures. The Parthians to the east, for example. A civil war would surely be the final straw. Once Rome's many legions had broken themselves fighting each other, barbarian hordes from all over would descend on them to pick the Roman carcass clean.

If these strangers from another time were to be believed, that correcting history would return the fate of Rome to a more stable footing, how it had been when he'd been a young boy, then that was worth surrendering this life for, wasn't it?

'Another version of Rome would be worth dying for,' he admitted.

'Oh, but you don't die,' said Liam. 'Not really. There'll be another you . . . another Macro, another Crassus.'

'Living the lives you should have lived,' added Maddy.

'And how do you intend to correct this history?'

'We believe . . . we're *hoping* really, that there may be technology – *devices* – left behind somewhere in Caligula's palace by the Visitors that we might be able to use to get back to our time. From there we can correct this more easily.'

The others looked like they were getting ready to come over and join them in the cool shade. 'It might be better if we keep this notion of travelling time like a road to ourselves,' said Cato.

Maddy nodded as they stepped into the shade beneath the portico.

'Does this brute of yours ever get tired?' grunted Macro as he slumped on to a bench and reached for a cup of watered wine.

Crassus took a seat beside Cato. 'It is time, I think, that we discuss matters in detail.' He reached for the jug, poured himself a cup of wine and lifted it. 'Something our new friends should know. This Roman officer to my left . . . Tribune Quintus Licinius Cato.' He was addressing Maddy and Liam in particular. 'This man is the one who has put our gathering of conspirators together. He is the one who has risked *everything* by whispering in dark corners to find the few of us willing to commit to treason.' He patted Cato on the shoulder affectionately. 'I would give my arm to have a small fraction of this man's courage.'

'Hear, hear!' barked Macro, filling his cup again and raising it. 'To Cato.'

Cato picked up his cup. 'To success.' He turned to Liam and Maddy. 'And to the return of better times, eh?'

'Aye, I'll drink to that,' said Liam.

CHAPTER 46

AD 54, Imperial Palace, Rome

An eternity of darkness. In here. This space. This world of his measured in mere feet. If he flexed his legs, his toes, his arms, his hands, he could brush the edge of his minute universe. He could feel the surface of it, worn smooth now, having been touched so many times.

But he didn't touch the edges of his universe any more. Not intentionally. He preferred to imagine the walls weren't there. He preferred to live within the endless corridors of his mind now. Dwelling on memories that were beginning to fade like old photographs pulled out into the daylight too often. He could wander through a few special childhood memories, could almost be there. Feel the sand beneath his bare feet, the warmth of the sun on his face. Smell his mother, hear his father and brother.

Only when he heard the doors creak open, and the ghosts of real daylight stole through the slits between the oak planks of his universe, was he pulled away from his memory-world. Once every day – the grim return to reality as someone, presumably one of the slaves, brought a bowl of water and that bitter-tasting barley gruel. Pulled open the feeding slot to his small cubed universe and pushed it through for him.

As the slot closed, the heavy doors outside creaked shut and his universe became a uniform, blank darkness once again; he would feel with his hands for his bowl of water and his bowl of gruel. If he could have talked . . . that once daily ritual might be his chance to communicate with someone, even if it was just to say a thank-you.

But he couldn't talk. He could grunt. He could whimper. He could howl. Oh yes . . . he could slobber and whine. But he couldn't talk.

He called the mask *Mr Muzzy*.

His muzzle. The only other permanent occupant inside this wooden box.

Me and Mr Muzzy.

The iron brace around his jaw with a protuberance, a tube of iron, that kept his teeth prised apart, mouth open, and pressed his tongue back preventing him from forming anything that sounded remotely like words; that was Mr Muzzy.

The gruel could be spooned down into Mr Muzzy's hollow tube; it slid down inside it and into his mouth where often he gagged on it several times before being able to swallow it. It took a long time to spoon his daily gruel into that. He imagined it probably took hours, but then in complete darkness, in almost complete sensory isolation . . . how does one measure time?

Mr Muzzy was his tormentor. The always-there taste of iron in his mouth. The sores where the brace rubbed his skin raw. Sores that constantly wept and crusted up, wept and crusted up.

Once — a million years ago, it seemed — Mr Muzzy broke. The brace had weakened: his constantly weeping pus had corroded the thin band of iron around his head enough that waggling it to and fro it had finally buckled and fallen away from his face. And then . . . oh God then. He'd screamed, hadn't he? His ragged voice had startled him. Terrified him. The sound of words instead of gurgling sounded alien, strange.

He'd screamed for hours, terrified by the babble of insanity that was coming out of him. Then the creak of the doors. The

247

faint hairlines of light entering his box. And the feeding slot opening.

Later the same day there was a brand-new Mr Muzzy. A much thicker, stronger iron band cinched tight round his head. And back in complete darkness once again he'd wept and wept and wept.

Ever since that time – however long ago it was – he'd learned that the best thing he could do was to try and live as far away as possible from this place. Wander the corridors of his mind and open doors into rooms full of gradually fading memories . . . and frolic and play in the twilight sunshine that existed in there.

One day those memories would fade completely . . . every room of his mind would be as empty and featureless and as dark as this place. And when that finally happened, he guessed he was truly going to be insane.

CHAPTER 47

AD 54, Rome

'An ingenious plot,' said Crassus. He looked at Cato. 'Devious even. Admirably devious.'

Macro nodded at that. 'Even as a snotty-nosed young *optio*, Cato was a smart-arse.'

'I had to be,' replied Cato. 'A young, soft strip of a boy in the legions? It was either be tough or be clever. And I wasn't much of a fighter back then.'

Macro grinned. 'Turned out all right in the end, though, didn't you, lad?'

Cato shrugged that away. 'The legions have a way of finding out what's in you.'

Liam smiled at the interplay between Cato and Macro. Clearly both men were fond of each other – brothers in arms. Over the last few days Macro had frequently come by, a visitor to Crassus's home of no particular interest to any of Caligula's spies that might be watching. He had plenty of tales to tell them of his time in the Second Legion, serving alongside Cato. Firstly as Cato's commanding officer and in the latter years, watching this young man mature and become a first-class officer who would eventually outrank him.

Liam saw a vague reflection of himself and Bob in these two. One of them the brains of the partnership, the other the brawn.

'Your plot?' said Maddy.

'Caligula may be insane, but he isn't stupid. He knows full well that the power of an emperor isn't in what the people, the citizens of Rome think: it's in the support of her legions. Treat the legions well and they'll do their best to keep you in power.'

Cato sat forward in his seat. 'When he first became emperor, he had a lot of money to make use of. Bought the support where he needed it. Now there's so little money left, he's stripped the assets from almost every wealthy family in the city and most of that money is going towards paying the Praetorian Guard and the only other two legions in Italy, the Tenth and the Eleventh. And paying them very well. All the other legions of the empire he's made sure to station as far away from Rome as possible, guarding our failing frontiers.'

'Far away because he's not paying them?' said Liam.

'Precisely. It's a foolish emperor that allows a disgruntled legion anywhere near home. The Praetorians, the Tenth Legion, the Eleventh Legion . . . those men will happily fight and die to keep Caligula as their emperor.'

'That doesn't sound promising,' said Maddy.

'The trick of this plot is deception. A sleight of hand. This plot hinges on being able to fool these two legions and the Praetorians into thinking the other is making some kind of a move against Caligula.' A wry smile spread across Cato's lean face. 'We're going to make them fight each other.'

Macro shook his head. 'I used to lose money playing dice with this lad.'

'We need to provoke the Tenth and Eleventh into marching on Rome. We need those men to believe the Praetorians are preparing to launch a coup against Caligula. At the same time, we need the Praetorian Guard to believe these two approaching legions are attempting to launch their very own coup. As soon as he hears the news of their marching on Rome, Caligula will have to react. He can't afford to appear weak or intimidated. He'll have to order his Praetorians out to face them. With nothing but a skeleton garrison left behind, guarding the government district and the Imperial Palace . . . I have a better chance of cornering and killing him. Provided your *Bob* can deal with the Stone Men.'

'Would he not have his men stay behind and defend the city?' asked Liam. 'That's what I'd do.'

'That's not how legions fight,' said Macro. 'Their strength lies in having room to manoeuvre. An open plain. If Caligula's guard are still stuck in the city when those two legions turn up, they'll simply be bottled up inside. Those legions will simply camp outside Rome and starve the fools until they come out weakened. Then, of course, their backs'll be against the wall.'

'Macro's right. Caligula will want them out and on the battle-ground of *his* choosing. As I say, he's not stupid.'

'So . . . how are you planning to get those two legions to suddenly believe the Praetorians are planning to turn on Caligula?' asked Maddy.

Cato sat back and let Crassus answer that.

'General Lepidus commands those two legions,' the old man replied. 'He's a career-minded general. He very nearly joined us. Came here to my home on several occasions. He's no friend of Caligula, but he's certainly not an idealist. He'll sit tight because his men are well paid, and so is he. But I have been working on him quietly, discreetly.'

'And he's prepared to help?'

Crassus laughed. 'No, of course not. The man is a coward. He became nervous and excused himself from our plans.'

'Isn't that dangerous?' asked Liam. 'What if he told Caligula about you?'

'He won't. He's already implicated. I've been doing my best to make the fat oaf look as guilty as possible of conspiring against Caligula. Bribes and gifts in certain places, correspondence in his name. A whispered word or two in Caligula's ear and he'll want Lepidus's head on a spike alongside mine.'

'The trick is,' said Cato, 'to let Lepidus know that someone is about to whisper of his treachery to Caligula. Lepidus knows that with Caligula there is no right of reply. He won't get a chance to try and prove his innocence. The only thing he'll be able to do is act quickly; either run for his life or make a preemptive move on Caligula.'

'But I thought you said his men would fight to defend the emperor?' said Liam.

'The men of a legion will always follow their general, up to a point that is. So, yes . . . he will convince them that they're marching on Rome to *protect* their emperor, not usurp him.'

'And how will he do that?'

Cato shrugged. 'The regular legions are always suspicious of the Praetorian Guard. Atellus, the officer you met the other day?'

Liam and Maddy nodded.

'He is one of Lepidus's tribunes. He'll feed Lepidus enough hearsay and rumour that even that idiot general can convince his men the Praetorians are up to no good. If those soldiers suspect for one moment their generous benefactor, Caligula, might be replaced with another emperor less generous,' Cato grinned, 'they'll be on their feet and marching towards Rome.'

Maddy and Liam looked at each other and grinned. 'That's clever,' said Liam.

'While Atellus is pouring suspicion into Lepidus's ear, I will be doing the same with Caligula,' added Cato.

'What?' Maddy sat upright. 'You meet with him?'

'I'm the tribune in charge of the Palace Cohort. Of course I do. Almost every day. I believe . . . he is beginning to trust me. Perhaps even likes me. Sometimes we talk and I'm as close to him as I am to you right now. I could try and have a go at him, but his Stone Men are fast.'

'You wouldn't stand a chance,' said Macro.

'Caligula does listen to me. He doesn't listen to the *praefectus*, but I know he trusts my advice. Perhaps if I can persuade Caligula to send some of his Stone Men into battle and get your *Bob* within the palace itself . . . it's possible he could overcome any of them left behind.'

'And us as well?' said Liam. 'Could you get us inside too?'

'Perhaps.'

'Bob . . .?' Maddy said in English. She patted the mound of one knee. 'You up for it?'

He replied in English, Cato, Crassus and Macro looking on in silence as they talked.

'The description we have of these Stone Men suggests they are third-generation military recon units. Designed to have normal physiques and pass more easily as human beings. As a full muscle-chassis combat unit, I am approximately fifty-five per cent stronger. This gives me a tactical advantage.'

'And you did sort out that other unit that came through the portal,' said Sal. 'And that was another big one, just like you.'

'But it was missing feet and a hand,' replied Bob. 'This also gave me an advantage.'

'But do you think you can take them down?' said Maddy. 'More than one?'

'Individually, yes. More than one at a time, this would be difficult.'

She sucked air through her teeth. 'We're rolling our dice on a pretty steep bet. We're helping these guys with their coup and there's no guarantee we get anything out of this. There may be nothing in the palace. No tech, no displacement unit, nothing.'

'In which case that leaves us stuck here,' said Sal.

'Right,' said Liam.

Maddy nodded. 'Right.'

'And without Bob . . . if those Stone Men kill him,' added Sal.

They looked at each other. A decision unresolved hung in the space between them.

'Actually, if computer-Bob doesn't activate that six-month window, his head chip's going to end up as helmet-spaghetti anyway,' said Maddy. 'He'll be a dribbling vegetable.'

The three Roman men were looking at them expectantly.

'Even if we end up successfully killing Caligula,' said Maddy, 'we might also not find anything in the palace that can get us back home.'

'Well, the way I see it is this: if we are goin' to be stuck here for good . . . I'd not want to live here with this Caligula fella still in charge.'

'There is that.' Maddy nodded slowly. 'If this is it for us, if this time we really can't put things right and we're stuck here for good . . . I think I'd rather Caligula wasn't around.' She turned to Bob. 'How does that fit with your mission priorities?'

His deep voice rumbled. 'This is an already contaminated timeline. If we cannot correct it, the mission has failed whatever course of action you choose to take.'

'Bit of a downer there, Bob,' said Maddy, 'but you're quite right.' She consciously switched back to listening to the translator burbling quietly in her ear.

'OK, count us in.'

CHAPTER 48

AD 54, Imperial Palace, Rome

Caligula felt a tremble of excitement course through his body. This place, this large chamber was once a temple to Neptune. Now it was a temple to . . . himself; more than that, an act of homage to his approaching destiny. Its large marble and tiled walls echoed his light footsteps as he walked among the artefacts inside. With those large heavy doors closed, the daylight outside was entirely gone, the only illumination the flickering flame of the golden oil lamp he held in his hand.

Objects that the Visitors left behind. He crouched down and picked through the strange-looking things.

'Incredible.' His voice echoed round the chamber. Such curious possessions they had brought with them. He never tired of looking at them.

There was a shuffling coming from the wooden cage in the middle of the chamber.

'But you see . . . that is something I find so fascinating. These devices of yours . . .' He picked up an empty hydro-cell. The smooth metal glinted in the gloom; a residue of liquid sloshed around inside its casing. 'I always believed gods needed *nothing*. That a mere wish, a desire, was all that was required for a thing to happen. And yet you and your friends brought with you all these odd contraptions. Objects you needed.'

A mewling whimper came from the cage.

He tilted the hydrogen fuel cell, listening to the liquid inside. 'Objects that stopped working for you eventually.' He smiled. 'Not particularly godlike.' He tossed it on to the pile of other items – empty ammo cartridges, guns, backpacks, first-aid packs, flashlights – and wandered over towards the cage.

He remembered how utterly bewitched he'd been when they'd first arrived. Such a stunning, remarkable arrival. Such noise, such spectacle. That day in the arena . . . like every other Roman citizen looking on, he was certain he'd been gazing upon heavenly beings. His heart had thrummed in his chest with the thrill of it and, of course, there had been an almost paralyzing terror at the idea of it. *Gods, or at the very least, emissaries of the gods . . . here . . . in Rome. Right before us!*

Caligula recalled that childlike wonder . . .

. . . approaching those enormous chariots and seeing up close the remarkably human-like passengers emerging from them. Some of them as fair-skinned as those barbarous savages in the northern parts of Germania. Some of them as dark as Egyptians. All of them wearing such delightfully strange garments. He'd been trembling like a leaf, fearful as a small child before an enraged parent.

The voice had boomed out across the floor of the arena and bounced off the stalls all around them. A thunderclap voice announcing in heavily accented Latin that they had come from above to enlighten them, to show them new ways. To offer them the gift of enlightenment, wisdom.

And finally, emboldened by the knowledge that several thousand of his subjects were watching, that a Roman emperor ought to be the one to lead the way, he had slowly reached out with a trembling finger and dared to touch one of them. Caligula had done that half expecting that at the first slightest touch of this creature from Heaven he would burn instantly to cinders as the power of Elysium itself flooded into him.

Caligula pulled the viewing slot of the cage to one side and peered at the darkness within. It stank of human faeces and stale urine. An appalling stench worse than any of those awful plebeian marketplaces or perilously tall, topsy-turvy apartment blocks. By the light of his oil lamp he could see the wretch inside, like a caged wild animal, restless and wide-eyed.

He realized now. Even back then, all those years ago, the moment his finger had touched warm skin damp with sweat, flesh just like his own . . . that the Visitors were just ordinary people. Not gods or messengers of the gods.

'Hello,' he uttered.

The man murmured and gurgled something behind his muzzle.

'I apologize. It's been some time since we talked,' said Caligula with a gentle smile. 'Quite rude of me.' He produced a bronze key, waved it so his captive could see it.

'Come here. I shall take your muzzle off . . . and you and I can talk.'

The man moved suddenly, like a wild animal, grabbing for the key. The viewing slot was wide enough for a hand of claw-like fingers to thrust out. Caligula took a step back.

'Uh-uh. Turn round . . . there's a good fellow.'

The man glared at him through the slot for a moment. Caligula could only see his eyes above the corroded bronze face mask and the gunk-encrusted hollow of the feeding tube, a dark, rigid oval frozen in a permanent corroded 'o'.

'Turn round,' he said, waving his key again out of reach of the waggling claws.

The glaring eyes disappeared into the darkness and then a moment later, Caligula could see the back of his head, the bronze padlock securing the brace and one or two tufts of lank hair drooping over, and the sore-ridden skin rubbed completely bald by the rough metal band.

Caligula reached through the slot, inserted the key and twisted. With a dull click, the padlock sprang open and the brace fell away.

The head instantly spun round, those glaring eyes on him once more, but now he could see the man's slim nose, and below that a thick nest of moustache and beard bristles clotted with dried mucus and rotten food. In the middle of it – like a pair of newborn, hairless rats in the bottom of a coarse nest – two lips mottled with scabs and abrasions old and new. They flexed and fidgeted, revealing bloody gums and the rotted black stumps of a few remaining teeth.

'Hello, my old friend,' said Caligula.

The man struggled to move his mouth, savouring the freedom for his tongue to actually wander around, his claw-fingers probing his crusted lips pitifully.

'It is the month of Sextilis once again. So . . . it's not so very long now, is it?'

The man was still flexing his mouth, relishing this fleeting moment of freedom from the mask.

Caligula suspected the crazed old fool was getting ready to cry out in that strange garbled language of his. He tried the same thing every time the muzzle came off. The same strangled word.

'Save your breath. Your Stone Men won't be able to hear you. The doors are closed and they are all on the other side of the palace. It's just you and I in here.'

The pitiful wreck of a man tried anyway, sucking in a lungful of fetid air then screaming. 'System . . . o-over-ride . . . en-enable . . . S-sponge –' His voice was a frail and feeble gasp like a faltering breeze across marshland reeds.

'Trust me,' smiled Caligula. 'They really can't hear you.'

Nonetheless, he tried again. This time his croaking voice had

259

a shrill and desperate power behind it: the asylum scream of some unhinged wretch. And it was the same meaningless word over and over again. Gibberish to Caligula.

   'SpongeBubba! *SpongeBubba!! SPONGE . . . BUBBA!!!*'

CHAPTER 49

AD 54, Rome

'So . . . Maddy, that thing about Caligula joining the gods? You remember? The information you got off your computer?'

Maddy nodded. She'd not forgotten. She looked ahead of them, at Sal and Bob. They were walking along a narrow avenue outside Crassus's walled garden. Traders set up temporary stalls along the base of the pink-painted wall early every morning. Stalls that could trade for a few hours before the mid-morning call to prayer sounded across the rooftops of Rome and Caligula's acolytes started patrolling the streets to be sure every citizen was obediently on their knees in homage to their emperor and god. The unlicensed traders and their illegal stalls were packed up and long gone before then.

Charcoal graffiti covered the flaking pink paint. Latin tags of one *collegium* or another, slogans, crude jokes and vulgar stick-man drawings. One clearly depicted the emperor: a stick man with an oak-leaf halo above his head and exaggerated booted feet. Maddy squinted at what it seemed to be waving around in its hand – without her glasses on, the entire street was in soft focus. It seemed to be a . . .

'Oh, per-lease . . .' She tutted in disgust.

'Joining with the gods?' prompted Liam. 'That's supposed to be soon, isn't it?'

'Yes.' There wasn't a date. But the data they'd pulled up did say something about it being in the summer.

'Should we not tell the others about that, though? I mean . . . it's important.'

'I . . . I'm not sure we should.'

'Why not?'

'Well, look . . . think about it. If they learn from us that actually Caligula might not be around for much longer, they'll abandon their plans. Right? I mean . . . why risk your life if you just need to be patient and wait a few more weeks, months?'

They watched Sal cajoling Bob into bartering with a trader. Maddy very much doubted any haggling was going to last particularly long with something as big and as intimidating as Bob on one side of the transaction.

'Liam, this "ascending to the gods" thing. It could mean anything. It's far too ambiguous for us to assume it means anything. It could mean he just got sick of a disease and died, and his priests decided to make up something that sounded suitably exciting and godlike.'

'Aye. True.'

'On the other hand,' she added, 'it could be a portal.'

He looked at her and grinned. 'Well, I was thinking the very same thing, so I –'

'It might be that there's some time-travel tech somewhere in his palace that's been in a dormant state and it starts to activate. Maybe something on a timer . . . a bit like one of our six-month windows, but much longer?'

She looked at him. 'See . . . that's why we've got to get in there. Before whatever happens to Caligula . . . happens. And Cato, and the others, they're our only way in.'

'We're using them,' said Liam. He didn't look entirely happy about that. She knew he'd warmed to those two, Cato and Macro.

'Yes.' She sighed. 'Yes, *technically*, we are sort of using them.'

'Doesn't seem right.'

'Oh sheesh,' she cursed under her breath. 'Why do I always have to be the freakin' bad guy? Huh?' Truth was, Maddy had learned to think of an alternate timeline as something not entirely real, almost cartoon-like. A virtual world even. These were lives that were not meant to have been lived. In some cases, perhaps they were better lives than they should have been; more often – at least so far – they'd been horrible lives lived through horrible timelines. Yes . . . perhaps she should have told Cato that *something* in this timeline was due to happen to Caligula very soon. But if whatever happened, happened in the palace on the Palatine with them sitting around out here and, God help them, they missed it . . . then that really might be their one and only chance to get back home wasted.

'We *have to* get in there, Liam . . . and we have to get in there *before* anything activates? Do you get it? This might just be our only way back home!'

He stroked the tuft of bristles perched on his chin thoughtfully. 'Aye . . . well, I suppose.'

'So, we don't tell them. We need them to act on their plans. The sooner the better.'

'So, then . . . our friend here is quite correct.' Crassus acknowledged Maddy with a nod. 'There is no need to delay a moment longer. With our conceit to lure away some of these Stone Men and with the help of yours, we have a chance for you to get to Caligula, Cato.

'The longer we delay, the more chance there is that one of

Caligula's spies will notice our gatherings.' Crassus looked round at the others; the two senators, Cicero and Paulus, had attended. Atellus had made a trip over from the Tenth Legion's permanent camp; Fronto the senior centurion of the Palace Guard cohort was there and, of course, Cato and Macro. 'I know Caligula already suspects me of whispers behind his back.'

Cato nodded. 'Agreed. We have a workable plan now. I say we proceed immediately.'

Although the gathered men stirred uneasily, there were no objections to that.

'Right.' Crassus reached into the folds of his toga and produced some scrolls. 'This is the evidence you can present to Caligula, Cato.' He handed Cato the scrolls. Cato unravelled them and scanned them quickly.

'This is correspondence between Lepidus . . . and *you*!'

The old man nodded.

'If I hand this over to Caligula, he'll have men outside your front door within the hour!'

'It has to be convincing.' Crassus smiled. 'My name on these letters will be enough to ensure Caligula sends for Lepidus as well. The moment he hears both he and I have been summoned, he'll know his involvement with us, albeit a fleeting one, has been exposed.'

'Crassus, if I do this, you should leave Rome. If —'

'No! If I run before they come for me, it will suggest I have foreknowledge. I must be caught red-handed by Caligula for this to fool him. More importantly . . . for him to fully trust you, Cato. He may already know you have visited me, met with me. You have to betray me, Cato . . . you have to hand me to Caligula as a traitor.'

He hunched his shoulders. 'I will comply . . . I will play the innocent old man and then, when he threatens me with torture, I will implicate Lepidus.'

Cato shook his head. 'We need you alive and well, Crassus! When Caligula is dead, we will need all of you!' He looked at Cicero and Paulus. 'We'll need every last one of you to rebuild the Senate —'

'The Senate needs men far younger than I.' Crassus smiled. 'Anyway, I don't plan to die. Caligula will want to keep me alive to execute alongside Lepidus in some elaborate public display.'

Cato looked at Atellus. 'Then we must be sure General Lepidus will make his move quickly.'

'He will,' smiled Atellus. 'He's already nervous about his meetings with you last year, Crassus. He has no wish to be made a martyr.'

'And his legions?'

'There's no love lost between the Tenth, Eleventh and the Guard.'

Cato nodded. 'Then it looks like this is our time.'

'When will you present this evidence to Caligula?' asked Cicero.

'On my return to the palace.' He looked at Crassus. 'They will come for you tonight. Are you ready for that?'

'My affairs are all in order.'

'Atellus, you should leave immediately then, and carry the news back to General Lepidus that arrests of suspected traitors are being made in Rome this very evening. That'll put the wind up him.'

'It certainly will.'

Cato held the scrolls of correspondence in his hand. 'As

soon as Caligula sees these letters, he'll issue an order for Lepidus's immediate arrest. I suspect the arrest order and a party of Praetorians will arrive not very long after you.'

Atellus grinned. 'There'll be no sleep for him tonight.'

'Let's just hope he decides to go on the offensive, and not turn and run.' He addressed the senators. 'You two should go into hiding. As soon as Crassus is revealed as a conspirator, Caligula may decide to round up the rest of the surviving Senate. Pick friends you can trust and stay out of sight until you hear that Caligula is dead.'

'What about me?' asked Macro.

'I want you to look after our new friends. Keep them safe. As soon as I have convinced Caligula to move the Guard out to confront Lepidus, I'll send for you.'

'How will you get us into the palace?' asked Maddy.

Cato gave it a moment's thought. 'You'll be my *property*. And Macro'll be bringing you into the palace grounds for safekeeping. A perfectly sensible thing for me to ask permission to arrange. There will be riots and unrest in the city when the people witness the majority of Caligula's Praetorians marching out.'

He took a deep breath. 'Tonight and for the next few days, few weeks, this city will be in a state of anarchy. Even after Caligula is dead, it will be a dangerous time. General Lepidus's men, the Praetorians and every other legion near Italy will be mobilizing to put their candidate on the throne. We need the Senate re-established quickly . . . and order restored fast if we're to avoid a civil war.'

'Rome's sickly enough without the prospect of that,' said Paulus.

'Quite. All of you should use tonight to prepare for this. Macro . . . you should make sure you have extra food in and be ready to fortify your apartments. This city will descend into Hell. The *collegia* will almost certainly make use of the chaos to raid and loot and settle old scores.'

'Right you are.'

'If we're very lucky,' said Cato, 'the majority of the blood-shed will be *outside* Rome. The Tenth, Eleventh and the Guard will incapacitate each other. The Palace Cohort will be right here in the city under my command, Caligula will be dead and we will have a small window of time to restore a Republic.'

Cicero looked at him. 'For a few days, Cato, you understand . . . you will in effect be the Protector of Rome. Quite possibly the only cohesive military force within a hundred miles of Rome.

'It takes a strong will to voluntarily surrender that kind of power back to the people.'

'Now's not the best time to start doubting me, Cicero.'

The politician looked taken aback. 'I was just say–'

Macro spat a curse. 'I'd trust Cato with my life!'

Cato glanced at Maddy, at Liam. A momentary meeting of eyes, a fleeting understanding.

'This was not meant to be. Caligula has to go before it's too late for Rome.'

'What if . . .' Fronto began.

'Go on, Fronto.'

'Thank you, sir . . . I just thought it might be worth saying. What if Caligula . . . really is, well, you know . . . a god?'

Atellus snorted with laughter.

'That's not such a stupid question,' replied Cato. 'Soldiers are a superstitious lot. Something we should be mindful of. A bad omen . . . a rumour, something as trivial as that can swing the allegiance of them at a time like this.'

'Most of 'em are semi-literate, wine-swilling knuckle-draggers,' grunted Macro, wiping his nose on the back of his hand. Cato looked at him, shook his head and smiled.

Macro scowled back. 'And what's that look supposed to mean?'

CHAPTER 50

AD 54, Rome

Late afternoon sunlight painted the clay-brick walls of every building a warm peach and cast violet shadows into every narrow alley and rat run. The streets were busy with vendors packing up their shop fronts and pulling shutter doors to for the approaching evening.

Liam and Bob flanked Macro; Maddy and Sal a few steps behind.

'What was it like in the legions?' asked Liam. Macro repeated the question.

Liam nodded. 'I've seen some . . .' He was going to say 'films', but stopped himself. Only Cato knew where and when they'd come from. That might change at some point, but for now, the fact that they'd come from some place beyond the known Roman world was enough to share.

'Well,' Macro shrugged. 'I'll be honest, I probably moaned all the way through my twenty-five years in the Second. It was either hard work or damned boring. And plenty of years spent shivering in cold, damp places I wouldn't wish on my worst enemy.' He smiled wistfully. 'But I'd have those days back if I could.'

They stepped aside for a pair of Caligula's acolytes wearing long green robes. It was approaching evening prayers and the calling horns would be sounding across the roof tiles soon.

'Why?'

'I miss the . . . I don't know. I suppose I miss the sense of *brotherhood*. They really are an ugly, stupid, foul-smelling lot of lowlifes . . . the lads in any legion. Not the sort you'd want to bring home to meet the family, if you get my meaning. But . . .' He shook his head, looking for a way to make his point. 'But together . . . you and those men, you're something *more*. Part of something greater. Do you understand?'

Liam nodded. He thought he probably did. He and the girls, Bob and Becks, even computer-Bob, they were their very own 'unit' . . . sort of. With someone else by your side, someone you know would throw down their life to save yours, somehow it made staring into a hopeless abyss possible.

Macro echoed his thoughts. 'Back then . . . I would have died for any one of my lads. And I know they'd have done the same, followed me into Hell itself if I'd ordered it. But now . . .?' He shrugged sadly. 'I see faces I recognize every so often. Lads retired from the legions, or even deserters. Just thugs and crooks some of them now. A lot of them hired men in the various *collegia*. I'd kill them without a second thought if I needed to.'

'How long did you and Cato serve together?'

'Oh now, I suppose it must have been about twelve years.' He laughed. 'Good times then. Most of it. Well . . . *some* of it. He came as a freshly freed slave from the imperial household of the Julii. As thin as a strip of willow and soft as a peach. And completely clueless about army life. I thought the lad wouldn't last a week.' He looked at Liam. 'I've told you that already, haven't I?'

Liam nodded.

'I suppose I took pity on him at first. Took him under my wing, taught him how to become a soldier. And in return he taught me how to read.' He laughed. 'Made this dumb old centurion appreciate some of the finer things in life.'

CHAPTER 51

AD 54, Imperial Palace, Rome

Caligula stood in the main atrium admiring the construction of these weapons. Every now and then he brought them out of the darkness and studied their smooth, well-honed lines and curves. There were no scrapes, scratches or the hammer marks of a craftsman. It was as if these things had been *born*, not *made*.

He gazed at them, spread out on a satin sheet. Beautiful, mysterious weapons.

His caged guest had once told him these things were called 'T1-38 pulse carbines'; weapons that spat death at the mere squeeze of a finger. Caligula had once, long ago, asked to have a go at using one. But the Visitor called 'Stilson', a man he found to be rather annoying and loudly spoken, had refused him, saying he was from a time too primitive to understand such things.

Caligula smiled at the man's breathtaking arrogance, at his assumption that their intellect was far greater than these Romans they'd come back in time to rule 'more wisely'.

Yes. Caligula had fully understood what they were. Certainly not gods – he'd known that almost from the first moment in fact. They were just men, men from a far future. His frequent private discussions with that dark-skinned young man had helped him to understand that, the Parthian-looking one who was called Rashim.

The one who had the *most* knowledge of such incredible

things. The one who could be promised the role of co-emperor of all and be foolish enough to believe it was genuine. The one who could be flattered so easily . . . young enough, naive enough to believe all the empty assurances and promises Caligula had given him.

Rashim.

They'd come here – the young man had told him all those years ago – because their world was no good any more; it was poisoned and dying. More than that, a pestilence had suddenly arrived that killed everything in its path. They'd had no choice.

Rashim had told him that they had knowledge of a science that allowed them to open a door on to an impossible dimension, to step through it and appear back in the real world at a time of their choosing. It was clear from the young man's description that he knew little of this dimension – it was knowledge beyond even his science. But Caligula thought he understood what it was they had passed through.

From Rashim's words: '*White like snow . . . infinite . . . endless . . . beautiful . . . terrifying,*' it could only be one place.

Heaven itself.

These short-sighted fools had passed directly through Heaven to come here and make themselves kings and emperors. If they'd had an ounce of wisdom between them, they would have realized Heaven was the true goal. To step through it . . . and actually leave it behind them? Now *that*, surely, was the very definition of madness.

It was only six months after the Visitors had arrived, made themselves at home in his imperial compound that Caligula learned his guests weren't quite as invincible as they believed they were. Their protectors, the Stone Men, were in a way – just like their other devices – merely tools that could be used for a purpose.

Used.

Switched on. Switched off.

One just needed to know how to do such things. The young man, Rashim, knew. He had an understanding of them, an understanding of how to give them instructions that made them behave very differently.

'Just a few words spoken by me,' Rashim had promised him, 'and they will follow your orders.'

'They will do *anything* I ask?'

'Yes, of course. It's a standby mode, a diagnostic mode.'

'And they will forever follow my commands?'

Rashim had nodded. 'Unless they hear the reset code sequence. Then they'll reboot and return to their last mission parameter set.'

'Then, Rashim,' Caligula had smiled warmly, 'you and I shall rule side by side.'

'I don't want the others hurt in any way.'

Caligula's assurance had been enough for the gullible young man.

It was a night of killing nine months after the Visitors had arrived. The palace's smooth marble walls had echoed with the screams of slaughter into the early hours of the morning as the Stone Men hunted them down one by one. Their leader, that arrogant fool Stilson . . . Caligula had made sure they captured him alive. His torment had lasted several days.

And Rashim?

Caligula giggled at the young man's naivety. The night of the bloodletting, as all the other Visitors had been enjoying his lavish hospitality, in a quiet room away from the main atrium, away from the noise of raised voices and laughter the twelve Stone Men had assembled as requested in obedient silence.

Rashim spoke his special sequence of words that unlocked

these automatons. The Stone Men had all seemed to momentarily fall into a trance only to stir moments later, a seemingly very different look in their cool grey eyes. Caligula's first order had been for the one called 'Lieutenant Stern' to silence Rashim before he could speak again.

And so . . . the night of bloodletting began. Eight hours later, dawn had shone into the palace, shards of sunlight across these very marble floors spattered with drying pools of blood. *His* Stone Men were already stacking the bodies in the courtyard and preparing a funeral pyre. And the young man, Rashim, was waking up in his cage, muzzled. Waking up to the realization that the rest of his life was going to be lived in that cage.

Caligula stopped stroking the cool, smooth metal of the weapons spread out like museum exhibits across the purple satin. He looked out at the panorama of Rome getting ready to bed down for the evening. A rich, warm dusk bathed the labyrinth of clay-brick and whitewashed walls and terracotta roof slates. Thin threads of smoke rose into the sky from every district, many of them from bonfires of the daily dead. Disease, spoiled water . . . the normal attrition of such a big city. He shrugged. Things would be better for his people soon.

When he returned.

He listened to the distant echo of horns across the city, summoning the people out of their homes to pay homage to him. He could see the dark outline of his marvellous stairway up to Heaven; a stairway he was going to descend to visit this world once he had stepped into the white mists of Heaven and finally become what he'd always been destined to become.

God.

His reverie was broken by the sound of bare feet whispering on the smooth floor. He looked up to see Stern step forward to intercept a slave and in a hushed voice ask him what message he had for the emperor. The slave prostrated himself immediately as soon as he noticed Caligula looking at him.

'What is it?'

'The tribune of the Guard wishes to see you,' replied Stern. 'Says it is important.'

Caligula sighed. He was tired. He rather fancied curling up on the satin alongside the weapons and resting his pounding head against that cool metal. Soothing. But this tribune of the Palace Cohort . . . yes, he quite liked this new one. Quite an intelligent and engaging man, for an army officer.

What was his name? He struggled to remember.

'Yes . . . all right, send him in.'

CHAPTER 52

AD 54, Imperial Palace, Rome

Cato entered Caligula's atrium. He'd been in here on only half a dozen occasions since being appointed to command the Palace Guard. The room was cavernous and every noise seemed to echo endlessly. He had only ever seen Caligula alone. The emperor it seemed preferred his royal family as far away as possible. Preferred his own company.

He was alone except for one of his Stone Men, the one called Stern, and, of course, half a dozen slaves waiting patiently by the walls for his bidding; almost unnoticeable, still like frescos, murals. Not really humans in Caligula's eyes.

Cato stopped a respectful distance from Caligula and saluted. 'Caesar.'

The emperor smiled a greeting. 'Ahh, yes, I remember now . . . it's *Cato*, isn't it?'

Cato nodded. 'Yes, sire. Tribune Quintus Licinius Cato.'

'Come on now, don't be rude, Stern . . . say hello to our visitor.'

The support unit looked at Cato, blank-eyed. 'Hello.'

Cato regarded him in silence for a moment. He had seen these things up close many times over the last few months. They unsettled his men. To be entirely honest, they unsettled him too. While he didn't believe in supernatural explanations, he'd always been certain there was something not entirely human about them. Now he knew what they were – man-made: constructions made from flesh and bone instead of wood and metal.

'What is it, Tribune?' Caligula settled back on a seat. He beckoned Cato closer. 'Come over so we're not barking at each other.'

Cato took a dozen steps closer. As he neared Caligula, he noticed the Stone Man watching him closely.

'Apparently it's something important?'

'It is, sire. I . . . I have come across evidence of a plot against you, Caesar.'

Caligula sat up. 'A plot, you say?'

'Plans to try and . . . well, to kill you, sire.'

The emperor's face reddened slightly and he offered a tired sigh. 'They never stop, do they?' He pulled himself to his feet and approached Cato. 'Kill me, you say?'

Cato nodded.

'All these conniving old fools. All they care about are their own petty agendas. Advancing themselves, the careers of their sons and nephews, marrying money to status or the other way round. Cutting each other's throats for profit. Awful people.'

He smiled sadly at Cato. 'It's the poor common man I feel so sorry for. Ruled by these inbred cretins for far too long.' He noted the scrolls clasped in Cato's hands. 'So then, which meddling fools want me dead now?'

Cato silently held out several scrolls. 'Correspondence, sire.'

Caligula snatched them from his hand, unrolled one and scanned it quickly. 'Crassus! That dried-up old fig? Why am I not surprised by that?' He looked up at Cato as if this was an old conversation they'd had many times over. 'You know, I should have had every last one of those gossiping old relics done away with. I'm too much of a soft touch, that's my problem.'

He looked back down at the correspondence and read on in silence.

'Lepidus.' Caligula looked genuinely surprised. 'Lepidus?'

'Yes, sire.'

Caligula opened the scroll and read further, his face turning a deeper red as his lips silently moved. 'The ungrateful, fat wretch. I've given him and his men everything! They take pay three times what they would have normally! They . . . he . . . Lepidus pledged his allegiance!'

He swiped his hand at a bowl of fruit on a stand. The bowl clattered noisily on to the floor and rolled across it like a cart wheel, finally coming to rest, spinning and rattling with a noise that echoed round the atrium's walls and off down the passage. Caligula spat a curse.

'Lepidus . . . that slug actually got on his knees and prayed directly to me. Prayed to me! Said he always *knew* I was more than a mere man . . .'

'The general tells you what he thinks you want to hear,' said Cato.

Caligula balled his hand into a shaking fist. 'The deceitful . . . He stood before me not so long ago . . . got on his knees before me and told me he believed in me! That he . . .!'

He turned on Cato. 'You believe in me, don't you, Tribune? You believe I will ascend to Heaven soon and take my place, don't you? Because you know it isn't long now! Not long at all!'

Cato hesitated. And realized in the space of several heartbeats that his hesitation was foolish. He should have anticipated this sort of question. Been ready and practised with an answer.

Caligula swung his hand up and placed a finger roughly against Cato's lips. 'No! Don't answer me.' His eyes were wide and glassy with tears of anger. 'Tell me! Why . . . why is it so very hard to believe? Why is it so difficult to imagine that I could be something *more* than human? Hmmm? I have wisdom. An infinite capacity for love. I know things no other man does. The Visitors came for me, you know, not anyone else! They came . . . and they told me *everything*!'

He leaned closer, lowering his voice to little more than a hoarse whisper. 'More than that, I have ambition. When I am taken up . . . when I step into the heavens and receive my powers, we won't need legions any more to pacify those barbarians in Germany, in Britain . . . we'll do it with my love, my compassion! I'll bless their crops, their water. I'll make the sun shine warmth and light on those cold, dark places and they will love me for it.'

Caligula's finger remained on Cato's lips. 'And, if that doesn't work, then I can just as easily send plagues on them. Turn the skies black with storms. Make them fear me.' He smiled. 'Love and fear . . . they are, after all, halves of the same circle. At some point on the arc, one becomes the other.'

Caligula was standing so close to him, Cato could feel the emperor's hot breath on his face. Cato's hands flexed by his side; his left wrist brushed against the iron pommel of his gladius.

I could kill him now. Reach for my sword and kill him right now.

Only he wouldn't get a chance. Stern was no more than a yard away and could move frighteningly fast. Cool, dispassionate grey eyes were regarding him closely right now, warily analysing the ticks of muscle in his face, noting the subtle flexing of his fingers near his sword. He could try and reach for it, but Cato doubted he'd even manage to get the blade out of its scabbard before the Stone Man had run him through.

'I . . . I am just a soldier, sire,' said Cato, his lips moving against the light touch of Caligula's finger. 'My only concern is your safety. That is all.'

The anger in Caligula's face, the faraway look in his eyes,

vanished in an instant. An ugly mask of rage whipped away and replaced with something that looked genuine: a warm, welcoming smile. He stroked Cato's cheek affectionately. 'I love the simplicity in that answer. No judgement . . . no doublespeak, no lies. The simplicity of a good soldier's mind. A task, a duty . . . and how best to perform it.'

Caligula stepped back from him. 'I will, of course, have both of their heads on spikes for this. Have Crassus arrested immediately.'

Cato nodded. 'And what about General Lepidus, Caesar?'

Caligula pursed his lips thoughtfully. 'It might be prudent if I were to summon him with no reasons given, rather than openly have him arrested. He may be a fat, spineless slug . . . but if he suspects he's shortly due to lose his head, he may try and do something rash.'

'Yes, sire.'

'Tell him . . .' Caligula rested a finger thoughtfully on his chin. 'Just tell him I wish to speak to him. Nothing alarming, do you understand? I merely wish to speak to him.'

Cato nodded. 'I will see to it immediately.'

'Good,' replied Caligula distractedly. 'Good . . . and let me know when you have got Crassus. I would like to have a little talk with him as well.'

'Yes, sire.'

Caligula turned away from Cato and strolled towards the window and balcony that looked out on the darkening city skyline.

'Ahh, now look. How annoying. I've just missed my sunset,' he uttered wistfully.

CHAPTER 53

AD 54, 18 miles north of Rome

'*What?*' General Lepidus sputtered wine across his desk.

'It's what I've heard, sir. This very afternoon.'

Lepidus stood up and the chair legs barked across the wooden floor. 'Arrests?'

The young tribune shuffled uncomfortably, his helmet respectfully under one arm. He was still puffing from his exhausting five-hour ride from the city.

'Come on, Atellus! What are you prattling on about?' Lepidus's voice sounded shrill and sharp, almost effeminate; he hated it when nerves, anxiety, made him sound that way.

'Arrests . . . Crassus was one of them.'

Lepidus's wide face instantly paled. 'Crassus!'

Atellus nodded. Lepidus slumped back down in his chair; it creaked under his heavy frame. He looked shaken. 'Crassus! Gods help me, he'll talk at the first sign of pain!' He looked at his subordinate. 'And names will be mentioned, Atellus. You and I . . .'

The tribune nodded.

Lepidus wiped his mouth, his skin already damp and tacky with anxiety. 'I curse that withered old prune for roping me into his bloody politics!'

A couple of visits, that's all. Him and Atellus. That had been enough for him to realize the old man was going to get

281

them all killed if he wasn't a great deal more careful. Lepidus had backed away quickly from the fool's small gathering of conspirators. Deliberately ignored his repeated invitations to rejoin them. He should never have gone in the first place . . . but ambition, vanity, had piqued his curiosity. Crassus had suggested Rome might need a Protector in the aftermath, should *something* happen to Caligula. Someone with power, popular with his soldiers, near to hand . . . and no great fan of the emperor.

Someone. Someone like himself.

Lepidus had brought along an officer he trusted, Atellus, expecting a lunch at the old politician's expense and a carefully worded conversation, a gentle probing of his thoughts on what direction Rome should take . . . should something, regrettably, happen to their emperor.

What he hadn't expected was an assembly of strangers . . . and such open, reckless, dangerous talk. And such a pitiful assembly of conspirators! Three senators, a tribune of the Guard and one or two others.

What he should have done, was leave the meeting immediately and report them all to the emperor just as soon as he could. But he hadn't. He and Atellus had returned and said nothing about the matter to anyone.

Enough right there to be deemed as guilty as Crassus and his conspirators in Caligula's eyes. And to make matters worse, Crassus had been badgering him to come back. Sending presents even.

'Dammit!' He reached for the cup on the desk in front of him, nearly knocking it over and spilling wine across the nest of scrolls in front of him, the routine and endless paperwork of a legion encamped. He emptied the cup quickly and wiped his mouth. 'That treacherous old snake has been playing games with me!'

'Sir?'

Lepidus winced, cursed under his breath. 'He sent me several gifts over the last year. Those Parthian horses? That attractive slave?'

Atellus nodded. He knew full well about them. Most of the camp did. The slave had been particularly well received by the general. 'Sir, surely those gifts have nothing to do with this –'

'Don't you see, you idiot? Crassus has been trying to make it look like I'm part of his mischief! He's trying to . . .' Lepidus stopped. His eyes widened. 'Gods help me!'

'What is it?'

'I wrote a letter to him . . . I . . . thanked him!' Before he'd attended that meeting he'd been almost seduced by Crassus's persuasive flattery. His eyes darted left and right as he tried to remember the precise wording of his correspondence. Crassus had sent his gifts with letters punctuated with carefully phrased criticisms of Caligula; subtly worded inducements for Lepidus to expand on that criticism a little more.

Sounding me out. That's what he was doing.

Lepidus remembered carefully avoiding any references to Crassus's less than flattering thoughts about the emperor and his appalling neglect of the affairs of the city in his reply. The general quite clearly remembered writing a polite and very neutral 'thank you' to the old man for his lovely gifts. But most importantly . . . *ignoring* those dangerously obvious phrases; phrases clumsily probing him for where his allegiance lay.

'Oh, help me!' he whispered.

'Sir?'

What he *hadn't* done . . . was immediately forward that correspondence to his emperor. What he *hadn't* done was warn Caligula of Crassus's treacherous mutterings.

Oh, the gods!

The general's thinking in recent years had been that sitting tight and keeping his head down – waiting this madness out – was the clever strategic game to play. With his two legions permanently encamped a mere day's march away from Rome, he was perfectly placed to sweep in and replace that insane fool the moment something happened to him.

And something inevitably would. Caligula was mentally unstable. Increasingly so. Believing himself to be a god, *immortal* . . . the crazy fool would end up either killing himself in some reckless chariot race to impress his people, or believing he could actually fly and stepping off a high wall. That or some desperate, starving citizen was going to get lucky with a slingshot or an arrow. Caligula's insanity seemed to be approaching some sort of a feverish crescendo. As if he expected something truly world-changing to happen to him very soon.

But this news? These rumours . . .?

Gods help him if that exchange of correspondence between him and Crassus should fall into the emperor's hands. *Not* participating in any conspiracy the old senator had been quietly organizing was not going to be enough to save him.

'Sir?'

Lepidus looked up at his tribune.

'We have to do something, sir. We could be next . . .?'

Caligula was going to have new heads on spikes all over the city by the first light of morning. *And two of them might just be mine and his.*

'Atellus?'

'Sir.'

'I want every officer from both legions assembled in my quarters in half an hour!'

'Yes, sir. What . . .?'

'What do I plan to do?'

'Yes, sir.'

'I have no choice, do I? Crassus has made sure of that.'

He thought he saw a grim smile play across his tribune's lips. 'Yes. Atellus, I want the men ready to decamp.'

'Sir . . . you are considering marching on Rome?' Atellus hesitated. 'Confronting Caligula?'

'Of course I am!'

'The men, sir . . . they may not take well to the idea.'

Atellus was quite right. The legions, officers and men's allegiance was broadly with the emperor. His was the hand that fed them and fed them very well. Lepidus couldn't be sure his men were going to be behind him. And should an order for his arrest arrive as well . . .

'Might I make a suggestion, sir?'

'Go on.'

'Let them believe the Guard is moving *against* the emperor.'

Lepidus nodded slowly. *Yes, of course.*

'Mobilize the men, sir. Let them believe we're marching on Rome to protect Caligula from a palace coup. Tell them the emperor will reward them for their loyalty . . . that the Guard will be disgraced, disbanded as a result of this treachery.'

Yes . . . there's no love lost there between the legions and the Guard.

'Atellus . . . every officer in here in half an hour. Move!'

'Yes, sir!' The tribune saluted, turned on his heel and swept out of Lepidus's private quarters.

By first light he was going to have both the Tenth and

the Eleventh assembled and ready to march. However the next few days panned out . . . whether he was going to need to confront the Guard or not, whether he was going to attempt to move against Caligula or not, it would be better to be ready for it; to have his men in their armour and on their feet.

CHAPTER 54

AD 54, Rome

Crassus heard the banging on the large wooden gates to his courtyard. He topped up his cup with the last of his wine as he watched his slave, Tosca, hurry across the courtyard clutching a flickering oil lamp to answer the insistent knocking.

Here they come. He tipped the wine insistently down his throat. A little crimson courage.

Crassus knew his strengths and his weaknesses. He wasn't a brave man. If he had an ounce of courage in him, he would have stood shoulder to shoulder with all the other senators who'd tried defying the emperor years ago.

Tonight he was going to try and make up for that.

The gates swung in and he saw the purple cloaks of a dozen Praetorian Guards sweeping in past his slave.

'Master! Master!' cried Tosca in a panic.

'Marcus Cornelius Crassus!' barked a centurion. 'I have orders for your arrest!'

Crassus recognized the voice. Fronto.

Cato had given the arrest order to an officer he trusted to handle Crassus humanely, gently.

Thank you, Cato.

'I am here,' he said shakily, stepping out of the shadows beneath his portico. 'Whatever is the matter?'

Fronto approached, flanked by his men. He adopted his best

officious voice. 'Marcus Cornelius Crassus, I have orders to escort you to the emperor's palace. He wishes to speak to you!'

Crassus smiled calmly at Fronto. 'At this time of night, Centurion? Is he lonely?'

Fronto worked to keep the flicker of a smile off his face. 'Best come along immediately, sir.'

The old man nodded. 'Yes, of course . . . can't keep a *god* waiting, can I?'

Tosca hurried forward with a cloak for him. 'Master! What is happening?'

Crassus patted his slave on the arm affectionately. 'Nothing to worry about, Tosca, old friend. I shall be back for breakfast no doubt.'

'Sir?' said Fronto insistently.

'Lock the door, Tosca,' he said quietly. He turned to Fronto, fastening the cloak round his narrow shoulders with a clasp. 'Centurion? I'm all yours.'

Caligula looked up from the small battle being fought between wooden figurines on the low table in front of him. He'd heard the clatter and jangle of armour, the slap of sandals on stone, all the way from the entrance hall.

'Ahh . . . good evening, Crassus.' He smiled coolly.

Crassus nodded politely as his escort of Praetorians came to a halt a couple of yards before the emperor. 'Your *divinity*.'

'Well . . . a curious thing happened earlier this evening. Would you like to know what it was?'

Crassus said nothing.

'Oh? Not in the slightest bit curious?'

'I suspect you plan to tell me anyway.'

Caligula grinned then frowned curiously. 'Hmmm, that's not like you, Crassus. You're normally so . . . so *meek*.' He leaned forward over his battlelines of miniature wooden legionaries and sniffed the air in front of the old man. 'Been drinking, have we? A little anxious perhaps?'

'I am working my way through the wine I have left. Before Rome falls into complete anarchy and is looted by the mob.'

'*Tsk-tsk.*' Caligula shook his head. 'I won't let Rome fall into anarchy. Soon every citizen will be showered with wealth . . . with their very own casks of wine.'

'Ahhh . . . you're still holding out hope for your special day, are you?'

'The day Heaven opens for me? Yes, of course. And it is very soon in fact.'

'If you say so.'

'I do say so.' Caligula's face tightened. 'You know this troubles me, Crassus; perhaps you can answer this for me. If those dirty savages in Judaea could believe a young, uneducated man, a simple craftsman of some kind I believe . . . if they could believe this mere troublemaker was to be the king of kings, the son of God . . . why is it so difficult to believe a Roman emperor could be –'

'You are quite mad,' replied Crassus. 'And a danger to Rome.'

Caligula was dumbstruck at the man's candour.

'There are no gods . . . or god. These are morality tales, nothing more. Any man with half his wits can see that.'

'Crassus . . .' Caligula's eyes widened playfully. 'You do seem to have found your tongue tonight.'

'You had a reason for bringing me here?'

Caligula stood up. 'Yes . . . yes, I do.' He looked over the old man's shoulder. 'Ahhh, Tribune! Come forward.'

Cato joined them and offered Caligula a crisp salute.

'Tribune . . . why don't you tell Crassus here all about your interesting find, hmmm?'

Cato turned to the old man. He kept his voice dry and officious. 'Correspondence between yourself and Quintus Antonius Lepidus, containing invocations to acts of sedition and treachery.'

'Pouring your poison into Lepidus's ears. Very, very naughty of you. Lepidus was a faithful man. A good man.' Caligula shook his head sadly. 'I'm sure he believed in me until you started working on him. Now . . .' He picked up a wooden soldier from the table. 'Now I really can't trust him any more, can I?'

Crassus laughed drily. 'You can trust no one. No one loves you . . . many fear you. Me? I just *pity* you. Your days are numbered.'

Caligula kicked the table between them, sending his wooden soldiers cascading on to the floor. 'Why? Why can't you all just wait! Just wait and see!!'

'Wait? Wait for you to become a god?!'

'YES!!!!' Caligula turned away from them all and screamed with frustration into the gloom of the atrium. 'Just wait!! Wait and see!!!'

Crassus glanced at Cato quickly to see the tribune shaking his head almost imperceptibly. The message was quite clear: don't provoke him any more. Not necessary.

The old man smiled at his friend. A smile that told Cato that he knew where this exchange was going to take them. That he was ready for it. But most importantly, that Cato should let this happen. To try and stop it . . . to try to save him, to try and lunge at Caligula would be futile; the emperor's Stone Men stood close by. Too close.

'You will never be a god, Caligula . . . "little boot". You are nothing more than a failed emperor and a deluded fool!'

Caligula whirled round. 'Tribune! Your sword!'

Cato looked at the emperor uncertainly.

'Give me your sword! NOW!'

Cato unsheathed it slowly and presented the handle to Caligula. 'Caesar, I suggest Crassus be kept alive! He will be a useful source of informa–'

Caligula ignored him and grabbed his sword. He pressed the tip of the blade into the hollow at the base of Crassus's throat. It drew blood, a small trickle that rolled along the old man's prominent collarbone, over the edge and soaked into the linen of his toga.

Caligula giggled at the sight of it. 'Crassus . . . you do seem to be full of surprises tonight. Do you have a death wish?'

'I am quite ready to die.' He glanced quickly at Cato. 'Ready to make way for a new generation of senators.' He turned back to Caligula and smiled defiantly. 'Senators who will very soon be replacing you.'

Caligula's face bloomed a dark crimson. He thrust the sword forward, hard, until it grated on bone somewhere inside the old man. He laughed excitedly as Crassus gurgled blood, his mouth jerking open and closed several times before he dropped to his knees and flopped forward on to the floor.

Caligula squatted down to examine the old man.

'Caesar.'

He looked up at Cato. 'Yes?'

'What are your orders?'

'Orders?'

'General Lepidus? You had a messenger despatched earlier? A message for him to report to you immediately? He will be warned now. He may even now be provoked to make a move on you.'

Caligula nodded, his mind clearing aside the dwindling rage. 'Yes . . . yes, you're quite right. We must do something about that.'

'May I suggest you mobilize the Praetorian cohorts

garrisoned outside the city? Lepidus has two legions at his command . . . and they are less than a day's march from here.'

Caligula stood up slowly, Crassus's body already forgotten about. 'Yes, we must move quickly, mustn't we?'

Cato nodded. 'Immediately, sire. If Lepidus already knows he's under suspicion, he could be readying his men to march on Rome right now. The Guard should be readied to march out and meet them.'

'You're right!' Caligula spat a curse. 'Where is your damned *praefectus*? I sent for him hours ago!'

Cato turned to Fronto. 'Find out where he is. We need his authority to –'

'No, we don't! *I'm the emperor!* I want word sent to all of the Praetorian cohorts to assemble outside the east gates on the Via Praenestina at first light. Is that understood!'

Fronto nodded. 'Yes, Caesar.'

'Well, go on, then! Now!'

Cato watched his centurion hurry out of the atrium. His gaze rested on Stern, standing to attention dutifully just behind Caligula. 'Your Stone Men, sire . . .? Might I suggest you send them along? They have something of a reputation.'

Caligula stroked his chin thoughtfully.

'And Lepidus has two legions to our one.'

'Hmmm. Maybe you're right.' He pressed his lips together thoughtfully. 'Although, if there are other whisperers like Crassus around, I would rather they remained by my side.'

Cato wondered how far he could push his advice. For the moment Caligula seemed to be listening to it, even welcoming it. 'You have my cohort here, sire, to guard you; to guard the palace and the government district.'

'Yes, perhaps I should send some of them . . .' Caligula was thinking aloud more than talking to Cato.

'Enough to be sure of a decisive victory, sire?'

'Hmmm . . . yes. It certainly needs to be *decisive*. Can't have every other disgruntled general out there following Lepidus's example, can we?'

'No, sire.'

CHAPTER 55

AD 54, Subura District, Rome

Sal looked out of the small window of their room down on to the narrow alley below. There were people emerging from their homes and the avenue was illuminated by the flames of oil lamps and torches carried outside by the curious.

'What's going on down there?' asked Maddy.

'People . . . gathering in the street. Something's going on.'

Maddy joined her, jostling for shoulder space to crane her neck out over the rough, flaking plaster of the ledge. 'It's like a town council meeting.'

'Something's happened already.'

Across the tiled rooftops they could see the walls of other narrow streets faintly illuminated from below by torches carried outside; the glow coming from dozens of window shutters opened, spilling light over the top of hunched shoulders and curious, craning necks.

'It's like Chinese whispers,' said Maddy. 'Something's going round.' Rumours in this city seemed to spread even faster than they used to back in her time. She laughed. No need for the Internet or Facebook or Twitter here in Rome, it seemed, when you could apparently just as easily shout through paper-thin walls or gossip across cramped courtyards.

'Maybe they've gone and killed Caligula already.'

'I don't know. It can't have been that easy . . . surely.'

Maddy looked down, past a shutter banging open directly beneath them and several more curious heads poking out. She could see the entrance to the rat run that led into their apartment block's inner courtyard. Down there, the unmistakable bulk of Bob moving around.

'Macro's right, though . . . whatever happens over the next few days, it's going to be complete chaos.'

'Altogether, lads,' grunted Macro. Liam and Bob and several other men from the apartment block hefted the cart up on one side. 'One . . . two . . . three . . . now!' barked Macro.

The cart clattered over on to its side, forming a rudimentary barricade blocking up most of the entrance to the rat run. There were gaps either side that needed filling and Macro started to bully his tenants into a human chain, ferrying bric-a-brac lying around the courtyard to stack either side of the overturned cart.

Liam stepped on a box and looked over the top, Bob standing beside him watching the gathering people.

'Can you make out what they're saying out there, Bob?'

'I will try.' He frowned, concentrating for a moment on the growing babble of voices out in the alleyway. 'They are discussing the news that the Praetorian Guard are leaving the city.' He cocked his head, listening more intently. 'There seems to be another rumour that Caligula has been killed by the Praetorians.'

Bob smiled. 'And there's another rumour that demons from the underworld have arisen from the sewers and are rampaging through the city.'

Liam watched as a cluster of young men emerged from a doorway further up the alley, all of them clutching knives, hatchets, clubs.

Macro joined Liam and Bob. Shorter even than Liam, he

stood on tiptoes on a crate to peek over the top. 'It's begun already, then,' he said.

'What has?' asked Liam.

'Troublemakers . . .' Macro sighed. 'First sign of a riot and out comes the scum of the earth looking for easy pickings.' He cursed and spat over the top of the cart. 'I tell you, if they even think about touching my property . . .' He pulled out his butcher's hatchet from a pouch on the leather apron tied round his waist. 'I'll give 'em what for. I'm tellin' you.'

Liam looked at the glint of light playing across the thick, rusty blade. 'So you, uh . . . you saw quite a lot of action when you were a soldier in the legions, Macro?'

Macro grinned a gap-toothed smile. 'You are joking with me, aren't you, lad?'

Liam's bud quickly translated that. But the incredulous look on Macro's face was more than answer enough.

CHAPTER 56

AD 54, Imperial Palace, Rome

Cato unrolled a map of the city across a table in the palace gardens, and weighted the corners down with several stones.

'Gather round, gentlemen,' he said to the assembled officers, the centurions and *optiones* of the first cohort. His men. Some of them roused from their cots only minutes ago were still bleary-eyed as they fiddled with the straps and buckles of their armour.

They pressed forward around the table as their tribune began to brief them quickly.

'I'm sure you've all heard by now that the rest of the Guard will be mustering outside the Castra Praetoria at first light.'

'What's happened, sir?'

Cato looked up at a bull-necked centurion with a flattened boxer's nose and a fuzz of blond hair clipped short almost to the scalp.

'It seems the general in charge of the Tenth and Eleventh has decided he's had enough of our emperor, Rufus. The Guard will be marching out to meet them.'

'Bit sudden, isn't it, sir? I thought Lepidus was the emperor's man.'

Cato shrugged. 'You know what it's like with these *equites* . . . they all think they're entitled to the job one way or the other. Anyway, to the point. Our cohort is being left behind to guard the city. When everyone wakes up tomorrow morning and hears of this . . . and they discover the majority of the Guard have packed up and gone, we're going to have riots in every district. A complete breakdown of order. So, it's going to be down to us to protect the city's infrastructure where we can.'

Cato leaned across the map. 'Starting with you, Rufus, I want your second century deployed over here in Campus Martius to protect the temple buildings. You as well, Lectus, your century over here guarding the Stratum. Sulla, Marcellus, I want your men protecting the aqueduct here and here. The rest of you, I'll be assigning perimeter positions in the Palatinus District to protect the government buildings.' He turned to Fronto. 'And your men, Fronto, will provide security for the palace itself.'

'Yes, sir.'

Rufus cocked his head. 'Just *one* century to protect the emperor?'

Cato looked at him. Rufus was like most of the men in the Guard: tough, but certainly not stupid. 'The emperor has his personal bodyguards.'

'The Stone Men,' uttered one of the *optiones*.

Cato disliked the term. It implied a supernatural quality about them. Now he knew they were just muscle-and-bone devices made by men from a more advanced time, the name smacked of superstition.

'He will be quite safe as long as he stays in the palace,' Cato assured them. He nodded at Fronto. 'Won't he?'

'Yes, sir. Perfectly safe, sir.'

Just then they heard a raised voice booming out across the flame-lit palace gardens. 'What the hell is going on here?!'

The officers all turned to see their *praefectus*, Quintus, striding towards them. He easily identified Cato's tall outline among the knot of men. 'Tribune! Who in the name of Jupiter took my authority and ordered the Guard to –'

'The emperor himself, sir!'

'What?' Quintus stopped in his tracks. '*Caligula?* But . . . only *I* have the authority . . . to . . .'

'Quintus!' Caligula's voice cut across the darkness. He emerged into the night, flanked by two of his Stone Men. The prefect's face paled. Nobody but a stupid fool bellowed the emperor's nickname across the palace grounds.

'Caesar, I . . .'

Caligula waved at him to be silent. 'I exercised my prerogative as emperor to mobilize them, since you were nowhere to be found!'

'But, sire.' Quintus swallowed nervously. 'There . . . there is a protocol that should –'

'More precisely, my prerogative as God-in-waiting,' added Caligula. He smiled. 'Say another word, Quintus, and I'll have your tongue removed from your mouth.'

His cool glare left Quintus staring down at the ground like a chastened schoolboy.

'Now then, where's that Tribune Cato? Ahhh, there you are!'

'Caesar?'

'I have decided that I shall in fact be *leading* the Guard.'

'What?!' He almost forgot himself. 'What's that, sire?'

'Yes, I think it's fitting that I come along. The men should be led by me and, of course, my Stone Men. It will truly inspire them.'

Cato glanced quickly across heads at the only other conspirator present: Fronto. 'But, sire, it would be much wiser for you to stay in the palace. The people need to see you right here in Rome. They need to see that Lepidus's . . . *foolishness* . . . is nothing that you're particularly worried about!'

'Oh, I'm not *worried*.' Caligula chuckled happily. 'In fact, I'm actually looking forward to having a splendid big battle! It's been too long.' He sniffed the evening air as if there was a faint scent that only he could detect. 'One last battle before I ascend to the heavens. How marvellous!'

He turned to one of his Stone Men standing behind him, holding his armour. 'And I really wouldn't want to miss seeing that fat, treacherous fool Lepidus grovelling at my feet.'

Cato struggled to keep his voice even. 'Sire! Please . . . it will be dangerous –'

'Dangerous! Oh, hardly!' said Caligula, lifting his arms up as one of the Stone Men helped him into his bronze cuirass. 'This is what the people need to see . . . what they need to realize; that I'm not just a god, but also a warrior, a great general.'

Cato clenched his teeth with frustration. The whole plan, for what it was, had relied on the certainty that Caligula would choose to remain in the comfort and apparent safety of his palace.

'Tribune,' said the emperor, 'you just make sure everyone behaves themselves while I'm away. I really don't want to come back to a messy city.' Caligula let the Stone Man finish tightening the straps at his side then turned to the prefect. 'Come along, Quintus! Don't stand around like an old woman! You better go and get your armour on too. We shall be moving out from the Castra Praetoria at first light.'

He turned to Cato and winked at him. 'I shall leave you three of my bodyguards to help guard the palace. I'm trusting you with my home, Tribune. Do try and keep it nice and tidy.' He turned back to Quintus and slapped his shoulder impatiently. 'Off you go, man!'

Cato watched Quintus turn and leave, and Caligula leading his bodyguards towards the imperial stables. He watched until the night swallowed them up then turned to his assembled officers.

'All right, then, gentlemen, you all have your orders! Dismissed!'

The officers saluted and then turned to gather their men. Fronto dismissed his own *optio* to go and organize the first century. Both men stood silently until they were entirely alone and out of earshot.

Cato cursed.

'Our plan is already broken so it seems,' said Fronto.

Cato nodded. The plan had rested on an assumption that Caligula would remain, and hopefully send out most of his Stone Men along with the Guard. Now he'd chosen to go, it was a battle that would probably go Caligula's way and embolden the madman even more.

'Unless Lepidus manages to be victorious. Do you think that likely?'

Cato shook his head. The Praetorians with those Stone Men in the vanguard were probably more than a match for Lepidus's men. 'All we have managed to achieve with this, Fronto, is to organize a few days' worth of blood sport for Caligula. That's all.'

He wondered whether there had been a moment during the last few hours when he could have reached for his sword and dealt the death blow. Certainly he would have been dead within seconds of the emperor. The Stone Men were quick and lethal. Quite probably it would have resulted in an unsuccessful lunge for Caligula, and him being wrestled to the floor and executed then and there.

Truth was, on his return Caligula was probably going to find out one way or another that Crassus had met with fellow conspirators. Cicero and Paulus were two men the emperor would probably have at the top of his list of people he'd like to have a little chat with, for sure. And how long before either of those old men let slip his name?

'If he wins, Fronto . . . if he's victorious and returns, then I shall make a try for him.' He looked at his First Centurion. 'Our names will come up soon enough once he gets back.'

'We will be dead men, then,' said Fronto.

'Indeed.'

CHAPTER 57

AD 54, Subura District, Rome

'I've never seen the streets so quiet,' said Macro.

Liam nodded as he scanned the empty avenue over the top of their barricade. Not entirely empty, though. Half a dozen bodies littered the cobblestone road. There had been fights all through the night, rival gangs settling old scores, people looting the small businesses that operated from alcoves beneath the apartment building opposite them. And something that had put the fear of God into the stocky old ex-centurion . . . a fire. Someone had set alight one of the small alcoves, a place selling bolts of linen and silk.

Macro had leaped over the top of their barricade, charged out across the avenue, roughly pushing his way through the mob of brawling young men to stamp the flames out before they got a firm hold of the place. He'd made his way back five minutes later, stinking of smoke, sweating profusely and muttering Latin obscenities to himself.

'If I'd known how flammable these shoddily-made buildings are . . . I'd have invested in a vineyard instead.'

It was mid-morning now, the sun spilling down from a smoke-smudged sky on to the cobbles.

'I suppose none of them food traders will come in today?' said Liam.

'No. Any merchant with an ounce of sense will steer clear of

Rome until the Praetorians return and restore some order. People are going to be hungry this morning.'

Liam looked back down the rat run into their courtyard. There was food there. Several sacks of grain bought in at an extortionate price yesterday afternoon, a dozen or so loose chickens and, of course, their two ponies. Liam guessed Macro had about a hundred tenants in his apartment block, a hundred mouths to feed for however many days this crisis was due to last.

'And they all know we've got food in here.' Macro nodded at faces peering at them from the three storeys of small shuttered windows and balconies opposite. 'Word'll spread quickly enough. We'll be fighting to hold on to it before long.'

Sal worked with the young man, a blond-haired slave from Gaul. She held the wooden stake steady as he sharpened the end into a spike. She guessed he was only fifteen, but it was hard to tell. His arms were all sinew and muscle, his face taut and lean. Not a square inch of flesh on him without a purpose. So unlike the puffy-faced friends she knew back in 2026.

'Steady, please,' he said, smiling at her fleetingly.

The bud translated that for her. 'Sorry.'

He worked the blade of the knife honing the end of the stake to a sharp tip then took it from Sal's grip and blackened and hardened it in the flames of a brazier.

'People say you and friends comes from far away,' said the boy.

Sal nodded. 'Very far.'

He glanced at her again. 'Someone whisper me . . . same place as the *Visitors*?'

She shrugged. 'Not really.'

To say 'yes' would have invited a barrage of questions she wasn't sure how she'd answer.

He looked at the stud in her nose. 'Is this mark of slave?'

She lifted her hand and felt it self-consciously. 'This? No . . . it's just . . . decoration, I suppose. To make me look good.'

The lad picked up another stake and offered her one end to hold. 'You look . . . different.'

'Different?' She looked down at herself. Her dark hoody, black drainpipe jeans and platform 'docker' boots were stored away in their room. She was wearing a sleeveless, burgundy-coloured tunic, hanging down to her shins, belted at the waist with a strip of leather, and sandals. No different from any of the other girls and women in the courtyard.

The young lad touched his own mop of curly hair. 'Hair like . . . short like boy.'

She made a face. It wasn't. If anything, it was too long. Her fringe seemed to hang in her eyes all the time. It had been far too long since she'd had it cut. But compared to every other girl or woman in this time, long hair pulled back and tied in braids that hung down to the small of their backs, yes . . . hers probably did look boyishly short.

'I like it like this,' she replied. 'It's the fashion where we come from.'

He cocked his head. 'They says you home is call . . .' He frowned with concentration as he tried to get the pronunciation right. '. . . A-me-ri-ca?'

America. Home? She smiled a little sadly. *Not really.*

'I'm from a place called India,' she replied. 'Mumbai.'

'*Marm . . . bye?*'

'Nearly. *Mumbai.*'

'Is this . . . same place as . . . you friends?'

How was she going to explain that? No. It wasn't. But then, she reminded herself, keep it simple.

'Yes, sort of. Quite close.'

He stopped whittling the stake for a moment. 'What is *Mumbai* like?'

She looked up at him, then at the courtyard, now filled with the apartment block's tenants working together on make-do weapons and barricades. She looked up at lines of laundry strung across the skylight above them, stretched from balcony to opposite balcony. There were parts of Mumbai that looked like this still, shanty towns of corrugated iron and breeze blocks stacked precariously high and ludicrously close. Tens of thousands of impoverished migrants from the now submerged lowlands of Bangladesh living on top of each other. Each towering shanty-block sharing several dozen overloaded electrical feeds, a handful of water taps and communal toilets that channelled untreated human waste down on to the mucky streets below.

Sal sighed. She realized she came from a time almost exactly two thousand years after this particular here-and-now, and yet things back then, back *home*, had been getting so bad, so overcrowded, resources so scarce, food and sanitation so utterly shadd-yah poor . . . that this downmarket district of Ancient Rome looked almost like a step forward in time.

Almost.

'It's not so good,' she replied. 'I think we might have ruined the place we came from.'

'What you mean?'

How to explain it all? 'Too many people,' she replied eventually. 'Too many people wanting too many things . . . I think.'

He nodded as if he understood that. 'Is like Rome, huh?'

Like Rome? She nodded. Rome fell eventually, didn't it? Crashed and burned, overrun by Vandals and left as nothing more than smouldering ruins. Maybe he was right. Maybe the far future and Rome had a lot in common.

'Yes, quite a bit like Rome.'

Just then she heard Liam's raised voice across the hubbub in the courtyard. She couldn't make out what he'd said, but by the shrill tone of his voice it didn't sound like good news.

Maddy, who'd been talking with Bob, called out. 'Liam? What's up?'

'We got company!'

Macro's voice boomed even louder, a parade-ground bark that bounced off all four towering sides of the courtyard and turned every head in the middle. The babel-bud in Sal's ear calmly translated his raucous cry into the relaxed, detached and emotionless voice of an elevator announcing a floor.

<Here they come!>

CHAPTER 58

AD 54, Imperial Palace, Rome

The palace was a quiet place normally. Caligula's notorious orgies, his peculiar excesses tittle-tattled about by Roman tongues all over the empire, were a feature of his younger years. Some of the older veterans in the Guard had shared with Cato tales of the emperor's extravagant behaviour after he'd first come to power. But they'd all agree that the Day of the Visitors was the day Caligula left that all behind him.

Since then the emperor's halls had become a place where conversations were spoken gently, and the guards that patrolled anywhere near where they thought the emperor might be, stepped lightly and muffled as best they could the clank and clatter of their equipment.

The palace was a quiet place normally, Cato noted, but today it was as silent as a tomb. The palace personnel, slaves and freedmen were confined to quarters for their own safety. The only people within the imperial compound were Cato, Centurion Fronto and his century . . . and the three Stone Men Caligula had chosen to leave behind.

And where exactly have they got to? He didn't like the idea of not knowing where those *things* were quietly lurking.

Cato did his best to look like an officer with duty on his mind, scouring the hushed, marble-floored hallways and private courtyards for any signs of intruders or looters. Out in the palace's herb garden he squatted down over a sewer grating and checked the grating itself was secure. Not that he particularly cared. But appearances were everything.

His mind was elsewhere.

A messenger from Prefect Quintus had arrived only several hours after the Guard had set off in a long column of purple cloaks. His message was that cavalry squadrons scouting ahead of the column had already clashed in several light skirmishes with scouts from the Tenth and Eleventh Legions. And that they'd caught a brief glimpse of Lepidus's column on the horizon. It seemed Atellus had successfully goaded the general into making his move.

Both forces would probably draw within a couple of miles of each other by noon, and then spend the remains of the day building temporary marching camps. Their men suitably rested overnight, the fighting would happen tomorrow.

What concerned Cato was the possibility of a parlay between Caligula and Lepidus. Perhaps the general might be able to convince the emperor that he'd been set up by Crassus and his fellow conspirators. How long into that conversation before Cato's name cropped up? And how long after that before a messenger and an escort of Praetorian cavalry arrived at the palace with orders for his arrest?

He could have lunged for Caligula. He should have tried while the emperor was distracted watching Crassus dying. He'd had a ghost of a chance then, hadn't he?

His mind turned to those young strangers: the two girls, the young man and their giant. Perhaps the only chance they had now was to get that creature *Bob* – a curious name – into the imperial grounds while it was mostly deserted. Then, on Caligula's return, he might somehow manage to pick the right moment, emerge and fight his way through to the emperor.

It wasn't much of a plan, but right now it seemed to be all Cato had left, other than wait for that inevitable messenger and arrest order to eventually arrive.

He returned to the main atrium and headed west, down along the main approach hallway to the front entrance of the palace. Fronto and several sections of his men were stationed there. Cato needed to speak to him. Halfway down the hall as he paced quickly, filling the echoing hallway with the noise of his own heavy footsteps, he stopped and looked at the drape to his left.

The temple was beyond that.

He took several steps towards it.

The temple that only Caligula entered. He wondered if the girl, Maddy, was right, whether hidden inside the room were those mysterious chariots, perhaps even the remains of the Visitors. He reached for the drape and pulled it slowly to one side.

'You do not have authority to be here.'

Cato jerked at the harsh voice. So this was where all three of them had been lurking.

'Please leave immediately,' said another, taking a threatening step towards him and reaching for the pommel of a sword strapped to its side.

CHAPTER 59
AD 54, Subura District, Rome

'Jay-zus! Get off, will ya!' yelled Liam as he swung the club down on to the bulging knuckles of a pair of hands grasping the top of the barricade. The club – the leg of a wooden stool with several lumber nails banged through it – crunched down heavily. Even through the din of the baying, jeering crowd that had amassed out in the street, he heard bones crack like eggshells.

There was another pair of hands in the same spot a moment later, the gathered mob working together as one, rocking the heavy cart forward and backward to make it topple over. Bob was doing his best to use his bulk to hold it in place, to steady it. But that wasn't working how they'd hoped. The wooden spars of the cart were stressing and creaking and loosening. The mob out there might not be able to push it over with Bob holding on to it, but that didn't matter; the thing was likely to rattle to pieces as soon as fall over.

Macro was busy prodding his old army-issue gladius at some of the desperate fools who'd pulled away the stacked clutter either side of the cart and were now trying to push through the gap there.

'Go on . . . get away!!!' he roared angrily at them. 'This is *my* property!!!'

A man a foot taller than him and armed with a similar army-issue sword swung down at him. Macro, thickset and carrying

311

a couple of stone more than he must have done as a soldier, was surprisingly agile as he sidestepped it. The blade bit deeply into the wood of a casket and lodged firmly there.

He grinned at the large man as he struggled frantically to wriggle it free. He smashed the pommel of his sword into the man's face and he fell back into the press of men behind him.

'Information!' roared Bob. 'This barricade will not hold much longer.'

Liam nodded. It was falling apart around them. They'd be better off – he, Bob, Macro and the three other men, Macro's tenants, holding the barricade – if they took several steps back now and formed a defensive line further down the rat run. 'It's going to collapse!'

Macro nodded; he could see that too. He glanced round over his shoulder. At the far end of the rat run was another low barricade of furniture and bric-a-brac. They could run back behind that and then have the advantage of all the other tenants being able to throw down stones and other missiles from the balconies around the courtyard.

'All right, then . . . after three, everyone back there!'

The other men nodded. Liam nodded at the whisper of English in his ear, barely audible above the noise. Although he'd already figured out what Macro was bellowing.

'One . . .!'

The other men stepped away from the rattling, rocking cart. Bob was still holding it.

'Two . . .!'

Liam swung his club down on another pair of hands, crushing them to a bloody mush.

'*THREE!*'

They all turned together and scrambled down the rat run, sandals slipping in the muck of animal faeces and night-water.

Liam heard the crash and clatter of the cart falling behind him as he vaulted over the flimsy inner barricade. Bob remained where he was, almost completely filling the width of the entrance to the rat run with his bulk and the arc of the short-handled blacksmith's hammer he was swinging wildly.

Now the cart was torn down and Bob fully exposed, missiles began to rain down on him from the avenue outside: stones, several arrows, dislodged clay bricks. Liam could see thickening blood trickling like syrup from a dozen nicks and gashes on Bob already. The support unit had faced far worse barrages than this, but Becks had been the example – one lucky arrow on target, one arrow puncturing the bone of his cranium and damaging either his walnut-sized organic brain or the computer nestling next to it, and he could be brought down like any other man.

'BOB! Get back here!' Liam cried over the cacophony of noise bouncing off the walls either side of them.

'Affirmative!' he heard Bob rumble in reply. He retreated slowly under the barrage, still swinging his hammer and holding the crowd back until finally he was able to quickly turn round and leap over the barricade to join the others.

A moment later, the mob crashed into the fragile second barricade. It wobbled and collapsed easily into a tangle of chair legs and shards of fractured crates, and through that pressed a forest of legs and arms, swinging clubs and knives and short swords.

The air above them buzzed and flickered with stones and short sharpened stakes, slingshots and grabbed handfuls of muck from the street. A neighbourhood brawl the likes of which Liam had never seen before.

The first few men through the tangle were quickly dealt with and collapsed amid the confusion of broken furniture; the rest quickly pulled back under the shower of projectiles raining down from the balconies around the courtyard.

Between Bob's swinging hammer and Macro's foul-mouthed jabbing swordplay, it looked like the pair of them in this narrow bottleneck were going to be able to hold the jeering, angry mob at bay for a while yet.

'Go on! Be off, the lot of you!' Macro bayed at the men hovering several yards beyond the probing tip of his sword. The bud struggled to find modern English alternatives for half of the stream of invective spewing out of his mouth. Liam found himself laughing nervously at the ex-soldier's coarse bravura.

'Aye! Go on, *get lost!*' he crowed defiantly as he ducked down and picked up a rock that had just landed at his feet and tossed it back into the crowd.

'Watch out!' Macro raised his shield, a battered and old curved rectangular shield that still sported the flecked paint insignia *Legio II* amid the forked lightning motif. He raised it over his and Liam's head as a large chunk of flint pulled up from the avenue outside arced over the heads of the mob in front and descended towards them. It clattered and bounced heavily, knocking a jagged gash through the shield before rolling on to the ground at their feet.

Macro lowered the shield and grinned at Liam. 'Just like the good ol' days!'

Liam had the distinct impression, even before he got the translation a half-second later, that the old boy was getting a kick out of this. Or he would have been . . . had he not heard someone scream, '*INCENDIA, FLAMMA*'.

'What?!'

Macro looked back into the courtyard, towards where the scream had come from.

'What's the matter?' asked Liam.

Above them they heard the unmistakable *whusk* of an arrow,

accompanied by a fluttering hiss. Liam saw the faint trail of smoke it left in its wake.

Macro spat rage and a stream of abuse. 'N-O-O-O-O!!!'

Several more flaming arrows zipped overhead, thudding into the wooden balconies, quickly setting fire to the dried wood, the woven-reed modesty screens and the hanging lines of laundry.

'*NO!*' Macro bellowed again. 'That's my *bloody property*!!'

CHAPTER 60

AD 54, Imperial Palace, Rome

Cato stood and stared at them; they calmly returned his silent gaze.

'This area is off-limits to you,' said Stern. 'You do not have authority to proceed any further. Please leave immediately.'

'I'm checking the palace for any intruders, looters,' said Cato.

'I understood that,' replied Stern calmly. 'However, I repeat: you have no authority to enter this particular location. Please turn round and leave.'

These men – no, not men . . . *things* – used to unsettle Cato. However, unlike the superstitious men he commanded, he'd never thought of them as supernatural beings. Just that they were decidedly inhuman. Odd. Creepy. But now he felt he had some sort of understanding of what they were.

Contraptions. Devices.

'You know who I am, don't you?'

'Affirmative. Tribune Cato.'

'And you understand I have the emperor's authority in his absence?' said Cato. 'I am in charge of palace security.'

'Affirmative.'

'So, what is behind those doors?'

Stern took a step forward. He cocked his head slightly as if listening to something only he could hear. 'That information is strictly classified, Tribune Cato. You do not have the correct security clearance for that information.'

Cato studied the Stone Man. His eyes were blinking repeatedly. There was an air of distracted uncertainty, of confusion about him.

Security clearance. Such odd words.

'You mean I don't have the authority? But you see, I do. The emperor put me in charge of –'

'Negative. This is a . . . *US military security zone* . . . this is . . .' Stern stopped. Cocked his head again awkwardly. 'In this current operational mode, the user designated "Emperor" has complete diagnostic control.' The confusion slowly cleared from his face as if another conflicting voice from within was coming through. 'We are authorized to use lethal force if you do not leave immediately.' Stern took a step forward, more certain of himself now. He reached for the hilt of the sword strapped to his side. 'You should leave now.'

Cato raised both his hands in surrender. 'All right, all right . . . I'm leaving.' He stepped back into the main hallway and allowed the drape to flop back into place, once more concealing the small passageway.

Cato realized the young woman from the future was quite correct. That beyond those sturdy oak doors was quite probably everything she wanted to find: the technology of her time. Her way home, and a way to correct everything.

He found Fronto a few minutes later, outside watching the sky above Rome laced with ribbons of smoke from riots that were breaking out right across the city.

'We should bring the others in now,' he said quietly.

'Yes, sir.'

'Take a section of men with you and get our friends back here as quickly as you can.'

CHAPTER 61

AD 54, Subura District, Rome

Sal was struggling to breathe. A thick pall of smoke from the fires above them had descended to fill the courtyard.

She had Maddy. Or rather Maddy had found her and was even now leading her by the hand through the churning sea of bodies. Five minutes ago the fight had settled into a stalemate; the looters held at bay in the rat run by the constant barrage of projectiles from above.

But now things had descended into a confused, misty chaos. The smoke from a dozen fires on the first and second floors had become a choking blanket. Macro's tenants were now no longer concerned with keeping their looting neighbours out of the apartment block, but instead were struggling with each other to escape the burning building.

Sal was jostled and bumped from all sides, nearly losing her grip on Maddy's hand as they became funnelled into a press of thrashing bodies. The rat run: five minutes ago it was a bottleneck that was proving to be their saving grace; now it looked like becoming a death trap for them.

Above her, amid the churn of smoke, she heard the crackle of flames taking hold of the building. 'Maddy, we've got to get out! We've got to find a way out!'

'I know!'

She had no idea where the others were. Last she'd seen, Liam and Bob had been manning the second barricade, successfully holding back the baying mob. But that was ancient history now. There were no more 'attackers' and 'defenders', not any longer, just a couple of hundred people fighting with each other to escape the building through a passageway littered with obstacles and bodies.

They heard a loud crack of snapping wood from above, and then a moment later, the balconies lining one complete side of the quadrangle came tumbling down through the smoke into the courtyard. An avalanche of blackened, smouldering slats of wood that exploded into a shower of sparks and embers that set fire to the tattered linen sun-awnings around the courtyard. Through a gap in the smoke, Sal caught sight of a woman with a child in her arms, trapped in the corner beside their two ponies that were rolling widened eyes at the flames around them; she and the animals were imprisoned inside a collapsed scaffolding of wooden poles.

The woman's eyes met Sal's – the only person now looking back into the courtyard. She was screaming for help. A fleeting moment, then the smoke closed on her and she and her child were gone. Items of burning clothing, embers from drapes and privacy screens and a million and one flammable household possessions were starting to rain down on the crowd that had completely plugged the rat run and were going absolutely nowhere, setting hair and more clothes on fire.

'Help!' Sal screamed. '*HELP!*'

Her voice was lost beneath a hundred others screaming the very same thing in Latin.

She couldn't see Maddy now. She still had hold of her hand, but their arms were twisted over the back and shoulder of some old man carrying a screaming toddler, piggyback.

'Maddy!' she screamed.

319

'I'm here!'

We're going to die. We're going to choke to death or burn.

Her mind flashed with memories of that day – the last day of her life. Standing in the ruin of that stairwell with the others on their floor who'd spilled out of their apartments. Her Mamaji and Papaji, like her with ghost-white faces of dust. The air thick with powdered concrete and toxic fumes. She remembered the choking, the panicking, being terrified. Then that sound, that end-of-the-world sound . . . a deep rumble like an approaching train, the floor trembling beneath their feet. Gasps, cries, screaming; a desperate collective horror that didn't allow them even a few seconds of stillness – a goodbye moment. A whispered farewell that might, just might be carried on some spiritual ether to those it was intended for.

And then Foster . . . extending a hand, offering her, just her, a way out.

Oh jahulla, not like this. Don't let me die like this.

'BOB!' she screamed. 'LIAM! *HELLLLLPP!*'

Liam looked at Bob. They were watching people pour out of the rat run on to the avenue. Not a fleet-footed escape but a molasses-like spill of the staggering, crawling, coughing and retching. People clambering desperately over a growing bed of collapsed bodies.

'That was Sal's voice!'

Bob nodded. 'Affirmative.'

'Ah, Jayzus . . . we got to go in and pull her out!'

'You must stay here, Liam,' said Bob. He turned towards the clogged exit.

'No! I'm comin' with –'

An iron grip held Liam's wrist. He turned to see Macro. 'Let your friend go, lad.'

Liam struggled to shake him off. But the Roman's grip was far too insistent and strong. 'Let him go, lad . . . if he's truly made of stone, then he'll live.'

Liam watched as Bob carelessly bulldozed his way through the emerging people and disappeared into the smoke spewing thickly out of the narrow rat run.

Above screams for help they could both hear the crackle of flames eagerly devouring the apartment block. Smoke, now growing a dark grey, pumped energetically out of seemingly every small window. The yellow-washed, clay plaster facade over the building's clay bricks was beginning to crack under the heat and crumble to the ground in chunks. Bricks and brittle mortar too . . . breaking, crumbling and falling, like the decaying flesh of a dead body; a body decomposing in fast forward, rendered from living flesh to skeleton frame in minutes.

Liam's weary, oxygen-starved legs buckled under him and he sat down heavily in the middle of the cobbled avenue, dropped, like a sack of coke off the back of a coalman's cart. He wasn't alone. The avenue was thick with others slumped on their knees, lying on their backs, gasping to fill their lungs with clear air.

Macro squatted down beside him, his eyes glistening with moisture. 'Stupid,' he muttered to himself. 'Stupid, stupid people.'

They heard something collapsing deep inside the column of smoke. Perhaps a wall giving way, filling the courtyard with fractured fragments of heat-shattered clay brick and glowing spars of charcoaled scaffold poles.

Liam felt his cheeks grow wet, tears creating two clean paths down his soot-blackened face.

They're dead in that. For sure. All of them.

The deafening clatter of collapse somewhere within the

smoke ceased, to be replaced by the growing crackle and roar of flames. The stream of people crawling, staggering out of the smoke had become a dwindling trickle, one or two dropping as they emerged. Surely the very last likely to step out of the pall. As certain as he'd ever been about anything, Liam knew the rest of the poor, unfortunate souls caught up in that death-trap space were either suffocated by now, burned to death or buried.

His vision, blurred with tears, became a kaleidoscope of refracting stars and spears of light. He felt a hand lightly on his back, patting him gently, and the deep grunt of Macro's voice far away offering a soldier's ill-phrased words of comfort.

But all Liam could do was hear his own choice of words. Hardly any more comforting.

They're gone . . . and it's just me now.

Just me.

Selfish words, he realized. Selfish to grieve at being left alone like this. To cry like this just for himself. Maddy, Sal and Bob . . . not just friends, but family — more like family in truth than the faint photo-album memories he had of a mother and father, uncles and aunts.

Macro's hand was still patting him.

If he'd had a greater presence of mind, been stronger, quicker, smarter . . . he should've reacted sooner. Left the stand-off over the barricade and gone to find the girls. There could have been a way out for them. They could have found another way out.

Macro's hand was thumping his back more heavily. Not a flat pat, more like a fist. Hardly a comforting, soothing gesture. He realized the bud in his ear was calmly, insistently telling him something, telling him what the old Roman was now bellowing loudly, repeatedly.

322

<Look. Look. Look!>

Liam did. Wiped muck and tears from his eyes. His blurred, refracted vision cleared. He saw what he expected to see: the thick column of smoke spiralling up from the skeleton of Macro's building and an avenue of soot-covered bodies.

But then he picked out the thick, round-shouldered outline of a bull charging towards him. Not a bull . . . it ran like a human on human legs. A minotaur, then.

No, not a minotaur. Those weren't horns on top – he could make out that much. He wiped his eyes again and realized Macro, still pummelling his back, was cheering hoarsely.

The minotaur, an enormous black creature, came to a halt in front of Liam. Hefted two blackened humps – what he'd mistaken for horns – from its shoulders and on to the cobblestones, where both began to wheeze, cough and retch.

'Minor burns and abrasions. There may be some minor scorching of the trachea and nasal passages. This will heal. But they will both be all right,' rumbled the minotaur.

Behind them the complete front wall of the apartment building collapsed backwards in on itself, sending a mushroom cloud of sparks, ember and ash up into the sky.

'Unlike your property, Lucius Cornelius Macro,' added Bob.

Just then they heard the *clack* of standard army-issue, nail-soled sandals on the cobbles and the approaching rattle and clatter of armour and harnesses.

Macro turned to look up at Fronto. 'You might have come a little earlier!'

Fronto gazed at Macro's retirement investment, fully ablaze now. 'It's like this right across the whole city. Riots in every district.' He turned to Maddy and Liam. 'Cato sent me to get you.'

Maddy, still on her hands and knees coughing up globules of

phlegm as black as tar, wiped her mouth and looked up at the officer.

'You . . . you can get us in . . . into the emperor's palace?'

Fronto nodded. 'Right now . . . yes. If we hurry.'

CHAPTER 62

AD 54, outside Rome

Caligula watched the ground, shifting and beetle-black: a thousand crows moving among the dead, more in the sky overhead swooping and buzzing the battlefield.

The dead stretched as far as he could see: the red tunics of dead legionaries; men from the Tenth and Eleventh dotting the olive-green grass of the hillside like wild poppies.

The deed was done before the sun reached midday. Two legions of men broken and routed within the space of an hour. Caligula had watched the battle unfold from the comfort of a wooden platform erected in the early hours of the morning. His small vanguard of Stone Men had formed the very tip of an advancing wedge that had plunged through Lepidus's predictable chequerboard formation. The Stone Men were soon lost from direct sight in the melee, but their precise location in the press of men was never in doubt; it was the source of the screaming, the source of the greatest amount of movement in the middle of the glistening sea of helmets and armour.

After the brief battle, Caligula could actually trace the path they took by the wake of horrendously dismembered bodies; almost as if someone had gathered up men and bits of men and laid them out like a narrow carpet, a road of ragged flesh, splintered bone and dented metal.

Almost indestructible, those Stone Men, but not quite. Four

of them had eventually been brought down by Lepidus's men. A concerted effort by his archers, leaving them for a moment staggering pincushion figures, like human porcupines, until they'd finally collapsed. But by then, of course, the damage had been done, the legions' formations were broken and the men were already beginning to turn and run.

Caligula glanced once more at the pitiful sight of so many good Roman legionaries dead on the field, carrion being pecked at by hungry birds. Difficult to savour victory for long when a sight like this was the aftermath. He sighed sadly then turned back round to face General Lepidus, kneeling, stripped of his armour and left with just his tattered and bloodstained tunic.

'This is what happens . . . when you decide to take matters into your own hands.' Caligula's hand idled on the pommel of his sword. 'What did you honestly think was going to happen? Hmmmm?'

Lepidus's eyes were on Caligula's idling, fidgeting fingers. 'I . . . I had no choice. I —'

'Well actually, I think you probably did have a choice.' Caligula pouted disapprovingly down at him. 'You could have come to me the moment that poisonous old man, Crassus, started sending treacherous little notes to you. You could have presented his letters to me and quite easily proved that I could trust you. But no . . . you chose not to.'

'I . . . Crassus was trying to make me look already guilty! He was wording his letters to make it look like we'd already spoken of . . . of . . .'

'Trying to kill me?'

Lepidus shut up and looked down, defeated.

'Even if Crassus's letters implicated you . . . you should have come to me. I would have understood. I would have been fair, merciful. Good grief, I'm not a monster, Lepidus.'

'I . . . it . . . I was misled. I was used.'

'Oh, you were misled all right.'

'I was frightened.'

Caligula crouched down before the general, lifted the man's ample chin with a finger and looked him in the eyes. 'Frightened? Of me? Why? What's to be afraid of? I only want what's best for us all, what's best for all Romans.'

He stood up again. 'Fear . . . that was your undoing. You're nothing but a frightened old man. I should have far better men in charge of my legions.' He began to pull his sword out of its sheath.

'Please!'

'Oh? Pleading, is it? So very sorry now, are we?'

Lepidus nodded vigorously. 'I . . . was left with no choice! I had to do something!'

'They goaded you . . . *coerced* you into trying to kill me, replace me.' Caligula smiled. 'And clearly you obviously thought you *could* replace me.'

'I, no . . . I didn't believe –'

'I don't think you were sorry this morning as you presented your legions for battle. I think you were looking forward to the idea of sleeping in my bed tonight, in my palace. Calling yourself emperor. Wearing my robes.' Caligula laughed. 'Not that they'd fit you.'

He lifted the tip of his gladius up and held it in front of Lepidus's face. Sunlight reflected off the polished blade, glinting into the general's eyes.

'I need better men than you in charge of my legions. Younger, braver men. Trustworthy fellows. Now listen to me, Lepidus, you can go some way towards making amends . . . if you were to let me know who else, other than Crassus, was involved in this ridiculous charade.'

The general licked dry lips quickly. 'I . . . I think my tribune,

Atellus, was in on it. Now . . . yes, thinking about it, yes, I'm sure of it.'

Caligula glanced at the tribune's body lying in the grass nearby. 'Well, he's not exactly going to deny that now, is he, Lepidus?'

'Others . . . I–I'm sure there were . . . Yes, Crassus used to have visits from Cicero . . . Paulus. Those two –'

Caligula nodded. 'Now that's a bit better. Yes.' He stroked his nose thoughtfully. 'I could imagine those two old relics would have been involved somehow. Who else? Hmmm? Any other faces you noticed keeping Crassus company?'

Lepidus's eyes darted left and right, trawling a racing mind for names . . . faces . . .

'Your palace tribune! The new one!'

Caligula frowned. 'What? You don't mean . . . Cato?'

Lepidus looked up, nodded vigorously again. 'Yes! He was involved! I . . . I'm sure of it!'

'Cato.' Caligula frowned.

'Crassus hinted to me . . . not long ago . . . said . . .'

'Said what?'

'He said he had someone in the palace . . . someone close to you. Someone who could get to you!'

Caligula cast his mind back to the few conversations he'd had with the man. The tribune had always seemed professional, reliable, competent. But then . . .

Your Stone Men, sire . . . Might I suggest you send them along? . . . You have my cohort here . . . to guard you . . .

Caligula spun round, looking for the *praefectus* Quintus.

'Quintus, take your cavalry back to Rome!' He nodded at the five remaining Stone Men, their olive-green armour spattered with dark droplets of dried blood. 'Take them with you as well! The tribune of the palace cohort is to be arrested!'

'Sire?'

'He's one of *them*, Quintus! A traitor! I want him arrested. And I want him *alive*! Do you understand?'

'Yes, sire.'

'And have the rest of the Guard assembled to march.'

'But, Caesar, they've just fought! They need . . .'

Caligula's look silenced him. 'Have them assembled,' he repeated softly.

The prefect nodded, saluted and turned to deliver his orders.

Caligula once more looked down at the man in front of him, an anxious, twitching face, bathed in sweat.

'Thank you, Lepidus,' he said absently. And then without much thinking about it, for good measure, he quickly swung his sword down at the general's neck. Even before the arc of blood had landed on the dry, sandy soil and arid grass of the hillside, Caligula had already turned on his heel and was heading towards his tent to change out of his uncomfortable armour. The march back to Rome would be a morning and an afternoon. They'd be back by twilight, he supposed . . . if they moved out soon.

Behind him he finally heard the thud of the general's body keeling over. While all around the orders he'd given to Quintus were being barked down the ranks, followed by the noise of five thousand men scrambling in response.

CHAPTER 63

AD 54, Imperial Palace, Rome

'I can't let you in, sir . . .' The *optio* grimaced uncomfortably at the thought of challenging his centurion's order. He craned his neck to look through the iron grille of the gate to get a better look past Fronto at the soot-covered people behind him. 'I can't let them into the palace grounds, sir.' He swallowed nervously. 'Standing orders.'

'Your orders, Septimus lad, are exactly what I say they are. Now open this gate!'

The *optio* looked unhappily at Fronto. Torn between the dressing-down his centurion looked like he was about to give him and fear of what would happen to him if ever Caligula discovered he'd opened the north-west gate and let in some uninvited strangers.

'Is this on the emperor's orders, sir?'

Fronto sighed. He was about to let rip at the *optio* with a blast of colourful language when Cato appeared beside him. 'It's all right. Let them in, Septimus. They're my property. I just wanted to bring them into the imperial grounds for safe-keeping.'

The *optio* nodded at his tribune. 'Right, sorry, sir . . . I just —'

Cato shushed him and smiled. 'Quite all right, you were doing your job.'

The bolt slid back and the iron gate swung inwards.

Fronto threw his *optio* a withering glare as he led his men and the others inside the gardens and the gate was slammed shut again.

Cato looked at his old friend Macro first, then at Maddy and the others. 'What happened?'

'A *fire* happened,' grunted Macro. 'It's all gone, my investment. My retirement fund, everything.'

'There are fires all over the city,' said Fronto.

Cato nodded. The smell of burning was on the air, and a pall of smoke hung in the sky. He spoke to Fronto. 'Best assign your men back to their posts immediately, Centurion.'

Fronto nodded. 'Right you are, sir.'

Cato waited until Fronto had finished barking orders and the legionaries had dispersed to their deployment positions around the imperial grounds.

'I can take you to the Temple of Neptune in the palace,' said Cato. 'I believe that's where you may find what you're looking for. The things belonging to the Visitors.'

Maddy glanced at Liam and Sal. 'He's found something!'

Sal looked heartened. 'What? A time machine?'

'Can you take us there right now?' asked Maddy.

'I can. But there's a problem,' Cato continued. 'Three Stone Men guarding it.'

Liam translated that for Sal. She sighed.

'Do you think your man could fight three of them at once?' Cato looked at Bob.

'They are lighter combat models,' replied Bob. 'I have a reasonable chance of success.'

'And we'll help you,' said Macro, 'if you need help, that is.'

All three units detected the faint signal at the same time; their eyes instantly locked on each other. It was weak and it flickered out of detectable range for a moment then was there again: an unidentifiable broadcast identification signal.

'It is not one of ours. A different systems manufacturer.' Stern narrowed his eyes. 'The carrier signal's ident tag has an older version packet header.'

The other two nodded in agreement. 'V2.3.11.'

'Agreed.' Stern's digital mind deconstructed the signal.

[Information]
Model Type – W.G. Systems Heavy Combat Model
Batch number – 4039282
Activation year – 2054
OS – V2.3.11

'Is this unit a threat?' asked one of them.

'If the unit compromises our user's standing orders,' said Stern, 'it is a legitimate target.'

'It's a Heavy Combat Model, Stern,' said the other. 'Heavier than we are.'

He looked at his squad member, mildly impressed by the note of anxiety in the unit's voice. An emotional stress indicator he must have picked up from a human and he was using quite convincingly now.

'There are three of us. We have a significant numerical advantage.'

'What if it has better weapons than us?'

Stern nodded. Certainly a concern. Although the three of them still wore their poly-graphene body armour, after all these years, their weapons were useless. It was strictly Roman-era swords and spears for them.

'Unit-Chuck? Unit-Butch? I have an order for you.'

Both units stood to attention. 'Affirmative.'

'Locate and observe. Identify what weaponry the unit is carrying and report.'

'Yes, sir.' Stern watched them push past the drape and listened to their heavy-booted footsteps recede. His digital mind had some simple calculations to make. Several combat scenarios to evaluate should this newly arrived support unit attempt to prevent him and his men from carrying out Temporary-User-Caligula's standing orders. But his actual mind, that tiny pink muscle linked by an umbilical cord of hair-thin data wires, was busy pondering how it was possible for another support unit, albeit a slightly older model, to be here in Ancient Rome.

CHAPTER 64

AD 54, Imperial Palace, Rome

'It's off the main passage beyond the entrance portico,' whispered Cato. 'Hidden behind one of the Thracian drapes on the right.' He turned to Maddy and Liam. 'Could your Stone Man attempt to lure them away?'

Maddy shrugged. 'It will depend on what orders they have. Won't it, Bob?'

'Affirmative. If guarding the doorway is a higher priority than attempting to eliminate a potential threat, then they will not attempt to pursue me.'

'In which case we'll just have to fight them,' said Liam. He turned to Bob. 'What do you think? Can we take 'em?'

'It is possible.'

'Possible?' Maddy sighed. 'OK . . . I guess I can go with "possible".'

Cato nodded. 'Shall we proceed, then?'

'One moment,' said Bob, cocking his head. His eyelids flickered.

'What's up?' asked Liam.

Bob nodded, satisfied with something going on inside his head. 'I am deactivating my local wireless communications system.'

'Switching your Wi-Fi off?' Maddy patted his back. 'Good idea.'

Cato led them across the east gardens of the Imperial Palace, approaching a cordon of Praetorians guarding the eastern portico. The men stared suspiciously for a moment at the soot-covered people accompanying their tribune. But Cato snapped stiffly at them to remain focused on their duties and keep a watch on the perimeter walls for any looters attempting to take advantage of the city-wide chaos.

He walked them past the guards, out of the afternoon sun and into the cool, dimly lit labyrinth of Caligula's palace, past marble columns and intricate, vividly coloured designs in mosaic tiles on the floor.

'Wow, this is totally bindaas,' Sal whispered softly, almost silently. Even so, her whisper echoed across the cavernous interior.

'The palace should be entirely empty now, except for the three Stone Men,' said Cato. 'The slaves of the palace have been confined to their quarters; my men are all stationed outside the building watching the entrances. The gardens. It is just *us* inside.'

'Which way?'

Cato nodded ahead. 'This leads to the main passageway.'

The tribune led the way, with Bob by his side, a short sword clutched in each fist. Behind them Maddy and Sal, hands clasped anxiously. Bringing up the rear Liam and Macro, warily glancing behind them and into the shadows between columns. Their breathing echoed in the gloom, the tap of their feet sounding precariously loud.

Presently they looked out on to a broad passageway, almost as broad as any Roman thoroughfare. The walls towered to meet a ceiling of murals that depicted heroic scenes of – presumably – Caligula. It was punctuated every now and then with small skylight openings that allowed meagre shafts of sunlight to pierce the gloom and angle down on to the mosaic tile floor like muted spotlights.

Cato indicated to the right and cautiously led the way.

They walked slowly along the broad passage until finally Cato stopped and pointed at a gently shifting drape.

The others nodded.

Bob crossed the passageway until he stood beside the drape. A draught of cool air was teasing it. Liam could feel it on his skin as he, Macro and Cato stood, weapons ready, beside him.

And there it was again, the same thing that cursed him every time he faced the possibility of imminent violence, his legs trembling like the whiskers of a rodent. His mouth as dry as parchment.

He glanced quickly at Macro, his dark beard splitting with a grin of excitement. Beside him Cato, a foot taller, poised with a face almost as stone cold and impassive as Bob's. Both men seemed utterly used to this – that moment of readiness before a fight. That final breath, that heartbeat before the calm became a bloody, thrashing chaos.

Liam sighed. *Why can't I ever look as ready as that?*

Cato checked the others were ready then quickly leaned forward and pulled the drape aside.

CHAPTER 65

AD 54, Imperial Palace, Rome

Maddy gasped at the sight of it. Standing there, legs planted astride, sword drawn almost as if it had been patiently waiting for them.

But it was the thing's appearance that surprised her: the breathtaking historical contradiction. Standing there, in the flickering light of a pair of oil lamps with a gladius held ready in one hand and a gladiator's shield in the other, was something quite unmistakably from the twenty-first century. A soldier in military olive green. A soldier wearing a polygraphene torso plate, shoulder and forearm armour plates, thigh and shin plates and black combat boots. At a glance – except for the sword and shield, that is – little different from the kind of special-forces guys she was used to seeing in grainy night vision sliding down ropes on to the terrace roofs of Al Qaeda hideouts.

'You are not permitted beyond this point,' it said almost politely. 'Leave immediately.'

Bob met its gaze. 'You must step aside.'

The soldier studied Bob for a moment. A flicker of recognition, comprehension in his eyes. 'You are a Heavy Combat Model.'

Bob nodded. 'Affirmative. You are a Multi-role Reconnaissance Model. A later version?'

'Yes, I am.' He smiled. 'Same manufacturer.'

Maddy could have sworn both clones nodded a quick 'nice-to-meet-you' greeting at each other.

'You must step aside,' said Bob finally.

'You are not permitted beyond this point.'

'Our priorities conflict.'

'Agreed.'

Both units' eyes flickered for a split second as they processed the same conclusion, but it was the soldier-unit who reacted first. He thrust his sword at Bob's neck – with the speed of a snake bite. Bob dodged to one side, but not fast enough to avoid the tip skewering him deeply just above the collarbone.

Bob retaliated with a roundhouse swing of the sword in his right hand. The soldier parried the heavy blow with his shield; a clatter and ring that sounded deafening. Bob thrust with his other sword at the unit's midriff. Its reaction time, or perhaps it was a module of combat-prediction code, *anticipated* the move and sidestepped it with an almost Becks-like ballerina grace, as it yanked its blade free from Bob's shoulder.

Macro took a step forward and thrust his sword at the unit. It swept its bloody blade down from Bob and effortlessly blocked Macro with a jarring rasp of clashing sword edges.

Bob tried again with his right sword: this time a thrust not a swing. The shield snapped down to intercept it; another clang filled the passageway.

This time, though, the guard of Bob's sword caught on the curved edge of the shield. Leverage for him; a chance to use his brawn. Bob flung his sword arm to the right, wrenching the small gladiator's shield out of the unit's grasp and hurling it against the passage wall.

The soldier-unit backed up a step. Eyes flickering from Bob to Macro, and now Liam as he took a faltering step forward to help them out.

'Liam! No, don't!' hissed Maddy.

'You will lose,' rumbled Bob. 'Stand down.'

'He's right,' snarled Macro.

The unit was crouched like a rattlesnake ready to strike, passing its sword deftly from one hand to the other. 'You do not have security clearance to pass. Please leave immediately.'

Macro and Liam were edging round either side of it, Cato warily holding his ground in front of it: a three-sided confrontation for the unit. But Maddy suspected it had already identified Liam's as the weak side. He was no soldier.

'Liam!' she cried. 'Please get back!'

'I'm fine, so I am, Mads!' he called back over his shoulder.

The soldier-unit took advantage of that – the split second of distraction.

It took a quick step in Liam's direction and thrust its sword at his gut. The blade disappeared into his linen tunic and Liam yelped in pain. The unit quickly pulled the blade back, the tip spattered with blood.

Liam clutched his side, a blossom of crimson spreading through the material as he dropped to his knees. Macro thrust his old sword into the unit's flank, exposed by the lunge towards Liam. Once again the unit's mind, working in nanoseconds of prediction, anticipated that and successfully dodged the thrusting blade.

With both arms committed now, however, one withdrawing from Liam, the other blocking Macro's thrust, the unit had nothing left to counter Bob's sweeping downward stroke. His blade bit deep into the unit's head – through the skull, deep enough to cause catastrophic, irrevocable damage to the organic-silicon processing centre inside.

Stern teetered unsteadily on his feet for a moment, a look of complete incomprehension in his grey eyes. A small trickle of dark blood ran between his brows, down the left side of his nose and on to his cheek.

He gasped something incomprehensible before falling forward, flat on his face. Quite dead.

'*LIAMMMM!*' screamed Sal, starting forward. She raced across the passage and scooted down beside Liam, still kneeling, holding his side. His face had turned grey, his skin waxy with beads of sweat.

'Ahhh Jay-zus! *This hurts!*'

Maddy was next to him. 'Liam?' Her voice was shaking. 'Liam, how bad is it?'

He grimaced with the pain. 'Do I look like a bleedin' doctor? I . . . I don't know!'

Macro and Cato joined the girls. 'Macro's looked after enough of his boys on the field.'

Macro nodded. 'Let me take a look at you, lad.'

Bob grasped Maddy's shoulder. 'We do not have much time, Maddy. The other units are nearby somewhere.'

'Your Stone Man is right,' said Cato. He nodded at the door in front of them. 'If whatever you seek is in there . . . then perhaps we should hurry?'

Maddy looked back down at Liam, now sprawled on the mosaic tiles, looking ashen, Macro ripping open the blood-stained tunic to get a look at the wound.

'Sal . . .' she said.

She nodded. Understood. 'I'll keep an eye on him. You go on.'

Maddy got up and followed Bob and Cato towards the door. A thick, iron locking bar ran across both doors and Bob easily slid it back with a heavy rasp that filled the short secret passage-way. Maddy reached for a handle.

'Be careful,' said Cato. He tapped the heavy doors with his

knuckles. 'These seem like doors built more to keep something in than keep intruders out.' The tribune took a deep breath, a sign perhaps that despite his rational mind, a part of him still held a wary suspicion that the supernatural realm of gods might just exist.

Maddy grasped the handle and pulled. The thick oak door rattled heavily, but didn't budge. She cursed. 'After all that, it's freakin' locked!'

Bob gently pushed against the other door. It swung inwards with an ominous creak.

'Negative. You just need to push, not pull.'

CHAPTER 66

AD 54, Imperial Palace, Rome

Maddy reached for a tallow candle and stepped inside the dark room. The candle's guttering flame picked out little detail. A vast room that echoed like a cavern. She could see a ceiling above, faintly. Frescos and decoration left for so many years in complete darkness. Bob and Cato entered behind her, another two candles marginally increasing the light in the room.

She took a dozen steps in until finally the candlelight glinted on piles of objects on the floor, laid out on several wooden tables. She went over to the nearest table and set her candle down on it.

'Bob! Over here!'

The support unit and tribune joined her. Bob studied the items on the table. 'Hydrogen cell powered pulse rifles,' he said drily.

'What are these devices?' asked Cato.

'Weapons,' Maddy replied. 'Weapons from the future.'

Cato's eyes widened. 'The stories of the Visitors . . . Cicero once mentioned they had "spears that roared".' He looked at them. 'These?'

'I doubt they'll "roar" any more,' replied Maddy, picking one of them up, blowing the dust off it and inspecting the weapon more closely.

'Information: without maintenance, the hydrogen cells will be dead by now.'

Maddy looked across the wooden table. There were other things, supplies of all sorts: medicines, emergency food packs, tools. 'This wasn't just a field trip . . .' She gasped. 'Those Visitors came here to stay! Do you think? To . . . to *colonize* Roman times?'

Bob nodded. 'That appears to be a plausible conclusion.'

She picked up her candle and wandered towards a pile of objects on the floor nearby. She squatted down and inspected them. Clothes. Shoes. Glasses. Some of them spattered with faded bloodstains. By the look of the mound of items of clothing there must have been a lot of them, perhaps hundreds. *And all of them massacred?*

'And this, then,' uttered Cato almost reverentially. 'This must have been one of the chariots they arrived in.'

Maddy turned to look. He was on the other side of the room now, holding his candle up to inspect something large that glinted dully in the gloom. She and Bob hurried over and a moment later, the three of them were inspecting the dusty, slanted metal sides of a large vehicle. To Maddy's eyes it looked like a cross between a Humvee and a hovercraft.

'Multi-terrain personnel carrier. With anti-grav thrusters for a limited-altitude vtol capability,' said Bob. 'This appears to be a more advanced model than the prototypes being field-tested by the US military in 2054.'

Maddy shook her head. 'This is completely crazy! The scale of time contamination . . . I mean this is insane. What the hell were they thinking?'

'Maddy?' It was Sal.

She turned round and saw her silhouette in the doorway. 'How is he?'

'Macro's bound him up.' She managed a relieved smile. 'Not serious, he said. Just a flesh wound.'

'OK . . . OK.' She sighed. 'That's good.' She looked round the room. There were plenty of other things to inspect. Perhaps, somewhere in this room, *please God*, a time machine of some sort. Something to get them back home. Now.

'Bob, if they've brought with them some sort of a time-displacement device, and it's in here somewhere, we need to find it.'

'Affirmative. But there is unlikely to be a viable source of power still.'

Bob clambered up on to the slanted metal hull of the vehicle. 'I will look inside the personnel carrier.'

'You do that.' She turned to Sal. 'We're going to find a way home, Sal. I promise. Stay with Liam, OK?'

Sal nodded and quickly disappeared out of the doorway.

A time machine. Please tell me you idiots brought with you a means to get back home. Please. You guys can't have been that stupid. Right?

Perhaps they weren't stupid. Just desperate.

She returned to the tables stacked with guns and ammunition cartridges and webbing and field equipment, hoping to find some first-aid packs. Anaesthetic for Liam, more importantly something antiseptic to cleanse the wound. Antibiotics to fight any potential infection. He wasn't going to make it if that sword wasn't clean. In this pre-penicillin time even a paper cut could finish you off if you got unlucky. She found a first-aid pack, unzipped it. It was fully stocked.

'Sal!'

Sal came back in. 'Here . . . unwrap Liam. There's an antibiotic spray in here. Use that and use these bandages; at least they're clean.'

Sal took the first-aid pack and hurried back outside. Maddy resumed looking round the vast room. Her candle picked out a large object in the middle. A box, a crate of some kind.

Crate? A protective crate?

She made her way quickly towards it, doing her best to stifle the growing hope it might actually contain a machine eagerly waiting to be switched on and ready to conveniently whisk them back home to 2001.

Life doesn't actually work that way, does it, Mads? Not for them at any rate.

Closer, she could see it looked less like a packing crate and more like the kind of travel cage you'd transport a wild animal in. She'd once watched a show on cable TV, a 'day-in-the-life-of' kind of show based on LaGuardia Airport. There'd been an episode with a sedated Indian tiger in a crate in the back of an aeroplane. Last of its kind or something. Anyway, the crate had looked not unlike this one. She stepped warily closer to it . . . expecting at any moment to hear the enraged snarl of a roused tiger or a lion coming from inside. She noticed a sliding trapdoor on one side of the crate.

Lion, tiger . . . or time machine. This crate, reinforced with iron brackets on the corners, had to contain *something* important. Gently she eased the trapdoor to the side, revealing a hatchway eighteen inches wide and six high. A viewing slot? A feeding slot?

She wrinkled her nose. There was an awful stench spilling out of it. Like sewage. Slurry. No, even worse. Decay.

A feeding slot, then. It had to be there was some kind of animal being kept in there. Or one that had died and was quietly decomposing. Slowly she raised her candle, its flickering glow beginning to pick out a few slats of wood on the inside.

'Hello?' she uttered softly. 'Anything in there?'

She heard a sudden scratching sound, the scramble of movement inside the box. Then a pair of eyes suddenly lurched into view.

Oh my God!

Eyes. Wide and milky. Almost human. Or perhaps human, but entirely insane, animal-crazy. Completely feral. The eyes were accompanied by a shrill, frantic, gurgling, whinnying cry. Its face – yes, a human face, she could see that now – was hidden from the bridge of the nose down to the chin by some sort of leather and iron mask strapped round the head and caked in scum and dirt.

'Oh God! Over here!' she cried. 'There's someone alive in here!'

CHAPTER 67

AD 54, Imperial Palace, Rome

Bob worked the reinforcing brackets off then pulled away the thick bars of wood that made the cage.

'Jeeez!' whispered Maddy as she caught her first glimpse of the rest of the pitiful creature cowering inside. 'Is that really a man in there?'

The frail, skeletal body inside looked like that of an old man, edges and bulges where bone pushed out against paper-thin skin. His skin was darker than Mediterranean skin; Middle Eastern, Asian perhaps. And hair. Lots of it, cascading down his narrow shoulders, once upon a time dark, but now grey threaded with white in places.

The man cowered in the corner at the sight of Bob pulling the cage open, bar by bar.

'Shhh! It's OK,' Maddy cooed softly. 'We're not going to hurt you!'

Cato stepped closer to get a better look at him. 'Is . . . is this one of the Visitors?'

The man in the mask glanced at him quickly. He nodded vigorously, manic, darting eyes growing even wider. He whimpered, mewed and gurgled, bony hands gesturing frantically at the mask over his mouth.

Maddy stepped forward. 'Let me take that off you. Is that what you want?'

The man scrambled unsteadily forward; his bare feet padded off a soft bed of trampled faecal matter – years' worth of human waste compacted into an almost compost-like bed – on to the cool, hard tiles with a gentle patter. He turned his back to Maddy and frantically lifted his long, matted hair to reveal a crusted iron band with a padlock on it.

'It's a lock. I'm . . . I'm sorry . . . I don't . . .'

'Let me,' said Cato. He pulled his sword out and carefully dug the tip of his blade into the lock's rusted clasp. With a sharp twist, it snapped and showered flakes of rust to the floor. Maddy eased the band away from his head, grimacing at the skin worn bald at the back of the man's head, the fresh scabs, the fading scars.

The old man untangled his matted hair, the long wisps of his beard and moustache, from the mask's locking band. He eased the mask itself away from lips crusted with scab and dried mucus. The feed tube, the outside of it coated in the slime of rotting food lodged in the front of the mouth, emerged from a largely toothless face; gums almost completely black with the ruined stumps of dead teeth.

'*Oh Jesus*,' Maddy whispered, controlling the urge to retch.

The mask clunked to the floor, the echo filling the cavernous, dark room.

'Are you one of the Visitors?' Cato asked.

The man seemed to be in a state of shock, hyperventilating. Gasping. His tongue, snaking out and tasting the air, relishing its release from captivity.

'Did you come from the future?' tried Maddy in English.

His darting eyes stopped on her immediately.

'English? You can understand me?'

His jaw flexed – trying to speak. Trying to form words with his ruined mouth.

Just then Bob stirred. 'Information.'

Maddy held a hand up to shush him. 'He's trying to say something.' The old man was gurgling something. Trying to produce a word.

'Caution!' said Bob more insistently. 'I am detecting two more idents! Approaching from the east quickly!'

'Two of them? We don't stand a chance against *two* of them!'

'What is your Stone Man saying?' asked Cato.

Maddy turned to look at the doorway. 'The others are coming!' she hissed in Latin to Cato. 'Sal!' She started towards the doors. 'SAL! Get Liam inside! HURRY!'

A moment later, she saw Macro and Sal with Liam dangling between them, shuffling inside.

'We've got to close the doors!' screamed Maddy. 'Help me!' She jogged across the floor and began to wrestle with one of the oak doors. Macro grabbed the other, the doors creaking on solid iron hinges. Bob was beside her a moment later and with a heavy, rattling thud, the wan light from the oil lamps in the small passage outside was gone.

By the light of her candle she could see there was no way to secure the doors, no locking bar on this side, no padlocks, nothing.

'They are twenty yards away,' said Bob.

'Everyone! We've got to hold the doors!' she barked, wedging her shoulder against one of them.

Cato was beside her now. 'No! They'll lock us inside and we'll be trapped in here!'

Macro nodded. 'Cato's right. We'll be dead men if we're stuck in here when Caligula returns.'

Cato drew his sword. 'We should fight them now. We have a chance against them.'

'They'll kill us all!' Maddy cried.

'Better that,' said Macro, 'than Caligula finding us in his palace.'

'They are now directly outside,' said Bob.

The doors suddenly boomed and rattled under the impact of something. A shaft of light spilled in as the doors momentarily parted. Bob threw his weight against them both and they clattered shut again.

'There's no knowing how long we have,' said Cato. 'Fronto's lads are loyal to the emperor and their prefect, Quintus. They're following my orders for now because they think I'm loyal too. But they catch a glimpse of what's gone on here . . . Do you understand? They're our men until they realize they're being fooled.' Cato shook his head. 'We have to find whatever contraption it is you need to put things right and we have to leave this place quickly.'

Bob's voice rumbled out of the gloom. 'He is correct, Maddy. We are trapped in here. This is not tactically advisable.'

'All right . . .' Maddy panted in the dark. 'All right . . . OK . . . we'll – ahh Jeeesus, this is freakin' crazy! So, I guess, what? We're gonna fight them?!'

'Your Stone Man, Macro and I . . . I say we have a chance.'

'Wait!'

The voice came from out of the dark. She heard the slap of bare feet approaching. 'Wait! I . . . know . . . this . . .' His voice was weak and brittle, the words slurred and almost incomprehensible.

'The word!' he croaked. 'The word! There's a word . . . I know it! There's a word!'

They didn't have time for this. 'Does everyone have a w-weapon?' Maddy whimpered nervously. 'Oh God, I can't believe we're doing this. We're going to die!'

'The word!!' cried the old man. 'I . . . I have the wo-o-o-o-ord!'

'Stand back, old man,' barked Macro, readying the sword in his hands.

'On three,' said Cato to Bob. 'You open those doors on three. Is that clear?'

'Affirmative.'

'Get back, Sal,' whispered Maddy, holding the hilt of a knife in trembling hands.

'Shadd-yah! Maddy? What? We're *letting them in*?'

'One . . . two . . . and . . . *three*!'

Bob pulled both doors inwards, stepping backwards into the room as the dancing light of oil lamps outside spilled in to meet them. He pulled the sword from his belt. The two Stone Men charged into the room, side by side – not a single microsecond wasted in offering a challenge.

'*S-s-s-s-SPONGEBUBBA!*' screamed the old man, an insane, wild, banshee scream that peeled round the darkness like the cry of some nocturnal forest creature.

The units instantly froze.

They dropped their swords and shields at their feet; a deafening clatter and rasp of metal on ceramic. Their heads dipped in unison, their eyes slowly closed as they straightened their posture, arms dropped to their sides, and they planted their feet heel by heel: soldiers standing to attention.

Ten, twenty seconds passed, the silence filled with a chorus of panting breath.

'What are they doing?' gasped Maddy.

Presently both units raised their heads and opened their eyes, gazed quite neutrally, almost benignly, at them.

'Diagnostic mode reinitialized,' they both calmly announced. 'Please state your username and password.'

CHAPTER 68

AD 54, Imperial Palace, Rome

Centurion Fronto heard the impatient clatter of hooves; nonetheless his *optio* called out the obvious. 'Horses, sir!'

'I can hear them.' He stepped towards the iron gate and looked out on to the Vicus Patricius. An hour earlier there had been several hundred citizens gathered out there, pleading to be let in, begging for food and water. No rough-talking plebeians these, but the better-off citizens, well-to-do merchants, friends and hangers-on of the court.

They'd been there grasping the iron bars and rocking the gate menacingly. He'd had to muster several sections of his century to form up inside the palace compound, open the gates and present an advancing shield wall to flush them away. They'd dispersed eventually, but not before a few of them had felt the probing tip of a gladius between their ribs.

Since then, it had been relatively quiet outside. Little but the occasional shout and scream echoed from back streets and across rooftops, the faint rasp and clang of blades here and there as *collegia* and neighbourhood militias fought each other.

He looked through the iron bars and saw a column of cavalry making their way hastily up the Vicus Patricius towards them. For a moment he wasn't sure if it was an advance party of scouts from Lepidus's legions or their own Praetorian cavalry squadron.

'Septimus? Can you make them out?'

The *optio* squinted. The sun was approaching the skyline of roofs and terraces; the men on horseback were a jiggling, silhouetted mass of helmet plumes, oval shields and the bucking heads of horses.

'Not sure, sir.'

But as they drew closer, Fronto caught a flash of purple tunic. His heart sank. Imperial purple. *They're ours.* That didn't bode well. If those had been red tunics, they'd be horsemen from the Tenth and Eleventh. It would mean Lepidus had won and Caligula was finished.

The column of horsemen drew up outside the gates and a decurion dismounted quickly, striding towards the gates. Fronto ordered the gates open and went outside to meet him. The young officer stopped and saluted him.

Fronto acknowledged the junior officer. 'Make your report. What's happened?'

'Sir!' The young man gasped for breath. Clearly he and his men had ridden hard. 'General Lepidus . . . has been beaten, sir!'

Fronto nodded, forced a grin on to his face. 'That *is* good news. And the general?'

'He's dead, sir.'

Fronto struggled to contain a sigh of relief. Dead, at least Lepidus wasn't going to be able to tell Caligula anything. Name any names. Hopefully he'd done the honourable thing and taken his own life before he could be captured alive.

'Sir! I have orders from the prefect.'

'Yes?'

The decurion seemed hesitant.

'Come on, what is it?'

'Your tribune . . . Tribune Cato.'

'What about him?'

'I have orders for his immediate arrest, sir.'

'What?'

'You are to arrest him immediately. The prefect . . . the *emperor himself* . . . wants him taken alive, sir!'

Fronto stroked his chin. His mind racing. 'My tribune? My commanding officer? He's . . . you're telling me he's *a traitor*?'

'Just have those orders, sir.'

'Right.' He nodded. 'Right, I . . . I'll have to . . .'

'He's to be taken *alive*.'

'Yes . . . yes, I understand. I'll have to . . .' He turned hesitantly to look at his men, watching from inside the open gate. All of this was out of their earshot. He could see an expectant look on their faces, eager to hear whatever news the messenger had just brought.

'Wait here, Decurion. I'll see to his arrest personally.'

'Yes, sir.'

Fronto turned on his heel and strode smartly back to his men. He picked out his *optio* and spoke in a lowered voice. 'Close the gates!'

'Sir?'

'Those men outside?' Fronto thumbed over his shoulder. 'They're traitors. They've turned against the emperor.'

The *optio*'s eyes widened. So did those of the other men close enough to hear.

'They're a part of General Lepidus's plot. They are *not* to be admitted into the imperial compound under any circumstances! Do you understand?'

'Yes, sir!'

Further down the avenue he could see another couple of *turmae* of cavalry arriving. A single squad – a *turma* – accompanying a messenger was quite normal. But others arriving? He wondered if Praefectus Quintus had despatched the *entire* cavalry wing.

'Close the gates!' the *optio* barked to his men. Several men dropped their shields and worked the iron gates closed.

The decurion called out something. Confused.

'TAKE ANOTHER STEP FORWARD AND YOU'LL GET A JAVELIN!' roared Fronto through the bars.

The decurion stopped in his tracks. 'What's going on?'

'Septimus!'

'Sir?'

'Send someone into the palace to find the tribune. Tell him we've got company out here.'

'Yes, sir!' The *optio* turned sharply and picked one of his men to take the message.

Fronto watched the decurion standing outside in the avenue, shrugging with bewilderment at the gate being closed on him. Fronto wondered how long he was going to maintain this confusion among his own men. Sooner or later they were going to question his orders.

'Lads!' he barked so that they could all hear. 'Those men outside have turned *against* our emperor! They are traitors! The emperor was *victorious* this morning . . . and our boys are already on the road back to Rome! We must protect the palace until then!'

His men eyed him uncertainly.

'No one is to enter!' roared Fronto. 'Not a single man . . . until our emperor returns! Until our emperor approaches up that avenue! Is this clear!'

His men chorused a 'Yes, sir.'

'Good!'

He looked through the bars at the decurion. The young man had caught most of what he'd just bellowed. His eyes met Fronto's and he shook his head gravely; he was perfectly clear on what the situation was now. That it wasn't just Tribune Cato who was to be taken alive. The decurion shook his head again. It said more than a mouthful of words could convey, a warning from one officer to another.

You are a stupid fool . . . sir.

CHAPTER 69

AD 54, Imperial Palace, Rome

Maddy and the others listened to the poor old wretch gabble. His cracked lips opened sores as they moved frantically; a trickle of blood and spittle rolled from his lips and into his thick, mucus-encrusted beard.

'. . . I *hacked* them . . . I . . . you see I . . . they were . . . reset to take his orders . . .'

'Slow down,' said Maddy. 'Please. Slow down. You're not making sense.'

'. . . chief technical officer . . . me . . . .m-me! See? . . . I was in charge! Exodus! *Exodus!*'

'Exodus?'

'P-project . . . the project. Exodus . . . I was chief t-technical officer.' The old man squatted down on the cool floor, his painfully malnourished body already exhausted from the rush of excitement.

Cato crouched down beside them. 'Ask him if he was one of the Visitors.'

'Oh, I think he must be,' replied Maddy.

'R-Rashim . . . m-my name . . . it . . . it's Rashim!' he replied in broken Latin. 'Yes! I . . . I was one of them! I w-was there! I was THERE!'

Sal came over to join them. 'I've bound Liam up and . . . Jahulla!' Her eyes took in the ruined facsimile of a human being, tucked into a foetal huddle on the floor. She stifled a gasp. 'Who is that?'

'We think he's one of the Visitors,' Maddy whispered in reply. She turned back to the man. 'What happened to you?' she asked. 'What happened to the others?'

Rashim's wild eyes danced from Cato to her. 'B-betrayed! My fault . . . oh my G-God it . . . it w-was all my fault I . . . I j-just wanted to . . . I never thought that . . . I . . . *Oh God!* OhGodOhGodOhGod –'

Maddy touched his hand, held it to calm him down. 'Shhh. It's OK, it's OK. You're safe now. We're going to get you out of here.'

'No . . . m-must listen. Y-you must listen to m-me now!' He snatched his hand from her. 'Time! Not m-much time! It . . . it . . . it h-happens *soon*!'

'What does?'

'Tell me . . . tell m-me the day! What is . . . the *day*? *WHATIS-THEDAY?*'

'Date? Is that what you want? You want the precise date?'

Rashim's head nodded vigorously. '*TELL M-ME!*' His thin voice was almost a childlike scream.

Maddy looked at Bob.

'Information: today's date in the Roman calendar is twenty-nine Sextilis, in the Twentieth Year of Gaius. In the contemporary calendar that would be twenty-ninth August AD 54.'

Rashim's eyes rolled, showing the whites, and his eyelids drooped down, almost closing. His cracked and bloody lips fluttered silently, counting, calculating.

'What is it?' asked Maddy. 'Rashim? *Rashim* – is that your name? What are you doing?'

He raised a bony finger tipped with a long claw-like nail to shush her, his lips still silently twitching and leaking bloody spittle into his beard.

'Rashim? What's up? What're you doing? Are you counting? Is that it?'

'*NO-O-O-O!*' Rashim bellowed suddenly. 'No-no-no-no ... too soon, too soon, *too soon*. *TOO SOON!*'

Cato grasped Maddy's arm roughly. 'Tell me! What is he saying?'

Too many things, too much hitting her at once. Maddy was ready to scream along with this crazy scarecrow of a man on the floor beside her.

'Rashim! What? Tell me, *what* is too soon?'

His eyes locked on her. 'I am c-coming!! I will be here!!!'

'What are you talking about?'

'B-beacons ... *BEACONS*! L-light, to show the way! ... I ... I came ... I came years b-before! I w-was here! To show the way!!'

She shook her head. That meant nothing to her. It was complete gibberish.

'R ... r-receivers ...' Rashim continued. 'I p-placed th-them. T-t-tachyon b-beacons —'

Maddy looked up quickly at Bob; his inert face flickered with a reaction.

'Rashim, did you just say *tachyon*?' asked Maddy. He was burbling nonsense again, the half-whisper of a deranged mind. She grabbed his shoulders firmly. 'Rashim! You said the word *tachyon*! You're talking about time travel! Yes?'

He nodded frantically. 'Yes ... yes! M-markers! S-signals.'

'Madelaine.' Bob hunkered down beside her. 'This could be an alternate time-displacement method. Marking out a locked location, a time-stamp.'

Rashim's face lit up hearing that, his deranged whispering

brushed aside in an instant. 'Yes . . . y-yes! Understand?' He grinned manically, looking at Bob then Maddy. 'T-time travel! Exactly! We came through . . . all those, all those years . . . but I came through *before* the others. See? Yes. It was me. I had to set it up, you understand?'

'You placed out . . . what, some kind of time-stamp markers?' asked Maddy. 'Beacons? Is that what you're saying?'

'Yes! Y-yes! Then we a-all came through. We *all* came through! *Exodus!*'

'*Exodus?* What is that? Is that the name of your . . . your group or something?' She recalled a name stamped on the side of the first-aid pack. *Project Exodus.*

'Project Exodus?'

'P-project! Yes!' He huffed air into his lungs. 'We came . . . the future is *dead*! We came back. We c-came back here! That . . . that is – was – m-my project. My project. My project!'

They heard the gravel-rasp of Macro's voice, an exchange of voices outside the temple in the short passageway. A moment later, he was standing in the pooling light of the doorway.

'Cato . . . we've got some company.'

'Lepidus?'

Macro shook his head slowly. 'No such luck.'

Cato cursed. He looked at Maddy. 'Caligula's on his way back. We may not have much time left.'

'Can you buy us some more time?'

He gestured at the piles of dust-covered technology. 'So, can we *use* these things?'

Maddy shrugged. 'Maybe. Maybe there's a way out of here. I just . . . I . . .'

Cato nodded. 'I'll do what I can.' He got up and headed to the doorway.

They watched him go until Bob broke the silence. 'It is possible Rashim may have been part of an advance party that arrived in this time to deploy markers in order to plot out a safe arrival area for a much larger group.'

Rashim nodded. 'But . . . calculations, I . . . made mistakes. So many m-mistakes.' He shook his head, eyes leaking tears on to his scab-encrusted cheeks. 'Too many new p-people. They made me guess. *I had to guess!*' His eyes darted wildly in their sunken sockets. 'You . . . can't just . . . guess. This . . . has to be precise. Time t-translation, you *MUST* be precise! You understand? *PRECISE!*'

Maddy nodded. 'Oh yes . . . I know that.'

'I-I . . . I got it wrong. W-we lost half of them.'

'Lost? Do you mean in *chaos space*?'

Rashim stilled. '. . . chaos? Chaos?' He worked the word round his mouth. 'Chaos . . . yes. Or Hell? Hmmm? Hell?' He licked his dry, cracked lips, shook his head and began to giggle manically. 'This is my Hell . . . my Hell, my Hell, my hidey-hole Hell. My hidey-hole Hell. Me and Mr Muzzy. Mr Muzzy and me –'

'Rashim!' She shook him by the shoulders. 'Rashim, come on, stay with us!'

His face steadied; the insane smile slid off his lips and vanished into his beard. 'I lost them in chaos. Lost s-souls now.'

'You said half of them. What about everyone else? What about the rest of you? You came here, right?'

Rashim laughed again. Bitterly. 'Arrived . . . seven . . . seventeen years too early.' Strings of blood-tinted spittle hung from his lower lip. 'Wrong time . . . wrong time . . . wrong Caesar.'

'Bob . . .' said Maddy. 'I'm just trying to figure this out. He's saying he made a hash-up of things and his group what? *Overshot* these time-stamp markers?'

'Correct. That is what I believe he is saying. They went back seventeen years earlier than intended.'

She looked at him. 'And that happened about seventeen years ago? That's when "the Visitors" supposedly arrived?'

'Affirmative.'

She shook Rashim from his manic reverie. 'Rashim! Is that what you're saying? Your deployment team are going to appear sometime *soon*? Appear to place out those beacons?'

He nodded. '*He* knows too.'

'He? Who?'

'*God.*' Rashim chuckled.

'God?' Bob looked confused.

'Right,' said Sal dismissively. 'He's a nut.' She looked at the others. 'And we're *listening* to him?'

'No, wait!' said Maddy. 'He's talking about Caligula, aren't you, Rashim?'

'I told him . . . it was this year . . . this summer . . . I told him.'

'Oh my God! You actually told him about your advance party appearing? About there being a portal?'

Rashim nodded. 'He . . . his . . . his doorway to Heaven.'

Maddy looked at Bob. 'Could we use it? Could we use this portal to get home?'

'I have no information. This must be a time-displacement technique developed after my inception date. After the agency's database was set up.'

'But it's got to be similar . . . the same basic technology, right?'

'Correct.'

'If it's a beacon . . . could we use it to communicate forward to computer-Bob?'

Bob nodded. 'Theoretically. The only way to transmit data is a tachyon transmission.'

The big question was whether computer-Bob was still in one piece, capable of receiving anything.

'Rashim . . . you said it's soon. A few moments ago you said

362

"soon". You were talking about the advance party appearing, right?'

He offered her an appalling gummy smile. 'Too soon . . . too soon,' he replied in a sing-song voice. 'Three days.'

'Three days' time?'

Rashim nodded.

'Do you know where? Can you tell us exactly where?'

He was mumbling to himself in that unhinged, sing-song way.

'Rashim!'

'I know . . . I remember . . .' He tapped his skull of tatty, wiry hair. 'All in here. Don't worry, me and Mr Muzzy know.'

Sal cocked an eyebrow at her.

CHAPTER 70

AD 54, Imperial Palace, Rome

Cato strode down the dimly lit main passageway towards the front portico.

'I said . . . they're not *actually* from Britain.'

Macro looked at him. 'They're not?'

'No . . . the place they come from is . . .' Cato made a face. 'I'm still struggling to make sense of it myself, as it happens. The place they come from is the future.'

'The future?'

'Yes, the very same place as the Visitors. Time ahead of us.'

Macro frowned as his mind worked on that. 'Years yet to be?'

Cato nodded. 'But from a place more than a thousand years yet to be.'

He expected his old friend to struggle with that concept. Instead, he nodded casually. 'Well, that explains quite a lot, then.'

'Macro, I don't understand what's going on with that prisoner we found. They're talking about something. Perhaps they're discussing some of the Visitors' devices. Perhaps their chariot. I don't know. But all I do know is we have got to find a way to give them some more time.'

'Cato, there's you and me, your centurion, Fronto, and that giant of a man back inside.'

'Bob.'

'Yes, *Bob* . . . strange name. Anyway, I'm not sure how long the four of us can hold back the entire Praetorian Guard, Cato. That's a fool's errand.'

'We have Fronto's men. That's enough men right there to hold the front gate for a while if it comes to a fight.'

'That's if they'll fight on our side.'

'True.'

They strode through the entrance portico. Cato nodded at the section of men stationed there. They carried on down several steps outside into the courtyard. He could see Fronto's men across the courtyard drawn up in an arc round the iron gates. Through the iron bars he could see a body of troops outside. Dismounted *equites*. Cavalry on foot acting for the moment, very reluctantly, as infantry.

He picked out Fronto and approached him. 'Centurion!'

'Sir!'

'What's going on here?'

Fronto nodded to the decurion still standing outside the gates. Beyond him Cato could see in the failing light of the late afternoon what looked like two or three hundred men and their horses. Still more of them in the distance, a column on horseback trotting up the avenue.

'This traitor, sir!' Fronto barked loud enough for his men to hear him clearly. 'Wishes to loot the emperor's palace.'

'I see.'

The decurion caught Fronto's reply above the noise of his own men assembling in ranks behind him. 'That's not true! I have orders from the prefect!' The decurion looked at Cato. 'Orders for your arrest.'

'It's common practice in the Roman army to address a senior officer as *sir*, Decurion.'

'Open the gates immediately!' the decurion snapped as

Fronto's men lined up behind their shield wall. 'This tribune is to be arrested for treachery!'

Macro snarled angrily and took several steps towards the gate. He grabbed the iron rails in his hands. 'This tribune is your superior officer!'

The decurion offered him a patronizing smile. 'And you? What are you, you fat old man? Nothing. Not even a soldier.'

Macro ground his teeth then spat through the bars. 'I could still take you on . . . boy.'

The officer ignored him. 'You will open the gates immediately or you will ALL be treated as traitors and punished accordingly!'

'Lads!' Cato turned to face his men. 'Those men outside the gate . . . have become deserters! Mercenaries! They're here to fill their pockets and then flee the city before our emperor returns! It is our sacred duty to hold this gate!'

'He's lying!'

'Quiet!' snapped Macro, smacking his fist against the bars of the gate.

'Men!' Cato shouted. His voice was never going to match the parade-ground roar of Macro or Fronto, but it carried the authority of rank and experience. 'The emperor has entrusted this cohort and this particular century to guard his home. He favours us. He trusts us. If we allow those men outside,' he laughed, 'those horse-maidens to come in . . .'

The men shared his amusement. There was little love lost between any legion's foot soldiers and its squadron of cavalry. *Equites* who considered themselves a class above the rest.

'. . . then we are breaking his trust and disobeying a direct imperial order!'

The decurion sighed, shook his head. 'Right . . . have it your own way.'

Cato joined Macro beside the gate. They watched as the young officer turned away from them and headed back to rejoin his men.

Fronto joined the pair of them. 'Well done, sir,' he said quietly. 'Some of my lads were looking a bit twitchy for a moment there.'

'This stand-off's only going to last until someone turns up with a higher rank or a written order,' said Cato. 'Then those men will turn us over.'

'Maybe not . . . they're good boys all in.' Fronto shot a glance at the anxious faces of his men, eyes glinting in the shadow of their helmets, eyes on their centurion. 'They're a loyal bunch.'

'Loyal enough to be branded traitors alongside us?' replied Cato. 'To face Caligula's wrath?'

The centurion pursed his lips, not entirely sure of his answer.

'Like I say . . . this stand-off's going to be over the moment we get a higher rank out there.'

'Stand-off?' Macro sucked air through his gap-teeth. 'It looks like we're up for a bit of a scrap if you ask me. Look.'

Cato followed the direction he'd nodded in and saw a cart being rolled forward through the assembled ranks. It was stacked high and heavy with sacks of animal manure, pushed by several dozen men and beginning to roll under its own momentum.

He reached up and tightened the strap on his helmet. 'I think you might be right there, Macro.'

CHAPTER 71

AD 54, Imperial Palace, Rome

The front rank of dismounted *equites* sidestepped to allow the trundling cart through. Its large iron-rimmed wheels clattered noisily across the paving stones of the square before the palace's north-east gate.

'That's coming right through,' grunted Macro.

Cato nodded. The iron gates were more decorative than they were utilitarian; the cart was going to knock them right off their hinges without any trouble at all.

'Fronto, form up your men closer to the gate.' He pointed to stone posts either side, and the eight-foot wall that continued all the way round the Imperial Palace. 'Once they've barged those gates open we can hold them in that bottleneck for a while.'

'Right you are, sir.'

Fronto advanced his men to within twelve feet of the gates, ready to press forward into the open space the moment the cart was pulled back to allow the *equites* in.

'Where do you want me, Cato?' asked Macro.

Cato smiled. 'Where you feel most at home.'

'In the thick of it, then.' Macro flashed a dark grin at him. 'Like old times, eh, lad?'

'Like old times.'

The cart outside had found the gentlest incline and now was

rolling freely towards the iron gates, shedding several sacks as it bounced and vibrated across the flagstones.

'Steady, lads!' bellowed Fronto.

Cato watched Macro shoulder his way in among the front rank of the centurion's men. 'Come on, ladies, make a hole!' he heard his friend growl at them.

Like old times.

Cato remembered his first skirmish in the army. He was just a boy only a couple of weeks into basic training; Macro, on the other hand, had been little different from the way he was now: short and stocky, an impenetrable wall of foul-mouthed confidence. He remembered that first skirmish, being petrified beyond belief, but somehow, even in the middle of the clash of arms and the screams of the dying, knowing that standing right beside his centurion, right beside Macro . . . he was safe. That he'd always be safe. As if a cloak of invincibility surrounded that cantankerous old man.

'Here it comes, boys!' shouted Macro. 'Who's up for teaching these horse-girls how to fight?' The men either side of him roared with nervous laughter.

Cato grinned as he stood beside Fronto. 'You'll have to excuse him.'

'You once served under him?'

Cato nodded. 'Oh yes . . . and he was just as bad then.'

The cart closed the final few yards and crashed into the iron gates, knocking the left gate so hard its hinges exploded from the stone pillar in a shower of dust. The gate collapsed inwards and they heard a roar from the Praetorian cavalrymen outside.

A moment later, the cart lurched as men behind it began to work it back, clear of the tangle of bent and crimped iron bars. The other gate, hanging from just one twisted hinge, clattered over on to the ground and, caught up on the cart's axle, was dragged away as the cart was pulled clear of the gateway.

'Advance!' ordered Fronto.

The front rank, sixteen men wide, advanced behind their presented shield wall. One step at a time they approached until they finally filled the gap between the stone pillars.

Cato spotted the decurion now joined by a cluster of several others still mounted. He saw the plume of another ranking officer trotting through the kicked-up dust and haze outside. The *praefectus alae* . . . commanding officer of the Guard's entire cavalry wing.

He cursed. The last thing he needed was that officer talking round Fronto's men. Better that the talking was all done and the fighting had begun. He decided to hasten things along.

'Fronto . . . let's give them an opening volley.'

The centurion nodded, and barked an order for his men to ready-and-release on his command. The men, two ranks of sixteen, all took a step backwards, javelins drawn back in their right hands.

'RELEASE!'

The modest volley arced through the air across thirty yards and picked out no more than a dozen victims. Not enough to make any sort of a difference, but enough to ensure the time for parlaying was over. The *equites*, many of them foreigners from across the empire – Batavians, Sarmatians, expert horsemen, but certainly no match for legionaries on foot – began to advance on the gateway in a ragged, loosely formed line, short spears protruding between their shields, a line of light oval shields designed for dextrous horseback melee, not closed formations. Spears instead of their swords . . . another cavalry habit. They were used to wielding a weapon with *reach*.

Cato pointed that out and Fronto nodded. 'Idiots haven't got a clue how to fight on foot.'

A moment later, the gap between them was closed and the

clatter and ring of blades on shields and spear tips on armour began to fill the ominous stillness that had descended over the smoke-shrouded city.

CHAPTER 72

AD 54, Imperial Palace, Rome

'We have to get out of Rome!' said Maddy. 'I mean, like, *now*!'

Bob nodded. 'That must be our mission priority.'

She joined Sal and Liam beside the doorway and hunkered down beside them. 'How is he?'

'It stings like hell,' Liam winced. 'Burns.'

'He's not bleeding any more.' Sal pointed at the bandage wrapped round Liam's waist. 'I don't think any veins or whatever were cut.'

'What about internal bleeding?'

Sal shrugged. 'I don't know what to look for.'

Nor did Maddy; it was just a phrase she'd heard often enough on hospital dramas. 'Right, well, when we get him back home, we'll get him looked at by someone.'

'Get back home?' Liam laughed sarcastically. 'Good luck with that.'

'We're *going* to find a way out of Rome. There is a way home. A window . . . a return window, and we're going to try and use it. OK?'

The other two nodded.

Bob brought Rashim out, supporting an emaciated elbow in one large hand. He blinked and grimaced at the modest light of several flickering oil lamps.

Maddy had a thought. 'Rashim? Could we use that hover-vehicle thing back in there?'

He shook his head, shading his eyes and wincing. 'Uh-uh . . . a big d-dead dragon now. Yes, it is.'

She shook her head. She didn't have time for his wittering madness. 'What the hell does that mean?'

'Information,' said Bob. 'The vehicle is hydrogen cell powered. The cells will have needed maintenance. They will not be any good to us now.'

'Rashim?' He was muttering to himself again. She grabbed his arm. 'Rashim! Where this portal is . . . is it close enough that we can get there in time on foot?'

He hunched his narrow shoulders. 'Time flies . . . time flies . . . tick tock, tick tock . . .'

'We're wasting our time with him,' said Sal.

'He knows where to go, Sal. We need him.' Maddy pushed a loose tangle of hair out of her blinking eyes. 'And we've got to escape this palace, the city somehow.'

'Cato . . . he can help us,' she replied. 'He knows this palace.'

'Where did he go? Did you see which way?'

'I think he's outside, at the front of the palace with all the other soldiers.' It was then that they heard it, the faint sound of metallic ringing and raised voices. Maddy and Sal looked at each other. 'Is that someone fighting?' said Sal.

Maddy cocked her head to listen for a moment. 'I think it is.'

'Then we're too late, aren't we? We're trapped!' She looked up at Maddy. 'Jahulla! We are, aren't we?'

Liam winced. Opened his eyes. 'No way I'm getting stuck in here!'

'We'll have to find a way out,' said Maddy. 'Can you move, Liam?'

'I'm sure as eggs not bleedin' staying!' He tried to sit up, groaning as he held his side. 'Ahhh! Ow! Ouch!!! It bleedin' well stings!'

'Bob, you carry Liam. Me and Sal, we'll help the old guy,' she said, nodding at Rashim.

'Which way are we going?' asked Sal.

'Let's try and find Cato. Maybe he can help us.'

A moment later, they pushed the hanging drape aside and emerged from the concealed passage and stepped into the main hallway, Liam groaning, carried piggyback, his arms wrapped round Bob's neck. Rashim shuffled between Maddy and Sal, giggling and warbling gibberish to himself.

'That way,' said Maddy, nodding to the left, towards the increasing sounds of battle.

They made their way down towards the entrance portico.

Closer, Maddy caught the flickering of glinting armour bathed in the blood-red light of sunset. 'What's going on up there?'

They arrived inside the high-ceilinged portico to find it swamped with wounded men bleeding out on the marble floor. Through the archway, down the steps, she could see the Palace Guard were drawn up in three lines along the bottom of the steps.

The courtyard was filling with other soldiers.

She caught a glimpse of Cato's horse-hair crest among the men, organizing the defensive lines across the steps. She pushed her way through the mass of men and finally stood beside him.

'What's going on? Who are they?'

'Caligula's Praetorian cavalry. All the damned alae. Five hundred of them.' He looked at her. 'Did you find what you were looking for?'

She nodded. 'Look, Cato . . . we need to talk.'

'Well, as you can see, I'm a bit busy right now.'

'There's a way we can fix all this . . . make it not happen! Please . . . we need to talk. I'll explain.'

Cato looked out at the *equites*. They were flooding into the gardens. They'd managed to push his men back from the gateway through sheer weight of numbers. This was their next best bottleneck to try and hold – the portico. But it was all but over for them now anyway. They were into the palace compound now. There were other entrances to the palace buildings. Soon enough they were going to be overwhelmed.

The portico was going to be a last stand for them. Plain and simple.

Cato grabbed Macro's arm. 'Macro!'

'Yes?'

'Give me a few moments. I need to talk to our friends. Quickly!'

Macro's brow cocked. 'Can they weave some kind of magic for us?'

He shrugged. 'That's what I'm hoping.' He nodded at the remnants of Fronto's century. The centurion had gone down five minutes earlier. The thrust of a cavalry spear to his throat. He'd gone down thrashing angrily with his sword, managing to at least catch and give a life-long scar to the man who'd killed him.

'They're all yours, Macro.'

He nodded. 'Right you are.' The men exchanged a salute then Macro turned and started bellowing a barrage of coarse language over the heads of the few dozen men drawn up on the steps.

Maddy led Cato back inside, into the portico where Liam, Sal, Bob and Rashim were standing. They stepped through a carpet of the writhing wounded to join them.

She pointed at Rashim. 'OK . . . he knows a place where a time window will open.'

'A time window?' Cato's eyes narrowed. 'That's a device that lets you travel through –?'

'Through time, yes. Exactly. And this window opens in three days.'

He shook his head. 'We're not going to last three more hours . . . let alone –'

'It's somewhere outside Rome.'

'You wish to find a way out? Escape?'

Maddy nodded.

'And what? We're to stay here and die?'

She had no answer to that. She spread her hands. 'Look, it's very hard to explain . . . but if we can travel home, we can change history back to how it should be. So this never happens.'

Bob stepped forward. He'd been listening to their hasty exchange. 'Information: Emperor Caligula's reign lasts only four years. He is assassinated in AD 41 by officers of the Praetorian Guard, and his uncle, Tiberius Claudius Caesar, is made emperor in his place.'

Cato made a face. 'Claudius? That stuttering cretin couldn't lead a beggar to coins.'

'He will be a very successful ruler. During his reign, Britain is successfully conquered and added as a province to the empire. So are Thrace, Lycia and Judaea. He is known for ruling fairly and –'

'Not now, Bob.' She placed a hand over his mouth. 'Point is the last seventeen years should have been very different. Everything that's happened since the Visitors arrived . . . it's all wrong. Them arriving here is what made it go wrong. It changed history from what it should have been.'

Cato studied them both silently for a moment. 'You can make all of this happen?'

'Yes!' replied Maddy. 'But only if we can get back home.'

Cato pinched his nose thoughtfully.

'Can you get us out . . . somehow?'

'I'm thinking.'

CHAPTER 73

AD 54, Imperial Palace, Rome

Macro finished threading the loops of leather through the fastenings and tightened up the *lorica segmentata* round his thick torso. It was snug, but he nodded with satisfaction that his portly gut could still be contained by the one-size-fits-all segmented armour.

'All right, lads!' he barked as he put on a helmet. 'Those girls across the garden are probably more frightened of you than you are of them!'

A grim cackle of laughter rippled among the men.

'Without their horses, they're just a rabble of rank amateurs. So let's not worry about 'em too much, eh?'

The red stain of twilight bathed the gardens with their stone pathways and small bushes, young olive trees and the decorative scattering of bodies. The evening was strangely quiet and still. After the last fifteen minutes of fighting, the clash of arms and the roar of raised voices, the silence seemed almost complete.

But Macro heard a low murmur of voices, from men still outside the imperial compound. A low murmur rolling forwards and spreading across the men inside like a wave riding up a shingle beach.

What's going on out there?

Then he saw movement, over between the stone columns of the gateway, several men on horseback picking their way through the men filing in. All of them roaring support as they suddenly recognized the men on horseback.

Macro cursed as he realized who they were.

Caligula and the Praetorians' prefect, Quintus.

'Cato!' He turned round and looked up the steps. 'What are you up to?' he muttered under his breath.

The *equites* on the far side of the gardens roared with glee at the sight of their emperor and *praefectus*. Macro watched as they dismounted and disappeared among the mass of men, only to appear a few moments later as the front rank of soldiers parted respectfully to let them through.

Caligula walked slowly towards them, flanked by two of his Stone Men. Quintus had dropped back a dutiful three steps behind.

A dozen yards away he stopped, raised his hands to quieten the *equites* behind him. An obedient hush swiftly settled across the gardens.

'I wonder now . . . what are you lot doing in my home?' He looked around at the grounds, littered with bodies, the shafts of javelins poking out of the dirt. Divots of displaced soil and trampled flowerbeds.

'What an awful mess you've made!' He sighed. 'On any other day, I'd be quite annoyed. But today . . . today has been a very good day. Soon – very soon now – something truly wonderful is going to happen. I will transform from a man to a god! And Rome will be showered with riches once more. Today . . . I defeated the last few men who doubted me. Two legions of fools, commanded by their foolish general . . . wiped out.'

'Praetorians!' He took a step closer. 'My good men,' he said with hands spread. 'I hear you have done your duty well, defended my home against those you thought had come to ransack it. For that I thank you all . . . and I *forgive you*.'

Macro took a step back from his line of men, climbed the half-dozen steps up to the portico entrance. He saw Cato deep in conversation with the others.

'But I'm afraid you have been misled . . . tricked,' continued Caligula. 'Tricked by officers who were in league with General Lepidus. Conspirators, fellow disbelievers, traitor—'

Macro put two fingers in his mouth and whistled. Cato looked up. Caligula paused and an expression of irritation at the rude interruption flashed across his face. The three ranks of sweating, grim-faced and blood-spattered soldiers on the steps swivelled their heads to look up at Macro.

An entire battlefield frozen in a moment, silent, and every pair of eyes on him.

Macro shrugged then grinned. 'Load of bollocks!' he roared loudly.

It sounded like a breeze rustling through the small orchard of baby olive trees. But in fact, it was a ripple of gasps spreading among the men on both sides.

'You're not going to be a god. You're just an idiot!'

That rustling breeze again. Followed by a silence. He could see the 'o's of mouths open, aghast, in every direction.

Stuff this.

He spotted an unused javelin on the floor nearby. And in one swift movement bent down, picked it up and hurled it towards Caligula. It arced lazily through the air, every pair of eyes on the seemingly endless trajectory of the wobbling wooden shaft and glinting iron tip until it dug into the dirt between Caligula's planted feet with a dull thud.

Caligula stared wide-eyed at the shaft as it wobbled in front of him. He reached out for the wooden shaft, pulled it free of the ground and then tossed the javelin to one side. His face split with a grin as he laughed with delight.

'Do you see now? No one can kill a god.'

Fronto's men began to stir and fidget unhappily.

Macro backed up across the entrance portico towards the others, nearly tripping over and losing his footing on the legs of one of the dying.

'A full pardon for all you men!' cried out Caligula. 'And a thousand sestertii for the one who brings me that man's head!'

'I think we'd better run!' rasped Macro.

Cato nodded. 'I think you're right.'

Together they turned and headed back into the dimly lit halls of the palace as some of the quicker-witted Praetorian Guards began to climb the steps in hungry pursuit of their bounty.

CHAPTER 74

AD 54, Imperial Palace, Rome

Cato led them all back down the palace's main hallway. They passed by the secret passageway they'd emerged from five minutes earlier.

'Where are we going?' called out Maddy.

'There's a slaves and merchants' entrance on the far side of the palace. If we're lucky, that idiot, Quintus, won't have thought to block it off yet.'

'He's not exactly the sharpest arrow in the quiver,' said Macro, puffing as they jogged.

'Which is the main reason Caligula appointed him,' Cato added. 'If we're quick, the section of Fronto's men I posted there won't yet know there's a bounty on our heads.'

The hallway ended at the grand atrium and, as they emerged into it, they saw on the far side a dozen soldiers emerging from the hallway opposite. Not men of Fronto's century but *equites*.

'On the emperor's orders, you there! . . . Stay where you are!' echoed a voice.

Cato hissed a curse. 'Too late!'

'We're going back!' cried Rashim. 'Back to my cage!'

'Be quiet!' grunted Macro as they reversed into the flickering, lamp-lit gloom of the main passageway again.

'This isn't good,' said Maddy. 'We're going to be trapped!'

'My cage!' trilled Rashim. 'Going back! Yes! My cage! My Stone –'

'I said *be quiet*,' Macro snapped, raising a threatening fist.

'The Stone Men!' said Maddy. 'He's right! Rashim . . . he could *reboot* them!'

The word didn't translate well for her and Macro offered her a puzzled glare. 'Put some boots on them? What the –?'

She tried again. 'Reactivate them! *Awaken* them!'

Cato nodded. 'Yes . . .' He turned to Rashim. 'Can you do this? Make them take your orders?'

'Oh yes, yes . . . I can make magic work!'

Cato pointed his sword back the way they'd come. 'Then back! Back there quickly!'

They turned. Cato grasped Rashim's painfully thin wrist and dragged him along as he jogged ahead with Macro. Bob bounded after them, Liam bouncing and groaning on his huge back. The girls kept pace either side, looking anxiously back over their shoulders at the clatter and jangle of armour and harnesses and the slap of pursuing nailed army sandals on the stone floor.

'Here! It's this one!' shouted Sal suddenly. 'This one!!'

She stepped towards the drape, pulled it aside to reveal the concealed passageway. They stepped in just as some more voices challenged them from further up the main hallway.

'IN! IN! IN!' screamed Rashim.

They stepped through the opened oak doors into the darkness inside. Bob placed Liam down on the floor, retrieved the locking bar from outside and brought it in. Then he quickly pushed the heavy doors to. He slid the locking bar across both sets of looped handles on the inside. The doors were secure for the moment.

A candle still flickered beside Rashim's opened cage and by

its light they saw the Stone Men, standing where they'd been left, calmly watching the commotion going on around them.

Rashim shuffled over to the nearest of them, out of breath and struggling to keep on his bow legs and arched feet. Sal hurried over and held an arm before he collapsed.

'Thank you . . .' he whispered. He turned to the Stone Man in front of him.

'You are . . . you are in full diagnostic m-mode? Yes?'

'Affirmative. All systems are nominal.'

Cato whispered to Macro in the dark. 'I've only ever heard their leader talk,' he said. 'And only on one occasion.'

'They sound like devils,' Macro growled suspiciously.

'I . . . I wish to talk to you.' Rashim's voice seemed to have settled. A lower, calmer timbre; a less manic delivery. 'What is your current . . . mission status?'

'I have no stated mission.'

'That's very good. And tell me, who was your last authorized user?'

'Temporary-User Gaius Julius Caesar Augustus Germanicus. Also known as Caligula.'

'Your . . . your last registered user is no longer authorized to issue you commands. Is . . . is that understood?'

The clone nodded. 'You will need to provide me with a system password before I accept that as a command protocol.'

'Of course. Of course.' Rashim frowned for a moment. Long enough that Maddy felt her heart sink. *He's forgotten*. Perhaps not surprising given that his hacking of these support units happened so many years ago.

'Ahh . . . yes!' Rashim slapped his head several times. '. . . I . . . I have it. I have it!'

'Please state your password,' the Stone Man calmly repeated.

'The pass . . . the password is *Patrick Starfish*?'

384

The Stone Man's eyes glinted by candlelight as his head slowly swivelled down to regard Rashim. 'Your password is correct and accepted.'

'I am your user now,' muttered Rashim.

The clone nodded. 'That is correct.'

'And these people are my . . . *friends*. Protect them.'

It looked up from Rashim at the others, a smooth, cool sweep of machine-like eyes. 'Affirmative.'

Rashim giggled. Pleased with himself. 'Transmit your updated status and accepted password to your friend . . . over there.' It nodded and began blinking rapidly. A moment later, the other Stone Man stirred to life and swept the chamber with its gaze.

Rashim turned to look at the others and spread a gummy smile. 'Our friends now. Yes indeed.'

The oak doors suddenly rattled under the impact of something outside; the locking bar jumped as a vertical thread of light from outside appeared momentarily between them.

'They've found us,' said Bob.

Maddy looked at him then the others. 'Well, that's just fantastic . . . now we really are trapped!'

CHAPTER 75

AD 54, Imperial Palace, Rome

'NO!' shouted Rashim. He pointed to the ground. Dropped down to his knees and spread his fingers on the floor, caressing the stone almost tenderly. 'Below . . . I hear it whisper . . . every night! My ocean . . . in my world!'

Cato looked at Maddy. 'What is that mad fool saying now?'

She shook her head. He was talking in English. Gibberish. Might as well have been in Mongolian.

Rashim rolled his eyes with frustration. 'Water, you fools! Dripping water!' And again in Latin for Cato and Macro's benefit.

'Of course!' Cato dropped down to his knees. 'Running water!' He looked up. 'A network of sewers beneath the palace! Somewhere beneath this floor . . . we just need to dig –'

'Dig?' Macro shrugged. 'With what?'

The oak doors boomed and rattled again, more insistently this time. 'They are using a battering ram,' said Bob. 'These doors will not last for long.'

Cato pulled his gladius from its sheath and dug the tip of the blade into the hairline seam between the stone tiles. With a soft crack, the clay cementing the tile gave up its hold and the tile dislodged with a puff of dust and grit. 'Come on, Macro! Help me!'

Macro produced his sword, knelt down and did likewise, both of them gouging at the floor frantically.

'Help them!' said Rashim, pointing. 'Dig . . . dig us a hole!'

Both Stone Men chorused an 'affirmative', produced their own blades and joined in hacking into the tiles.

The doors boomed again, accompanied by the sound of cracking wood. Bob braced his back against the doors, supporting the locking bar with his own substantial weight. 'We will not have long,' he cautioned.

Maddy looked at Liam. 'How are you doing?'

He grinned. 'Not so bad. Getting used to the sting now.'

'That's good,' she whispered and smiled. 'We're getting out of here, you know.'

Cato dug frantically at the dried clay floor beneath the dislodged tiles, his sword gouging out fist-sized chunks, rust-red and crumbly. The four of them quickly had a crater three foot across and several uneven inches deep. He cursed under his breath. 'How deep do we have to dig?'

'Water . . . down there!' hissed Rashim. 'Beneath our feet, yes? I hear it every night!'

Sal picked up a candle and headed towards the piles of dusty equipment.

'Where you going, Sal?' called out Maddy.

She pointed at the piles of artefacts on the floor. 'Maybe there's something we can use from over there?'

'Sure, uh . . . OK, go look.'

The chamber filled again with the sound of a deep boom and the crack of surrendering oak; hairline fissures of light stretched up and down each door.

'You must dig faster,' suggested Bob.

Cato peered down at the rust-coloured clay. His sword tip was hitting and sparking on stone again. Another layer. By the flickering candle nearby he could see little. Desperately he scrabbled with his fingers, feeling for another seam to wedge the tip of his blade into.

Sal squatted down next to the pile of things. Her hands pulled at the threads and edges of half-seen things: clothes, shoes, glasses, boots . . . a child's toy, the dark and cracked touch-screen of a long-dead holo-data pad. But nothing remotely useful.

Come on . . . come on!

The cavernous chamber boomed again.

She thrust her hand deeper into the piles of things, fumbling, patting, pulling, feeling for something that might help them. Her index finger caught in something and wrenched painfully as she struggled to twist her finger free.

It scraped out of something. A hole. She pulled clothes and boots aside until she found herself staring at a small iron grille in the floor. She could hear it, coming up through the grille, the unmistakable soft trickle of water.

That's what Rashim had heard. That's where the noise had been coming from!

'Over here!' she cried. 'Over here! There's a grille!'

The men looked up from their digging, a moment's hesitation – no more. Not a clue between them as to what she was saying. She wished she had one of those buds. 'Shadd-yah, Maddy! Tell them! There's like a sewage grating or something! Right here!'

Maddy did, and both Romans were out of their shallow crater and beside her moments later.

Once again Cato used the tip of his sword and levered the iron grille out of the floor. Macro helped him, grunting as, between them, they slid it to one side.

'That's it,' said Cato, leaning over the small hole and peering down into the darkness. The faintest reflection of candlelight glinted back at him. The foul smell of rancid effluent was overpowering.

'Oh, that's it all right,' said Macro, curling his lips in disgust.

The doors boomed again and this time a strip of oak from the left-hand door clattered on to the tiled floor.

Cato picked out the shape of Maddy near the doors, a comforting arm around Liam. 'You! You two, come here!'

Maddy helped Liam to his feet and they both came over.

'This sewage aqueduct, you have to follow the direction of the flow!' said Cato. 'It leads to the river.'

She nodded. 'OK.'

'You should go now.' He glanced at the doors. 'They'll be through soon enough.'

Maddy nodded. She turned to Sal. 'Can you help Rashim down?'

'Right.'

Sal lowered herself down through the hole in the floor. 'I can't feel the bottom. I think it's a drop.'

Maddy peered through a gap to the side of her, until she caught the flicker of reflected candlelight. 'I don't think it's far.'

'Here goes, then.' Sal lowered herself down until her arms were fully extended then let go. Maddy heard the echo of a viscous, muddy *splut*.

'It's OK, not far.' Her voice reverberated as if it was at the far end of an underpass. 'Ughh! But it's total chuddah!'

Maddy grabbed Rashim's hand. 'You next.'

Another deafening boom and more fragments of splintered wood clattered to the floor. Thick shafts of light speared into the darkness, and she could see the glint of helmets through the fractured doors.

Liam pulled himself painfully up to a seated position.

'Liam? You OK to . . .?'

'I'm fine, Mads . . . I'm OK. I can get myself down.'

'Your friend . . . then you, Maddy and your Stone Man,' said Cato. 'But hurry!'

'What about you?'

Cato glanced at Macro. Macro returned a subtle nod. An unspoken understanding between the pair of them. 'We need to cover over the sewage trap. And perhaps we can buy you some time.'

She looked from one to the other. 'They'll kill you!'

'Of course they will,' Cato smiled. 'But then, as you said, you can make it so this never happened? Am I correct?'

She nodded. 'Yes, but . . .'

'Then you should go. Now. Give us both a better end than this one.'

Rashim was down. Liam eased himself into the hole, groaning with pain as his arms worked and his torso flexed.

Boom. The cavernous room echoed with Bob's deep, angry roar as he thrust his sword through the jagged hole in the left-hand door and there was a yelp of agony from outside.

They heard the echo of a muddy splat and Liam's voice groaning at the impact.

'Bob!' cried Maddy. 'We're leaving! Get here now!'

'I must remain by these doors!'

Cato stood up and approached the Stone Men. 'Will you two take my orders?'

'Affirmative,' they both replied. 'You are to be protected.'

'Then kill anyone who comes through.'

Both clones drew swords from their sheaths and crossed the floor to stand in front of the shuddering, flexing oak doors.

Bob nodded at them as he passed by. 'Good luck,' he offered. They paused to look at each other briefly, both clones bemused by such an oddly human gesture of compassion from another support unit. Then they took up their positions before the fragmenting remains of the oak doors, legs apart, a two-handed grip on their swords, braced to kill.

'Go!' said Maddy, slapping Bob on the shoulder as he squatted down beside her.

'You first, Madelaine. I will guard the rear.'

Cato seemed to understand Bob's intent. 'He is right. Let him be the rearguard.'

She was about to drop down through the hole, but hesitated. She leaned over and kissed Cato on the cheek. 'I'll make things right . . . I promise you that!' Then she grasped Macro's forearm. 'I'll make it right.'

'Go!' said Macro. He grinned. 'Go on . . . don't worry, we've been in tighter spots than this.'

She lowered herself down into the sewer and landed with a splat. Bob quickly followed her down, squeezing, *barely*, through the hole in the floor.

Both Cato and Macro reached for the iron grating and eased it back into place as a final crash against the doors sent them juddering open. The clones stepped forward together into the light of flickering torches and braziers and engaged the Praetorians stepping across the splinters of wood and twisted iron bracing.

Cato picked up his sword as Macro pulled the rotting and dusty artefacts across to cover the manhole.

'Is that the truth, Cato? They can change this?'

He bent down and picked up a shield from the floor. 'Perhaps.'

Macro pursed his lips as he gave that a moment's consideration and finally nodded. 'Good enough for me.'

'That's what I've always liked about you, Macro.'

'What's that?'

'You never overthink things.'

Macro laughed. The two clones were doing a lethal job so

far, holding the doorway and filling it with a growing pile of squirming bodies.

'I hope our *other* fate sees us both as old men,' Cato grinned. 'Old and rich. How does that sound?'

Macro flexed his arms, sword in one, shield in the other. 'I always figured we'd go out like this, you and me.'

Cato smiled at his old friend. 'Ever the optimist. Shall we?'

He shrugged. 'No point standing here gossiping like a pair of old fishwives.'

CHAPTER 76

AD 54, outside Rome

They emerged into the night. No shining light at the end of the tunnel, just the darkness of full night, the stars and moon lost behind clouds and a pall of smoke from the many fires across the city.

They took several steps down a delta of silt and sewage into the cool water of the River Tiber to wash the muck off. Rashim shuffled over, savoured the cool tickle of water on his skin, cupped it in his hands and drank and drank.

'Eww . . . I wouldn't drink from here,' whispered Maddy, watching him.

'Liam? You OK?' asked Sal.

He was holding his side, wincing with pain. 'I'll hold together . . . I think.'

Maddy washed her hands clean and waded over to him. She pulled her glasses out from beneath her tunic. The arms were bent. She fiddled with them for a moment then put them on crookedly. 'Let's take a look.'

'You won't be able to see a thing in this light,' replied Liam.

She reached out to his side. 'Is it bleeding?'

'It's OK, I think.' He touched the tight binding Macro had fastened round him. 'It's dry.' It burned painfully – literally *burned* – but it seemed his exertions hadn't opened the wound.

'Macro did a good job,' said Liam. He looked up at her, an

expression on his face that told her what she already knew. He'd grown rather fond of the ex-soldier.

Maddy nodded. *Me too*. Between gasps back in the tunnel she'd explained that the pair of them had decided to stay behind and cover their escape.

'We owe them,' she said sombrely. She looked around at the city, dotted with the flickering light of fires. 'We'll fix this for them. I promised them that.'

'Aye. Then we'll make sure we do it.'

'No time for this!' said Rashim. 'No time! We must leave Rome now! Aye, skippa! Yes, indeed!'

Sal nodded. 'I'd really like to leave now.'

Maddy looked up and down the river. To their right a bridge running across stone arched supports. To their left, further along, a rickety-looking bridge made from wood.

'Which bridge?'

'Neither,' said Rashim. 'We follow . . . see?' He pointed along the bank of silt to their left. 'Takes us round the bottom of the city, then we go . . .' He frowned as he thought, tapped his temple with his knuckles as if to shake loose a memory.

'Are you *sure* you know where this portal's opening?'

'Yes! Yes!! . . . We go north-east from Rome . . . for some hours.'

'Can you be more precise than that?'

Rashim tapped away at his scabby temple. 'In here . . . all in my head! Let me . . . let me get it out!'

'Information.' Bob lifted his head. 'If we are within several miles of the correct location, I may be able to detect tachyon particles.'

'As it opens . . . yes,' said Maddy, 'but if it opens for just a couple of minutes and we're a mile or two away, we'll miss it!' She turned to Rashim. 'We need the *precise* location. We need to be in exactly the right place!'

'So long ago . . .' Rashim muttered. He closed his eyes. 'I . . . I remember coming along a road into the east of Rome.'

Bob's eyelids flickered, accessing his database. 'The Via Praenestina?'

'Yes! Long road! A big archway! A . . . a market!'

'Go back. Remember it backwards,' said Maddy. 'Before entering Rome . . .?'

'Can we go now?' said Sal, looking back at the sewage outlet they'd emerged from. 'Can he remember and walk at the same time?'

Maddy followed Sal's gaze. If Caligula's soldiers had figured out they'd escaped through the sewage outlet, it surely wasn't going to be long before they saw the faint flicker of torches emerging.

'She's right. Let's get going.'

CHAPTER 77

AD 54, outside Rome

Dawn saw them on a dusty track flanked by rolling fields of parched soil and withered wheat stalks on one side and an orchard of fig trees on the other. Rashim's weak bow legs had long ago failed him and now he was fast asleep on Bob's broad shoulders.

Sal walked beside him in thoughtful silence, occasionally sharing a word or two with Bob, but mostly lost in her own thoughts.

Liam walked beside Maddy, still holding his side protectively. There was a slight limp to his walk as he favoured his right leg with a longer stride.

'You're made of tougher stuff than I've given you credit for,' said Maddy.

'Ahh, I may not be whinging like a little girly-girl, but that doesn't mean to say it isn't hurting me like there's a pitchfork stuck in me sides.'

'Liam.' She looked at him. 'You took a sword in the gut!'

He shrugged at that. 'I took a glancing blow. Looked a lot worse than it was, I'll wager.'

She wondered. In the heat of the moment of that fight, she'd actually thought that it was all over for Liam. That he was going to hit the floor dying. Liam was right — a glancing blow. If it had skewered him, like she at first thought it had . . . that surely

396

would have meant a ruptured spleen or stomach or kidney or liver, leaking all manner of toxic acids into his blood. A painful, agonizing way to go. Certain death for sure.

'You're incredible, Liam,' she said, hugging his narrow shoulders gently.

'Incredible, yes,' he winced, 'but not a bleedin' Stone Man.'

'Sorry.'

He shrugged. 'Maddy?'

'Yes?'

'When we return . . .' he said, 'we're going to be walking into trouble, are we not?'

'I don't know. I don't even know if we can get back to our field office. It might not even be functioning any more.'

Sal overheard them. 'What if we went back to whenever these Exodus people came from?'

'I don't even know when that is.'

'It'll be *after* 2001, surely,' said Liam.

'Well, obviously.'

'The Exodus Project occurs after 2056,' said Bob.

'How do you know?'

'The Stone Men were running AI software that is a later generation than mine.'

'2056?' Liam turned to Maddy. 'Is that *when* our agency came from?'

'That's a safe-ish guess, I suppose.'

'What about it?' asked Sal. 'What if we go into the future?'

'Why, Sal? You know better than me and Liam what it's like. It's grim.'

Liam nodded. 'That man who came through to Robin Hood times . . .' He tried to remember his name. '*Locke* . . . I think it was. I remember he said something about hearing rumours of our agency in the 2060s, so. He said it was bad then. Really bad.' Liam met her gaze. 'Sort of end-of-the-world kind of bad.'

The end. Words that were all too familiar to Maddy.

Maddy stopped walking. 'Guys . . . that message in the Voynich Manuscript. You know Becks has it in her head. All decoded and everything?'

Liam and Sal stopped walking and turned round. 'What about it?' said Sal.

'You know I said Becks couldn't tell me what it was?'

They both nodded.

'Well actually, Becks told me she could only tell me what the message was when certain conditions arose.'

'What *certain conditions*?' asked Sal.

'She said "when it's the end".'

'The end?' Liam laughed scornfully. 'Great! What's that supposed to mean?'

'I dunno,' Maddy shrugged. 'But I get the feeling we're all headed for something pretty nasty.'

'We?'

'Everyone! I'm talking, like, *mankind*.'

Liam made a face. 'Well, that's cheered me up no end, so it has.'

'See . . . I think something awful happens one day. Something that wipes us all out. That's what I think Pandora is. It's a warning about that.'

'That poor man . . .' said Sal. The other two knew who she meant: that unfortunate soul who'd arrived out of nowhere back in New Orleans, 1831. An arrival that had been catastrophic, that had inadvertently caused the death of a young man called Abraham Lincoln. He'd arrived presumably without properly probing and checking his destination. He'd arrived in a hurry . . . presumably leaving his own time in a hurry. Arrived and instantly fused with the bodies of a pair of horses.

'That man was the one who was warning us about Pandora,' said Sal.

'Joseph . . .' Liam looked at her. 'That's what he said his name was, didn't he?'

'Yeah. He was the one that left you that note, Maddy.'

'Yes.' She sighed. 'Yup . . . I know.' She shook her head. 'But what do we do? Huh? So we've got a warning from some guy from the future that something awful happens to mankind. What the hell was he trying to tell us? Change history so it – whatever *it* is – doesn't happen?'

Sal nodded slowly. 'I think so.'

'But we've also got a duty to make sure history *doesn't* change,' said Liam. 'That's what Foster told us. Remember? *For good or bad . . . history has to go a certain way.*'

'My point exactly,' said Maddy. 'I just don't know what we're supposed to do any more, Liam. And now we've got whole freakin' platoons of support units being sent back to kill us. So, obviously we're making somebody angry. Doing something wrong!'

'Or something *right*?' volunteered Sal.

Maddy rolled her eyes. 'See? Welcome to *my* world. The world of Not-Having-A-Freakin'-Clue-What's-Going-On.'

They stood silent, in the middle of the road, the rising sun making hard shadows that stretched long and slender across the cobbles.

'I'll tell you what I think,' said Liam after a while. 'I trust Foster. He said we should keep history as it is. For good or bad it has to go a certain way. Well . . . if that means that one day there's an end,' Liam pressed his lips together – a conciliatory smile, 'then, well . . . I suppose it is what it is.'

'We're *just following orders*,' said Maddy.

'Aye.'

'You know who said the very same thing?' Maddy didn't wait for him to pull out an answer. He wasn't going to know. 'Nazis, that's who. Concentration camp guards.'

'So, what are you saying we do, Maddy?'

She turned to Sal. 'I'm saying I don't know. I just don't feel like trusting anyone right now.'

Liam nodded at that. 'Let's just get home, then?'

'Let's get home. If we can. And then we'll figure it out from there.'

CHAPTER 78

AD 54, outside Rome

Rashim had mentioned that the Exodus group had travelled most of the one-hour journey on a broad brick road. Winding the memory backwards, he said that it eventually became a broad dusty track. Two lanes, busy with cart and foot traffic. The old man had said it had taken them an hour . . . but they had travelled quite slowly because their multi-terrain vehicles were heavily laden: people crammed in below, equipment stacked all over. Slow, then. Not much faster than a person could jog. His words. Hardly precise.

But he did mention a range of hills. Nothing too spectacular, hills that would be on their right coming out of Rome. And one hill beyond a gently rolling valley with a notably flat top.

As it approached midday, Maddy scanned the horizon. There were hills ahead of them, as he'd said. And beyond their smooth outline, on the far horizon, the more distinctly sharp-edged silhouette of a range of mountains.

'Rashim!' she called out.

He twitched slightly on Bob's back.

'Give him a prod, Sal.'

She obliged.

He lurched, opened his eyes then howled at the bright daylight. His eyes instantly clamped shut. *'What is this?* Where am —!?'

'It's OK! It's OK!' Sal reached up to calm him. 'We escaped, remember?'

The old man winced and covered his face with his hands at the glare of daylight, or perhaps it was some sort of agoraphobia – a mortal terror of the infinite openness all around him. Maddy wondered how much of her sanity would be left if she'd spent seventeen years cooped up inside a large packing crate.

'Rashim, over there . . . those hills? Are they the right ones?'

Bob eased him down to the ground and he shaded his almost completely shut eyes against the painful brilliance of the morning sun. 'I . . . think . . . yes. Or maybe . . . I'm not sure.'

'Come on! We need to be sure.'

His face looked pained as he studied the rolling line of hills to the right of the dirt road. Then his eyes widened as he spotted the flat-topped hill. 'That one! There! You see it! Yes!'

Maddy followed the direction of his claw-nailed finger. The hills followed each other in almost symmetrical humps, some topped with villas, spilling hair-thin threads of smoke into the morning sky. But the one with the flat top was distinctive, as if a cheese-slice had scooped its crown off.

'You sure?'

'Yes! *Y-yes!*' His eyes narrowed, his mouth widened with a manic grin. 'Needed a flat place! Big . . . open . . . flat! Yes? An open place to mark out! Yes! Me and SpongeBubba!'

'SpongeBubba?'

Rashim ignored her. 'That's it! That's it! That's the place!' His eyes were wet with tears. 'I never thought . . . I . . . I . . .'

'And how long have we got?'

'He said three days last night,' said Bob. 'Which would mean we have two days now.'

Maddy wiped sweat from her eyes and squinted through scratched glasses at the distant hill. It wasn't that much of a hike for them. An hour at most. Then, once they were certain they had the precise location, they desperately needed to find something to drink. Even spoiled water would do. Anything. She'd worry about disease some other time – when they got back home.

'Are you sure Caligula doesn't know where to come?' asked Sal.

Maddy bit her lip. 'Does he know, Rashim? Does he know where your people arrived?'

Rashim smiled. 'Stories . . . and stories. Mr Muzzy and me –'

'Rashim! Does he know?'

He cocked his head. 'We . . . kept secrets. We told . . . stories . . . we –'

'I'd take that as a no,' said Sal.

Maddy reached out and grabbed Rashim's thin arm. 'But he knows it's sometime soon? Doesn't he?'

Rashim nodded.

'And by now he'll know you're missing.' Maddy frowned. 'He'll be looking for you, won't he? Does he know the Exodus people travelled in from the north-east?'

Rashim closed his eyes. 'The day the Visitors came . . . in chariots of gold . . .' His sing-song reverie wandered off into gibberish again.

'There is only one main road into Rome from that direction,' said Bob. 'It is this one.'

'Then let's get off of it!' Maddy scanned the road in both directions. It was deserted, except for a pale speck kicking up dust a mile away. A solitary cart or trader. Hopefully. Or perhaps a Praetorian scout – one of many sent in every direction, along every road out of Rome, looking for them. She didn't want to waste another moment finding out.

'Come on,' she said, pointing towards the flat-topped hill.

She could see there were trees around the base of it, even though it was a bald hill on top. They could hide somewhere in there for a day or two; wait it out until Rashim's advance party were supposed to arrive.

'Let's go.'

CHAPTER 79

AD 54, outside Rome

'Dry wood, that's the secret,' said Liam. 'If it's totally dried out, like charcoal, you don't get any smoke at all.'

Maddy gazed at the fire. It was barely visible in the daylight. A few wisps of smoke from the cones and branches they'd thrown on, turning grey as transparent flames consumed them and the air above danced with the heat. There was, of course, the pleasant, always welcoming smell of a fire. It would carry, but no one was going to see where it was coming from. Certainly not from that road they'd left earlier.

She raised a hand to her eyes, and peered through the gently wafting evergreen branches of cypress trees at the road, two or three miles away. The weather was so dry this summer, anybody using it would kick up a plume of dust. She could see nothing.

Sizzling on a wooden spit were several wild hares Bob had caught for them, skinned from neck to lean shanks and naked except for furry heads and furry booties. Normally she'd be queasy at eating an animal she could recognize, but her mouth was salivating at the smell of them cooking, the savoury tang of crisping meat.

Rashim sat hunched over beside the fire, drooling at the glistening meat, chuckling at the sound of fat spitting into the fire.

Maddy glanced out once again through the branches of the hillside wood at the distant road. 'I think we're safe now.' They'd seen a party of cavalry thundering along an hour ago, leaving dust trails behind them. From this distance they could have been anyone, but they'd seemed to have a purposeful, disciplined look about them.

Rashim had laughed gleefully as they'd passed by. Laughing that Caligula was going to miss his precious 'rendezvous with Heaven'. They'd seen no one else since then, though. She looked at him curled over beside the fire. She studied the pitiful skeleton of a man. Malnutrition and complete darkness for so many years: she wondered how a human body could cope with that.

Downhill, through the trees, she could hear the faint splash of water. Bob and Sal were rinsing their tunics in a small brook. Clean water. Drinkable water, not like the rancid Tiber. They'd bring some back when they were done.

Maddy wandered over to where Liam sat, perched on a boulder that afforded him a view down the side of the hill. 'I guess we ought to get some air to your wound.' She nodded at the bandage tied firmly round his waist. There were a few spots of dark, dried blood that had soaked through. The wound must have opened while they were fleeing the palace, wading through sewage. Actually, as soon as they got back home, they were probably going to have to pump Liam so full of antibiotics he was going to rattle like a pill bottle.

Liam shrugged. 'All right. Just be gentle with me now, Mads.'

'Oh, *tsk-tsk*. Don't be such a baby.' She worked the bandage loose. 'I'll be careful.'

He winced as she unravelled the material. 'Sorry. Hurts?'

'Naw, not exactly. A little tender . . . just —' he looked anxiously at her — 'just worried this is the only thing holding me together.' He laughed edgily. Not entirely joking.

'Oh, I think you'll mend.' She smiled. There was something about Liam that felt indestructible. Maybe it was that stupid lopsided grin of his. Maybe God really did exist and spent his full shift every day looking after devil-may-care idiots like him.

'Ouch! Go easy!'

'Sorry.'

Even though she could see traces of ageing in his face, the silver flecks in his hair, that plume of grey hair at his temple . . . somehow she couldn't quite imagine him as Foster yet. As that poor, frail, dying old man. Or perhaps maybe she just didn't want to.

He should know.

'Here we go,' she said. The last layer was still damp. Blood that was not quite dry. She eased the material away from his skin, stuck to it as if by glue.

'More slowly, please,' he whimpered nervously.

'Sorry, sorry, sorry.' She grimaced as his pale skin tugged at her soft pull.

She eased the last of it away and realized, as she looked at the puckered line of his wound, there was never going to be the *perfect* time to tell him . . . just *a* time. Too many secrets had already got in the way of them as a team, as friends. This was the last of them. She looked across at Rashim, muttering like Gollum as he sat on his haunches and studied the glistening meat.

'Liam?'

'Aye . . . how is it?'

'Liam . . . you're dying.'

'What? It's just a cut –'

'No, Liam, listen . . . time travel, it's actually killing you.'

He frowned. 'What the devil are you going on about now?'

'Foster told me. Going back in time, it ages you. It accelerates the ageing process.'

That silenced him.

She pointed at his temple. 'Liam, come on, you must have noticed –'

'Of course I have. I'm not blind.' He took the bandage out of her hands and began winding it back round himself. 'I'm not stupid either.'

'Liam. I –'

'It's killing me.' He sighed. 'I know that.'

'You know?'

He paused then nodded. 'I suspected as much.' He busied himself winding the bandage again. 'When we came back from the Cretaceous time. Edward Chan, that girl, Laura? I think I guessed it then that time travel made them sick.'

Maddy nodded. 'They both took a lethal hit. It's a bit like radiation poisoning – there's no recovery. It does its damage and there's no way back from it.'

'That doesn't sound so good.'

'No, not good.' She heard something in her voice she didn't need right now. 'Here, let me help you.' She took the bandage back off him and finished the job with a knot. 'I'm so sorry, Liam. I'm so very sorry. I should've told you as soon as I knew.'

She expected anger. Instead, she got a smile out of him. A heartbreaking one; the wistful, moist-eyed sort that old war veterans give on Patriot's Day.

'Liam?'

'I got some extra time, Maddy. That's a bleedin' gift, so it is.'

Oh God, Liam, why can't you just be angry with me? That would have been easier to cope with.

'And I've already seen so many incredible things with that time.' He grinned. 'I'm up on the deal. What's to be all down about there, eh?'

'There's something else.'

'What?'

'Liam . . . you're Foster.'

'Uh?'

'You are Foster.'

He laughed. 'I'm not as cantankerous as that old –'

'No. Liam . . . I'm saying you *are* Foster. You're the *same* person.'

For the second time in as many minutes she'd managed to shut him up.

'I don't know how that is. I don't know how it works that you two are the same person; it's just what Foster told me.' She was struggling to explain it. 'Maybe it's something to do with the loop we live in. Maybe we've all been here before and we don't remember it. Maybe history and us, we're on some big wheel that just goes round and round. I don't know. All I know is what Foster told me.'

'Right . . .' Liam's eyes were on Rashim's sunken, tortured body, folds of skin drooping from bones that seemed to almost poke through in places. 'Right . . .'

'There are no more secrets now, Liam. That's it. You know everything I know.'

He looked down at the hands in his lap. 'Old man hands,' he whispered. 'That's what me mam always said I had. All knobbly knuckles.'

'Liam . . .?' She rested a hand lightly on his arm. 'Liam . . . I don't know exactly what it means that you and Foster are the same, but it's something important. Important to all three of us. We have to think it through. We need to talk it through. When we get back, we'll do that. The three of us, we'll –'

She could hear branches cracking, Bob and Sal's voices. They were returning from the brook.

He nodded. 'OK.'

Just then they emerged from beneath the shade of a tree with a cracked clay jug in Bob's arms. 'We found this!' said Sal. 'So Bob's humped some water up for you.'

'About time,' croaked Liam. He even managed that stupid goofy grin for the pair of them.

'We should eat,' said Maddy.

Rashim nodded. 'Yes, eat! Eat!'

'Aye! I'm bleedin' starvin'! We was just about to start on them coneys without you, so we were.' He looked at Maddy. 'Right?'

She could have wrapped her arms round him then and there, squeezed him blue just for Liam being Liam.

'Yeah.'

CHAPTER 80

AD 54, outside Rome

'Are you absolutely *positive* it was today?'

Rashim nodded, although not as vigorously or as confidently as Sal would have liked. 'Today, yes, of course, of course, *of course* it is! . . . I remember!' he muttered irritably.

They sat in a line in the shade of a row of bushes looking out across the flat top of the hill. Wild parched grass and heather swayed gently in the light breeze. They'd been sitting here in the shade as the day had warmed up, gradually sweltering, cooking in their own sweat as the morning passed interminably slowly and the sun beat down on the arid countryside.

Sal sighed. She wasn't so sure this mad old fool was going to be their ticket home. He was too *skittish*. Too unhinged. Too completely weird and schizo to seem reliable. She looked at his lean face, all ridges and old scars; his wiry grey hair in tangled tufts, bald patches here and there like an attack of alopecia. Worst of all, his mouth: rotten gums and brown stumps of dead teeth. His breath was almost unbearable – like decaying meat.

She wondered how old he was. Seventy? Eighty? It was almost impossible to guess. But then, as Maddy had eloquently pointed out last night, seventeen years spent in a wooden box was going to 'mess anyone up pretty good'.

'Midday. Midday. Oh yes! Yes! It was about midday,' Rashim muttered to himself.

But then again he'd said last night they'd arrived first thing in the morning, which was why they'd been sitting here like a row of gullible morons since daybreak.

'Maddy?'

'Uh-huh?'

'If we do manage to get back to the archway, what if those "Bobs" who were after us are still there? You know? *Waiting* for us.'

'We'll just have to be ready to fight them.' Maddy closed her eyes. 'There were two of them left, weren't there? A male and a female.'

'I think so.'

'Bob can handle the male . . . the rest of us –' she glanced at Liam – 'I'm sure between us we can handle the female one.' She shrugged. 'That's if we can even get back.'

'It may be possible that the tachyon beacons can be adapted to return a signal to our field office,' said Bob.

If they turn up. And frankly Sal was pretty sure today was going to pass by without incident, the four of them listening to this old loon muttering, '*Tomorrow* will be the day . . . of course it is . . . I remember now!'

And the next day. And the next.

'I don't want to be stuck here,' she said.

'I know,' sighed Maddy. 'None of us do.'

'It is coming soon,' said Rashim. 'I promise. Yes!' His rheumy old eyes took in the wild meadow. 'This is the place . . . for certain, yes.' A long slender finger pointed out at the swaying grass. 'Right there . . . me. That's the spot I arrive.'

Sal nodded, less than convinced. She wanted to say, 'Yeah. But what if you're a whole year out? Huh? What then, Mr Genius?' But she didn't. It wasn't going to help any. The mood was already pretty sombre out here. The other two, particularly

412

Liam, seemed unusually quiet and distracted. Normally they could count on him to fuel them all with a generous helping of unrealistic optimism. And if not that, to say something pretty stupid and make them laugh.

'Maybe I'll go and get us some more water,' she said.

No one answered. 'Liam? You thirsty?'

He seemed to be a million miles away.

'Maddy?'

She stirred as if she'd been poked. 'Uh?'

'Water? You want some?'

'Uh . . . er, yeah. OK, yes, that would be good.' She looked across and smiled. 'Be careful, 'kay? Remember to keep out of sight. Those scouts are out there.'

They'd seen a few more yesterday, in pairs, careering along distant tracks and roads, almost certainly looking for them.

Sal picked their cracked jug up, got to her feet and turned to head down the slope, through the trees to the babbling brook at the bottom of the hill. She decided she might just sit with her feet in the cool water for a while. And there were several fig trees down there. She could pick a few and bring them back for lunch. That might cheer this miserable lot up.

'Be back in a bit,' she said. Not that anyone seemed to hear her.

Sal ducked beneath the low branches, picking her way slowly downhill past the humps of tree roots that surfaced from the hard clay soil like the backs of writhing sea serpents.

'Wait, Saleena!' A deep voice.

She turned to see Bob crouching under the low, thorny branches to join her. 'Maddy sent me to watch you,' he said as he ducked past her and pushed his way through undergrowth and low pine needle branches.

'Oh, so I'm not the invisible girl today, then?'

Bob looked back at her. Puzzled. 'No. I see you quite clearly.'

She joined him. 'Bob, can I ask you something?'

'Of course.'

'I'm scared of those things . . . those other support units. Why –' she stepped over a gnarled root – 'why were they trying to kill us?'

'I have no information on their mission, Saleena.'

'You saw one of them, though, right? They looked exactly like you. Did they come from the same place as you? Are they like brothers and sisters or something?'

He stepped ahead and pushed the branches of a thick bush aside for her. She could see the glint of the stream below, a thread of silver curling its way through weather-worn boulders of flint and sandstone.

'The unit I saw appeared to be almost identical. Most likely from the same foetus batch. I registered his AI ident only briefly. His software was only one iteration newer than mine. Inception date 2057.'

'Hold on.' She run-stepped the last few yards down a steep bank and stopped herself against one of the boulders, blistering hot to the touch. 'Hold on,' she said again, 'you make it sound like the same people . . . the same *company* made you.'

Bob scuttled down, keeping an ungainly balance. 'Correct. The unit I encountered was also manufactured by W.G. Systems.'

'Who are they? W.G. Systems? They like a weapons manufacturer or something?'

Bob settled down on the hot stones beside the stream. 'I will fill your jug if you like.'

She handed it to him. 'Thanks.'

'They are one of the largest profitable organizations at the time of my inception. I have only common-source market information on them.'

414

'Well, that'll do.'

'The company was founded in 2048 by Roald Waldstein. The same year –'

'You mean the time travel inventor?'

'Correct. He filed a number of technology patents in the same year. In the space of less than six years, he becomes the third richest man in the world.'

'And he's the one that set us TimeRiders up, right?'

Bob shrugged. 'That is not information I have. I have, however, heard Maddy make that speculation.'

'Is she right, do you think?'

'This is possible. Waldstein campaigns *against* time travel. Waldstein also has access to the resources and technology to have set up this agency.'

'But you're saying it's also Waldstein's clones that were trying to kill us?'

'Affirmative.'

She settled down beside him, letting her feet drift in the cool water. 'So . . .' She frowned. 'Does that mean he wants us dead now? Why? If he went to all the trouble of *recruiting* me, Maddy and Liam . . . huh?'

'I do not have that information. It is possible they were units that were acquired and programmed by some other organization.'

That made more sense to her. 'I thought we were top secret, though. That no one else knows about us?'

'It is possible, Saleena, that you are *no longer* a secret agency. Remember, Liam mentioned that man *Locke*?'

'The Templar Knight?'

'Correct. If he is to be believed, there are people who are aware of the existence of this agency. Whether they actually know for cert–'

She looked up at him, momentarily frozen. 'Bob? Are you getting a . . .?'

'Particles. Yes.' He returned her gaze. 'It appears that Rashim was correct. Today is the day.'

CHAPTER 81

AD 54, outside Rome

Maddy and Liam watched the young man in silent dismay. Long dark hair pulled back into a ponytail, sunglasses, a checked shirt and jeans. She turned round to see Rashim, staring out, wide-eyed and trembling.

'My God! That's you?'

He nodded, his fingers absently probing the sunken contours of his old face.

'But he's so young!' whispered Liam.

'Yeah,' said Maddy, 'he . . . he looks, like, twenty-something?'

'Twenty-seven,' said Rashim wistfully. 'Twenty-seven.'

It didn't make sense to Maddy. Rashim said the Exodus group had overshot by seventeen years; that he'd been stuck here for just *seventeen years*. That made him just forty-four? She turned and studied his feeble frame again. Not old age, that wasn't why he looked like this . . . but abuse, malnutrition. Borderline starvation . . . and the sheer terror of being Caligula's caged pet.

'What's that yellow thing?' whispered Liam.

She saw something about a yard high, box-like, waddling through the tall grass behind the young man as he paced across the field, several metal rods under his arm.

'It looks like . . .' She giggled a little manically. 'No, surely . . .'

'What?'

Am I losing my freakin' mind? Is that what's happening?

417

'Maddy? You all right there?'

'Liam, it looks like . . .' She shook her head. 'It looks exactly like a stupid cartoon character I used to watch on cable.'

The old man's face split with a nostalgic gummy smile. '*SpongeBubba!*' he crooned softly. 'My little *SpongeBubba*!'

They watched as the young Rashim stopped pacing across the field, pulled one of the iron rods out from under his arm and rammed it into the hard-baked earth. He squatted down beside it, as the SpongeBob-like robot joined him. She saw him talking to it, listening as its goofy plastic mouth flexed an answer, and then fiddling with something on the rod – a touch-screen or a keypad. The top of the rod began to blink green, like a navigation light.

From behind she heard the careful placing of approaching feet. She turned to see Bob and Sal quietly creeping forward under the low branches of the bush to join them.

'Who's *that*?' hissed Sal.

'Him.' Liam nodded at the quivering older Rashim.

'And SpongeBob SquarePants,' added Maddy, not quite believing she was saying that.

'So what do we do, Maddy?' asked Liam.

'I guess one of us has to go out there and talk to him. Let's try not to totally freak him out, though. We don't want him to run away.' She looked at the others. Rashim looked like a wild, completely insane hermit. Bob, thoroughly intimidating, still spattered with dots of dried blood. And Liam and Sal were looking at her expectantly.

'I guess it's me, then.'

Rashim squatted down in front of the second translation array marker and wiped the sweat from his forehead with the cuff of his shirt. He was torn between getting this job done quickly, getting the hell back home to the twenty-first century . . . and taking the time to breathe in this clean air, to savour that rich blue sky untainted by pollutants. To take a moment and really drink in the sensation of actually existing in history; actually standing on a hilltop in Italy . . . a mere fifty-four years after the birth of Christ!

He was entirely alone out here. His decision. The less mass to transmit, the higher the safety margin. It was just him and his lab unit. A five-minute errand into ancient history to deploy and test the translation array markers. That's all.

He kept looking anxiously over his shoulder, for some reason half expecting an entire Roman legion to descend on him at any moment with horns blaring. Silly really, he noted, the clichés one associates with well-branded history.

'Give me the reference sequence again, will you? I need to check it offsets correctly.'

'Righto, skippa!' SpongeBubba said enthusiastically. 'The sequence is . . . are you ready, Rashim?'

'I'm ready. Fire away.'

'Nine. Zero. Seven. Two. Two. Three.'

Rashim tapped those into the rod's touch-screen. 'Go on.'

'Two. Nine. Seven . . .'

A pause. He looked at his lab unit. 'Yeah, I'm waiting . . . go on.'

'Uhhh . . . Rashim?'

'Yes?'

'There's a person coming towards us.'

'Uh?' Rashim stood up and saw a young woman in a burgundy-coloured tunic and with a mane of frizzy strawberry-blonde hair striding through the grass towards them. He cursed under his breath. They'd checked this hilltop hundreds of times over for passing density shifts. Apart from signals that might be the occasional bird, or a passing goat . . . no one came here. Ever. Until now apparently.

Dammit.

He'd learned a smattering of Latin – a requirement for all the Exodus candidates. He quickly removed his sunglasses before she got too close, wincing at the brightness of the day. The clothes and his bright-yellow lab unit he couldn't do anything about. As she drew up in front of him, he offered the young woman his most charming smile.

'Uh . . . *Salve.*' He was pretty sure he'd just mangled up the pronunciation right there.

And then, rather belatedly, he realized she was wearing glasses. 'Hey,' she replied with a casual wave. 'How's it going . . . Dr Rashim Anwar?'

Rashim's jaw swung open and hung there uselessly.

She offered him a hand. 'Yup, I speak English. And yup, I know precisely who you are. My name's Maddy by the way . . . pleased to meet you.'

'How . . . how . . . who . . .?'

'I know. You've got a lot of questions.' She smiled. 'Don't worry – I know exactly what that's like.'

He stared at her outstretched hand.

'I know all about Project Exodus, Dr Anwar. So look, I'll cut to the chase. I work for some people. We're . . . well, you won't have heard of us, but our job is preventing foolish things like this from happening.'

Rashim's mouth finally closed. 'You . . . you're from *that agency*, aren't you?'

She frowned. '*That* agency?'

'The freelancers! Rumours! Jesus! I've heard rumours. Not sure I ever believed them! But –'

'Rumours?'

'Yeah . . . about the agency. *The* agency. They say that billionaire nutcase Waldstein's involved in some way. Is . . . is it for real?'

Maddy shrugged. 'I can't say exactly who I —'

'My God, it is! Isn't it?' Rashim didn't know whether to be begging for an autograph from her, or running for his very life. International law on time travel was unforgiving. And very final.

'Jesus! I thought it was just *us*, you know? Just us with a viable time-translation system!' He laughed nervously. 'But how the hell . . .? I mean we've had trillions of defence budget dollars, *trillions*, thrown at this and we've only just managed to get the system reliable enough to risk *human* translations!'

She lowered her hand. 'Look. We really need to talk with you. Project Exodus is going to fail badly, Dr Anwar. I've seen the results for myself.'

'What? You . . . you've *pre-empted* us? You've arrived here before now?'

She nodded. 'You're going to miss this time-stamp by a mile. It's going to go badly wrong and you're all going to die. This project has to stop right here.'

She offered her hand again. 'Dr Anwar . . . *Rashim*, I'm not here to arrest you, or hurt you or threaten you. I'm just here to stop this nightmare happening. Can we talk?'

CHAPTER 82

AD 54, outside Rome

Dr Rashim Anwar looked at the old man, stick-thin arms wrapped round knees that bulged like arthritic knucklebones.

They were sitting together in the shade of the trees. He sipped ice-cold Protein-Plus solution from his cell-powered thermos flask, offered it to the young Indian girl beside him.

'He . . .?' he said, pointing at the old man. 'He's *me*?'

Maddy nodded. 'The Exodus group's translation overshoots those beacons you were putting out.'

'But . . . it shouldn't. They should anchor the particle signal. They should –'

'Mass,' the old Rashim hissed. 'Mass. We miscalculate . . . you and me. We get it wrong. Yes!'

The young man shook his head vehemently, his ponytail swinging like a pennant. 'No, I've calculated and recalculated the figures. Run simulation after simulation on the total mass we're planning to send.'

'It changes!'

'Changes?'

'The translation day is hurried f-forward . . . candidates *changed* . . . last-minute panic. It's a *mess*!' The old man muttered more, but it was lost in his gurgling throat.

'Why?'

The old man was muttering a one-sided conversation with

himself. The young scientist leaned forward and grabbed a stick-thin wrist. 'Tell me! Why is Exodus hurried forward? What happened?'

The old man's black and brown peg-tooth smile looked revolting. 'The end . . . young me!'

Maddy looked at him. 'Did you say "*the end*"?'

He cackled. A sad, dry laugh. 'We finally do it . . . wipe ourselves out.'

'What?'

'Kill the planet with drips of poison . . . then finally kill ourselves. Tidy finish, hmm?'

'What is it, bombs?' said Maddy. 'Is that "the end"? Is that what happens? A nuclear war?'

Rashim rocked gently on his haunches, distracted as he spoke. 'Oh no! Bombs some of us could survive. But this? No . . . no-no-no. No one survives this!'

'What is it?'

The old Rashim grinned. 'Elley! Elley! Elley!'

'Who's *Elley*?' asked Sal.

'He means an ELE. An Extinction Level Event,' replied Rashim. 'Like the K-T event wiped out the dinosaurs: an aster-oid.' The young man shrugged. 'I wouldn't be surprised, the way things are. It's –'

'Not an asteroid,' said the old Rashim. He giggled. 'It is God! Punishing us with a pestilence! Yes!'

'You mean a virus?'

The old man cocked his head. 'A pestilence.'

Maddy sipped from the flask and passed it back to the young Rashim. 'You need to know that your Project Exodus will cause a time wave that will completely rewrite history. You should know there's no New York, there's no America in 2001, thanks to you.'

'It's all jungle,' said Sal. 'Nothing.'

'Christ! Time contamination is exactly what we *want* to achieve! The future's a dead end for us! Don't you see? There's no way forward for mankind! Only backwards! The goal of Exodus is to export the executive branch of the United States back to Roman times. We've got weapons, we've got medicines, technology databases, experts in absolutely every field! Soldiers –'

'Well, whatever you *intended* Exodus to be . . . it ends up a disaster.' She nodded at the old man beside her, once again lapsed into distracted muttering to himself. 'That wreck of a human over there is the sole survivor of Project Exodus. That's you, Dr Anwar! That how you want to end up?'

'Then I'll go back and suggest we reduce the translation mass. We can take less and that'll reduce the potential error margin!'

'You're not going back,' said Maddy.

'What?'

'I can't let you go. Your people have to think your deployment technique failed. That your translation method is too unreliable to continue any further with.'

Rashim swallowed nervously. 'Please . . . I have to get back.'

'Sorry,' she replied. 'This is the way it goes.' She looked across at Bob and Liam inspecting the display screen of one of the beacon rods and the lab unit looking anxious as if they intended to use the thing as a cricket bat. 'We're using your beacons to try and get back to our time. To 2001 . . . and I'm afraid you're going to have to come with us.'

Bob finished tapping in the data on the small touch-screen and a light flickered green from the top of the rod. 'This should now be sending a thread-signal of particles that can be detected by our transmission array.'

'You shouldn't be interfering with that!' complained the lab unit. 'It's not yours!' SpongeBubba stuck out a petulant lip. 'Very naughty!'

'Do you think it will work?' asked Liam.

Bob shrugged. 'If the equipment in the archway is still functioning and undamaged and there is enough power remaining to deploy a time window, then there is no reason this should not work.'

'My skippa will be very angry with you!' chimed the lab unit.

Liam gave Bob a tired smile. 'What would we do without you?'

Bob missed the affectionate rhetoric. 'Grow another unit?'

CHAPTER 83

AD 54, outside Rome

'I . . . I am not going in *there*. I am not going with you!'

Maddy looked at the old man. She'd expected they'd have to get Bob to wrestle the young Rashim through the portal, but not the old one. 'What? Why?'

He shook his head. 'Want . . . want to die right here.' He nodded slowly. 'Here . . . this place. This hilltop. Open space . . .' He closed his eyes, sniffed the air as the gentle breeze made the long grass before them and the leaves above them whisper together.

'Shadd-yah! You don't have to *die*,' said Sal. 'We can get you some help back home! Decent food. Get you looked at by some doctors or something! You're going to be just fine!'

'Already dead,' he rasped. He looked at his younger self. 'Don't become *this* . . .' he said, touching his own cheek with a claw of a finger. He smiled and closed his eyes. 'I found you. These people must stop you . . . stop us.'

'None of you understand, do you?' said young Rashim. 'The world's pretty much finished in my time. We've poisoned every-thing. The world's a garbage pit. What's left that isn't flooded is . . . is *landfill*. There's no hope for us any more!'

'Whatever mess we made of earth . . . we can't toy around with time like this,' said Maddy. 'We're *all* going back and leav-ing this history as it's meant to be.'

'No!' The old Rashim's eyes opened. 'God . . . He's in there.' He nodded towards the strobing beacon that Bob was holding in his fist. 'In that place . . . is *chaos*!'

Young Rashim shook his head with mild disgust at the rambling old man. 'There's no way that crazy old fool's me.'

'. . . *if I he finds me . . . me and Mr Muzzy*,' he gabbled, '. . . *if he finds us in there, we'll be sent straight to Hell for what we did. Straight to Hell! Straight to Hell . . .*'

'Why don't we let him stay?' said Liam.

Maddy turned round. 'What?'

'Let him stay.' Liam looked at the old man with pity. 'Look at him . . . the poor man's completely terrified.'

'We can't just leave him here! He'll starve or –'

'He won't survive, Maddy. He won't make it through. Look at him.'

Maddy did. And she could see Liam was probably right. It looked like a strong gust of wind would kill him, let alone being bombarded with cell-rupturing tachyons. 'All right, then.' She squatted down beside the old man and put a hand on his arm. His wild rambling stopped.

'Is this what you want, Rashim?'

He turned to look at her with milky madness in his wet eyes. She wondered if he was even seeing her.

'Rashim? Can you hear me? Do you want to stay here?'

'Yes.'

'You'll be on your own? We all have to go.'

He nodded, smiled. 'Have Mr Muzzy with me.'

Maddy shook her head. It felt wrong leaving him out here. His mind was mush. She wasn't even sure he knew where he was, even who he was any more.

Then there seemed to be some purpose in his eyes. He smiled. 'You go. I want this . . .'

'What? What is it you want?'

He spread his arms. '*This*. Let me have this.'

She looked around at the flat hilltop. The soft hiss through the dry grass, the unbroken blue sky above. A horizon of distant lavender-tipped mountain peaks. And peace.

Peace and almost infinite space.

Maddy got it. She totally got it.

'All right,' she whispered softly to him. 'All right . . .' She smiled, squeezed his arm gently. 'Savour it, Rashim. Savour every moment of it.'

He looked at her with a glimmer of sanity. 'Thank you.'

She stood up and beckoned the others away, leaving the old man sitting hunched in the middle of the tall grass, his head cocked, listening to the gentle whisper of the wind.

'Fill up that jug for him. Let's at least leave him some water.'

'He's not coming?' asked Sal.

'Nope.'

CHAPTER 84

2069, Project Exodus, Cheyenne
Mountain, Colorado Springs

'Still nothing?'

The technician shook his head solemnly.

Dr Yatsushita watched the proxy density display on the main holo-screen. It was flatlining. The density equivalent of white noise. Just an interdimensional soup. He took his glasses off and rubbed weary eyes. It was return-time plus over three hours. Even at one minute past due, the implication had been pretty clear. Just as there was no such thing as being 'slightly pregnant', there was no such thing as being *nearly successful* with time translation.

We lost them. Dr Anwar and that ridiculous customized lab unit of his.

He sat back down in his chair. The other technicians in their monitor-high cubicles sat up to get a look at the project leader, wondering how to read his body language. Their heads bobbed above partitions like a coterie of meerkats.

Yatsushita balled his fists. He'd just lost the brightest mind on his team and in a limited field like this . . . where do you go to recruit a replacement?

'Dr Yatsushita?'

He looked up. One of the beacon deployment team was

standing over him. 'We uh . . . we picked up a faint signal. One of the beacons squawked a signal for about a minute, but that's all we got.'

'Nothing now?'

He shook his head. 'It's like it just got switched off.'

'Or it malfunctioned?'

The man shrugged. That was probably a more likely answer. The translation of Dr Anwar and his armful of beacon markers and that stupid yellow robot probably ended up with them being fused into a layer of rock in the middle of some mountain range or simply lost in that horrific subatomic broth that reduced the calculations of the world's best particle physicists to little more than *eeny-meeny-miney-mo* guesses.

Their system was still far too unreliable for human transmission. It appeared that Dr Anwar had been too confident with his own calculations. Yes, their system could send an apple fifty minutes, fifty hours . . . fifty days, even fifty years into the past. But once every two or three times, they lost it; that or they brought back apple purée.

'All right, shut it all down.' He sighed. They were burning gigawatts of power that couldn't be wasted endlessly. Not in this resource-poor time anyway. 'Shut it down!' he snapped louder. The deployment team technician nodded and turned away quickly.

A few moments later, the deafening hum of power surging through the giant Faraday cage running across the roof of the hangar died away, leaving a hollow echo behind.

Losing Rashim was going to set them back months. Maybe even years. If they couldn't even reliably send a single human test subject there and back without losing him, they certainly weren't even close to ready for the proposed party of three hundred.

'Let's get the diagnostics running!' he called out. Overall the system had been powered up for a total of three hours and twenty-nine minutes – when Dr Anwar had stepped confidently into one of the translation grids and disappeared. They had countless terabytes of diagnostic data to sift through. Hopefully somewhere in there they might locate a single solitary variable that was miscalculated. But he doubted it.

Time travel seemed horrifically, frighteningly *random*.

More like magic than science.

CHAPTER 85

2001, New York

The archway was empty. A single webcam iris on top of a computer monitor in the middle of a messy desk studied the still darkness. There was no sign of movement. No sign of anyone: none of the team and none of the unauthorized intruders. They were dealt with. For now.

Computer-Bob was on his own and was going to have to wait.

Through the iris of the webcam, computer-Bob noted that the shutter door was smashed open, bent slats of corrugated aluminium hanging from one side down to the ground on the other, and outside pale daylight, filtered green by a canopy of foliage, seeped into this gloomy brickwork cave.

Computer-Bob calculated the generator could keep the one running PC going for another seventy-seven hours. A lot more if he shut down the growth tubes in the back room, effectively killing Becks and the other foetuses held in suspended animation.

But he couldn't do that. Or didn't want to. Not yet at least.

No external feeds of data to examine and explore. Just this still archway. Just this one view across a messy desk, a half-empty can of Dr Pepper, sweet wrappers.

If the monitor hadn't been in sleep mode, one would have seen a cursor dance across a dialogue box.

>**Information: Maddy is messy.**

Like he didn't already know that.

His idling AI moved on to consider more important matters. Who were those intruders? Who sent them?

>Information: the intruders had W.G. Systems idents and AI software.

>Information: the intruders had mission logs authorized by user: R.G. Waldstein.

Two things occurred just then at almost the same moment in time.

Firstly computer-Bob picked up a clear and distinct tachyon signal. The time-stamp location was precise and the message was perfectly straightforward, for once. 'Open a portal at this time-stamp immediately.' Computer-Bob at once began directing power to the displacement machine. It would require approximately two minutes of recharging, enough to flip one of the LEDs on the display back from amber to green. Enough of a safety margin to ensure a stable portal force field.

The second thing was the arrival of a fresh breeze stirring the woodland outside, teasing the branches of a cedar tree directly beyond the entrance, right in the middle of what was normally a rubbish-strewn alleyway.

The hum of the displacement machine competed with the hiss of whispering leaves shifting excitedly as the breeze picked up and became a somewhat blustering gust of wind.

Computer-Bob recognized the wind for what it was. A bank of air pushed by the sudden shifting of reality, the emergence of possibilities wrestling with each other deep within an enormous wall of approaching change.

The gust stirred rubbish inside the archway, paper cups and burger wrappers chasing each other in a game of tag on the breakfast table. The curtain that hung beside the bunk beds from an improvised rail fidgeted impatiently like a bored child swinging from a parent's hand. The hum, meanwhile, rose in pitch as it sucked in power from the generator; the hum was like a cockerel announcing dawn, desperately wanting to tell the empty archway that it was nearly good to go.

Once again the cursor blinked across its black dialogue box.

>Ready to transmit displacement field.

>Activating field–office bubble.

Computer-Bob didn't have emotions. Not really. He had files. They were useful back when he used to live inside a W.G. Systems wafer-processor, inside an engineered human body when those files could be used to stimulate muscle movements . . . a smile, for example. He missed that. Missed the ability to use those files in a meaningful way. Oh, but actually he decided he could. It wasn't quite the same thing, but it was good enough. The tachyon signal appeared to be good news. It seemed that his team, or at least some of them, were alive still. Cause for some sort of a celebration.

The cursor scuttled along, albeit briefly, to form three ASCII characters.

> 8-)

CHAPTER 86

2001, New York

Air was displaced inside the archway as it gusted noisily in from the outside. A sphere of pulsating energy blinked into existence and lit the gloomy archway with a bright Italian sky and a parched, rust-coloured field of baked earth and dry grass.

Dark silhouettes clouded the dancing image then, a moment later, one of them, the biggest by far, stepped into the archway. Bob crouched, legs apart, sword drawn and ready to swing it. His eyes swept quickly round the dim archway, into the dark corners. He ducked down to look under the bunk beds. He crossed the floor and pulled aside the sliding door into the back room. The chugging of the diesel generator spilled out as he checked inside. He returned to the main archway as the wind outside began to become a hurricane-like roar.

Standing beside the shimmering orb of Mediterranean blue, he beckoned the other dark shapes to join him. 'The archway is clear!' he roared above the deafening whistling of wind outside, and the thrashing branches of the woodland.

They came through one after the other: Liam, Sal, Dr Rashim Anwar and his lab unit, and finally Maddy.

She emerged into the archway swearing as she almost tripped over SpongeBubba. 'Goddammit! Out of my way!'

'Sorr-*eee*!' SpongeBubba cried out in his sing-song voice, and waddled a few steps back from her.

'*Close the portal!*' she shouted above the scream of wind from outside. The portal collapsed behind her.

'*What's going on here?*' shouted Rashim above the roar of wind outside. '*Is this a storm?*'

'*Time wave!*' she shouted back.

'*A what?*'

'*A TIME WAVE!*'

Liam hurried across to close the shutter and stopped dead in his tracks as he realized the door was ruined. '*What happened to our door?*'

His words were lost in the roaring wind.

It went completely dark outside. The tree trunk right there, a yard beyond where their concrete floor became dirt and flora, *liquidized* . . . spun into strands of insubstantial matter, like a wispy tendril of sugar in a candyfloss tumbler. Amid the pitch-black it became a swirling maelstrom of fleetingly seen things: another different tree, a rock formation . . . a tipi . . . a wooden shack . . . an Easter Island monolith.

And then, all of a sudden, it was a brick wall covered in graffiti and lined with rubbish along the bottom.

The roaring receded quickly, fading into something else entirely: a commuter train rumbling over the Williamsburg Bridge's old tracks above their heads; the sound of impatient traffic, bumper to bumper, coming from the intersection at the end of their alleyway. The distant *whoop* of police sirens. The soft chop of a helicopter swooping across the East River. Somebody somewhere nearby had a thumping sound system in the back of their car.

Noisy . . . but so much less noisy than it had been a moment ago.

'We're back,' cried Sal, running towards the opening and the alleyway outside. 'We're back! We made it!'

Liam nodded. Subdued. 'We're back,' he replied.

Maddy crossed the floor and joined both of them standing in the ruined doorway. She stared out at the brick wall, the rubbish piled against it. She listened to the noises of Brooklyn, the irritable, impatient noises of blissful ignorance. Millions of normal lives being led . . . all of them content with their little decisions, their little dilemmas, the day-to-day jostle of office politics and the nightly family squabbles.

'Maddy?' said Sal. 'You OK?'

'What do we do now?' said Liam.

They were all looking at her. Sal, so much like a little sister, lost without her leading the way. Liam – *oh God, poor Liam* – was putting a brave face on things, but she knew he was affected badly by what he'd discovered about himself. Bob. Useful, helpful, loyal like a Labrador, but – let's not fool ourselves here – nothing more than a database on muscular legs.

And now this Dr Anwar and his stupid SpongeBot, the pair of them looking like lost sheep right now.

And I'm everyone's mom. I've got to come up with the 'what-do-we-do-next' bit.

Funny thing was that for the first time in a long time she knew exactly what they had to do next.

'We've got to get out of here,' she said.

'Huh?'

Maddy stepped back from the ruined shutters. 'Somebody out there knows exactly *where* we are, they know exactly *when* we are . . . and *who* we are. And they want us all dead. We've got to grab what we can, whatever we think we're going to need, and we've got to get the hell out of here.'

Liam raised his eyebrows. 'Leave this archway?'

'Yes.'

'You mean . . . like *now*?'

Maddy nodded. 'I mean, like, *right now*.'

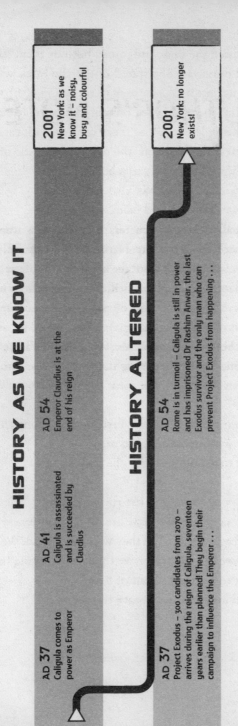

HISTORY AS WE KNOW IT

AD 37
Caligula comes to power as Emperor

AD 41
Caligula is assassinated and is succeeded by Claudius

AD 54
Emperor Claudius is at the end of his reign

2001
New York: as we know it – noisy, busy and colourful

HISTORY ALTERED

AD 37
Project Exodus – 300 candidates from 2070 – arrives during the reign of Caligula, seventeen years earlier than planned! They begin their campaign to influence the Emperor . . .

AD 54
Rome is in turmoil – Caligula is still in power and has imprisoned Dr Rashim Anwar, the last Exodus survivor and the only man who can prevent Project Exodus from happening . . .

2001
New York: no longer exists!

AUTHOR'S NOTE

Cato and Macro are two characters that I've long wanted to cross paths with the TimeRiders team. They actually have their own series of books (the Roman Legion series by Simon Scarrow) in which we see them as much younger men serving in the legions of Rome. If you've enjoyed their company in this book, I heartily recommend giving this series a go, starting with the first book *Under the Eagles*. A big thanks again to my brother, Simon, for letting me use them. As always, those two fellas have been great fun to be with.

WANT MORE ACTION? MORE ADVENTURE? MORE ADRENALIN?

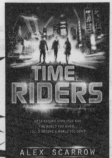

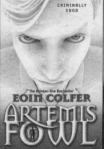

GET INTO PUFFIN'S ADVENTURE BOOKS FOR BOYS